Piers Anthony was born in Oxford in 1934, moved with his family to Spain in 1939 and then to the USA in 1940, after his father was expelled from Spain by the Franco regime. He became a citizen of the US in 1958 and, before devoting himself to full-time writing, worked as a technical writer for a communications company and taught English. He started publishing short stories with *Possible to Rue* for *Fantastic* in 1963, and published in SF magazines for the next decade. He has, however, concentrated more and more on writing novels.

Author of the brilliant, widely acclaimed *Cluster* series, and the superb *Split Infinity* trilogy, he has made a name for himself as a writer of original, inventive stories whose imaginative, mind-twisting style is full of extraordinary, often poetic images and flights of cosmic fancy.

By the same author

PIERS ANTHONY

Bio of a Space Tyrant
Volume 1: Refugee

PANTHER
Granada Publishing

Panther Books
Granada Publishing Ltd
8 Grafton Street, London W1X 3LA

Published by Panther Books 1985
Reprinted 1985, 1986

Copyright © Piers Anthony Jacob 1983

ISBN 0-586-06259-9

Printed and bound in Great Britain by
Collins, Glasgow

Set in Times

Contents

Editorial Preface

There have been many biographies of the so-called Tyrant of Jupiter, and countless analyses of the supposed virtues and vices of his character. He was, after all, the most remarkable figure of his generation, as even his enemies concede, and will no doubt be ranked with the other prime movers or disturbers of history, such as Alexander, Caesar, Attila, Genghis Khan, Napoleon, Hitler, and the like. But his personal model was Asoka, who was also called a tyrant in his day, though he may have been the finest ruler the subcontinent of India, Earth, ever had. It is virtually certain, however, that neither the inimical nor the sanitized references adequately describe the real man.

Now that the Tyrant of Jupiter is dead, his voluminous private papers have been released to researchers. These reveal some phenomenal secrets, confirming both the best and worst aspects of his reputation. It turns out to be true, for example, that this man was personally responsible for the deaths of between fifty and a hundred human beings before he was sixteen years old, and thousands more thereafter – but still, it is not fair to call him a cold-blooded mass murderer. It is also true that there were many women in his life, including several temporary wives or mistresses – the distinction becomes obscure in some cases – but not that he was promiscuous.

The legal name of the Tyrant was Hope Hubris, literally reflecting the hope his family had for him. He was of Hispanic origin, and the name Hope was at that time an unusual appellation for a male of his culture. It is perhaps a measure of his impact that it is so no more. He was, throughout his life, literate in two languages, and able to speak others. He was, in any language, always possessed of that particular genius of expression any leader needs.

Hope Hubris was charged with many terrible things, and his seeming unwillingness to deny or clarify many of these charges appeared to lend credence to them. It was said that he watched his father being murdered without lifting a hand; that he sold his sisters into sexual slavery; that he permitted his mother to practise prostitution in his sight; and that he killed his first girlfriend in order to save himself. He was also accused of practising incest and cannibalism, of trafficking in illegal drugs, and of being a coward about heights. There is an element of truth in all these charges, but appreciation of their full context goes far to exonerate him. As he himself wrote: 'We did what we had to. How can that be wrong?'

Hope was fallible in the fashion of his kind, especially in his truncated youth, but he did possess a single and singular skill, and there was a certain greatness in him. His early and savage, if limited, experience in leadership was to serve him excellently later in life, as Tyrant. He seldom repeated his mistakes. Remember, too, that he suffered tribulations such as few survive. How pretty do we really expect the survivors of the holocaust to be?

The Tyrant was not a bad man. This assessment is well documented by the series of autobigraphical manuscripts he left, each written with disarmingly complete candor. It seems fitting that the final word on his nature be his own. The intelligence and literacy of young Hope Hubris, who wrote at age fifteen in a secondary language, is manifest, coupled with a quaint naïveté of experience. This is, however, no juvenile narration!

Herewith, edited only for clarification of occasional obscurities, and for separation and titling of episodes, but otherwise uncensored, is the earliest of these five major documents, editorially titled *Refugee*.

HMH

1

Rape of the Bubble

Jupiter Orbit, 2-8-2615 – The shell of the bubble was opaque, for it had to be thick and solid to contain the pressure of air and to insulate against the cold of empty space. But there were portholes, multiple glazed tunnels that offered views outside, and naturally I was interested.

The view really wasn't much. Jupiter, the colossus of the system, dominated as it always did, about the apparent size of my outstretched fist. Its turbulent cloud-currents and great red eye were looking right back at me. The planet was almost full-face right now, because the sun was behind us. Our progress towards the planet was so slow that the disc seemed hardly larger than it had been when we started three days before. But giant Jove was always impressive, however distant and whatever the phase.

'Ship Ahoy!' our temporary navigator cried. I didn't know whether this was standard space procedure, but it was good enough for us, who were less experienced than the rankest of amateurs.

A ship! Excitement rippled through the refugees massed in the bubble. What could this mean?

Soon we all saw it through the portholes: a somewhat bloated barrel with attachments. Of course streamlining was not needed in space, and a tub like this one was never intended to land on any significant solid body. Still, I felt a certain disappointment. Perhaps I had been spoiled by all those dramatic holographs of the Jupiter Space Navy in action, with needle-sleek missileships homing in on decoy drones and exploding with instant fireballs. I had always known that real spacecraft were not like that, and yet my mental picture remained shaped by the Jupe publicity ads.

The ship overhauled us readily, for it had chemical jets to boost its gravity shields. It closed on us, and its blunt nose clanged against our access port with a jolt that shook us all. What was it up to?

I turned to discover my big sister, Faith, immediately behind me. She was absolutely beautiful in her excitement, though as always I pretended not to notice. I had the chore of staying near her during this voyage, to discourage mischief. Faith attracted men the way garbage draws flies in the incredible films of old Earth – perhaps it would be kinder to say the way flowers draw bees – partly because no man had touched her. We Latins place importance on that sort of thing; I understand there are other cultures that don't.

'Who are they?' Faith asked.

'Maybe traders,' I answered, feeling a mild burgeoning of importance in the expressing of such an opinion. But I felt a slow clutch of apprehension. We were refugees; we had nothing to trade.

In any event, we were powerless to oppose their boarding. Our bubble had only one weak propulsive jet; we were virtually free-floating in space. Our main physical motivation was the selected gravity of Jupiter and the forces of inertia. We could not have performed an evasive manoeuvre had we known how. The entry ports could be operated from either side; this was to prevent anyone from being trapped outside. Our competence was such that this was a necessary safety feature, but it did leave us open to boarding by any craft that chose to do so.

The seal was made and the port opened, making an open window to the other craft. There were of course safety features to prevent the lock opening both doors simultaneously when the pressure was unequal, but the normal air pressure of the ship did equalize it. In space, safety had to be balanced by convenience; it would have been awkward to transfer any quantity of freight from one vessel to another if one panel of the air lock always had to be sealed.

A burly, bearded man appeared, garbed in soiled yellow pantaloons, a black shirt, and a bright red sash. He needed no space suit, of course; the merged air lock mechanism made exit into the vacuum of space unnecessary. Most striking was his headdress: a kind of broad, split hat like that of the classical buccaneers. There is a lot of conscious imitation of the past, so archaic costumes are not unusual.

Buccaneers. I had been uneasy before; now I was scared. I was aware that not all of those who emulated buccaneers in costume were playing innocent games. Some took the part more seriously, particularly in this region of the system. 'We've got to hide, Faith,' I said, in our natural Spanish. The translation of course is not perfect, and neither is my memory; allowance must be made.

Her clear brow furrowed. 'Why, Hope?' she asked. 'I want to meet the traders. Maybe they have soap.' She had been unable to wash her luxuriant tresses, and so she fretted. It was the way of pretty girls.

'They're not traders,' I snapped. 'Come *on!*'

She frowned. She was three years older than I, and did not like taking orders from me. I could hardly blame her for that, but I really feared the trouble that could come if my suspicion was correct. I took her by the arm and drew her along with me.

'But you said—' she protested as she moved.

It was already too late, for several more brutish men had crowded through the open port, and they were armed with clubs and knives. 'Line up here on the main floor!' their leader cried. I found it mildly anomalous that he did not use the proper term, 'deck'. Maybe he did not consider our little bubble to be a true spacecraft.

The refugees looked at our navigator, who seemed to be the most likely authority in a situation like this. He looked suddenly tired.'I think we must do as they say,' he said. 'They are armed and we are not.'

'Stay back,' I whispered to Faith. 'Stand behind me. Try to – you know – make yourself inconspicuous.'

'Oh, no!' she breathed. She had a very feminine way of expressing herself, even when under stress. She had the business of being pretty down virtually to a science. 'You don't think—?'

'I think they're pirates,' I said, trying to speak without moving my lips as I faced the intruders, so they wouldn't know I was talking. 'They're going to rob us.' I hoped that would be the limit of it.

We moved slowly to merge with the mass of people forming on the designated portion of the deck. Fortunately the bubble's spin was high at the moment, so there was enough centrifugal gravity to hold us firm. Our concentration at this spot did cause the bubble to wobble slightly, however.

'Now, I'm called the Horse, because of the way I smell,' the red-sashed leader said. 'I run this party. That's about all you need to know about me. Just do what I say, and no one will be hurt too much.' He chuckled, but none of us saw any humour in this. We were frightened.

The pirates spread out around the bubble, around the curve of the deck, poking into things. The leader and several others attended to the refugees. 'All right, come on up here, you,' the Horse said, beckoning an older man.

'What?' the man asked in Spanish, startled.

The pirate leaped and grabbed him by the arm, hauling him roughly forward. 'Move!' he shouted.

The man recovered his balance, nonplussed. 'But, Señor Horse—'

Deliberately, yet almost carelessly, the pirate struck him on the head, backhanded. It was no token blow; the man cried out and fell to the deck. A trace of blood showed on his lips as he put one hand to his face.

12

'Check him,' the Horse said brusquely. Two others stepped up, hauled the old man to his feet, and searched him roughly. They found his wallet and a small bag of golden coins, his fortune. They dumped these in a central box and threw him to the side. I think the violence upset him and us more than the actual robbery did. We were plainly unprepared for this.

'You,' the Horse said, pointing to a middle-aged woman.

She screamed and shrank back into the crowd, but he was too quick for her. He caught her by the shoulder and dragged her into the open. 'Strip!' he ordered.

Horrified, unmoving, she stared at him.

The Horse did not repeat his order. He gestured to the two assistant pirates. They grabbed the woman and literally ripped the clothing from her body, shaking it so that all objects in her pockets fell to the deck. These were mostly feminine articles: a comb, a mirror, a vial of perfume, and a small change purse. The pirates took the change and cast her aside, naked and sobbing.

Now the pirate's eye fell on Faith. My effort to conceal her had been unsuccessful; there were too many of the intruders scattered around the bubble. Also, the curve of the deck meant that those of us who stood behind the group actually were more visible than those near the centre, because the curve had the effect of elevating us. 'Here's something better than money!' he exclaimed, beckoning her.

Faith shrank away, of course. My father shoved his way out of the crowd. 'She has nothing!' he cried.

One of the peripheral pirates strode forward to intercept my father. Another went after Faith. My father was not a man of violence, but he could not tolerate abuse of his children. He raised one fist in warning as he met the pirate. It was not that he wanted to fight, but that he had to give some signal that the limit of our tolerance had been approached. Even confused refugees could only be pushed so far.

The pirate drew his curved sword. 'Get back!' another refugee cried, catching my father by his other arm and drawing him back into the throng. The pirate, satisfied by this act of retreat, scowled and did not pursue.

Meanwhile, the other pirate reached Faith, who now stood close beside me, no longer protesting my leadership. He caught her by the elbow. She screamed – and I launched myself at the man.

I caught him in a clumsy tackle about the legs, making him stumble. This brought a feeling of *déjà vu* to me, the sensation of having been here before. My mind is like that; I make odd connections at the last convenient times. A teacher once told me that it is a sign of creativity, that can be useful if properly harnessed. I had tackled a man before, rescuing my sister—

A fist like a block of ice-rock clubbed me on the ear. There is a peculiar agony to the injured ear; my very brain seemed to shake inside my skull.

The pirate had knocked me down with the same almost careless contempt the Horse had applied to the old man. It was as effective. I sat up, my ear seeing red stars. For a moment I was disorganized, not doing more than hurting and watching.

The pirate hauled Faith into the open. She screamed again and wrenched herself away. Her blouse tore, leaving a shred in the man's grip. He cursed in the manner of his kind and lunged for her again.

I scrambled up and launched myself at him a second time. This time I didn't tackle, I butted. The man was leaning towards me, reaching for Faith; I brushed past her and struck him dead centre with the top of my head.

His arms were outstretched; he had no protection from my blow. His mouth was open, as he was about to say something. I was braced for the impact; even so, it was one spine-deadening collision.

The air whooshed out of the pirate like gas from a

punctured bag, while I dropped half-stunned to the deck. Now my whole head saw stars, and they had heated from red to white! We were both lightweight in the fractional gravity of the bubble, but our inertial mass remained intact; there had been nothing light about the butt!

I lay prone, waiting for the shock to let go of my system. I was conscious, but somehow couldn't get my limbs to co-ordinate. I heard the pirates shouting, and Faith's voice as she turned about and returned to me. 'Hope!' she cried. 'Are you all right? Oh, they've hurt him!'

I presumed that 'him' was me, news for a third party. I tried to tell her I would be all right in a moment, when the universe stopped gyrating quite so wildly and my head shrank back to manageable dimension, but only a grunt came out. Maybe that sound actually issued from the pirate next to me, who was surely hurting as much as I was. Maybe with luck, I had managed to separate his ribs.

But now other pirates charged in. 'Hack that boy apart!' the Horse cried, and rough hands hauled me into the air. My dizziness abated rapidly; there is nothing like a specific threat to one's life to concentrate one's attention!

Faith screamed again – that was one thing she was good at! – and flung her arms about me as my feet touched the deck. The scream was ill-timed; at that moment all the pirates were doing was standing me on my feet and supporting me as I wobbled woozily. Their intent was unlikely to be kind, but in that instant no one was actually doing me violence, despite their leader's orders. Maybe it had been intended to cow the other refugees, rather than to be implemented literally. I make this point, with the advantage of retrospection, because of the importance of that particular scream.

Ill-timed it was, but that scream electrified the refugees in a manner no prior event had. Suddenly they were acting, all at once, as if choreographed by a larger power. Four of them grabbed the pirate beside me, stripping him from me.

Others jumped on the one I had stunned with my butt. Still others went after the oncoming pirates.

The refugee throng had been transformed from an apathetic, frightened mass to a fighting force. Faith's third scream had done it. It remains unclear to me why her first or second screams had not had that effect. Perhaps the first ones had primed the group. I like to understand human motives, and sometimes they defy reasonable explanation.

At any rate, in moments all the pirates except their leader had been caught and disarmed, surprised by the suddenness and ferocity of the refugee reaction and overwhelmed by our much greater number.

The Horse stood, however, not with a drawn sword, but with a drawn laser pistol. This was another matter, for though a laser lacked the brute force of a sword, it could do its damage a great deal faster, particularly when played across the face.

'Turn loose my men,' the Horse said sternly.

My father spoke up. I knew he did not like this sort of showdown, but he was, after all, our leader, and with Faith and me involved he was also personally responsible. 'Get out of this bubble!' he said. 'You're nothing but robbers!'

The Horse's weapon swung to cover my father. I tensed despite my continuing discomfort, knowing that little weapon could puncture a man's eyeballs and cruelly blind him before he could even blink.

'Who are you?' said the pirate.

'Major Hubris,' my father responded.

'You're no military man!'

'It's my name, not a title. Fire that laser, and the rest of us will swamp you before I fall.'

The Horse grinned humourlessly. 'I can take out five or six of you first.'

'Two or three of us,' my father corrected him evenly, and I felt a surging pride at his courage. My father had always had the nerve to do what he had to do, even when he disliked it. This was an example. 'And there are two hundred of us. We've already got your men. You stand to lose, regardless.'

The pirate leader considered. 'There is that. All right – you release my men, and we'll leave you alone.'

My father turned to the crowd. 'That seems fair enough.' He noted the scattered nods of approval, then turned back to the pirate. 'But you have to leave the things you stole from us. No robbery.'

The Horse scowled. 'Agreed.'

By this time I had recovered most of my wits. 'Don't trust him, Father!' I cried. 'These are pirates!'

'I am a pirate,' the Horse said. 'But I keep my word. We will not rob you, and we will leave the bubble.'

My father, like most men of honour, tended to believe the best of people. He nodded at the men who held the pirates, and the pirates were released. They quickly recovered their weapons and rejoined their leader, somewhat shame-faced.

The Horse stood for a moment, considering. Then he indicated me. 'That's your boy who floored my man?'

My father nodded grimly. 'And my daughter, whom he was defending.'

As I mentioned, thoughts scurry through my head at all times, not always relevant to the issue of the moment. Right now I wondered where my little sister Spirit was, as I didn't see her. I don't know why I thought of her right then. Maybe it was because, the way my father spoke, it sounded as though he had only two children, when in fact he had three. Of course, he wasn't trying to deceive anyone; the pirate hadn't asked how many he had, just whether I was one. It was just that my meandering brain insisted on exploring surplus details.

'And when she screamed, the others rallied around,' the Horse said. 'We misjudged that, it seems.'

'Yes.'

'So we'll just have to try it again,' the Horse concluded. He made a signal with his hand. 'Take them.'

Suddenly the nine other pirates advanced on us again, each with his sword or club ready.

'Hey!' my father protested. 'You agreed—'

'Not to rob you,' the Horse said. 'And to leave the bubble. We'll honour that. But first we have some business that wasn't in the contract.' He looked at Faith and me. 'Don't hurt the boy or the girl or the man,' he ordered. 'Bring them here.'

Pirates grabbed the three of us. In each case, two men menaced the refugees nearby while the third cornered the victim. They were much more careful than before. It was not possible to resist without immediate disaster, for the Horse backed them up with his laser. More than that, it was psychological: The remaining refugees, rendered leaderless again, did nothing. The dynamics had changed.

That's another phenomenon that has perplexed me. The mechanism by which a few uninhibited individuals can cow a much larger number, when both groups know the larger group has the power to prevail. It seems impossible, yet it happens all the time. Whole governments exist in opposition to the will of the people they govern, because of this. If I could just comprehend that dynamic—

'Bind father and son,' the Horse said. 'String them up to the baggage rack.'

I struggled, but lacked the strength and mass of any one of the pirates. They tied my hands behind me, cruelly tight, and suspended me from the guyed baggage net in the centre of the bubble. My father suffered a similar fate. We hung at a slight angle, overlooking the proceedings, helpless.

Now the Horse turned to Faith. He whistled. 'She's a looker!' he exclaimed. His vernacular expression may have been cruder, but that was the essence. Faith, of course, blushed.

'Leave her alone!' I cried foolishly.

18

'No, we won't let this piece go to waste,' the Horse said, running his tongue around his lips. 'Prepare her.'

The pirate held Faith and methodically tore the rest of her clothing from her struggling body, grinning salaciously. Oh, yes, they enjoyed doing this! In my mind they resembled burning demons from the depths of Hell. Someone among the refugees cried out, but the swords of the other pirates on guard prevented any action.

When Faith was naked, they hauled a box out of the baggage and held her supine, spread-eagled across it. The Horse ran his rough hands over her torso and squeezed her breasts, then dropped his pantaloons.

There was a gasp of incredulity from the refugees. This was not because of any special quality of the Horse's anatomy, which was unimpressive and unclean, but because of the open manner in which he exhibited himself before such a company of men, women, and children. The man was completely without shame.

I am striving to record this sequence objectively, for this is my personal biography: the description of the things that have made me what I am. I strive always to comprehend the true nature of people, myself most of all. There is a place for subjectivity – or so I believe. My feelings about a given event may change with time and mood and memory, but the facts of the event will never change. So I must first describe precisely what occurred, as though it were recorded by videotape, uncluttered by emotions, then proceed to the subjective analysis and interpretation. Perhaps there should be several interpretations, separated by years, so that the change in them becomes apparent and helps lead to the truest possible comprehension of the whole.

But in this case I find I cannot adequately perform the first requirements. My hand baulks, my very mind veers away from the enormity of the outrage and hurt. I can only say that I loved my two sisters with a love that was perhaps more than brotherly, though never would I have thought that there was any incestuous element. Faith was beautiful, and nice, and I was charged with her protection, though she was a woman while I was a mere adolescent. I had in fact never before witnessed the sexual act, either in holo or in person and never imagined it to be so brutal.

It was as if that foul pirate shoved a blunt dagger into my sister's trembling, vulnerable body, again and again, his face distorted in a grimace of urgency that in ironic fashion almost matched her grimace of agony, and his body shuddered as if in epileptic seizure, and when he stopped and stepped away there was blood on the weapon.

And I – I with my absolute horror of that ravishment, my hatred of every aspect of that cruelty – I found my own body reacting, as it were a thing apart from my mind, yet I knew it could not truly be separate. There was some part of me that identified with the fell pirate, though I knew it was wrong and more than wrong. My innocent, lovely sister Faith possessed certain attributes of Heaven, while now I knew that I possessed, at least in part, an attribute of Hell. I looked upon the foul lust of Satan, and felt an echo of that lust within myself.

I cannot write of this further. It is no pleasant thing to confess an affinity to that which one condemns. I can only say that I swore a private oath to kill the pirate Horse: some time, some way. And the pirates who followed him in the appalling act. I tried to note the details of each of them, so that I would not fail to recognize them if ever I encountered them again. I saw that several of the pirates, however, did not participate; they obeyed the Horse in all other things, but would not ravish a helpless woman. Even among pirates, there were some who were not as bad as others.

Apart from that effort of identification, my mind retreated from what was happening. My sister, I think, had fainted before the second pirate readied his infernal weapon, and that was a portion of mercy for her. She, at least, no longer knew what was being done to her body. I knew – but chose not to see.

I fled into memory, into that sequence that was the origin of my feeling of *déjà vu*, for it related directly to the present situation. Probably I should have commenced my bio there, instead of with the shock of Faith's violation, for I see now that the true beginning of my odyssey was then. This bio is more than a record of experience; it is therapy. Biography, biology, biopsy – all the ways to study a subject. Bio – life. My life. Not only do I seek to grasp the nature of myself, I seek to strengthen my character by reviewing my successes and my mistakes with an eye to improving the ratio between them, painful as this process can be at times.

Therefore I will now illumine that prior sequence, demarking it with a new dateline, and will try to keep my narrative more coherent hereafter. I would perhaps dispose on my 'false start', but my paper and ink are precious as is my evocative effort. After all, if once I begin the process of unwriting what I have written where may it end? Every word is important, for it too is part of my being.

2

Faith and Spirit

Maraud, Callisto, 1-2-2615 – My sisters and I walked home together after school, because there was a certain safety in numbers. Faith, eighteen years old, resented this; she claimed her social life was inhibited by the presence of a skinny fifteen-year-old little sibling. The vernacular term she was wont to employ was less kind, and I think not completely fair, and does not become her, so I shall not render it here. Yet she smiled as she said it, deleting much of the sting, and I think there was some merit to her complaint. It is true that a fifty-kilo sibling is not much company for a fifty-kilo girl. Our weights were similar, in full Earth gravity, but the distribution differed substantially. Faith was about as pretty a girl as one might imagine, with the rich ash-blonde tresses and grey eyes that made her face stand out among the darker shades that predominated in our culture, and a generously symmetrical figure and small extremities. I was young and not versed in social relations between the sexes, and I was her brother; even so, I understood the impact such physical qualities had on men.

Faith was not really intelligent, as I define the concept, though she did well enough in scholastics. It was said that a single look at her was enough to raise her grade before any given class commenced, and that may not have been entirely in jest. She lacked that ornery attitude that passes for courage in others; these qualities of intelligence and courage were reserved in healthy measure for her sister. Spirit was as bold and cunning a gamin as could be found on the planet. Technically Callisto is merely the fourth Galilean satellite of Jupiter, a moon, but its diameter is almost 5,000 kilometres, the same as Mercury and greater than Pluto, so only the accident of its association with the Colossus of the System prevents it from being accorded the dignity of planetary status, and so I think of it as a planet, though the texts disagree. But I was describing my little sister, Spirit, who even at age twelve was a person to be reckoned with. I fought with her often, but I liked her too and envied her her survivalist nature. Theoretically I was the guardian of our little group, for I was the male, but my appreciation of the complexities of people was too great for me to perform this duty as well as Spirit might, had she been me. Once she set her course, she pursued it with an almost appalling efficiency and dispatch.

On this day, precisely one month following my fifteenth birthday, we experienced what is termed an 'incident'. How I wish I could have foreseen the consequences of this seemingly minor event! We have on Callisto a society of classes arising somewhat haphazardly from the turbulent history of our satellite. The government has changed often, but the mass of the populace has sunk slowly into the stability of poverty and dependence. Interactions between the classes are fraught with complications.

My father had mortgaged his small property and gone into debt to ensure a decent education for all his children. Thus the three of us, unlike the vast majority of those of our station, were literate and well informed. Faith and I could speak and read English as well as Spanish, and Spirit was learning. We had applied ourselves most diligently throughout, aware of the sacrifice that had been made for us; but for me the pursuit of knowledge of every kind had become a obsession that no longer required any other stimulus.

We hoped this good education would facilitate Faith's marriage into a more affluent class and my own chance to enter some more profitable trade than that of coffee technician. Then we could begin to abate the debts of our education, bettering the situation of our parents who had toiled so hard for our benefit. We could also achieve higher status and greater economic leverage to benefit our own children, when they came. It was a worthwhile ambition.

But such aspirations were fraught with mischief, as this episode was to demonstrate.

As we three walked a side street of the city of Maraud – named after the days when Marauders of Space had made Callisto a base of operations, a quaint bit of historical lore that was not so quaint in its remaining influence – a mini-saucer floated up. It bore the scion of some wealthy family. He was handsome and wore jewellery on his quality coat, steel caps on his leather shoes, and the sneer of arrogance on his face that only one born to the manner could affect. I disliked him the moment I saw him, for he had all the ostentatious luxury of situation that I craved, yet he had been given it on the proverbial platter, while my family had to struggle constantly with no certainty of achieving it. He was about twenty years old, for he looked no older and could not have been younger; that was the minimum age at which a person could obtain the licence to float a saucer.

'You're Hubris,' he said to Faith, hovering obnoxiously near, so that the downdraft from the saucer's small propeller stirred the hem of her light dress and caused more of her legs to show. Here within the dome, the climate varied only marginally and was always controlled, so that heavy clothing was unnecessary. This was fortunate, for we could not afford anything more than we had. Still, the untoward breeze embarrassed Faith, who was of a genuinely demure nature in the presence of grown men.

'I've seen you in school,' the scion continued, his eyes travelling rather too intimately along her torso. He must have meant that he had watched her at her school, for he would not have attended school at all; he would have had hired tutors throughout, and computerized educational programmes and hypno-teaching for the dull material.

'You look pretty good, for a peasant. How would you like a good kiss?' Only 'kiss' was not precisely the term he employed. Our language of Spanish has nuances of obscenity that foreigners tend to overlook, and translation would be awkward. Something as simple as a roll of bread can become, with the improper inflection, a gutter imprecation. He surely had not learned such terms from his expensive tutors!

Faith blushed from her collar to her ears. She tried to walk away from the insulting man, but he coasted close and took hold of her arm. I saw the several rings on the fingers of his hand, set with diamonds and rubies, displaying his inordinate wealth. The hand was quite clean and uncallused; he had never performed physical labour. 'Come on – you low-class girls do it all the time, don't you? I'll give you two dollars if you're good.' The Jovian dollar – that was our currency too – had been revalued many times, and currently was worth about what it had been seven hundred years ago, back on Planet Earth. That was one of the things I had learned in the school it had cost my father so many of those same dollars to send us to. I also understood the ancient vernacular significance of the two-dollar figure. It was an allusion to the fee of prostitutes.

My anger was building up like pressure in the boiler of a steam machine, but I contained it. Slumming scions could have foul mouths and manners, but it was best to tolerate these and stay out of trouble. All men are not equal, in the domes of Callisto.

Faith tried to wrest her arm free, but the man hauled her roughly in to him. She screamed helplessly. I suppose it would have been better if she had kicked or scratched him, but she had practised being the helpless type so long it was now second nature.

Then Spirit did what I had lacked the nerve to do: She put her foot against the rim of the saucer and tilted it up. Its gravity lens made it and the man aboard it very light, so it responded readily to her pressure. The shield was partial, so that the saucer would not float away when not in use. About ninety-five per cent of the weight of vehicle and user was eliminated, enabling the propeller in the base to lift and move the mass readily. The null-gee effect was narrow and limited, so that the air above was not unduly disturbed. The first saucers, when gravity shielding was new, had borne their users along in perpetual clouds of turbulence, and minor tornadoes had been known to form above them, contributing to the awkwardness. But the refinement of the shield to make a curving and self-limiting null-gee zone had solved that problem, and the saucers were now quite common. (I use 'shield' and 'lens' interchangeably here. I should not, but the technical distinctions are beyond my expertise, so I go with the ignorant majority in this case. As I understand it, there is no shield, but the lens performs the office admirably.) The saucers use very little power, and though they aren't generally fast, they are fun. Larger saucers can do considerably more, of course.

But I|digress, as is my fault. The point is, it does require fair balance and skill to ride such a saucer for the passenger's weight reduction is proportional to the amount of the body within the region of shielding and the angle of the shielding disk. It is a common misconception that a gravshield angled sideways abates gravity sideways; of course that could never be true. Such an angle merely reduces the size of the null-gee region. Thus a person floating too high can always bring himself down by tilting the shield. Properly managed, the saucers provide precisely controlled individual flotation, with the rider drawing his body into the shielded region to increase lift, and extending it beyond that region to increase weight and make a gentle descent.

So when Spirit tilted the saucer two things happened. Its cross section intercepting the planetary gravity diminished slightly – and the man aboard it found himself angled to a greater extent outside that field. Naturally the saucer sank under his increasing weight. It also threw him off balance, so that yet more of his body projected from the shielded zone.

Balancing on a gravity lens has been described as similar to balancing on a surfboard or skateboard – which provides modern folk a hint of the fun the ancients had – and a slight miscue could quickly become calamitous.

It was so in this case. Only the man's grip on Faith's arm steadied him, enabling him to jump off the saucer instead of being dumped on his face. Shaken and furious, he whirled about – just in time to spy the burgeoning smirk on my face.

I had not done the deed, but I was certainly guilty of appreciating it. 'I'll teach you!' he cried angrily in that idiomatic expression that means the opposite. He released Faith and concentrated on me. Behind him the vacant saucer righted itself and hovered in place, as it was programmed to do. It had not failed him; he had failed it, with a little help from Spirit.

The scion was substantially older and larger than I, for five years can be a tremendous distinction in this period of life, and I was afraid of him. I did not want to fight him. I have never regarded myself as a creature of violence in the most propitious circumstances, and this one was least propitious. At the same time, I was aware that this development had distracted his malign attention from Faith, and that it would return to her the moment he settled with me. Therefore I could not seek to elude him. Not until my sister was safe. That was the onus attached to my privilege of being male.

'Get on home, girls,' I snapped peremptorily.

Spirit started to go, knowing it was best, though she didn't like leaving me. By herself she would have stayed, but she was aware that the real threat was to Faith, who had to be moved out of danger.

But Faith, less perceptive of the realities of the situation, had the endearing loyalty of the Hubris family. She did not go. 'You can't fight him, Hope,' she protested, her voice quavering with reaction and fear.

'I won't fight the twerp,' the scion snarled. Again I take a liberty with the translation, ameliorating the essential term, 'I'll only jam his head into a wall to teach him his place. Then I'll deal with you.' And he made a small gesture of universal and impolite significance.

Emboldened by my awareness of the peril of our situation, I never paused to see the horrified blush I knew was crossing Faith's face. I punched the scion in the stomach.

It was a foolish gesture. He was not only larger than I, he was in better physical condition. He looked clean and soft, but he had access to expensive complete-nutrition foods tailored to his specific chemistry, while my stature had been somewhat retarded by sometimes inadequate diet. He could go regularly to a private gymnasium for expertly supervised exercise crafted to be entertaining and efficient, while I got mine playing handball in the back alleys. Even if I had been his age and size, I could not have matched his training and endurance. This was a gross mismatch.

The scion smiled grimly, well aware of these aspects. He might not have completely enjoyed the various facets of his training, since he might have preferred at any given time to be out slumming in the city, as he was now, but he had nevertheless profited from them. He assumed a competent fighting stance, body balanced, fists elevated. I had hit him; I had not hurt him, but I was committed by the convention of our culture that transcended the difference in our station. A person who hits another had better be ready to fight.

The scion stepped forward, leading with his left fist, his right cocked for the punishing follow-up. In that moment I saw Faith standing frozen to my right and Spirit to my left.

My older sister was terrified, but my younger one, who now had a pretext to stay, was intrigued.

I ducked and dodged, of course. Fights were an integral part of youth and though I never sought them – perhaps I should say *because* I never sought them – I had had my share. I am a quick study on most things, and pain is a most effective tutor. I had been hurt so many times that my response had become virtually instinctive. It was not that I had any special competence to fisticuffs or any delusion about winning, but I could at least put up a respectable defence, considering the disparity in our forces. Like the scion, I had been an unwilling student, but I had mastered the essentials.

The scion turned with a sneer, unsurprised at his miss. Only a complete fool stands still to take a direct hit. He retained his poise. He had only been testing, anyway. He stepped forward again, jabbing with his left, still saving his right for the opportunity to score. He was too smart to swing wildly; he knew he would catch me in due course unless I fled, in which case he would have undistracted access to Faith. This was, in its fashion, merely a preliminary to that access. He was, perversely, showing off for her, impressing her by beating up her little brother. He had no need of her pleasure or her acquiescence, just her respect, to feed his id. He was the dragonslayer who would get the fair maid – in his own perception.

Young as I was and inexperienced as I was, I still understood that the sexual drive is superficial compared to the human need for recognition and favour. This man could have bought willing sex elsewhere, or possibly even had it from Faith had he chosen to dazzle her with some costly gift or tour of the realm of the rich. But that would have lacked the cutting edge of this drama. The thing a person works for has more value than the thing too easily obtained. Also, it seemed to be a requirement of his need that the girl he got be inferior, someone to be coerced in an

29

alley rather than wooed like a lady. A certain kind of upbringing fosters that attitude. To that type of perception, sex could not be enjoyable unless it was dirty.

Meanwhile I dodged again, not allowing my thoughts to interfere with the immediate business of self-preservation. The scion shifted to face me again, satisfied to bide his time while Faith watched. Now I was fielding information about him: the way he moved, the standard procedure he employed, the glances he made at Faith to be sure he was sufficiently impressing her. He was larger and stronger and healthier than I, but not actually faster, and certainly not more versatile. He was using no imagination in his attack, relying solely on basic moves. He was in fact limited by his arrogant attitude and his certainty of success.

He came at me a third time, and I ducked a third time – but this time I did not dodge aside. I launched myself at his knees, tackling him, my shoulder striking his thigh in front and shoving him back. The force of my strike and the surprise of my attack gave me an advantage I lacked in conventional combat. But this was not convention; this was the street. The rules were not exactly what the scion might have been taught, here.

The scion stepped back, surprised, but did not fall. He had maintained good balance, as he had been trained to do, and it is in fact very hard to dump a balanced opponent. But he had lost his poise. As I had anticipated, he was unprepared to deal with atypical strategy. The odds remained uneven, but not as much so as before.

I scrambled away before he could adjust and club me. I had hoped to dump him on his back, but simply lacked the force. Still, my confidence grew, and I began to hope I could after all take him. I have been an excellent judge of people, whether that judgment is positive or negative; it is my special talent. This was now my key to victory. An opponent understood is an opponent potentially nullified. Had this one simply gone after me with full force at the outset, he should have pulverized me; because he preferred to posture, he had given me opportunity to utilize my own strength.

The scion came at me another time, shaken and angry. He had intended an object lesson; now he was serious. I had heightened the stakes.

He feinted with his left hand as usual, expecting me to duck again. Instead I pulled back. His knee came up in a manner that would have cracked my chin, had I performed as before. As it was, it missed – and I stepped in to grab his leg.

I had learned this early: A person on one foot is largely helpless. This is a liability of such martial arts as karate or kick-boxing; blows with the feet are powerful, but if the other party gets hold of a foot, that's trouble. I hung on, preventing him from recovering his balance while staying out of the reach of his fists. He hopped about on his other foot, absolutely furious at his loss of dignity, especially with Faith watching, but unable to do much about it. His training evidently had not covered the handling of such an exigency. Spirit tittered, which didn't help.

I had him, but I didn't know what to do with him. I couldn't really hurt him in this position, and the moment I let go I would be in trouble. It was like riding the tiger: how does one safely get off?

Of couse he could have broken my hold quickly by lying down and grappling for my own feet. But I knew he wouldn't do that; it was counter to his self-image. That was my advantage of understanding again.

But I had grown too confident myself and made an error. I had not judged what he would do if trapped in a position of indignity.

The scion reached into his shirt and brought out a miniature laser weapon. It flashed, and the beam seared into my left side, causing my shirt to smoke and burning a line across my flesh. I yelped and let go, for I had to get

31

clear of that beam before it penetrated to an inner organ and cooked it. A laser can do a lot more damage than shows, because of the invisible heat-ray component. It doesn't have to vapourize the flesh to make it useless.

The man made an exclamation of victory and stalked me, aiming his laser. It scorched my buttock, making me leap out of the way. He laughed. I could not dodge that beam of light!

If I fled him, not only would I lose the fight but Faith would be subject to his will. If only she had fled when I gave her the chance! If I did not depart, he would soon score on my face, perhaps destroying my vision. I was in real trouble!

Then the scion cried out and dropped the laser. I took immediate advantage of his distraction and charged in to the attack. Those burns had eradicated any faint reticence I might have had . I stiffened my fists and clubbed him on ear and neck as hard as I could.

He fell back, seeming hardly to notice my blows though I knew they stung. He bent to pick up his weapon with his left hand, and I kneed him in the nose, exactly the way he had intended to knee me before. In a moment blood was flowing across his face. The laser skittered away from his misdirected hand.

He turned, one hand to his face, cupping the blood, and jumped for his saucer. It lurched upward; it seemed he still had sufficient command of his body to control it. In a moment he was gone.

Now I looked at Spirit, realizing what she had done. 'You used your finger-whip!' I cried as though accusing her.

She smiled smugly, whirling her finger to re-coil her weapon. The finger-whip was a spool of translucently thin line that hooked to her middle finger. When she flicked her digit just so – she had practised this diligently in private – the weighted tip carried the line out rapidly to its full length of a metre. That, plus the reach of her arm, gave her a fair

32

striking distance. Invisible the whip might be, but she could snap coins out of the air with it. That line could really sting, and sometimes cut into the skin. Spirit had savaged the scion's weapon hand, disarming him.

It had not been a fair tactic – but of course the laser itself had not been fair. She had rescued me from a nasty situation. This was not the first time, though it was the most significant.

I decided to drop the matter. Children were not supposed to have weapons, but Spirit had won the whip on a bet a year before and had made a point of mastering it. She had become the junior champion of the schoolyard, partly because of her finesse with her finger and partly because of her indomitable fighting spirit. Oh, yes, she lived up to her name! Once she had been tagged four times by an agile whip opponent, suffering scours on a leg, both arms, and one ear, but only came on more intensely, until her opponent, a boy of her own age, had lost his nerve and yielded the issue without being struck himself. He had realized that if he continued, Spirit *would* score, and her flicks had already come so near his eyes that it was obvious that discretion was the better part of valour. Pain could make her scream; it could not make her yield. Nerve, not skill, had won her that battle – but since then her skill had increased. Of course a finger-whip is a little thing, not capable of dealing death – but I knew from that time on that I never wanted to have my little sister truly angry with me. I had never betrayed her secret and neither had Faith, and we were not about to now.

'We had better not tell our folks about this incident,' I said, picking up the scion's laser and pocketing it after noting that its charge gauge read about half. Several good burns remained in it. Now I had a secret weapon too, and the others would keep my secret.

Silently, Spirit nodded acquiesence. I put my arm around her small shoulders and hugged her, my thanks for her help. She melted against me, letting down now that it was over. However tough she was in combat, she did need emotional support, and this I could offer. We understood each other.

Faith came out of her stasis. 'You shouldn't have done that, Hope,' she reproved me shakily.

I exchanged another glance with Spirit. We both knew Faith's naïveté was a necessary aspect of her self-image. 'I guess I got carried away.'

'Did you see his nose splat!' Spirit said enthusiastically.

'I didn't really mean to do that,' I admitted. 'I was aiming for his chin, but he went down too fast.'

'All that blood!' Faith said, horrified. She seemed oblivious of what could have happened to her had we not driven the scion off, and this was just as well.

Faith had some clothing-patching material that she kept for possible emergencies in connection with her dress. She used this to repair and conceal the damage the laser had done to my clothes. The burns on my flesh would simply have to heal.

We hurried on home, and by the time we got there Faith, too, had agreed that it was best that we not mention this incident to our parents.

3

Hard Choice

Maraud, 2-2-'15 – They came resplendent in the military uniform of the Maraud police, delivering the foreclosure on our property. I mentioned the debt and mortgage our father took on to ensure an education for his children. He was in arrears on the payments, of course, because all peasants were. That was the way of life on Callisto.

My father, Major Hubris, was an intelligent man with minimal formal education. He knew very well that the big landowners were systematically cheating the peasants, but didn't know how to stop it. I had progressed far enough in my education to have a fair notion of the situation, and was confident that by the time I reached maturity I would be able to set about reversing the downward trend for our family. But until that time, the Hubrises were vulnerable – and that vulnerability had abruptly been exploited.

Foreclosure – that finished us before we could begin to fight back.

We had three days to vacate unless we could pay off the mortgage in its entirety before that deadline. Of course we could not. People do not get into debt if they have the wherewithal to escape it. That clause of the contract is an almost open mockery of the hopes of the peasants. If there had been any reasonable hope of paying on demand, you can be sure the landowners would have passed a law to eliminate that hope.

My father put in a call to our creditor, who had been reasonably tolerant before. This was Colonel Guillaume, of an ancient military family, now retired to his wealth and not really a bad person as creditors went. That is, he cheated the peasants less than some creditors did, treated them with reasonable courtesy, and did seem to have some concern for their welfare. The colonel did not speak to my father personally, of course; the secretary of one of his administrative functionaries handled that matter. That was all we had any right to expect.

'Why?' my father asked, and I perceived the baffled hurt in his voice. 'Why foreclose with no warning? Have we not behaved well? Did I make some error in the tally? If I have given any offence, I shall proffer my most abject apology.'

I did not like hearing my father speak this way. To me he had always been strong, the master of the household, a column of strength. Now his darkly handsome face showed lines and sags of confusion and defeat, as though the column were cracking and crumbling under a sudden, intolerable and inexplicable burden. His newly apparent weakness frightened and embarrassed me and made my knees feel spongy and my stomach knot. I saw little beads of sweat on his forehead and shades of grey in his short, curly hair. But his hands bothered me more, for now the strong fingers clenched and unclenched spasmodically behind his back, out of the view of the secretary in the phonescreen but in full view of my eyes, and the tendons flexed along the back of his hand as if suffering some special torture of their own. But most of all it was his voice that bothered me: that cowed, self-effacing, almost whining tone, as if he were a cur submitting to legitimate but painful discipline, sorry not so much for the strike of the rod on his flesh as for the infraction that caused this punishment to be necessary. I had never before seen him this way and wished I were not seeing it now. A bastion of my self-esteem, rooted ineluctably in my perceived strength of my father, was tumbling. This is an insidiously unpleasant thing for a child. It is as if he stands upon bedrock and then experiences the first tremor of the earthquake that will destroy his house.

The secretary was female, of low degree, not unsympathetic, but compelled by her own employment to deliver the cruel response. 'The Hubris account is three months in arrears on payments – '

'Of course,' my father cut in, showing at least this token of mettle. 'We are all behind on payments. But I am due for a promotion to tallyman for my quadrant, and that will enable me to recover a month this year, perhaps two months if there is no sickness in the family – ' He paused, disliking the sound of his own voice pleading. ' The honoured colonel must have some specific reason – '

The girl looked at him sadly. 'There is another message, but I don't think I should read it.'

My father smiled grimly. 'Read it, girl; you know I cannot.' Actually, he was partly literate, having taught himself a little by looking at Faith's homework assignments, but he preferred not to have this generally known. Ninety per cent of the peasant population was illiterate and most of the rest were not clever readers, and it seemed the big landowners and politicians preferred it that way. Literacy could lead to peasant unrest. In this, I was sure, the authorities of Callisto were quite correct. Illiteracy meant ignorance, and ignorance was more readily malleable.

How was it, then, that Faith and Spirit and I had been permitted to enroll in one of the few good schools, expensive as it was? There had to have been a bribe, making it more expensive yet. I had never inquired about that and never would; if we children had our secrets to preserve, so also did our parents have theirs. I knew that if my father had done it, there had been no other way.

The girl frowned. 'If you insist, señor.' She was being overly polite, for peasants were normally not dignified by the title 'señor', or, as it is in English, 'mister'. Peasants were supposed merely to be things rather than people. 'It seems to be a notification of a charge of truancy and abuse against your children,' she said, looking at the document.

'My children!' he exclaimed, baffled. 'Surely, señora, there is some mistake!'

'B. Sierra, scion of a leading family, has lodged a charge of unwarranted aggression against the children of Hubris,' she said apologetically.

Suddenly it made awful sense. I looked at Spirit who nodded. *We* were to blame! We should have told our father, instead of concealing the episode. I had never thought the boorish scion would report us. It should embarrass him too much to have it known that a fifteen-year-old peasant boy and twelve-year-old peasant girl had balked his attempted rape of their older sister.

'I cannot believe this,' my father said. 'My children are well behaved. I have sent them to school beyond the mandatory age—'

'The charge is that they made an unprovoked attack on him as he passed on his grav-disk. He took a fall, smashing his nose, but managed to recover his disk and get away. Because they are only children, he is not demanding criminal action, but they must vacate the city.' I wondered, as I heard that, whether that could be all there was to it. If the scion had been angry enough to make a formal complaint, he must seek more revenge than our departure.

My father turned to look at me. He saw the guilt on my face. 'Thank you, señora,' he said to the screen. 'I did not properly understand my situation.'

'The colonel says he is sure it is a misunderstanding,' the girl said quickly. 'But it is better for you to leave. It is awkward to offend such a family as this. The colonel will make a domicile available for your family at the plantation – '

'The colonel is most kind. We shall consider.' The call closed and the screen faded.

Spirit and I both started to speak as we returned to our house from the pay-phone station, while Faith blushed. My

38

father silenced us all with a raised palm. 'Let me see if I have this correctly,' he said, with a calm that surprised me. Now that he had a better notion of the problem, it seemed, he had more confidence about dealing with it. 'The young stud floated up and accosted Faith, and you two fought him off.'

Silently, I nodded.

'The scion burned Hope with his laser,' Spirit said, 'We had to do something.'

My father looked at me again, and I pulled out my shirt and showed the burn streak on my left side, now bright red and painful. It was a certain relief to have this known, for I had had to keep myself from flinching when I moved my arm.

He sighed. 'I suppose it was bound to happen. Faith is too pretty.'

Faith blushed more deeply, chagrined for her liability of beauty. She was the lightest-skinned among us, strongly showing that portion of our ancestry that was Caucasian, and which accounted in part for her pulchritude. I never understood why beauty should not be considered equal according to every race of man, and every admixture of races, but somehow fairness was the ideal. Spirit's developing features of face and body were almost as good as Faith's, but her darker skin and hair would prevent her from ever being called beautiful.

I was perversely glad to see the tension relieved. 'You're not angry?'

'Certainly I'm angry!' my father exploded. 'I am infuriated with the whole corrupt system! But we are victims, not perpetrators. I only wish you had found some more anonymous way to defend your sister. We are about to pay a hideous price for this mishap.'

I felt the rebuke keenly. How could I have saved Faith without antagonizing the scion? I didn't know, and now it was too late to correct the matter, but I knew I would be pondering it until I came up with a satisfactory, or at least viable, answer. Actually, 'hideous price' turned out to be an understatement, but none of us had any hint of that then.

'Now I must explain our situation,' my father said. My mother had quietly joined us as we returned to our house, our forfeited house, and now she sat beside Faith and took her hand comfortingly.

My mother's given name was Charity, and it was an apt designation, though it did not match the normal run of names any more than the rest of ours did. We were a family somewhat set apart, being, I think, more intelligent and motivated than most, and it showed in our names. Our surname, Hubris, meant, literally, the arrogance of pride; it was a point of considerable curiosity to me how we had come by it, but I also had certain arrogant pride *in* it, for it did lend us distinction.

My mother, Charity, was not, and had never been, as pretty as Faith was now, but she was a fine and generous and supportive mother who, though I should blush to say it, still possessed more than a modicum of sex appeal. She was not a creature any man would be ashamed to have at his elbow. We three children were as different from our parents and each other as it was feasible to be, yet Charity's charity encompassed all our needs. She had a very special quality of understanding, an aspect of which I believe I inherited; but her use of it was always positive, in contrast to mine. Seeing her now, her dark hair tied back under a conservative kerchief, her delicate hands folded sedately in her lap – Faith inherited those hands! – her rather plain features composed – yet should she ever take the trouble to enhance herself the way Faith did, that plainness would vanish – I felt an overflowing of love that lacked, at the moment, any proper avenue of expression. She was my mother, a great and good woman though a peasant, and I sorely regretted bringing this affliction to her. Had I only known – yet of course I *should* have known! How could I have thought we could humiliate a scion with impunity, here in a dome on class-ridden, stratified Callisto?

'Colonel Guillaume has offered us a place in the plantation dome,' my father said. 'We must consider this offer on its merits, which are mixed. We must move from the dome of Maraud; the charge against our family can only be abated that way.' He held his hand aloft again, forestalling Spirit's impetuous interjection. 'Yes, dear, I'm sure the incident was not as the scion states it, and theoretically in a court of law both sides should be heard. But our republic of Halfcal –' Callisto, I must clarify, is actually two nations, of which ours is the lesser. Thus the other is called the Dominant Republic of Callisto. But I interrupt my father's speech: '– is weighted towards the wealthy, and it would be your word against his. There would be no justice there! We have been given the chance to avoid such a legal confrontation, and indeed we must avoid it, for it would surely lead to penalties we can't pay, and therefore prison.' Spirit subsided; she grasped the distinction between the ideal and the practical when it was explained to her. No peasant ever prevailed in an encounter with the elite class. The whole system was engineered to prevent that.

'The advantage of the plantation,' my father continued, making a fair presentation, for he always tried to be fair and usually succeded, 'is that that is my place of employment. I would no longer have to make the daily trips between domes, and that would save time and money. I could be with my family more, and perhaps begin to gain on our mortgage arrears.' He smiled tiredly. 'I should clarify that even though we are being foreclosed and evicted, our debt remains as a lien against our family line, and must eventually be cleared if we are ever to achieve higher status. There will be a rental on the plantation domicile; the good colonel did not get rich by being foolish about such details. But it will be a convenient and pleasant accommodation.' He paused, and we knew there would be another side to this. There was always another side to anything in Callisto that seemed too positive for a peasant family.

'The disadvantage is that the coffee plantation is maintained at half Earth gravity. I am not sure you children quite appreciate what that means. Half gravity may be fun for occasional play, and it is possible to spend several hours in it each day without harm, but permanent residence within it is deleterious to human health. The living bones decalcify and weaken, until it is no longer possible for a person to survive in normal Earth gravity, such as is maintained in the dome of Maraud. The process is gradual and painless, and harmless as long as residence in that gravity is maintained; it is the body's natural accommodation to the changed environment. It would be possible to return to full Earth gravity within a year, physically, though with some discomfort, but it becomes more difficult with time, and after two years no one returns.'

'But – ' Spirit burst out,

My father nodded. 'It is, as my daughter points out, no temporary choice we are making today. If we go to live in the plantation dome, we shall have an easy and peaceful life, for we can be sure no scions reside there, but our branch of Hubris will never be anything but coffee handlers. It is not a bad employment; there is honour in doing any job well, and half our national export is coffee – but we should never again have any choice. Now, it would be possible to ferry you children to school in Maraud for the rest of the current term, but after that you would have to join us full time at the plantation, for your scholastic district will be there. Unless we arrange to have you legally separated from the family—'

'No!' my mother exclaimed. That ended that; she would tolerate almost anything for the sake of family unity except the dissolution of it. Family is important to us of Callisto;

42

we are, as I explained, a Latin breed, reputed to be hot-blooded, and in this respect perhaps we are. Whatever we did we would do together, as a family. It was our weakness and our strength.

My father glanced at Faith, giving the eldest child leave to speak. But Faith wrung her hands without opinion. 'Whatever you decide, Father.'

He glanced next at me. I was naturally bursting with questions, but had to settle for one: 'We have to get out of Maraud. The coffee dome isn't good. Where else can we go?' It was really half rhetorical, for the planet outside the domes was airless and trace-gravity. The only place to go was another dome city, in the other half of the planet, the Dominant Republic, where there would be no charge outstanding against the Hubris family. But I knew from my school studies that the Dominant Republic was just as hard on peasants as Halfcal was – and we had no connections there. No job, no friends, no residence. If they admitted us at all, which was doubtful, we might just be worse off than we were here.

There was a silence, as each of us turned the grim reality over individually.

'Jupiter!' Spirit exclaimed.

My father glanced questioningly at her.

'We can emigrate to Jupiter,' she explained. 'We can bubble off from Callisto and float to the big planet where everyone is welcome and everyone is rich, and be happy ever after.'

My father did not suppress her foolish notion directly; that was not his way. Instead he asked her leading questions, letting her find her own way towards the truth. 'What bubble did you have in mind?'

'Well—' she faltered. 'There are tourist and trade bubbles, aren't there? And big freight bubbles.' She turned to Faith. 'You've taken Contemporary Economics in school, haven't you? Don't bubbles go through the whole

43

Jupiter System all the time?'

'Yes,' Faith said. 'But the moons of Jupiter are mostly Latin, while most of the commerce is done by United Jupiter, which is mostly Saxon. We don't speak the same language – that is, our people speak Spanish and theirs speak English – and they don't like our governments, what with the Saturnian bias of Ganymede and the dictatorships of Europa and Callisto.'

'*We* don't like our governments!' Spirit blurted. 'That is why we want to leave!'

'And we, the Hubrises, do speak their language,' I put in, warming to Spirit's notion as I got into it. 'That's the big advantage of the schooling we had. Faith and I can write it, too.'

'But Charity and I cannot,' my father pointed out. 'Still, the Colossus of North Jupiter does claim to accept freedom-seeking refugees, and there are many Latins settled there. We could probably find some bubbles there that conduct much of their business in Spanish, or at least are bilingual. But that's academic; the Halfcal government would never grant us leave to emigrate.'

'Why not?' Spirit demanded. 'They want to get rid of us, don't they? They should be happy to help us on our way.'

My father shook his head. 'Not so, child. They have assorted international agreements and covenants that restrict free emigration, and in any event Halfcal would hardly care to advertise that its own people are eager to leave. They may want us gone, but they won't let us go.'

'I always knew our government was crazy,' Spirit said, pouting.

'There's a way,' I murmured hesitantly.

All eyes centred on me. 'What, flap our arms and fly there?' Spirit inquired sceptically.

That angered me. I made a motion of sticking someone in the posterior with a pin, and Spirit jumped, and that diluted my anger, for she always did play our little games well. 'A bootleg bubble,' I explained. 'There's one hiding in Kilroy Crater, in the Valhalla complex, right now, just waiting for a full load.'

My father whistled. 'You children have sources of information the government lacks?'

'Well, it's just gossip,' I admitted. 'But I believe it.'

'The government knows about it,' Faith said. 'They just don't care. They consider it pirate business.'

Pirate business. That suggested volumes. Callisto had first been settled by Spanish-speaking colonists five centuries ago, who brought in slave labour to work in the first plantation domes. Then French-speaking buccaneers raided Halfcal and used it as a base for their operations. The name of our great city, Maraud, is a legacy of that period. In due course the slaves revolted. There were massacres, and finally, two centuries ago, the buccaneers were expelled. But their influence remained in this area, barely covert, and it was said that modern pirates of space had influence in the Halfcal government. Certainly there was a lot of pirate money around from the illicit drug trade, and we all knew the corrupting power of money. So it was not surprising that officials winked at innocuous or even illegal activities. I doubted that pirates were actually involved in refugee bubbles, for there could not be much money in that, but certainly individual entrepreneurs could be.

'You would go on such a bubble, rather than to the coffee dome?' my father asked, and I grasped now that he had not really been surprised by the suggestion. Adults, too, had their private sources of information.

'Oh, sure' Spirit agreed immediately. 'It would be fun!'

Oh, my Lord, how little she knew!

'There could be danger and discomfort,' my father warned.

'But if the family stayed together—' my mother said.

That was, I believe, the turning point. After that we found ourselves committed to the exodus.

We would flee Callisto!

4

Flight Into Vacuum

I have only an inkling of what my father did to organize for our horrendous trek across the surface of Callisto. (I have not run a dateline for this entry because it follows the last without change of locale. A foolish consistency, as Señor Emerson said many centuries ago, is the hobgoblin of little minds.) Probably he did not want us to know, for it could hardly have been completely legal. Officially, we were preparing to vacate the premises; actually, we meant to vacate the planet.

All of our private holdings were liquidated on the grey market and the money used to buy third-hand surface suits for each of us, together with compact food packs and water filters. There was enough left over to cover the down payment on a junky low-gravity transporter.

That was all. We could not keep our toys and dolls and treasured books. Surface suits had very little room for extra things, even if we hadn't needed the pittances the sale of those things brought. Spirit tried hard to conceal her tears, no longer quite so thrilled about the journey, and I went bleakly about the business of cashing in. We knew what was at stake.

I kept the laser pistol, however, squeezing it into an exterior pocket, and I knew Spirit kept her finger-whip.

As far as I know, no final payment was made on the mortgage. It was not that we sought to cheat Colonel Guillaume, who had done the best he could for us within the limits of his philosophy, but that the foreclosure already represented a fair profit for him, since we had built up a fair equity over the years which he would not have to transfer to the coffee-plantation residence. Perhaps he knew what we intended and did not report us to the authorities for that reason. As long as his hands were technically clean and he made a fair profit, he did not mind our effort to seek a better life elsewhere. Certainly he could have stopped us, had he wished to.

We left at night, in order to avoid any police watch. Again, it would not have been possible to escape the dome of Maraud if the authorities had really cared to prevent us. But we were only peasants; they were hardly concerned if we took it upon ourselves to depart the good life we supposedly had here.

I should explain that leaving a dome is no simple matter. Callisto is an airless world, terraformed only in particular spots. It is the same with all the moons of Jupiter, and indeed throughout the Solar System other than Earth. The domes are made of huge bubbles grown in the massive atmosphere of Jupiter, floated to the local surface by means of standard antigravity shields, cut in half, and cemented to surface plates. The fit had to be strong and tight, or the pressure of the air inside would blow the dome apart and right off Callisto. So entrance and egress were only by air locks, and these were not carelessly supervised.

The city-dome of Maraud is 1.3 kilometres in diameter, so that each of its 100,000 (approximately) inhabitants can have a floor space of at least ten square metres. Of course family units like ours increased their effective floor space by living in two-storey homes. Anyway, there were only two locks big enough for vehicles, and only one of these functioned at night, so that part of our course was set.

Mother and the girls bundled down in the cargo cage, while I got to sit up front with my father. I know this is teen-age foolishness, but it made me feel important, and I felt as if I were a real adventurer in the control cabin of a sleek Jupiter Navy spaceship, co-piloting through the starry galaxy. Of course Navy ships do not cruise the galaxy; the relativistic limitation confines mankind largely to his own Solar System. Still, this was the way my imagination went. Imagination allows more leeway than does reality, which is perhaps why we come equipped with it. What a horror it would be to be forever restricted to reality!

'Special order of garbage,' my father called out to the technician in charge of the lock. That damped my fantasy somewhat; garbage is not exactly the stuff of high adventure. Still, this too was a kind of fantasy. At least I prefer that description to the alternative of calling my father a liar.

My father proffered a folded paper. The technician took the paper and glanced at it. It was a standard twenty-dollar bill, an obvious bribe. 'The authorization seems to be in order,' the man agreed, pocketing it. 'Get that garbage well away from here.' He pressed the buttons and the air-lock panel slid clear.

The 'garbage' of course was my mother and two sisters, hunched in the cage with our limited supplies. I wondered whether they appreciated the humour.

My father drove on. It was pedal car, of course, as few motors operated conveniently in a vacuum and very little power was needed on the airless, low-gravity surface. Inside the dome the pollution of ordinary motors was unacceptable and distances were short, so the pedallers made sense there too. It occurred to me that the dome of Maraud was very like an ancient walled city, small and crowded but secure from the enemies without. In this case the enemies were vacuum and low gravity and terrible cold. This was also one reason that projectile weapons were not used inside the dome; the substance of the dome could reflect a laser beam fairly harmlessly, but a powerful enough projectile just might make a hole, and such a nightmare was not to be risked.

We secured our suits, which hung on us awkwardly,

made sure the three in the back were secure, and sealed our helmets. The lock panel slid closed behind us, the warning klaxon sounded, and the air pressure dropped. I had been outside the dome before, of course, on field trips in school, so I knew what to expect. But this time it was excitingly real, for we planned never to return. There was no hospital tank along to rescue us if we suffered a suit blowout, and no home for us to relax in if we turned back. They might not even open the lock for us. We were committed with an uncompromising finality that awed me in a somewhat squeamish manner.

Faith sat up suddenly in the cage, pointing to her left leg. That leg was not very shapely in the suit, but that was not the point. A thin plume of vapour jetted from a pinhole there. Hastily my mother slapped a seal patch on it, pressing it tightly in place. These were old, battered suits, which was why we had been able to afford them. Some problems were to be expected – but this served to remind me, as if I needed a reminder, that the danger was real and immediate. If any of us suffered a full-scale blowout, that person would be lost.

Our suits inflated and grew taut as the last of the air went, without any other problem. Fortunately there is not much actual force behind a pinhole leak, and an external patch can readily contain it. I gave a silent sigh of relief.

The outer panel on the lock slid open and we pedalled out onto the barren surface of Callisto. We were truly on our way!

The distaff contingent of our spaceship (as I fancied it) sat up and more or less joined us once we were clear of the lock. We could not readily talk with each other, for these primitive suits lacked radios, and of course there was no atmosphere to conduct our sound. But there *was* sound; it was conducted through the vehicle and our suits. We heard, as it were, through the seats of our pants. It wasn't very clear, since there was also the rattling of the pedal car, but it was better than silence.

Spirit leaned forward over the top of the cage and touched her helmet to mine. 'Isn't this fun?' she cried, so loud that I jerked my head away. Head-to-head conduction was much more efficient! 'Valhalla, here we come!' That last was through the seat, much dimmer.

Valhalla is the monstrous system of concentric rings associated with a huge old crater, extending out about fifteen hundred kilometres from its centre – a significant fraction of the planet's surface. Maraud is about one hundred kilometres outside that formation, and the bootleg bubble was hidden in an old crater hangar about two hundred kilometres within it, so we had a good three hundred kilometres to go. We could travel up to forty or fifty kilos per hour in this trace gravity, however, so that was all right.

The city domes, you see, use gravity lenses to concentrate gravity inside them, bringing it up to Earth norm, what we simply call gee. This is actually another aspect of the gravity shielding used to make saucers float above ground and bubbles float between planets. There is no such thing as blocking out gravity, but it can be diluted or intensified in limited regions by the lenslike shields, somewhat the way light itself can be affected by a properly curved lens. That's a considerable oversimplification; the actual science of gravity manipulation is far too complex for an amateur like me to comprehend. But I am sure that gravity variation is the key to the human colonization of the Solar System, because it makes both travel and residence feasible anywhere in space. Not easy, understand, but feasible, because of the enormous savings in energy required for these activities.

My mind reviewed what I had learned in school, for it was suddenly more relevant to my immediate existence. The human species had originated on the Planet Earth, but population had expanded voluminously until there really wasn't room for everyone. For reasons that weren't entirely clear to me, this caused people to react violently, and they were afraid there would be a bad nuclear war that would destroy everything. But then the discovery of gravity shielding, popularly and not too accurately called anti-gravity or null-gee, had enabled the extra people to emigrate to the other planets and moons of the Solar System, and the threat of internecine war had faded for a while.

For a while – that is a significant qualification. According to my history texts, the crush of overpopulation on Earth and diminution of resources had been set back by some five or six hundred years. As it happens, those years have passed, and we are now back to the point, population/resource-wise, where we were just before the discovery of the technique of gravity manipulation. So we face the problem again – only this time grav-shielding isn't enough to abate it. That makes me nervous, when I think about it.

The early colonization of the Solar System proceeded rapidly, for the shields enabled man to hoist huge masses into space. The problem of air and food and water remained, however, so there were limits. It was like man's discovery of the lever: It enabled him to multiply his force, but not indefinitely. One enterprising company had fitted a gravity lens to an ocean liner and sailed it through the air. But it was clumsy outside its natural element, subject to errant winds, and when it sailed too high, the passengers suffered from the thinning of the air. Aeroplanes had similar problems, actually, as they flew beyond the normal atmosphere. Efficient as an aeroplane may be in air, it becomes clumsy in vacuum, for its wings cannot plane through nothing. So in the end the compact, simple, tough bubble became king of space. From the outside a bubble most resembled a planetoid with portholes, or a little round meteor with craterlets on it, but inside it was a temporary world.

Bubbles floated out to all the other planets and moons and fragments, carrying gravity lenses and construction equipment that could operate in a vacuum. Bases were established throughout the Solar System in the course of the first century following the null-gee discovery. New nations sprang up in the likeness of old, as individual Earthly governments operated competitively to establish their domains in space. The American continents of Earth centred on the richest prize, the gross planet Jupiter and its moons, while the Asians settled for the next-greatest prize, beautiful Saturn, with its rings and many small moons. The smaller or more distant planets, considered less desirable, were left to the lesser powers of that day: the Africans, who got the hot inner worlds of Venus and Mercury; the Europeans, who got Uranus; the Moslem states, who got Neptune and its oil-rich satellite Triton, and the remainder somewhat haphazardly distributed among other special interests. A number of the other powers claimed shares of frigid Pluto and its satellite Charon, hoping eventually to discover and exploit rich resources there. There was no established population on Charon or Pluto, however; they were just too far out, and the sunlight there was too dim to be usable for power.

This was part of the education I had suffered in school, which I now parrot back as if it represented original thinking on my part. Would it were so! I happen to have a flair for geography, so I did well, but most of my fellow students professed to find it boring. I could make fairly precise matchings of each planet or moon with an equivalent political entity of six hundred years before on Earth; no one else saw any point in such a game, and I can't honestly claim it is more than idle entertainment.

Oops – did I write that the Moslems of Earth took Neptune? I would have flunked that question on an exam! Already my school learning fades and becomes confused. It was Mars the Moslems took; Neptune was – let me think now – that went to the Australians. Yes, now I have it straight!

I experienced queasiness that interrupted my chain of thought described above. I tend to think too much, as I may have confessed before. 'Say, fun!' Spirit exclaimed brightly against my helmet. 'We're passing out of the lens!'

True enough. The lens concentrated gravity in Maraud to Earth normal, but outside the dome gravity thinned out, since this was the depressed area three or four times as broad as the dome. Gravity doesn't come from nothing, after all. Now we were coming into the true natural surface attraction of Callisto, which was a little more than a quarter Earth norm. From one gee to one-tenth gee to one-quarter gee – it was vaguely like riding ocean waves. I have not had direct experience with any large body of water, but can imagine it. Maybe we were riding gravity waves.

The outer surface of Callisto is bleak, barren, and frankly, dull. Our world is the most heavily cratered significant body in the Solar System, for the past billion years of new meteoric strikes have only replaced old craters with new ones, not changing the total number. One might suppose this would make for a singularly variegated terrain, but that is not so. Right here on the surface it simply wasn't that interesting. On other planets there may be deep oceans and high, jagged peaks; not so Callisto and our sister planet Ganymede. These are two iceball worlds, of low overall density because of the ice, and, though the surface is crusted with rock and dust, the thick mantle of ice below prevents any really spectacular mountains from forming.

I'm not sure I'm getting this across. You see, ice is as hard and stable as any other rock at the local temperature of one hundred degrees Kelvin – I'm not as good at figures as geograpy, but that's an easy one to remember, one hundred degrees Celsius above absolute zero – but at the local noon (which of course has no relation to the Earth time we use inside the domes), it can be fifty degrees warmer, and deep down below the pressure can heat it some too, so in the course of millions of years that ice does soften and flow a little. This planet has been around for four billion years or so, so the flow obliterates the extreme features. Result: shallow, rounded craters standing, as it were, shoulder to shoulder, rim to rim, and one inside another, and overlapping: This world is made of craters, and none of them are any effort to navigate. There are no cutting edges on Callisto. You might say the features of the surface have been eroded by water: not water coursing over from above, as on Earth, but slowly squeezing out from below. That's why we were moving along so well in our wheeled vehicle; there was very little natural obstruction.

The sky was more interesting. This was night, on the surface as well as inside the dome, but Jupiter was full, and his baleful light flooded the rolling rills of Valhalla. Jupiter was anything but dull, with his violently contrasting bands of atmosphere and the various gaseous eyes staring at us. Surely Jove was watching our puny efforts with disdain – but he was our destination. I was, of course, sorry to leave my home world, for all my experience was invested here on Callisto and all my prior hopes for success had been defined by the Halfcal culture and hierarchy. But I knew that in those bands of turbulent colour on the Jovian Planet was opportunity as vast as Jupiter himself. We would certainly be better off there; we would no longer be peasants, there!

I looked directly up, trying to see the other gravity lens, the one above us, close. Such lenses don't just fix the gravity inside the domes, they govern the light we receive. This can be hard for people who don't reside on moons to understand, so I'll try to make it simple: Light is affected by gravity, technically the curvature of space that we call gravity, so a lens that bends gravity waves also bends light waves. Properly formed, a large gravity lens can be used to focus the light of the distant sun on a smaller area, making it proportionally more intense. There's a lot of energy in light, as a magnifying glass can demonstrate when used to set fire to things. Since the sun's light is much less intense out here at Jupiter's orbit than it is at Earth's orbit, we need to focus it to match what our bodies and our plants are used to. We are all transplants from Earth, really, though we may have been born or seeded here; a few centuries can't erase a few billion years of evolution.

So above each dome-city is a huge gravity lens that is twenty-seven times the area of the dome, and the lens focuses the wan sunlight to that amount, and it shines in through the dome's transparent roof to light and warm the city, exactly as would be the case on Earth. Well, not exactly; Earth's copious atmosphere filters out many deleterious aspects of the radiation, so our twenty-seven-times-concentrated sunlight would burn us if we took it straight. But the material of the dome is designed to filter out the harmful radiation, substituting for the missing depth of atmosphere, and so the net effect is similar.

The same is true for the agricultural domes; they are literally greenhouses. This is convenient to do on an airless planet, since nobody lives outside to complain about being deprived of sunlight. Naturally the focused brilliance at the dome is at the expense of the twenty-seven-times-as-large area around it, which receives very little light. We had not noticed any difference because we pedalled through this zone at night. But it would have been night by day also, near the dome, if you see what I mean.

It's really more complicated than that, because Callisto's day is the same as its period of revolution around Jupiter: sixteen and two-thirds Earth days. One face – Halfcal's – always faces Jupiter; the other always faces space. So we have eight and a third days of continuous light, and then a night just as long. We humans don't like that; it doesn't match our biological rhythm. So we exchange light with a sister city around the globe: San Pedro, in the Dominant

55

Republic. San Pedro is always in darkness when Maraud has light, and vice versa, so there's always sunlight one place or the other. We never have clouds or bad weather, of course, the way Earth does; in fact, we have no weather at all. When Maraud is in sun, we use it for twelve hours, then refract it around the planet, in the form of a concentrated light beam, using a chain of vertical gravity lenses, to San Pedro.

In this manner we have our night in the middle of the Callistian day, while they have their day in the middle of their night. When they are light, they send us twelve-hour segments of daylight. This is the most fundamental and absolute system of co-operation between the two nations of our planet, and is inviolate. If Halfcal and the Dominant Republic went to war with each other – and sometimes, historically, it has come to that, for we are a bickering culture – neither would abrogate the light exchange. Without it, life as we know it would be virtually impossible on Callisto. We depend on the sun for almost all our energy, for we have no great deposits of oil or uranium and lack the technical and industrial base to establish a hydrogen-fusion power plant.

But my glancing was wasted, for the huge elevated gravity lens was not visible. Not only did it operate only in daylight, it was not physical at all. It was generated in space, forming between key points. There was nothing to see. Still, my eye sought it out, much as it sought the gaze of a person in a picture looking in another direction. This foolishness in inherent in my nature; I seek constantly to relate to people and things directly, even when I suspect it is unwise or impossible.

My attention wandered to the other large moons of Jupiter, all closer in than ours. Ganymede, off to the side of the Colossus, its brightness at three-quarter face; it was almost halfway in toward Jupiter, from our vantage. That is, its orbit is just over one million kilometres out, while

Callisto's is just under two million. We would pass that inner orbit on our way to Jupiter, but would not pass close to Ganymede itself, because it revolved about the planet more than twice as fast as we did and would rush to the far side when our bubble passed, as if avoiding us. Just as well; the recent political revolution there seemed to have made things even worse for peasants than before. As the ancient poet Coleridge put it: 'They burst their manacles and wear the name/Of Freedom, graven on a heavier chain!' But of course Europa was little better, while the innermost big moon, Io, zooming all the way around Jupiter in less than two Earth days, was hardly habitable, even with terraform domes. No, no hope for us on the other moons.

Down near the horizon behind us I spied a speck of light I didn't recognize. It wasn't a star, for it was moving, shifting somewhat erratically above the landscape, as if guided by some human hand.

'Saucer!' I exclaimed. 'What's it doing out here at night?' For there was very little interdome travel by night, as Callisto is essentially a hinterworld with no major industry, other than agriculture. Unlike the hyperactive denizens of major worlds, we preferred to sleep at night.

'The Maraud authorities wouldn't chase us, would they?' Spirit asked. My parents were consulting with each other, helmet to helmet, but I couldn't hear their dialogue, to my annoyance.

'Shouldn't,' I agreed tersely. 'We're not breaking any law. We're just leaving the city, as ordered.'

'And the planet,' she added. 'If they found out about that – and they might suspect, the way we snuck out.'

'Maybe,' I agreed uneasily. I would have disparaged the notion out of hand – since I knew the Maraud authorities did not care about us – except for the fact of the saucer. There had to be some reason for it to be out here, and we could not safely assume that reason had nothing to do with us.

The light zoomed towards us. In moments we recognized a private pick-up craft, used by explorers to collect samples of minerals from the planet's surface. Callisto was extremely shy of heavy minerals, which made them all the more valuable. Prospectors were constantly ranging out with metal detectors to search for what few nuggets there were. A lode of iron ore could make a man's fortune. Even mineral dust was far more valuable on Callisto than it was elsewhere, except on Ganymede. Most of our metals had to be imported from the inner planets of the Solar System, and even with the gravity shields, that was expensive.

This craft was typical. It had a nether power scoop and a fair-sized storage compartment and a sealed cockpit with windows looking forward, upward, and down. That meant the occupant did not have to suffer the inconvenience of wearing a space suit, the way we peasants did. Cheaper saucers were not sealed; they might be hardly more than flying platforms, and a miscue could dump the operator off. Not so this one. I envied whoever could afford this sort of vehicle: sealed afloat instead of suited and landbound like us.

The saucer came right up to us, evidently using a metal detector to spy us out. The metal was the main value in a pedal car; it could be melted down and lose only a fraction of its price, and it would be very easy to spy from the dome. However, there was not a great deal of metal here, for most of the transporter's mass was plastic; for a saucer to come out in the hope of salvaging a vehicle like this – no, that didn't make sense.

It all came back to the original question: why would anyone be looking for us? Legal or illegal – I think our status was now hazy – we remained only refugees, nothing people, completely unimportant to anyone except ourselves.

The saucer paused to hover directly over us, putting us in shadow. That hardly mattered; we weren't trying to draw on Jupiter's pale radiance for power. Then a bright beam of light speared down at us from a unit by the cockpit, blinding to our Jovelight-acclimatized eyes. It found us and blinked off and on again, rapidly, several times.

The saucer was signalling us. It was, of course, impossible to communicate by sound through the vacuum when there was no direct physical contact. Saucers used radios to talk to each other and the city domes, but of course we didn't have a radio. We didn't have a flashlight either, and in any event didn't know the blinking communication code. We didn't have anything that wasn't essential to our progress across the surface or our journey through space, because everything cost precious money. We were unable to make any meaningful response. So my father just waved and pedalled on.

The nether hatch in the saucer opened. The scoop pincers descended slightly, holding something. They were going to drop us a message!

The pincers descended, in order to get below the gravlens. It was possible for objects to pass right through it without interfering with its function; gravity does not obey ordinary rules. Once below, the pincers cranked open to release the message capsule. It was a bright-orange cylinder that seemed almost to glow, even in the shadow.

Suddenly our transporter swerved violently to the left. I was jammed into the right wall of the vehicle. We must have hit a craterlet. Craters aren't all landscape-sized; they graduate on down to pinhead size, and some of those can be almost as deep as they are broad. they have less mass to flatten them out – no, I'm wrong, how can a hole have a mass? – or maybe it is that they are fresher, so have not yet melted down to gentleness. Geologically speaking, any crater less than a million years old is an infant, born yesterday. Yet my father surely would have seen it and avoided it. Anyway, it was a bad jolt. Spirit, perched high, had to grab my head to keep from being flung out of the vehicle.

5

Fight For Life

Belatedly I remembered that capsules were colour-coded in an obvious manner, as it could be exceedingly awkward to open them in a vacuum to check their contents. Glaring orange was the code for explosives.

Explosives are normally used for excavation work. It is not feasible to light fuses or whatever in a vacuum – oh, yes, they do have a fuse that burns in empty space, with its own oxygen built in – but it takes special equipment to start it going. So most small explosives are contact-detonated.

The effect of this one did not seem great, but of course this was a mine-charge, and the debris settled out almost instantly, because there was no air to buoy it. Had that bomb struck our transporter, those of us who were not directly injured would have died from suit destruction. Even a little bomb is devastating when it detonates in your face! My father had caught on and swerved just in time; we had struck no craterlet.

The saucer swerved to get above us again. I saw its pincers, holding another bomb. There was no doubt about its hostile intent! But, though the immediacy of the threat somehow abated the fear I should naturally have felt, my curiosity remained undimmed. Who was trying to do this to us, and why?

My father swerved again and braked, and the second bomb missed us to the left front. This time all of us were hanging on firmly, so neither the swerving nor the jolt of the ground from the explosion dislodged us. The forward bumper took the brunt of the flying debris, and we all ducked low so the rest passed harmlessly overhead. This was nervous business, though. Sand is sharp, and while space suits are tough, they aren't that tough.

Still the saucer pursued. It was more manoeuvrable than we were, and faster; I knew we could not escape it long. I didn't know how many bombs it had, but all it needed was one score on our vehicle. Each cylinder was small, and the saucer's hold could contain hundreds of them. Weight wouldn't make much difference, with the gravity shielding; a full hold weighed about the same as an empty one.

The pincers carefully lowered each bomb below the shield before releasing it, as I mentioned; otherwise, instead of dropping, the cylinder would remain in the chamber until it banged into something there, and—

That gave me a notion. If I could somehow jam a bomb back into the hold, or set it off before it dropped—

I got out my laser and took a shot, but the two vehicles were jogging about so violently relative to each other – I'm sure it was mostly us, but it seemed at the time like the saucer, which is a useful exercise in perspective – that I couldn't aim well, and I missed. I wasn't at all sure the laser beam would detonate the bomb anyway. Light and heat were one thing; abrupt collision was another. In any event, if the bomb did explode above us, shrapnel could rain down on us and wipe us out. Even if it also took out the saucer, what good would it do us then? Maybe it was best that I had failed. I had no business depleting the charge in the weapon uselessly.

The third bomb missed behind us as my father accelerated, once more outsmarting the saucer pilot. Actually, it is very hard to align with an erratic target; pure chance gave us the advantage, if you consider having a chance to survive such a threat an advantage. The saucer was in no danger; it was the aggressor. These misses were too close; I knew they couldn't go on much longer.

Then Spirit jammed her helmet against mine. 'Look!' she

yelled. 'The ice caves!'

She meant the excavations made by the city of Maraud to mine clean ice. A community of a hundred thousand people needed a lot of water, and the recyclers were always breaking down and it was too expensive to replace them with new and reliable ones, so it was simpler just to quarry the water out of the ground. If there is one thing Callisto has in abundance, it is ice! The bedrock ice is very close to the surface in some places, and here there was a combination trip-and-tunnel mine. The top ice at this site was blended with minerals, but the deep ice was as clean as nature had formed it four billion years ago. Huge chunks of it were blasted free with bombs similar to those being used against us now, and gravity shields were used to float the icebergs to the dome, where smaller pieces were cut and taken inside for melting and using. There was always an iceberg perched near the dome, our guarantee that one thing we would never suffer was thirst.

I leaned over to touch helmets with my father, who was intent on his pedalling, steering, and the saucer. He was really working hard, but he kept his helmet still for me. 'The ice caves!' I shouted. 'We can hide in them!'

'Get rope!' he yelled back, and I realized he had been angling for this all along. I didn't know what good rope would do, but I scrambled out of my seat and across Faith in the back, delving for the flexible cable every outside vehicle had for towing and such.

In a moment I found it, as the vehicle swerved in crazy patterns, preventing the saucer from getting a good line on us. I realized the saucer was floating too high, so my father could see when the capsules were being released, and could dodge out of the way before they arrived. Things didn't fall very rapidly out here in quarter-gee. Faster than they would in atmosphere, of course, as the prompt settling of the dust showed; but any distance made the slower pattern of natural acceleration evident. Human reactions, geared for

Earth-type acceleration, were quite ready to cope with Callisto acceleration.

The saucer, however, was catching on. First it angled towards the ice mine as if to block us off from it; then, realizing that this ploy was ineffective because we could zigzag towards the mine anyway, the saucer floated lower, so as to cut the fall time and prevent us from dodging effectively.

My father made a throw-gesture with a free arm, and I caught on. I could use the rope against the saucer! It had been floating too high for the rope to reach, before, but now it was coming down close enough. My father was still out-thinking it.

I made a lasso noose as I eyed the saucer. If I could loop that extended pincers, I could put it and the saucer out of commission. The lower the saucer got, the more in reach it got.

I flung the loop, but missed. I wasn't experienced at this; I didn't know how to lasso a moving object in low-gee. The dynamics were all wrong. In addition, that hovering bomb made me excruciatingly nervous. If it dropped now, could I catch it – and do so gently enough to prevent it from detonating? I doubted it.

Spirit climbed back to join me, moving lithely. She always had been an active type, able to fling herself about like a little monkey. She put her helmet against mine. 'Dad says jump!' she cried.

'And desert the family?' I retorted, 'No.'

'With the rope, dummy! Here, I'll do it.' She reached for the lasso.

Then I understood. In low-gee we could jump much higher than normal. It wasn't as simple as jumping four times as high in one-quarter gee; it depended on technique and the centre of body mass. I hadn't had much practice at this either, but I had a general notion.

As the saucer swooped low, lower and closer than before,

I launched myself upward, carrying the loop of rope in both hands. I imagined myself a rocket, jetting from a planetary berth with an important payload. It felt like straight up, but of course it was at an angle, with the inertia of the vehicle's forward motion slanting me. There was no atmospheric drag to slow me; I shot straight for the saucer. I was amazed, though I shouldn't have been; the power of my leap should have taken me up a metre within the dome, which translated to somewhere in the vicinity of four metres here, allowing for the uncertainties of the situation. That was how high the saucer now floated.

I came right up under the bomb, and with my two hands looped the rope around the extended pincers. Then I fell away to the side, slowly – and saw to my horror that I had dislodged the bomb, or at least failed to prevent it from being released.

I grabbed for it, but that was futile. I was already out of reach, and it was falling at the same rate I was. It was travelling right towards the transporter.

I watched helplessly as that terrible cylinder descended. Time dilated for me; everything was in slow motion. My family faced destruction – and I could only watch.

Then Spirit jumped up and caught the bright capsule in her hands. Still aloft, she flung it from her, behind the vehicle. She had been alert, bless her, and had done what I could not. Once again she had backstopped me, and perhaps saved us all.

The bomb exploded as Spirit and I landed on either side of the transporter. Both of us managed to get turned to face forward and hit the ground running, for we still had that forward inertia. It was rough, but I managed to keep my balance, and so did she. We jogged to clumsy stops well behind the transporter.

The rope was tied to the saucer pincers at one end, and anchored to the land vehicle at the other. The two machines were tied together.

The three oldest Hubrises were in the transporter – and who was in the saucer?

Spirit rejoined me, touching helmets. 'Sierra,' she said.

'What?' My mind was distracted by more important things than her chance remarks.

'The scion on the saucer!'

Suddenly it came clear! The one we had humiliated! Naturally he was out to get revenge, and he had *not* been satisfied with our departure from the dome of Maraud. Out here at night he could destroy us and get away with it! We had fled the dome of our own volition, leaving the protection of its law, such as it was; we had become fair targets. There wouldn't even be any inquiries.

Sierra must have been keeping track of us, unsatisfied without the taste of blood. The arrogance of scions was almost beyond belief; a personal humiliation by a peasant was justification for murder, in this person's view. But not open murder, for then it would be known that he had acted in a cowardly manner, bombing a pedal-powered vehicle from a saucer. The nature of his humiliation might also become known. So his revenge had to be private and complete. Yes, it made sense at last.

The saucer wrenched upward as its pilot realized that something was wrong – and it skewed crazily as it snapped on the end of its tether. The rope provided with out-dome vehicles is tough, for it has to stand up to the abrasion of sharp rocks and the stress of hauling a vehicle out of a mine cave-in. That saucer could not break free!

With a gravity lens, a saucer can lift any amount that will fit in its hold, because the load has no weight – provided the lens is between the load and the planet. But the rope anchored the saucer to the transporter below the lens, with its full quarter-gee weight. This was too much to lift. The propulsive rockets (no propeller out here in vacuum, of course) weren't designed for significant lifting, only for ward thrust. What a lovely trap!

With its pincers unit immobilized, the saucer couldn't drop any more bombs. We had muzzled it as well as tethering it. Because the pilot was sealed inside, he couldn't go to the airless cargo hold to untie or cut the rope. Not unless he had a space suit – which was unlikely. Trying to scramble into one of those bulky things in the confines of a cockpit was so awkward as to be something a scion would not consider, anyway.

On the other hand, we couldn't let the saucer go without being in trouble again. It was similar to the way I had grabbed the scion's foot, really incapacitating us both. Only then he'd drawn the laser—

Oops! If he had a laser now—

No, that seemed unlikely. No laser cannon was mounted on the saucer itself, as lasers weren't very useful for cutting this ice of the mine. It simply melted, flowed, and refroze in an instant, absorbing an enormous amount of energy in the process. It takes as much energy for a laser to do its work as it does to do the work any other way; there is no such thing as free power, other than what we draw from the sunlight. So the ice had to be cut physically, without wasteful heating.

Anyway, if the scion had had a laser, he would have used it instead of the clumsy blasting cylinders. So it seemed we really had evened the odds.

Then my mind, which never knows when to stop, brought up another thought: The scion could have a laser in the cockpit, but not have used it because that would have holed up our suits and killed us without destroying the evidence of the murder. A person or a family could run afoul of blasting cylinders by error, perhaps, but there had to be another party to fire a laser at five separate people. So I could not afford any complacency on that score.

The transporter reached the ice mine, hauling the saucer along on its tether. On the shallow-crater region of the planet the saucer had the advantage, when it was loose, for there was no place for a vehicle to hide or avoid it. But the mine was deep, convoluted, and jagged, not having had the necessary billion years or so to melt into anonymity. This terrain was no picnic for a ground vehicle, but it was downright dangerous for a low-flying saucer on a tether. If we let the scion go here, he would probably just have to float home.

But if we did that, and the saucer did not go home, we would be trapped in the mine, unable to proceed to our rendezvous with the bubble. Safety in the mine was no good when we had a time limit for crossing the landscape. The saucer could hover indefinitely, outwaiting us. We had no great supplies of food or water, and in any event had to reach the bootleg bubble before it departed without us. So we had to hang onto the saucer. But could we haul it all the way to the bubble? That was unlikely – and if we did, the operator of the bubble might decide to take off before we arrived, fearful that the saucer represented the authority of an official. Our predicament had changed its nature, but not its urgency.

My father was no expert driver, since few peasants ever got much practice with vehicles of any type, and his legs had to be tired from all that pedalling, but he was strongly motivated. Spirit and I came to the brink of the mine and watched the action. There were roads winding around and down past tiers of blank ice walls, and the whole cavity was like a giant inverted dome, with high ridges of ice-rock projecting between many of the levels and spires rising where there were turnarounds. Any of these could smash up the saucer pretty badly, if it happened to be unlucky enough to collide with them. The gravity lens made the saucer light, but it could not change its mass; a crack-up would be just as devastating as one in full gravity.

The winding roads were designed for exactly the kind of vehicle my father was driving, by no coincidence, so now he had the advantage of the terrain. He wheeled around the spires, dragging the saucer along, trying to snag it on a projection. He knew it was not safe to let the saucer go, and he was not a forgiving man. The scion had tried to kill him; he would now try to put away the scion. I felt a certain horrified elation of battle, and pride for my father. He was normally a reasonable man, but the time for reason had passed. Spirit and I had humiliated Sierra before; my father was out to finish him.

But the saucer followed, skilfully manoeuvring around the obstructions, keeping the rope slack. Scions had plenty of leisure to learn to master their craft; this one floated with precision. I saw that this tactic wasn't going to be enough. There were too many open spaces in the mine, and the moment the saucer had the chance to get clear, as it might by snagging the rope on a sharp edge of ice-rock so that it would saw through the rope, or if there were any alternative way to drop a bomb—

My eye was distracted by Spirit's motion. There were whole piles of ice-rock fragments that had been bulldozed clear of the roads, and she was checking through one. She was always curious about things. How could I blame her? I had the same attitude.

She saw me watching and made a throwing motion, empty-handed. Then I caught on. These rocks were weapons!

We started in with a will, hurling head-sized rocks at the saucer. The quarter-gravity and irregular edges made it easier to grasp and throw large pieces, but they didn't go very fast and our aim wasn't very good. Again we faced the problem of mass: Weight is only one element of substance, one of its many dimensions, and it was as hard to accelerate a large chunk here as it would have been in full gee. Maybe harder, for the weight we did heft caused our muscles to assume that this was the amount of mass we had to throw, so we constantly misjudged it. Soon we shifted to smaller chunks and schooled ourselves to overthrow, and then we got the range and power and began scoring on the saucer as it trailed the transporter in a diminishing spiral down into the centre of the mine. Those rocks might be light and slow, but they were as ornery in their stopping as in their starting, and solid enough to dent the saucer's metal hide and shake the whole mass of it as they struck.

A bomb exploded below the saucer, and we knew one of our rocks had jogged it out of the hold. Those capsules were only lightly anchored, so that the pincers could take them without risk of setting them off; now they were being shaken loose, and that could mean a whole lot of trouble for the pilot!

Still, it wasn't good enough. The saucer was getting too far away from us, so our rocks were losing accuracy and effect. We had to keep up the distraction, or it would get above the transporter and shake loose a bomb. This would be difficult and risky with its pincers incapacitated, but if any bombs were floating free in its hold the scion needed to get rid of them anyway. Certainly it was too much of a risk for us to tolerate. That wasn't just a transporter down there; that was our family!

We jumped down the slopes, bounding from level to level, as each was separated from the next by only two or three metres. Soon we were back in range, because we were going straight in, while the vehicles were travelling in spirals. A straight line really *is* the shortest distance between two points!

Then I saw that they were approaching a major staging area, where the various vehicles normally operating in the mine could load and turn around. Here the saucer would have plenty of manoeuvring room. I'm sure my father would have avoided this region, but he lacked our vantage and probably could not see it coming, and in any event his road was curving right to it without any turnoff. We had to resume our barrage, keeping the saucer occupied.

But as they entered the clear area, while Spirit and I

desperately hurled more ice-rocks, the saucer dropped almost to the floor of the mine. Had its gravity lens malfunctioned? I doubted it, because those units were very stable and reliable. They resembled, in a fashion, permanent magnets, and lasted almost indefinitely once activated, requiring no external source of power. That was part of what made them so useful. A gravity lens is like a sail on an ancient Earth ship, a tool to utilize the forces around it. A sail taps the immense power of moving air; a lens does the same with the ubiquitous gravity in the universe. Neither sail nor lens is likely to break down if properly used.

A beam speared out from the saucer. Oh no! My mental reservation had been correct. The scion did have another hand laser, and now he was firing through the transparent forward port. This was not the most effective way to use a laser, because of the dispersion caused by the glass, but even a weakened beam could readily hole a suit. Presumably the exigency of the moment forced the scion to get out of this trap any way he could; maybe if he killed my father with the laser, he would then have leisure to shake loose a bomb and cover up the evidence. The threat was immediate.

Spirit touched her helmet to mine. 'I'll foul the glass!' she cried.

'You can't go down there!' I protested.

I should have known better. She was already taking off, carrying an ice stone. Spirit seldom let the voice of reason stand in the way of direct action. I leaped after her, knowing this was folly; the scion's laser would spear her before she ever got close to the glass. But she had a lead on me, and she was an athletic elf and I couldn't catch her. We both went tumble-running down almost on top of the saucer, carrying our rocks.

Spirit took a final leap and landed on the low saucer. She had excellent spacial judgement that way. I did not. I missed.

Naturally she was affected by the gravity lens when she touched the saucer's surface. The typical lens makes an onion-shaped distortion in the gravity-wave pattern, into which the saucer or other object using the lens nestles. Above, that distortion narrows and winks out as the gravity pattern reasserts itself. Gravity is powerful, ornery stuff, despite its reputation as the weakest of the four universal forces; it can never be actually abolished, it can only be channelled slightly. If this were not so, true gravity shields would disrupt the natural order horribly. Imagine the havoc that could be wrought in an atmosphere, for example; the gas above the shield would be literally blown out of its world by the pressure of the surrounding gas. Perhaps a monstrous whirlpool or tornado would form around that dreadful leak, funnelling the atmosphere out into space until it all was gone, leaving the planet denuded and as naked as was Callisto. Lenses would be terrible weapons, with the potential to suffocate whole inhabited worlds. An enemy could simply drop a lens from space and let it wreak its havoc as it descended, since it itself would be subject to natural gravity and not be thrown clear of the planet. Well, maybe it would have to be tied down, to prevent being sucked up by the tornado it caused. A minor detail. And of course the first huge, crude lenses had caused considerable mischief, since their onion-tops had projected so high that there was some of that tornado effect. But fortunately the modern lenses were crafted to wink out at their tops fairly expeditiously, just a few metres from their lenses, and very little atmosphere was affected. Here on an airless world that didn't matter, of course, but it remained, to my mind, a significant matter. The Colossus Jupiter would hardly allow lenses to be used on the moons that had the potential to disrupt Jupiter's own atmosphere if dumped there accidentally or otherwise. There is obviously much politics in physics.

At any rate, Spirit lost her weight and had trouble

staying on the saucer. Then she caught hold of the ladderdents that were there for workers, and was secure. The dents actually curved inside the skin of the saucer, so that fingerholds were convenient. Sometimes it was necessary for a person in a suit to ride a saucer outside, as when helping to load it, so that was facilitated. A weightless person could normally support himself by one finger; even the slightest anchorage was all that was necessary.

I came to the foot of the slope and tried to be inconspicuous. I didn't know what to do at the moment, but had to be ready to do whatever offered, when it offered. I couldn't throw rocks for fear of hitting my sister, yet if I didn't, that laser might get her. I was terrified for Spirit, but was helpless.

I should clarify that the telling of this required much more time than the action did. Obviously the saucer was not sitting there quiescently for ten minutes while we set up to smudge its window. It may have been as little as thirty seconds, while the scion was trying to get into better position for a killing shot at my father.

Spirit squirmed across the saucer roof, awkward in her suit. Then she reached down to the front vision port and smeared her ice-rock across it. The glass was supertough and scratch-resistant, but some of the dust in the ice smeared. Maybe enough heat from the cabin radiated through the glass to cause the surface of the ice to melt a little.

It took the scion inside a moment to realize what was happening. Maybe he had felt the impact of Spirit's landing and assumed it was another big rock. The saucer was now so low that I could see his shape behind the glass. Then, furious, he aimed his hand laser at Spirit.

I don't remember digging out my own laser again, the one I had, ironically, acquired from him after our first encounter and tried to use to detonate one of the bombs. I had had it fastened in a compartment in my suit belt; now it was in my hand, as if possessed of its own volition. I pointed it at the glass, steadied my hand, and squeezed off a ray.

I don't think my beam could have had any deadly effect. I had only a mini-laser, with a little power, and the angle wasn't good, and the glass was dirty thanks to Spirit's continuing effort. But the ray could have splayed as it passed through the glass and temporarily blinded the scion inside. At any rate, he didn't fire again, and Spirit was able to finish her smearing job without getting her suit holed, no thanks to her impetuosity.

I scrambled across and pulled her off the saucer at last, not wanting her to take any more such chances. 'We have to get away from here before he radios for help!' I yelled as we touched helmets.

She nodded, understanding. We moved to the transporter, where my father was unloading. He knew we couldn't get that vehicle out of danger in time, uphill around and around the spiral roads of the mine. We had to abandon ship, as it were. We all got our belongings into our packs and strapped the packs on. Then my father started the transporter, fixing its steering wheel, and sent it rolling down a slope towards a drop-off. As the brink neared, he disengaged from the pedals and jumped free, letting the vehicle's inertia carry it and the trailing saucer over the edge, down the steep embankment beyond the staging area. With luck, both it and the saucer would wreck, and any pursuers would assume we all were dead – at least until it was too late to matter.

But the wrench did not drag the saucer down. The rope broke. Maybe it had been frayed in the course of the descent into the mine. The saucer drifted free at last, dangling a metre of rope, its pincers twisted crooked. It could not drop bombs, but once its occupant recovered, that saucer could be dangerous again. Too bad, I thought ungraciously.

My father led the way through the mine. He had been here

before; in his youth he had worked here, before he got the more pleasant and safer job in the coffee dome. I realized that age could be an advantage; it provided time for broader experience. The particular configurations of the mine would have changed considerably in the intervening years, but not its basic nature.

We saw two lights coming over the mine's horizon. There were the scion's allies! Probably other spoiled, rich, arrogant youths like him. I jogged my father's arm and pointed.

He looked and broke into a run. We followed, though running is not fun in space suits; it's not the weight but the clumsiness, since they are not as flexible as human bodies and one must run spraddle-legged. But we had to get to cover in a hurry.

Soon we came to a sort of crevice in the ice wall, broad enough for a man to enter. We plunged in, getting out of view of the saucers, and worked our way along it until we were safe from any discovery from above. We were lost in the deep shadow of the crack in the ice.

This was just as well, for through the crack I could see one of the saucers casting about. They were looking for us, certainly!

The crevice closed in tighter, so that we had to squeeze along in single file. I began to get claustrophobic; I was somehow afraid the separation in the ice would close up again, crushing everything within it. Of course I knew better; Callisto is a dead world, as these things go, with no volcanism or plate tectonics; even a tiny crack could remain undisturbed for a billion years if man did not interfere Such fears are not rational, but the perception of their irrationality does not necessarily make them depart. I willed myself to react sensibly; the planet presented no danger, but the saucers did.

That ice, as we slid along the walls, was extremely solid and cold; I felt its chill through my suit, psychologically.

75

The space suits were insulated and heated, charged for forty-eight hours continuous use – which was more than enough, since we had only twenty hours to reach the bubble, to be sure of catching it before takeoff.

And there, more than likely, was the real source of my chill: We had used up two hours – and lost our vehicle. Here we were, stuck in an ice crevice; how could we ever reach the escape bubble in time?

Then we squeezed into a regular tunnel. The workmen had reamed out this section of the crevice, preparatory to the next blast. It was much easier to break off an iceberg along natural lines of cleavage, cracking it away largely without heat, but the charges had to be correctly placed, or the whole thing would break up into clumsy fragments. I understand there is a whole science of ice blasting that it takes many years to master, as with any really specialized discipline. The acquisition of water is too important to be entrusted to amateurs.

The tunnel cut deep into the bedrock ice, then stairstepped up to the surface. There was no sign of the saucers. They had evidently given up the unpromising pursuit, uncertain after all whether we survived the demise of our vehicle and satisfied to get the scion back to the city before he got into any more trouble. That was our good fortune.

We had precious little other fortune, though. We would have an awful time crossing the surface of the barren planet afoot within our time limit.

My father pointed the direction to the centre of the Valhalla Crater. He had a good sense of direction, but it really wasn't difficult to fathom what we needed. All we had to do was proceed at right angles to the low rills that circled it. Of course, we weren't going all the way to the centre – *far from it!* – but this direction would take us to the smaller crater where the bubble was. Kilroy Crater.

We started off, making great low-gee bounds. We had a long way to go, and not enough time. Maybe.

At first it was easy enough. We covered many metres between landings despite the clumsiness of our suits. We sailed over the rolling ridges and down through shallow troughs. There is a technique to moving rapidly in low gee, and we were necessarily acquiring it. There is also a certain exhilaration to such velocity, a sensation of power; I thought of myself as some alien creature who existed naturally in these barrens, leaping from site to site searching out some completely inexplicable-in-human-terms item.

But anything becomes tedious or tiring in time. My pack became heavier, my suit started chafing in awkward places, the burns I had received from the scion's laser in the dome chose this time to make themselves felt more insistently, and I wished I could stop, but of course I couldn't. The alien creature I had imagined had more freedom and fewer pains; it deserted me the moment it tired of this quest and went to some more interesting site. I think it used instantaneous matter transmission to jump to another galaxy, a technology mankind has not yet developed and probably never will. That's the problem with alien creatures: they make us look inadequate.

Our pace slowed, not because of me but because of my mother. She was not used to sustaining such high exertion. If I found this travel uncomfortable, how much worse it must be for her! I went to help her, but she shrugged me off. It wasn't foolish pride on her part – there has never been anything foolish about Charity Hubris – so much as awkwardness; two could not jump as freely as one. Then Spirit came and took her right elbow and I the left, and after a few stumbles we were able to move together and boost her along fairly expeditiously.

Still, we had 160 kilometres to go in less than a day. We were travelling a good ten kilometres per hour, so theoretically we had time – but we did need to rest, eat, and even sleep, some time, and that cut us down. It was foolish to reckon without the fatigue factor, I now realized. We had been busy all day, getting ready to travel, and would ordinarily have been sleeping now.

After three hours, we had indeed covered over thirty kilometres, by my reckoning – but that was the first flush of energy. I was no longer sure I could make the full distance at all, let alone in the time remaining. Certainly my mother could not.

That damned scion in the saucer had succeeded after all in wiping us out. That must have been why there was no further pursuit; he knew we could not make it afoot. My brain seethed with impotent rage. If we missed the bubble because of him, if the foul scion won after all—

Then what? We would have nowhere to go, and no way to get there. We could not return to Maraud, and no other dome was within our range. We would die in the barrens of Valhalla.

I smiled with my private gallows humour. Our Ragnarok was at Valhalla!

We sat on a rock, resting. Eating was complicated in the suits, and so was elimination. We knew how to do both, but the whole business did take attention and time, and wasn't much fun.

We started off again, at a slower pace because of my mother. I didn't know whether to be glad for the relief it gave me or sad, because it made it ever less likely that we would reach the bubble in time. We were locked into our situation; what would be would be.

It was doom that we contemplated, but I found myself too busy just keeping moving to suffer proper gloom. In literature I had learned that work was supposed to be an answer to doubt, and this seemed to be the case. It takes effort to doubt, and I did not have effort to spare for such a non-essential. Still, some of it did leak through to my consciousness.

We travelled another three hours. By this time it was

obvious to us all that we would not make it. We stopped again, weary, and my father beckoned Spirit and me to him for a helmet conference while Faith and my mother helped each other.

'We'll camp here,' my father said. 'The two of you will stand watch while the women sleep.'

'Watch?' Spirit demanded. 'What for?'

'Other refugees,' my father said succinctly.

Spirit and I exchanged glances through our helmets. I suffered another surge of admiration for the foresight of my father. Of course there would be other people travelling to the bubble, from Maraud and other domes; it would hardly fill its load with just the five of us, assuming it even knew we were coming! We were now far enough along so that those other families should be converging on our route. If any of them had good-sized vehicles, and certainly some should—

Spirit and I, abruptly recharged, got on with it with a will. We were not dead yet!

We not only watched, we ranged out in an expanding circle, she going one way, I the other. We leaped as high as we could from the surrounding ridges, though these weren't really very high, trying to spot any moving thing.

I must say this about Spirit: She was twelve, a child, but she was always great to work with. She had enthusiasm and competence, and enough savvy to operate effectively. I liked doing things with her; such shared tasks always seemed to have more meaning than those I did with other people, or alone. Maybe she was just trying to live up to her name as she interpreted it; if so, she succeeded admirably. She was a child, but I hardly knew her like among children or adults. I fancied her dark hair flinging out as she bounded, though of course there could be no such effect out here in the vacuum or in the space suit; it was just the way I saw her in my mind. I realize it is not fashionable to remark about one's little sister in this manner, but I decline to let fashion interfere with truth.

We spied nothing. More hours went by, and the glare of Jupiter seemed to turn baleful, and our enthusiasm was slowly replaced by dread. We came in to report – and discovered that Faith's suit had sprung another leak. Actually it was the same leak; the patch wasn't holding quite tight. It was intended for temporary use, to hold an hour or two until the suit could be brought in for permanent repair, and now it was giving out. She had her hand on it, holding it closed, but that only slowed the leakage, and it was obvious she would not be able to travel well. We couldn't even return safely to Maraud, now, even if it happened to be politically feasible, which it didn't; that patch simply would not make it that far. We did have other patches, but it is a bad business trying to patch a leaky patch, and the effort tends to be wasted.

Spirit and I went out again. We *had* to find transportation to the bubble!

She spied it first, with her sharp eyes and intense juvenile attention for detail: a shape floating over a distant ridge. She waved frantically, attracting my attention, and then I saw it. At first I felt dread: was it the scion's saucer, coming to finish us off?

No, it was too large. Anyway, even if it had been the scion's saucer or that of one of his companions, we still would have had to approach it. We would perish out here alone, so we simply had to take the chance. We bounded after the shape.

We caught it, for it was travelling slantways past us so that we were able to intercept its path without matching its velocity. It slowed and hovered in place, waiting for us. What a lovely sight!

I stood bathed in the light of its headlamp and pointed the direction of the rest of my family. The floater moved in that direction. It was a large vehicle, a supply transport, presumably bringing food and water and fuel to the bootleg bubble. In that case, we were really in luck!

My guess turned out to be correct, but our luck was imperfect. The pilot held up a sign with a figure printed on it: the payment they demanded for the service of transporting us to the bubble. Truly has it been said: There is no free lunch!

We had to pay; we had no choice. But it left us no margin, after allowing for the thousand-dollar entry fee to the bubble itself. We were now, essentially, all the way broke.

Yet the ride itself was fun, and not merely because it represented our salvation from death in the vacuum. They didn't let us inside; we clung to handholds atop the vehicle and floated in its onion-field of null-gee over the terrain. In three more hours we were there.

Could we have made it on our own? I like to think we could have – but I really am uncertain. What counts is that we did get there.

6

Bubble, Bubble

Callisto Orbit, 5-2-'15 – We stood before the bubble at last. I was excruciatingly tired, but excitement fended off my fatigue for the moment. The bubble most resembled a cratered planetoid, only the craters were actually recessed ports sealed with tough space-glass.

The globe sat on the ground, but I knew its gravity lenses abated most of its weight so it was actually feather-light. It was about ten times my height; I'm less than two metres tall, but still growing. Call it a good sixteen metres for the diameter of the sphere; it's hard to judge with the naked eye, but that's a standard size for small space bubbles. They aren't uniform, actually, because their patterns of growth differ, but they do run pretty true to form.

The idea was that such a sphere would be halved, with one section reserved for equipment, supplies, baggage and such, and the other half providing eight cubic metres of living space to each of one hundred passengers. It all worked out mathematically; I had studied it in school. But it was different, seeing the great dull hulk of it looming before me, blotting out part of the horizon.

The air lock opened, and we scrambled in. The supply vehicle had a separate lock, designed for things that didn't need oxygen or air pressure for survival; my father had had to deposit our short-hop payment there before we got our ride. The bubble lock's outer panel slid closed behind us, and our weight decreased to about half its prior amount because of the effect of the shielding. The pressure came up, making our suits go slack. Faith was finally able to relax her hold on the leaky patch and straighten up. That must have been a tremendous burden off her mind!

'How many?' a voice demanded from a speaker. It was good to hear normal speech again!

'Five,' my father said, lifting back his helmet. The rest of us did the same.

'Fifteen hundred dollars, cash in advance,' the voice said.

My mother gasped. 'We were told two hundred apiece,' my father said evenly.

'The price has gone up. Pay or leave.'

We knew we couldn't leave. But we didn't have the money. It had been all we could do to raise what we had. I saw the little lines of desperation form in my father's cheek, but his voice was admirably steady. 'We haven't got it. You should have sent word.'

'Then get out. No freeloaders here.'

My father paused, signalling us to silence. Then he said: 'Put your helmets back on, folks. They don't want our money. We'll have to take another bubble.'

In shock, I fumbled at my helmet. Faith's face was as pale as death; she knew she would die if she had to go out again. But at the same time, I knew my father was bluffing; he would not let us all go out.

I looked at Spirit, and knew the same thought had come to her. If the fee was now three hundred dollars each, only three of us could go. Two would have to return to Maraud. My father and mother would sacrifice themselves to get the three children aboard. But that wasn't right!

Slowly, her little face set with unchildish intensity, Spirit nodded, answering my unasked question. We were the youngest, and most adaptable; we would volunteer to return, so that our parents could go. After all, we were the ones who had humiliated the scion and brought this trouble upon our family. We were the ones most deserving of punishment. We could conceal our identity, somehow, in Maraud, or maybe go to the coffee plantation. The notion was not pleasant, but it was viable.

'You really don't have the fee?' the voice asked, sounding disgusted.

'Only the fee we were told,' my father replied. 'One thousand dollars in gold. The supply vehicle took the rest, to carry us here.'

'In gold?'

'In gold. We had to liquidate everything we had.'

'That's enough for three, and some for extras.'

I opened my mouth, but my father put his hand out to silence me without even looking. How well he knew me! 'There will be other bubbles,' he said. 'We can wait for the next, and perhaps its fee will not have changed. Our family travels together.'

There was a sigh. 'Well, for good gold, it will have to do. Hand it over.'

'Not without guarantee of passage for our whole family,' my father said firmly. 'We must stay together. Unity is more important than schedule.' I knew my mother felt that way, but with Faith's suit leak, compromise seemed essential.

'We'll let you in. But you'll have to work, to make up the difference.'

'Agreed,' my father said, his face relaxing. I realized that the bubble pilot's lust for our money was greater than any principle he might have had. Gold was universal currency, unlike the chronically deteriorating scrip of the various moons. By threatening to leave, taking our gold with us, my father had bluffed him out. Even if we had perished on the surface of Callisto, that gold would not have gone to this bubble, so it was take it or lose it. The man had taken it. So we would have to work; why not? It was only a ten-day trip to Jupiter. How much better this was than the alternative Spirit and I had tried to offer!

'Shuck your suits,' the voice said.

We were happy to oblige. We helped each other get out

of our space suits and folded the bulky things and stacked them on the floor. We should have no further need for them, as the bubble would not again dock in vacuum, and the bubble personnel would have a storage room to store them. This, more than anything else, gave me a feeling of relief. A person could relax when he took off his space suit. We did, however, detach our packs and carry them in our arms.

My father produced our two bright gold coins. The inner panel slid aside. The panels were designed to move readily when the pressure was equal at either side, but to baulk when it was not: an automatic safety factor to counter human error. Hard experience in space has taught our species many useful little things.

There stood a man in a grubby pilot's uniform, his hand out. 'Cells 75 and 76,' he said as he took the gold. 'They're consecutively numbered; you can find them. Get in them and stay; keep the Commons clear.' He brought first one coin and then the other to his mouth, bit each and tasted it, and smiled with satisfaction as he put them away. I had not realized it was possible to identify a metal that way; I would have tried an immersion test for density, as gold is the most dense of the common metals, and anything with greater density is bound to be more valuable. The fact is, you can tell pretty well whether gold is authentic merely by glancing at its size and hefting it in your hand. But I'm not a trader or space pilot.

The man did not introduce himself or offer any other advice, so we moved along the passage. It really didn't matter where we stayed, so long as we were aboard the bubble when it lifted for Jupiter.

The passage angled up at forty-five degrees, then debouched immediately into what appeared to be a torus-shaped chamber. That is, we stood within a giant dough-nut, only it was hollow while the hole was solid. Its outer wall curved down on one side and up on the other. I should clarify that the outer wall of the torus was not the outer wall of the bubble.

We walked downwards into this torus, since the upper side curved until it was vertical. The lower side curved level in just a few metres – and just at that point the floor converted to a latticework of squares, each square two metres on a side, with a sliding panel in the centre. Some panels were open, showing cells below, about two metres cubed.

'Numbers!' Spirit exclaimed. 'See – here's 28 and 29 next to it. Is this a prison ship?'

'These are the passenger rooms,' my father said dryly. 'Eight cubic metres apiece.'

'But we're only assigned two numbers,' I protested. 'We should have five cells. Or at least three, for our entry fee.'

A head poked out of one chamber, startling us. 'They have doubled up,' the man explained. 'They make twice as much money that way.'

'But that's wrong!' my mother said.

'What law does an illegal craft follow?' the man inquired sardonically.

'What law indeed,' my father agreed. I realized that we – except for my father – had been naïve. Of course the refugee-smugglers would seek the greatest profit, by jamming as many people as possible into the bubble and overcharging those.

'We have cells 75 and 76,' Spirit said. 'Do you know where they are?

'Opposite side of the bubble,' the man said, pointing up. 'You'll have to climb. It's not hard, in this one-eighth gee, and there are handholds. Better hurry, before the next load comes. There'll be people scrambling every which way, stepping on each other's faces.'

So many refugees! I had supposed our situation was more or less unique, but apparently many others were as desperate to leave the planet as we were. It was a sad commentary on the nature of our society.

We thanked the man and hurried. We followed the numbers up and around the torus chamber. The handholds were really the ceiling lattice, which seemed to be formed of sturdy netting. The ceiling was close to four metres from the floor, but not hard to reach at eighth-gee. So we climbed it readily enough, and when it curved around towards the topside, we walked on that netting until we spied cells 75 and 76 in the new ceiling, which was really part of the same surface that had been the floor below, if that's clear.

It occurs to me that a verbal or written description isn't enough, so I will make a map of the complete bubble, as I came to know it. Turn to the next page for that map, and don't blame me if it does not match the standards of Space Navy specification blueprints!

'How ever are we to stay in those?' Faith demanded irritably.

'When we are in space, we'll rotate and the cells will all be "down",' I explained, feeling very educated.

'Idiot!' she snapped. Fatigue and nervous tension had worn out her temper, understandably. 'I know that. I mean *now*.'

Faith is a very pretty girl, but she was not very pretty now. I was about to make some sarcastic retort, but before I could work out something cutting enough for this occasion, my father interceded. Adults seem to handle fatigue better than do juveniles; maybe they are more accustomed to it. 'We'll manage,' he said mildly. 'As you can see, others are doing well enough.'

I peered up. Dimly through the translucent sliding doors I saw people in cells 74 and down, sitting comfortably on the floors; 77 and up remained empty.

'Now, if your mother and I take one, will you three children get along in the other?' my father asked, and the tone of his voice made the suggestion sound eminently

MAP OF THE BUBBLE

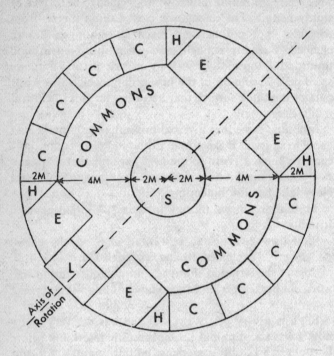

Scale: .5 cm = 1 metre

S—Storage

L—Locks, air

C—Cell, residential

H—head

E—Equipment

reasonable. That's another adult talent. It was, of course, more than a suggestion.

'We should have two and a half cages,' Spirit said belligerently. We were all very tired, and it was manifesting more openly as our certainty of survival increased. 'Even doubled up, that's our share.'

'If one of you can find a free space—' my father said, shrugging. He really didn't want to argue.

The hatch to cell 74 slid open. A boy about my own age poked his head down. 'I'll take a roommate,' he called. 'Are you nice people?'

'Well . . . ' Spirit began mischievously. She was never too tired for a flash of humour.

'I'll take it,' I said. 'It's no fun rooming with sisters anyway.' Actually, it would have been okay with Spirit; but Faith was too conscious of her maturity, and would have made things difficult in various minor but cumulatively overwhelming ways.

Spirit frowned but did not protest. She knew she would get along with Faith better than I would. It was my position in life to protect Faith from molestation on the street, and Spirit's to preserve her privacy in the home. It is a fair-sized responsibility to have a pretty sibling.

'Spring up and catch the edge of the opening,' the boy advised.

I touched Spirit's shoulder and gave it a squeeze. I would rather have roomed with her than with some stranger, and she knew it; this reminder was merely my gesture of thanks for her understanding. We could not put Faith in with a strange boy!

I tossed up my pack, then sprang up and hooked my fingers in the opening, then hauled myself on inside. Acrobatics are easy in eighth-gee! When I was clear of the entrance, the boy slid the panel closed, so we could relax without fear of falling through the floor. I didn't worry about my folks; I knew they'd manage.

I sat up and contemplated my companion. He seemed to be my height – it wasn't possible to be certain while sitting – but more slender of structure, with very thin arms. His hair was short and brown, like mine, and his eyes were brown too and seemed a bit too large for his face, but his features were well formed. I decided I liked him – but my sense-of-people signalled warning. There was something about him that didn't jibe.

'What's your name?' I asked forthrightly.

'What's yours?' he returned less forthrightly.

Still that slight wrongness. 'Hope Hubris. My father's a tallyman of the coffee dome. Was, I mean. I got into trouble with a scion, and now we all have to get out.'

He smiled. It was a fetching, compelling expression that transformed his face into something wholly likeable. Some people have practised smiles that are letter-perfect but that lack warmth; this was a natural one. 'I'm Helse. My folks are servants – when they find work. They can't support me, so I'm emigrating.'

'Helse?' I asked. 'That's an unusual name, for this planet.'

'And Hope isn't?'

I laughed. 'I guess a person can be named anything his folks want.'

'Helse is the plural of Hell, they tell me. I'm a hellion.'

I was already sure he wasn't that. Violence was not his way. But what he was, I had not yet fathomed. Maybe he had more urgent reason to emigrate alone than economics.

The ice was broken. We chatted a little about inconsequentials, and my awareness of the oddness about him intensified. He wasn't bad or dangerous, just subtly wrong. I liked him, for he was at least as well educated as I, and he wasn't mean. My judgment of people in this respect is infallible.

After a time I checked on my folks. Faith and Spirit were next to me, in 75, and our parents in the next one over.

They were already lying down for a nap.

'Go back and finish your conversation,' Spirit told me. 'It's interesting.'

But I was too weary for that, or even to be embarrassed. Naturally there was no privacy of sound in a situation like this; one would have to whisper to keep any secret from those in adjacent cells. Helse and I had not said anything confidential, anyway.

I saw I had other neighbours in cells 73, 71, and the two corners, and when the remaining cells filled up we would have eight neighbours in all. I see this isn't clear, so I'll make a chart, as I like to keep things straight. The band of cells extended all the way around the bubble's equator, four abreast, numbered consecutively by rows. With a circumference of about fifty metres at the equator, but less to either side of it, there was just room for twenty-four such rows, or ninety-six cells, and four more squeezed in somewhere around the edges. Our particular section was numbered like this:

| 65 | 72 | 73 | 80 | 81 |
66	71	74	79	82
67	70	75	78	83
68	69	76	77	84

The line along the centre is the bubble equator, the region of greatest centrifugal gravity when it is rotating. It wasn't really a line, any more than it is on any moon or planet, but it helps a person to align things. The cell numbers continued on either side, upwards and downwards, but it seems pointless to list all ninety-six. Anyway, I was sure that I would get to know the people in all eight bordering cells soon enough, once we were under way.

Right now the brief exhilaration of de-suiting and settling in and meeting my roommate was giving out, and I just had to rest. I returned to cell 74, handing myself along from panel to panel readily enough, said goodnight to Helse, though I suppose it was just about morning in Maraud time, and tuned out the universe.

Sleep came like a ton of sand, burying me, for all that a ton only weighed an eighth of a ton in this gravity. At one point I was dimly aware of other people entering the adjacent cells and of the clangs of the outer locks being secured. I didn't let any of it disturb me. Helse lay parallel to me, presumably sleeping too. I heard him speak once to someone outside, probably another person wanting to share the cell; there was a hassle, but it finally died down without the intrusion of any other person. So if my presence here in cell 74 had been an imposition, it was legitimate now. I had legitimized it by possession or squatter's rights. But Helse had been instrumental in that effort, for he could have had me booted. I owed him one.

I woke to a hand on my arm, steadying me. 'I didn't want you banging into a wall when the bubble manoeuvres,' Helse explained.

I looked about blearily. I was floating in air!

I flailed wildly for a moment, then realized I was not really falling. I used Helse as leverage to get to a handhold and secured myself to a wall. My stomach felt light, and I had to swallow several times before convincing myself that I wasn't about to throw up, but otherwise I was all right.

'We're taking off,' Helse explained. 'Null-gee. You can see out the port.'

I hadn't realized the cubic chambers had portholes of their own, and later I learned that many did not; we happened to be lucky. Actually, ours wasn't much; it was only ten centimetres in diameter, and the thickness of the outer shell of the bubble made it seem tubular. I set my nose against it, holding myself close by means of recessed handholds on either side, and peered out.

I really didn't see much. Our cube-cell was near the top

of the bubble-sphere as it rested on the ground – but it wasn't on the ground any more, so that was irrelevant. I knew the propulsion was from the vicinity of the axis, so here at the equator we would be looking straight out at right angles to our line of travel.

I see I have to explain about the drive. Like the little null-gee saucers, bubbles have to use some form of active propulsion. Gravity lenses are fine, but they do not *move* objects; they merely lessen or eliminate the pull of gravity. Now, you might think that all we had to do was cut off the gravity of Callisto, and Jupiter would pull us right in to itself. Well, Jupiter was trying, but we still weren't free to respond. We were, in fact, in orbit about Jupiter, as was Callisto. So we stayed right where we were. Releasing us from Callisto was only part of the job. We had not been released from the basic physics of our situation. So we needed a jet to make us move.

The jet was now boosting us up at an angle to the surface of Callisto; that much I could perceive. We no longer weighed anything, so didn't have to worry about falling back to Callisto, but our mass remained, and the jet wasn't strong, so it was slow. But gravity travel *is* slow, in practice; if you want to get anywhere in a hurry, you have to use a spaceship, not a bubble. The bubble is the rowboat of space; it is not exactly first-class travel. Which is why we refugee peasants could afford it, barely.

So all I saw, apart from Callisto, was Jupiter, and it didn't even seem to be getting closer. Perspective is like that; it seems you are getting nowhere. Jupiter was moving, of course, as our course wobbled somewhat uncertainly, but that was irrelevant. I pushed away from the port.

Now Helse looked out. 'Shouldn't we be going right towards Jupiter?' he asked.

I saw that I knew something he didn't. That gratified me. 'We *can't* go straight to Jupiter,' I explained. 'We're in orbit.'

93

'I know that,' he said, miffed. 'We'll approach Jupiter in a big spiral. Because our orbital velocity joins our approach velocity in a compromise vector. But at least we can accelerate towards Jupiter, to help tighten the spiral.'

'No good,' I said. 'The closer an orbiting object gets to its primary, the faster it orbits. We'd end up going so fast we'd bounce out again. What we have to do is *slow our orbital velocity*. Then we'll fall in naturally – though we'll still be orbiting faster.'

He shook his head. 'We slow – so we go faster? I don't understand that.'

'Lots of people don't,' I said somewhat smugly.

He let it drop. 'I'll be glad when they spin the bubble, so we have weight again.'

With that I agreed heartily. Free fall is fine for a moment, but it rapidly palls as the novelty wears off. I had spent all my life in gravity, mostly Earth norm; I could get along on less, but my stomach definitely didn't like null-gee. 'I think it'll be some time, though,' I said. 'The jet drive doesn't have much thrust, only enough to nudge us into the wall. This is no space liner.'

He laughed, with a surprisingly high pitch. 'No, this is a little sailboat!'

It was a nice enough analogy, better than my prior thought about a rowboat. Back on the historical oceans of Earth, a thousand years ago, there were all kinds of ships. It was impossible to go to space in an open craft, but the contemporary bubbles were as close to it as was feasible, using mainly the ambient gravity fields of space for propulsion, much as the little sailboats used vagrant winds on the planetary surface. Winds could let a person down – and so could gravity.

We waited interminably. The pilot made a circuit of the Commons – that was the torus-shaped central hall – and advised us to remain in our cells until we got clear of the planet, except for use of the heads. The heads were the

94

bathrooms; there were eight of them, which was supposed to be enough for one hundred people. But we had about two hundred people. So that meant twenty-five to a head. We organized it by the numbers – and cells 74 and 75 were at the line for head number 6. Suddenly my business there seemed overpoweringly urgent!

Helse seemed to be in even greater distress than I. 'May I talk to you privately?' he asked.

I realized that he meant he didn't want the people in the neighbouring cells overhearing. I moved close. 'Sure.'

'Will you keep a secret?' he whispered in my ear.

'Not if you plan to do anything illegal or unethical,' I whispered back, not certain whether I was serious. We were all doing something quasi-illegal by sneaking away from the planet like this. The feeling of oddness about him returned, and I wasn't sure I wanted to hear his secret. The very knowledge could compromise my own situation, somehow.

'Nothing like that,' he answered me. 'But awkward – and I'll need your help. Please do not betray me.'

I squinted at him. The urgency in his voice was manifest; he was not joking. I was becoming excruciatingly curious about his oddness. 'I'll keep your secret, so long as it doesn't hurt me or anyone else,' I said. 'But if you have, for example, a contagious disease, common sense should indicate that secrecy is not—'

He smiled instantly. 'No, nothing like that!'

'But I don't promise to help you,' I finished. 'The secret is one thing, inactive; help is another.'

'All right.' He took a breath, then leaned close to my ear again. 'I'm a girl.'

'So that's it!' I exclaimed in a whisper, as the oddness fell into focus.

His – her brow furrowed. 'You knew? What gave me away?'

It was my turn to smile. 'I didn't know, but – well, I have

this sense about other people. I know what their strengths and weaknesses are, and what motivates them, and how far I can trust them. It's not psychic; it's just a judgment I have, after I interact with them a little. Maybe I pick up private signals from the body. I don't know. With you there is something wrong. *Was* something. I knew you were a nice person, but you didn't quite fall into place. Now I realize it's because I was trying to fit you into a masculine mode, and you were – are feminine. That's a relief.'

'You don't mind?' she asked uncertainly.

'I like to solve mysteries. You aren't odd any more. I mean, not to my special perception. Probably no one else would have felt it at all, but I – well, that's my one real talent, the thing that distinguishes me from other people. I'd really hate to have it be wrong.'

'I deceived you, pretending to be a boy. You might have refused to room with me, otherwise.'

'I don't care what sex you are, if you don't care,' I reassured her. 'I have two sisters; I was going to share a cell with them, but this is more fun and less crowded.' I considered, looking at her with a changed perception. 'How old are you? You're my size—'

'Sixteen,' she said. 'Girls don't get as big as boys.'

'I know. My sister Faith is eighteen, and she's the same size as me, and I'm not big. But I fight for her, because – you know.'

'I know,' she said, smiling herself. Now, with my perception of her as feminine, the expression was cute. She wasn't as pretty as Faith – wouldn't be even if she were all garbed and coiffed like a girl – but of course *no one* was as pretty as Faith – but she was nice enough. There is something sort of special about any girl; they're a distinct and intriguing species. 'I have no brother to fight for me, so I became a brother.'

'Makes sense.' It did indeed! 'The way men go after Faith – that's really why we're here. I stopped a scion from getting at her.'

'Scions are bad ones,' she agreed. '*Any* man is potential trouble. I don't mean you; you're a boy. No offence.'

'And you don't want to room with a man,' I said, working it out. 'He would make demands – I guess we should have had Faith join you. But we didn't know.'

'No, I wanted you,' Helse said quickly. We were still conversing in barely audible whispers, of course. 'It would look funny, a mixed couple unrelated, even at our ages, and I still have to hide my nature. I don't know who may be aboard this bubble, or what may be expected when things get dull. Please don't tell anyone.'

'I promised,' I said a little stiffly. 'It's your secret. I'll keep it.'

'And I'll need your help, if you will give it. You see, the bathroom—'

The rest of her problem illuminated. 'You'll have to use the male head! That'll be awkward, if—'

'If there's anyone else there,' she finished. 'Will you help me?'

'It's something no person can do for another,' I pointed out, embarrassed.

She blushed. She would have to watch that, in public. 'I need someone to cover for me, in case—'

'Oh, to stand by the door and make sure no man interrupts,' I said. 'I'll try.'

'Oh, thank you! I'm most grateful.'

'Actually, I'm glad to get a half share of a cell, instead of a third share. You don't have to be grateful to me.' The truth was, sharing a cell with a young woman not my sister was a prospect that promised to be interesting. Like most adolescent boys, I had dreams of the opposite sex, but lacked the courage to implement them. It wasn't that I envied youths like the scion; he was obviously a heel from the outset, and should come to a bad end, if we had not succeeded in ending him. It also wasn't that I had any overwhelming procreational urge; as far as I can tell, mine is normal for my age. But there are few convenient avenues of general acquaintance with girls available to boys in my situation, and none for full sexual expression. I knew girls were not mere sex objects – after all, Spirit is a girl – but when society places a sexual emphasis on association, it is hard to relate to the opposite sex as regular people. Here was my chance to really get to know a girl who was not my sister.

Helse was looking at me as if trying to assess the nature of my agreement. I fathomed her concern. 'Don't worry,' I said. 'I'm a boy, not a man. I won't be grabbing for you.

'Thank you,' she said, smiling wryly.

Yet I was close enough to manhood to feel the desire *to* grab for her. I had told myself that I valued the opportunity to have a young woman for a friend, and I did – but there was an insidious and powerful undercurrent of sexual interest too. I would have to guard myself, because if she got the notion that I might appreciate her sexual qualities, she would surely seek some other roommate, and that would abolish all speculations, licit and illicit. I had a secret of my own to keep, now.

Our turn for the head came. We slid open the panel and floated down. Head number 6 was alongside the quadruple row of cells; it was more triangular in cross section, because of the curve of the bubble shell. The Commons was a doughnut, but near the bubble's axis the chambers were lined up parallel to it. This left a wedge-shaped space between the cellblock and the axis, where storage sheds, fuse boxes, and bathrooms were squeezed in. The bubble didn't need space for bathtubs or shower stalls, as there was no spare water in space for this sort of nonsense. People were expected to wash their bodies with small sanitary sponges that could be rinsed with half a cup of water. We didn't even bother with that; no sponges were left. People were going to have to stink. Fortunately the air recycling removed odours as well.

I was going to let Helse go in alone, but she gestured me to join her. I saw that there were other people nearby, who might deem it odd if two boys our age showed such deference to each other. Feeling a trifle guilty, I crowded in with her.

Now the details of Helse's problem showed starkly. There were two apertures for body excretions, one for solids, the other for liquids. It was important that the functions be separated, because the recycling processes were different. Solids would clog the liquid system, and the liquid would saturate the dry-compost mechanism of the other. I had known this intellectually without considering the practical side of it. Actually, on a ten-day hop the solid recycling would not be done within the bubble; the holding tanks would be emptied elsewhere, providing rich organic material for some agricultural dome. The water, however, would be cycled through many times while we travelled.

With the facilities already being overworked by the crowding of the bubble, any abuse could be disastrous. Helse would not urinate into the solids aperture; such wrongdoing would soon be apparent as the tank fouled up. She had to use the liquids aperture – and there was a problem. Either sex could use the solid-collector funnel, as that was set in a sort of potty chair with handholds to keep the floating body proximate. But the liquids funnel was set at waist height in the vertical wall. The wall that would be vertical when spin began, I mean. At the moment, in complete free fall – for they seemed to be using the propulsive jet intermittently, saving it for some later need, so there was not even the trace thrust of acceleration – all walls were of indeterminate orientation.

I had no trouble with the liquids funnel, of course. I merely hooked my toes in the toehold slots in the floor so that my body was fixed parallel to the wall, and directed the flow appropriately. There was a slight suction that brought the fluid in; otherwise it might have floated out into the chamber in disintegrating bubbles, an obvious liability. The presence of a young woman did not bother me unduly, for our family had never been squeamish about such things; we had had to share a single bathroom, and my sisters and I had long since passed the exploration stage. But Helse—

'You'll have to hold me against the wall,' she said. Her face was somewhat ruddy, as mine would have been in a similar circumstance. Obviously she hadn't *wanted* male co-operation; she had had to have it.

That was the solution, of course. I hooked my toes, leaned back, and caught her as she floated close. She dropped her trousers, or rather drew them down about her legs in the absence of gravity, baring her bottom. Then she doubled up her legs and squatted against the funnel, while I held her by the shoulders and gently shoved her in to the wall. Otherwise she would simply have floated away from it, especially when – well, a rocket moves in space by jetting gas, and a person would move similarly by jetting liquid.

I closed my eyes, in deference to her modesty, after the first guilty glimpse that verified that she definitely was not male, but could still feel the slight motion of her body and hear the fluid striking the funnel. Then, abruptly, it became very exciting for me, though my reaction embarrassed me. I was lucky to have urinated first; had I done it last, I would have had more difficulty than she, albeit for a different reason. I chided myself; after all, she was only urinating. Why should this essentially pedestrian activity excite me so strongly, in that fashion? Yet there was no question that it did.

Then I opened my eyes and looked again, not to further titillate myself, though that was a consequence; I realized I had seen something odd. Yes, there it was – a small mark, or tattoo in the crease where her left leg connected to her body. Three letters: *QYV*.

She finished and drew her trousers back up. 'Thank you,'

she said. 'That was the help I needed.'

'Sure,' I mumbled, knowing I was blushing. I hoped my erection did not show. One advantage the female of the species has is the ability to conceal sexual awareness if she wishes.

'In the female section they have bidets,' Helse said. 'You'd have almost as much trouble using one of those.'

'Umph,' I agreed, preferring to change the subject, though I was curious about what a bidet was.

We returned to our cell, and two men headed for the head, passing us in the Commons. I could tell the men didn't suspect anything; we were just two teen-age boys. My blush must have faded, or maybe it just didn't show well in the partial light, against my naturally dusky complexion.

'A female roommate couldn't have helped this way,' Helse murmured as we climbed back into our cell.

She had certainly figured it well, and played it correctly. She had of course been lucky I was available, but luck is a fickle mistress that is powerless unless intelligently exploited. Helse had gambled, to the extent she had to, and won, and I respected that.

Then a complementary notion occurred, 'If I ever have to use the female head—' I began.

'Yes, of course I'll help you,' she agreed quickly. 'There could be an occasion.'

We settled down for more rest, as there wasn't much else to do. But now that my roommate's femaleness had been so unequivocally brought home to me, I could not quite relax. That sexual barrier was up between us; I kept thinking of the private glimpse of her posterior vicinity I had had. Certainly I had seen it on my sisters – though not recently, on Faith – but this was not my sister. That made an enormous difference. I wondered what the rest of her looked like, when it showed. She had done an excellent job of masquerading as a boy; nothing showed. Her chest looked just like a masculine chest. Maybe she was flat-breasted. No, that was unlikely, because her buttocks were too rounded and her – she was at the age of nubility, and the upper part of her would certainly conform.

And my own reaction to her urination – I suppose it was because her act called more specific attention to that portion of her anatomy and the functioning of it. A person may be stimulated to hunger by seeing another person eat; why not a similar stimulation in genital matters? At any rate, I had learned something about my own organic responses. The first requirement in the understanding of other people is the understanding of oneself.

'Anyway, thanks,' she said. I jumped – which didn't get me far, in free fall. I felt nervous, thinking about someone that way, when she was right there with me. I did not believe in telepathy, but my disbelief weakened at moments like that.

'Welcome,' I said, and that at least was honest.

7

Betrayal

I must have snoozed – certainly I needed more rest! – because I was jolted awake when the warning klaxon went off. We had separated far enough from the planet and were about to go into spin. That meant gravity, or a reasonable facsimile, and we didn't want to be sleeping in mid-air when it started. I had, of course, been doing exactly that.

But it started gently enough. I heard noises from the hull and realized someone was out there in a space suit, doing something. 'They're moving the drive unit around to the equator,' I said, catching on. 'If they angled it sideways at the pole, it would start the bubble turning pole over pole, and it's not designed for that. So they have to fasten it where it belongs for proper spin.'

Then the room began to drift to the side. 'Now they're starting the spin,' I said, working it out in my own mind. 'But at the start it's spin acceleration, so we feel it mostly sideways. Once it gets up to proper torque, we'll feel it outwards. But it's not much of a jet, so it's slow.'

'You're good at physics,' Helse said.

I wasn't good at physics. I'm not, if the truth must be told – and I suppose it must, here – much good at anything apart from my judgment of people. Oh, I'm smart enough in a general way; that runs in our family, except for Faith, who got beauty instead of brains. But I owed my comprehension of the present situation more to the fact that males tune in to these things more than females do, by training and inclination. I knew Helse was gratuitously complimenting me, and the words meant nothing in themselves. But I was flattered that she *wanted* to flatter me. After all, she was a year older than I, a real girl, a young woman. I was sure that in normal circumstances the likes of her would not even have noticed the likes of me. Of course, she needed my co-operation for the bathroom, so she could keep her secret; it figured that she would try to keep on my good side. Still, I was unreasonably pleased. I would have been pleased if a boy had complimented me similarly, but I knew it would not have had the same force. I wanted a genuine young woman to respect me; it made me feel almost like a young man instead of an awkward adolescent. So she was trying to manage me – and I was eager to be managed.

Slowly the spin increased until the outer wall became the new floor and the sliding door became a ceiling exit. The slight push of the jet sideways was constant, not increasing, while the effect of centrifugal force was cumulative, so that it came to dominate. It was good to have weight and orientation again!

In due course there was a jolt. Helse looked up, startled.

'Just the drive unit being disconnected,' I explained. 'They have to take it back to the pole and set it up again for normal forward thrust. Now that our spin is established, it will maintain itself; the rocket is needed to continue our acceleration towards Jupiter. We'll hardly feel it pushing at right angles to our new gravity, but the bubble will get up respectable velocity in due course.'

She smiled, complimenting me again, and I felt unreasonably good again. Helse had done nothing, really, to turn me on like this, but I was thoroughly turned on. For the first time in my life, I was coming to appreciate the potency with which a woman could affect a man – just by being near him.

We had been sitting on the new floor, wary of standing while our orientation was shifting. Now we stood – and I felt abruptly dizzy and had to lean quickly against a wall for support. I saw Helse react similarly. Naturally I had to set my brain scrambling for a facile explanation, lest my newfound status as a knowledgeable person suffer erosion. 'The spin!' I said. 'This is a small bubble, so we feel the effect. When we stand upright, our feet are moving faster than our heads, and maybe they weigh more too. So we get dizzy, and we tend to fall sideways, because of the physics of the situation.'

'So it's not something I ate,' Helse said. 'I don't have to get sick.'

I wish she hadn't said that word! We struggled with our equilibrium and our psychologies and managed to get ourselves less queasy and more balanced. But we could hear the sound of someone retching in a neighbouring cell.

'Let me try something,' I said, struck by a notion. I took my comb from my pocket, held it aloft near the ceiling just above head level, and dropped it.

The comb took about one second to reach the floor – but it didn't fall straight down. It drifted four feet to the side and banged into the wall.

Helse gasped. 'How—?'

'It's the spin, again,' I said, pleased. 'The hull is evidently providing us about half Earth-gravity, which I think is standard for a bubble this size. It has a diameter of about sixteen metres, which means a circumference of just over fifty metres, and so if it spins in ten seconds—'

'Wait, wait!' Helse interrupted. 'I want to understand, really I do, because I think comprehension makes me less queasy. But I've had most of my education in Jupiter measurements, you know, inches and feet, and—'

Oh. I wondered how she had picked up that education, since it was normally affected on Callisto only by the rich landholders and politicians who had dealings with the Colossus Planet. But I did have some conversance with that clumsy system, so I rose to the challenge. 'The bubble's radius in feet would be perhaps twenty-five,' I said. 'And

105

it's circumference, here just inside the hull, may be one hundred and sixty feet, roughly. So if it completes a full turn every ten seconds, which seems reasonable, a point on the hull will travel sixteen feet every second. That gives us a velocity of sixteen feet per second – no, I guess it doesn't because the deviation is tangential, not straight—'

'That's all right,' she said quickly. 'Now I understand the principle. But why did your comb fall sideways?'

'Well, the floor of the Commons, our ceiling, is a little over six feet farther in, so while the hull moves sixteen feet, the ceiling moved only, let me see, twelve feet. So that's the velocity of my comb at that level. When I drop it, it can't match the velocity of the hull, so it falls four feet behind.'

'Oh, yes!' she exclaimed. 'Yes, of course!' And yet again she was flattering me.

'So when we go up into the Commons, 'I concluded, 'we had better lean a little to compensate for the effects, and watch out how we jump, because we may not land where we expect. And our weight will be less on the Commons – about three-quarters what it is here. If this is half-gee here – and I really can't tell, now, so maybe it's quarter-gee, like Callisto – the Commons will be three-eighths gee, or three-sixteenths, or whatever. Anyway, less.'

'I feel better already,' Helse said. 'Maybe some time I'll have the chance to explain something as useful to you.'

She was giving me too much credit, but I could live with it. It was time for us to go abroad and meet our neighbours.

I reached up, opened the panel, and hauled myself into the Commons. Spirit had done the same thing, and other passengers were popping out of their holes, some of them looking greenish. Yes, I understood their nausea! Soon a number of us were standing on the new concave floor of the doughnut, meeting each other. Camaraderie was easy, for we all shared some significant experiences: fleeing Callisto and adapting to spin-gravity.

I introduced Helse formally to my family. 'He's travelling alone,' I explained. 'His family couldn't support him any longer.' I made sure I made the 'he' plain, so that Helse would know I was honouring her secret. I suppose technically this was lying, but I had given my word, and it would have been a greater wrong to betray her. Still, I felt a twinge and resolved to cogitate upon the ethics next time I had cogitation time on my hands. Is a lie ever justified by circumstances? That's one you cannot answer in an off-hand way.

Our neighbours, as it turned out, were basically similar to ourselves. They had been ground into intolerable poverty by the system, or had incurred the wrath of some person of power, or had simply come to the conclusion that they were on a dead-end street on Callisto. They were not the very poorest, for those could not even have raised the fare; they were the descending middle class, like us, or the disillusioned specialists who could no longer tolerate the system.

There was a lot of demand for the heads at this point, as people tried to get their motion-sick stomachs in order. Helse and I had overcome our problem, so were all right in that respect. I saw that a number of people were remaining in their cells, probably too sick to emerge. Time would help cure that, I was sure.

The immense if cloud-shrouded lure of Jupiter summoned us all. There we would somehow find the reprieve life had so far denied us. It was a giant mutual dream, and if it was short on practical details, at least it was better than dwelling on the problems behind us. How much better to float towards a dream than to sink into potential nightmare!

Now at last it was time to eat. Those of us who were not sick were famished, after the ardours of our departure from our lifetime homes. A bubble crewman dispensed packages of food and drink from the storage space in the centre of the vessel, dropping them down through a hole in the net. People watched, amazed, as those items angled to the side.

travelling twice as far horizontally as vertically. I spread my explanation around, but found that quite a number of people had already figured it out for themselves. Spirit, always one to get into the spirit of these things, practised jumping up to the net, which she could do with much less distortion by adjusting the angle and velocity of her take-off, then spreading her arms and flapping them as if flying, on the descent. Soon she had all the children doing it, and I suppose it was a good experience. A person should always be properly conversant with his environment.

The food was staple stuff: all-purpose vitamin/mineral/protein cakes and globed water. No gourmet fare, but quite good enough to sustain us. This was, after all, not a pleasure excursion.

'We have to see to the orientation of the lenses,' the pilot announced, as we squatted in groups on the Commons floor near our cells. 'We need a volunteer to supervise the air lock while we're outside.'

'I'll do it,' an older man said. 'I've floated a bubble before.'

'Fair enough. I'll appoint you temporary captain for the interim. Your name is—'

'Diego,' the man said. 'Bernardo Diego.'

'Take over, Captain Diego,' the pilot said, making a mock salute. Then he entered the air lock with his two crewmen.

Diego settled down by the lock, and the rest of us returned to our repast. Helse ate with us, seeming almost to become part of our family, and I guess that was just as well. No one seemed to suspect her true nature, not even Spirit, who could be unconscionably perceptive when that was least convenient. But she was more interested in her flying and in the other people around us, learning their names; she was as good at that sort of thing as I was poor. My talent is judging, not remembering people. That's why I am not naming people freely here; I did know their names, but I have already forgotten them, and there is nothing to be gained by cudgelling my memory to recreate every last one.

We finished our meal, and Helse and I took our turn at the head again, lining up by the cell numbers as before. We, as a group in the bubble, were fortunate that the male-female ratio of the total was just about even, for there were four heads of each type, and an imbalance would have been awkward. I helped Helse again; no one found it remarkable that two teen-age boys entered the room together, for that was the nature of boys. My mother and sisters went to their head together, though three was crowding it, and my father shared his turn with another family man. It was really working out quite well, considering the crowding. One person could use the liquid collector while another used the solid collector, and then they switched; in this way no more time was taken than it would have for one person at a time. We seemed to have a good group here, for all that it had been randomly assembled. Maybe there just happened to be a large percentage of intelligent, motivated people who couldn't abide the repressive Halfcal system.

Time passed. 'How long does lens adjustment take?' I asked. 'They can't stay out there forever.'

'Lens adjustment?' a neighbour asked. 'Was that what they said? I was in the head when they went out, and didn't hear.'

'Orientation of the lenses,' I informed him. 'They appointed a temporary captain from our number while they were out.'

'But a gravity lens is not oriented from outside,' the man protested. I remember his name now: it was García. 'The lenses are not physical objects; they are fields, generated by a unit in the centre of the bubble. It has to be that way; otherwise the spin would interfere with the gravity shielding, and we'd be jerking all over the cosmos. I used to be a technician. I'm not expert, but that much I do know.'

'That's right!' I agreed, chastened for not realizing it

myself. I excuse myself in retrospect by pointing out that we were then in a new situation, adjusting to the spin in various ways, eating our first bubble meal, and meeting our neighbours, so that the affairs of the crewmen were not uppermost in our minds. Probably that was the way our crewmen had intended it. 'They had no reason to go out for that – and one of them would have had to stay inside to change the settings if they were wrong.'

'We had better investigate,' my father said.

He and I and García made our way to Diego to present our concern. Diego looked stricken. 'You know, you're right! They don't need the lifeboat to check the lenses!'

'Lifeboat?' I asked, experiencing a sinking sensation that my trace weight could not account for—

'This lock opens to the lifeboat,' Diego explained. 'That's why they didn't need space suits this time. The boat's sealed, with its own supplies. I believe they stored the gold in there, for safekeeping—' Now his face was as aghast as mine had been.

It took us some time to verify and believe it, for our resources and information were limited and we didn't *want* to believe it. We had to get out the space suits and go outside the air lock to search for the lifeboat that wasn't there. But it was true: The three bubble crewmen had decamped with the gold. We were abruptly on our own, without even a lifeboat, in space.

We organized a meeting to discuss the situation and work out our options. Most of the refugees were in a state of disbelief; surely the crew would come back! They couldn't leave us stranded in space! Who would pilot the bubble? How would we get to Jupiter? But as time passed, more people believed. We realized that there was close to $50,000 in gold involved, and that this old bubble, converted from a retired pleasure craft, could not be worth more than $5,000. Perhaps a similar amount was invested in supplies. The crewmen had the money, so weren't bothering to carry through with their commitment. They were thieves or swindlers – and we had been taken.

Some women became hysterical. Some people retreated to their cells, refusing to face our situation. But a solid nucleus remained to tackle the problem. After all, if we ignored it, we would all perish. We could not simply float forever in space.

Diego argued in favour of reversing our thrust and descending to Callisto and taking our chances there. But too many people had cut their ties to the society below; return would mean harsh treatment by the government of Halfcal.

My father argued that if we could manage to operate the lenses and jet well enough to descend safely, we could use them as readily to proceed on our original mission. We could float the bubble to Jupiter ourselves!

There were arguments back and forth, but in the end we took a vote and my father was elected to be the new captain, since he had spoken for the majority. He immediately appointed Diego lieutenant captain. 'If something prevents us from going forward, you will be the one to take us back,' he explained to the man. 'You will need experience in handling the bubble, just in case. We are still a long way from Jupiter! Meanwhile, you're in charge of bubbleboard operations.'

Diego, who had been working up an irritation of temper when he saw the vote going against him, became mollified. My father had acted to preserve harmony in the bubble, and I noted this and learned from it. A person who opposes you does not have to be your enemy.

'Anyone who knows anything about navigation, come to me now,' my father announced. 'We need all the expertise we have, because I'm no space mechanic. We're a long way from the coffee plantation now!'

'And anyone who knows anything about supplies, atmosphere, recycling, sanitary facilities, or human motivation come to me,' Diego announced. 'We've got to keep this bubble healthy while it's going wherever it's going.'

I hesitated, then went to join Diego. Helse tagged along with me.

As it turned out, we were fairly well off. Diego found people to monitor the pressure and oxygenation equipment and check the funnel toilets. He glanced at me, and I was about to explain that I was good at human motivation, but he spoke first. 'You're Hubris's boy, aren't you? You'll be in charge of food supplies. First thing you'll want to do is get up there in the net and make a count, just to be sure we have enough.'

'Uh – yes, señor,' I said, realizing that he was doing the same thing my father was: appointing a potential malcontent to a responsible position. My father had made Diego second-in-command, so Diego was giving recognition to my father's son. It was a mutual backscratching operation, but I suppose it did alleviate tensions.

'And take your friend,' Diego added.

Helse was glad to participate. She had been staying close to me so she wouldn't have to tell her secret to anyone else. How this suddenly critical situation would affect her personally I didn't know, but it was unlikely to facilitate her serenity.

We clambered into the webbed chamber. I profited from my reasoning about the distortion caused by our spin, but still it took me two jumps to catch the entrance aperture in the net. Our weight was much less here, for we were near the centre of the bubble. In fact, some of the packages were floating, glancing off each other like molecules in motion. It was a good place for storage, since even the heaviest article could readily be moved here in free fall. This doughnut hole space was only four metres in diameter, so just by standing on the lattice net we had our heads just about banging the globe that encased the lens generator. It was a strange sensation: feet with trace gravity, head with none.

But we really could not conveniently stand, because the food packs and water bags and such mostly filled it. Some refugees had stored baggage up here, sensibly enough. So counting the food packs was a problem, because they didn't stay put very well. We could end up counting some several times and missing others completely. It might average out and lead to a correct count – but this was too important to leave to chance. Without food we would be in deep and early trouble.

I stuck my head down, out of the hole of the lattice. I spied Spirit, who was naturally curious about what I was doing, and tired of playing. 'Tell Señor Diego we need a bag or something to count them into; a big bag,' I called to her.

Soon she was back with a voluminously bulging armful of the kind of netting used to sweep rooms clean in free fall. She scrambled up with it, using this pretext to get in on the fun. It was all right; we were able to use her help. Spirit could be extremely helpful when she wanted to be.

We counted food packs into the net. There were quite a number, but in time we got a close enough figure: about 2,800.

'How many will we need for ten days' travel to Jupiter?' Helse asked.

I did some quick computations. 'Three per person, per day, for two hundred people – that's six hundred. Times ten days—' I broke off. 'Oops!'

'That's not enough!' Spirit said.

I worked it out another way. 'We've already had one meal, so that's two hundred. We must have started with three thousand. That's enough for a normal load of one hundred people – but we're overloaded. So there's only half enough.'

'Why didn't they pack more?' Helse asked.

Suddenly it all fitted together. 'They must have planned for one hundred, but twice as many refugees showed up, so they took us all. Because of the money. Then they realized they couldn't feed us all, so they took the money and flew.'

'Leaving us to starve in space!' Spirit exclaimed angrily.

'So it seems,' I agreed wearily. 'They planned a legitimate venture, but greed overwhelmed them, and we are left to pay the price. We'd better make a private report to Señor Diego, so the people won't panic.'

We glided down, hitting the Commons deck running so as not to be swept off our feet by its higher velocity. I noticed this time that there was a constant movement of air, for it had the same problem we did: differing velocities at different elevations. It tended to drag at the floor and to rush at the net ceiling. Well, that helped circulate it, so the purifiers could operate effectively.

We approached Diego. 'How many?' he asked.

'Twenty-eight hundred,' I murmured.

He leaned against the curving wall. 'You sure?'

All three of us nodded solemnly.

He led us to my father, who was at the control section of the bubble. 'Tell him,' Diego said to me.

'There're only half enough food packs,' I said.

My father considered the implications. 'I'll call another meeting,' he said grimly.

Soon it was done. My father summarized the situation.

'So it seems we don't have enough food to make our journey,' he concluded.

'How do we know the count's correct?' a man demanded. 'Diego doesn't want to make the trip, so he could have—'

'My son made the count,' my father said. And I realized how neatly Diego had arranged it. He must have suspected that the supplies would be short, so made sure no suspicion would attach to him. Regardless, it was true; we didn't have enough food.

'What about oxygen?' the man asked.

'There's enough,' Diego replied. 'Another crew checked

that. And most of the water is recycled. It's only food we're short.' And I realized that, whatever his preferences, Diego was trying to do an honest job. Had I interacted with him longer and paid more attention, I would have perceived what I now did; he was an honest man, expressing honest judgments. He had not urged our return to Callisto because he wanted to be a leader, but because he truly believed that was the best course. Snap judgments are treacherous.

'We could travel on half rations,' my father said. 'We would be hungry, but we wouldn't starve, and for ten days it should be bearable. If it were longer, we could try to use our refuse to grow edible plants, but we really aren't set up for that, and in ten days that won't work. But we can do it on what we have – if we wish to make the sacrifice. I won't insist on that unless there's a clear consensus.'

There was debate. The democratic process does take time! Then we took a vote. It was about four to one in favour of going on to Jupiter. Diego, amazingly, voted with the majority. 'We have better leadership than we had before,' he explained wryly to those who looked askance at him. 'I think we can make it now, with Don Hubris.'

My father smiled. 'Thank you, Don Diego.' And there was a minor ripple of appreciation, for there is this about that polite title of *Don* in our language: It is generally used with the given name, not the surname. They should have said Don Major and Don Bernardo – and indeed, thereafter they did so. I am not sure why they elected to misuse it this one time; there are aspects of adult humour and interaction I have not yet mastered. Perhaps Diego had simply not known my father's given name before.

The navigation crew had a fair notion what it was doing. Señor García explained it for those of us who were interested, and at this point most of the refugees were. All of us wanted reassurance that we were not travelling into doom. The details were somewhat technical for me, but here is the way I understand it.

8

Adjustment

Jupiter Orbit, 10-2-'15 – I need not repeat the sequence of
the pirate raid that occurred two days before this dateline,
and the horror that befell my sister Faith. It was a brutal
awakening for all of us; we had not before believed in the
reputed savagery of the outlaws of space. Yet for me
especially it was a turning point; my belief in the
fundamental goodwill of all men had been destroyed by the
Horse.

The Horse! Damn that pirate for what he did to us all, to
our minds as much as to Faith's body. It was necessary for
me to reconstruct my philosophy of life, to cope with the
ugly new reality. I did not agree with this reality, or even
understand it, but I had to live with it. I am not sure I can
successfully present the tides of my changed awareness, so
this may be disjointed or fragmentary, but I will try.

On Callisto, in Maraud – ah, that name had a changed
relevance now! – I had succeeded in defending my sister
from the lust of a strange man. Here in space I had not.
True, my entire family had paid a gross penalty for my
prior defence, having to flee the planet – but what was the
penalty for my failure this time? I simply could not grasp it.
Would it have been better to let the scion have his way?
Could anything he might have done to Faith have been
worse than what the foul pirate had done? I had to ask
myself whether my victory over the scion had been illusory,
and I was uncertain of the answer. Of course I could not
have let the scion have his way – yet how could I have
reacted to truly preserve my innocent sister? I had a deep

and terrible guilt to settle in my own mind, apart from the other present problems of existence.

I was jogged to awareness by friends – they had been only casual acquaintances, but suddenly now they were friends who were lowering me from my prison of suspension and untying my hands. Oh, it hurt as the circulation returned, for even my trace weight had caused the bindings to constrict – but it was in my mind that I deserved such pain, as part of my punishment for my failure.

The pirates were gone. The Horse had kept his word, such as it was, departing with his crew, leaving our valuables behind. He had not promised not to rape, merely not to rob or kill, and to leave us alone. There was, it seemed, a kind of honour among criminals, but it was subject to a savage interpretation. It galled me anew that I could not entirely condemn the Horse; he did have some spark of humanity in him, though he was a bad man. I would much rather have cursed him absolutely.

Faith lay as she had been left, not even trying to cover her shame. I think she was still unconscious. My mother rushed up to minister to her, and the other women closed in, as though whatever they might do was no fit matter for the eyes of males. Perhaps they were correct. The men, in turn, clustered around my father and me, as we stood chafing our hands and wrists and wincing from the pain. 'We didn't know,' they murmured. 'We *couldn't* know!' 'The pirate gave his word!'

'He kept his word,' my father said, his voice oddly calm. 'The agreement wasn't tight. Maybe he did us a favour – teaching us the reality of space without killing us.' He turned to me, and there was something blank about his countenance. I had been concerned with my own horror – what, then, of his? He had watched his daughter ravaged! 'My son was right. We should not have given up our advantage.'

'But that laser—' another man protested, then halted.

118

The deal with the pirates, had, in fact, traded the lives of several men, including my father, for the violation of my sister.

An aspect of reality laid siege to my awareness at that point. Which was worse: the death of my father or the rape of my sister? If I had had the power to choose between the two, knowing . . .

Helse came up and took me by the hand and led me to our cell, and no one objected. They knew I needed to be out of it for a while.

She put me on the floor as a nurse might place a non-resisting patient on a bed, then jumped up to close the panel in the ceiling, separating us from the rest of the bubble. Then she kneeled beside me. 'I understand,' she murmured. 'I can help you, Hope.'

'What do you know of rape?' I flared.

She took my unresisting hand and squeezed my fingers gently. It was foolish, I told myself, but I was reassured. The cell was deeply shadowed, since only a little light filtered through the translucent panel from the Commons, and that was just as well, for admixed with my horror was the shame of unmanly tears. 'I know a lot about it,' she said.

'Oh, sure!' My pain was turning on her, the nearest object. I knew this was unfair, but I had little control. The savagery to which my awareness had been subjected was too much for me to control; I could not react in an intelligent manner.

She leaned down, wrapped her arms around me, and lifted me in the partial gravity and drew me close to her, my head against her chest. She wore a tight band to flatten her breasts, to make her torso look masculine; now she paused to release this, and cradled my face to her abruptly feminine bosom, and it was marvellously compelling. She was indeed a woman, and soft in the way only a woman could be, and I felt her measured breathing and heard her steady heartbeat, and I was pacified.

'I'll tell you about me,' she said, speaking in a low and even tone so that others would not overhear. I think she was talking in order to distract me from the raw shock of what I had just seen, to give my soul a small time to heal, but before long the nature of what she was saying penetrated, and I really was distracted. Of course her monologue was not as succinct as I render it here from memory, but it was as important. I listened, and was slowly amazed.

Helse came from a family larger and poorer than ours, living in one of the smaller city-domes. She had been a pretty child, and in order to gain money on which to survive, they had rented her at the age of six to a middle-aged bachelor landowner as concubine. This was legitimate, socially, in that dome, though it has no legal status. There was merely an understanding that permeated that limited society from the poorest to the wealthiest; it had existed thus covertly for centuries, and it seemed no one really wanted to change it.

This landowner had never married, because he was unable to relate to adult women; he liked children, and had the wealth and power to indulge his propensities. His appetite was generally known but never openly bruited about, and he was generous to those who indulged him. Thus Helse's family, possessed of a pretty female child, had not been directly coerced to put their daughter into his hands; they had seized upon the opportunity to alleviate their poverty for the few years during which they had something worth selling.

Helse had called him 'Uncle' and he had called her 'Niece'. This was to facilitate a nonexistent relationship that would satisfy any question that might arise among occasional visitors or business acquaintances. Uncle was not a bad man, and he did not brutalize her. Far from it! He fed her well and gave her nice clothing and toys and presents. If she expressed an interest in something, she would have it the next day. He also provided her with a series of excellent tutors who set about giving her a proper upper-class education. Yet this was not an adult-child relationship; it was a courtship.

He courted her, and she was delighted. She regarded her position in his mansion as the privilege of being desirable; other girls her age had vied for it, but she had been chosen. But she knew she had to submit to whatever he chose to do with her body, and not all of that was fun. This was the price of her gifts and good life. If she ever once said no, or intimated that she objected, it would be over. She had the constant option of returning to her family – and this was not a promise, it was an unspoken threat. It was not that she didn't want to go home, but that it would be disaster to be *sent* home. She had to succeed. The kissing and fondling was easy enough, but the culmination was painful. He was a mature man and she was a child; no amount of gentleness could completely alleviate that.

Yet there were physical and mental devices, and she knew he did not mean or want to hurt her. He was driven by adult urges she did not understand, but he wanted to believe that she liked what he did. She learned to take relaxant medication and to dissemble her real reaction, for Uncle was most generous when most pleased. Experience made it easier, and in time she developed a certain pride in her competence. She became proficient in pleasing this man.

She was no prisoner. She was able to visit her family, sometimes for an hour, sometimes for a night. She brought them nice gifts that made all of their lives better. This was done with the approval and co-operation of Uncle, who wanted her to be happy. It seemed she pleased him more than others had, and now reaped commensurate rewards. But no direct word was ever spoken of her real place in Uncle's household; she was his niece, with certain poor relatives she liked to help.

In fact, she was now the principal provider for her family. Her father found work only intermittently, but Helse's work was steady. She became important in her own eyes, and perhaps she became arrogant, but this was her right.

For four years Helse was a little princess in Uncle's mansion, her every wish catered to by his other servants. He had an excellent staff, and they too understood their situations perfectly; there was no covert unkindness to her or embarrassing leaks of information. They were, in a fairly real sense, an extended family, each concerned with the welfare of the group. When a high official of the city visited, expressed a certain curiosity about rumours he had heard, and spread some money privately to confirm them, the staff members accepted the money and assured him with absolute sincerity that there was nothing to the rumours. When he questioned the naïve child Helse, she gave him similar assurance with marvellous innocence. Yet he knew, for he had other sources of information. 'I'd like to know your secret,' he confessed ruefully. 'How do you compel their loyalty?' And Uncle had smiled and not answered. This official was known to beat his own servants. The fact was that, apart from his sexual aberration, Uncle was a good and kind man, and his staff protected him because all its members genuinely cared for him. Wealth alone could not purchase that.

But at age ten Helse was getting too old, past her prime, as it were, and had to make way for a younger girl. She stifled her savage jealousy, knowing there was no percentage in it. She had known this would happen from the start; the staff had made it clear. She had to master adult grace in the face of the inevitable, and if she was unable to stifle a genuine tear in parting, this was not objectionable. Uncle gave her a generous separation bonus, and it was over. She was retired.

'You liked it!' I exclaimed, appalled. 'You wanted to stay with the child molester!' For, though I have rendered her narration as politely as I can, I have no sympathy with it. My family upbringing simply does not provide me with much tolerance for this sort of abuse of children.

'I liked the life, and I respected the man,' she qualified. 'I wish I could have been his real niece. He was not a molester, merely a person with a specialized taste. Some men like young, nubile women; some like fat women; some like other men, or boys; this one liked children. Uncle never raped anyone.'

That shut me up. Obviously her 'uncle' was a better man than the pirate Horse. I had to broaden my definitions.

There were, however, openings for experienced intermediate-aged children, Helse continued, and her family always needed money. So she went to work for a new employer. But this one had more violent tastes. For him there had to be humiliation and pain. It was not exactly rape, for he had paid for what he wanted and obtained prior acquiescence; it was more like submitting to necessary surgery with inadequate anaesthetic. The money was good, however, and she learned to endure this too. The one thing she insisted on was that no injury be done that would leave a mark or scar on her face or any portion of her body that normally showed.

I expressed curiosity, so she showed me some of the scars she did have, on her abdomen and back. I shuddered; the origin of those must have been painful indeed. She certainly *had* had experience of being tormented by men.

'But finally I got too old for any of that stuff,' she concluded. 'I could no longer earn enough to support my family. Not without risking my health or life. I had no better prospect than a life of formal prostitution. So I squandered my nest egg on this voyage and concealed my nature, so there wouldn't be any more trouble. I've had enough sex, especially painful sex, to last me a lifetime.'

That I could appreciate. I knew she was telling me the truth. Her ploy had been effective; the pirates had never even thought of raping Helse.

'But my point is, a girl can survive it,' she said. 'What happened to your sister is terrible, because she wasn't prepared for it, but there are worse things. I have survived worse.'

Again I believed her. Obviously she had prettied up her story for me. Helse was a nice girl – but she had had experiences I had never dreamed of. She maintained her emotional equilibrium; her mind had not been devastated. I realized that if Faith could adjust her thinking similarly, she would suffer far less. 'I wish you could talk to Faith,' I said.

'I will – if you want me to.'

I reconsidered. 'No, that would give away your secret, and I don't know that it would help her. I'll talk to her myself.'

'She could learn to pass for male,' she suggested. 'That could save her a lot of trouble.'

'Faith just isn't the type,' I said. 'But Spirit—'

'Your little sister is in danger too,' Helse said. 'This time the pirates went after the obvious, and were satisfied. Your sister Faith stands out in a crowd; every man's eye was on her from the start. You tried to shield her, but it was impossible. Next time they could go after the rest. There are men like that. I know.'

She certainly did! I thought of my little sister getting raped in the manner of my big sister, and a kind of blackness clouded my mind's eye. 'Spirit's a good kid. She can fight, and she can keep a secret. Will you teach her how to pass?'

'If you ask me to.'

There was something about the way she said that. I realized that I did not yet completely understand her. 'What do you want in return?' I asked.

'I like you.'

'I don't understand.'

'That's why I like you.'

'I like you too. But this is business! If there is something you—'

'What I want can't be bought. Just ask me to teach your sister.'

'All right,' I said, slightly nettled. 'I'm asking you.'

'Then I'll do it.'

My sense about people, as I've mentioned, is infallible. But that's a matter of comprehending motive, not of understanding every nuance. It is possible, for example, to know that a man is honest without knowing how to operate his business. Helse was not deceiving me. Yet she did want something from me – and she would not tell me what. That was a paradox of a type I had not encountered before, and it baffled me.

Then I remembered something else. 'Would you answer a question – if I asked you?'

'Yes, Hope,' she said.

'When you – when we were in the head, the first time – I didn't mean to look but I saw – what is that tattoo on your thigh?'

She sighed. 'I promised to answer. But you must promise not to tell.'

'All right,' I said.

'I told you I used my nest-egg money to pay for my passage on the bubble, but I didn't tell you how I got the money. My family had used up all that I had from Uncle and the other employers, and they don't pay that amount for – you know. But I was still friends with Uncle, and I phoned him privately—' She paused a moment, frowning. 'His current niece answered the vid. She was the second one since me. A cute little girl. I couldn't tell her I knew, of course. It jolted me, though.' She shrugged, then returned to her explanation. 'I asked Uncle how I could get to

Jupiter. I wasn't asking for money, just advice, and he knew that. I think he was flattered that I should think of him in that connection. He sent me to a man, and the man didn't want sex. He asked my why I wanted to go to Jupiter, and I told him it was to find a better kind of work. He said he couldn't guarantee the work, but that he could facilitate my trip there. All I had to do was carry a message to a certain person, whose name was Kife, or so it sounded. For that service I would be given the money to get passage and would be protected on the way. The tattoo is my protection.'

'That tattoo – three letters where no one can see them? How do they protect you?'

'They spell Kife,' she said. 'Hard Q, vowel Y, hard V. All I have to do is say the word to any criminal who threatens me, and he will stop. If he doesn't I can show him my tattoo – he's bound to see that anyway, if he means to rape me – and that will prove I'm authentic. But the mere spoken word is supposed to be enough. So I will not be molested by criminals, and of course law-abiding men will not bother me.'

I shook my head. 'You believe that?'

'No,' she confessed. 'Not completely. That's why I conceal my sex. But if I really am threatened, I'll try the word. Maybe criminals really are scared of Kife. After all, if he can afford that kind of money just to deliver one message, he must have a lot of power.'

'What's the message?' I asked.

She shrugged. 'That's the funniest part. I wasn't given any.'

'You were paid a thousand dollars to deliver no message?'

'Three hundred, for an individual. The man said Kife would understand when he saw me.'

I was having trouble with this. 'Just the sight of you would tell him something? Are you sure you aren't – I mean, that it is you he—'

Helse laughed. 'For sex? Hope, I'm hardly that special! I'm third-hands goods. No one would pay three hundred dollars for my body! For your sister's maybe; for mine, no.'

She was probably right. The going rate was less than a hundredth of that – as it had been for Faith. Pirates didn't pay for what they could take by force. 'Did the tattoo hurt?'

'No. The man gave me a sniff of gas, and when I recovered consciousness it was over. It didn't even sting.'

'Gas! Then he could have—'

She put her hand on my arm. 'No, Hope. There was no sex. I can tell. I was surprised, because that is usually a matter of course with such men. If he had wanted sex, I would have done it, and he knew that. I just wanted to get to Jupiter, the land of hope – no play on your name, Hope – whatever the price. I was put under so the tattoo wouldn't hurt; that was all.'

I sighed. 'I was curious about the tattoo. Now I'm twice as curious! There's something we don't know.'

'That's what you get, for curiosity,' she said, smiling in the shadow. She was very pretty, that way. 'But please don't tell anyone. Just in case it *is* important.'

'I won't tell.' At this point I almost wished I hadn't asked. I hate unsolved riddles.

However unconnected all this may seem in retrospect, I have to say that Helse had succeeded in what she set out to do: She had broken my mood of shock, enabling me to function more or less normally, for the time being.

My father plunged into the task of navigation; evidently he had come to his own terms with the situations of the bubble and of Faith. Adults seem to have greater resources in that respect than people my age do. Diego got to work on bubble defence. All of us who weren't otherwise occupied went to classes on combat. There was a retired martial artist among the refugees, an old man whose days of competition were decades past, but he possessed a lifetime of devastating knowledge. Had we had any warning about the raid of the pirates, he could have prepared us for them, but he too had been caught unawares.

He explained at the outset that there was little we could master in one or two days that would baulk armed pirates, so it was best that we concentrate on fairly simple, crude defences. He showed us how to fashion weapons of incidental objects, even wads of paper, and how to protect ourselves when disarmed. 'A girl does not have to to submit to rape by a lone man,' he said, getting right down to the point. 'The one we saw – there she was helpless. But usually it is just one man at a time. She has teeth, she has knees, she has fingers. The rapist has a nose, and testicles, and eyes.'

We listened doubtfully. 'I will demonstrate,' the instructor said. He dug in a bag he had and produced a rubber mask with bulging Ping-Pong-ball eyes and a huge beak of a nose. 'A young woman for a volunteer, please.'

Spirit jumped forward, naturally. I suppose she had not understood what had happened to Faith, so was not devastated. 'No, not a child!' a woman protested.

I glanced at Helse, understanding something she had said. 'Pirates don't worry much about age,' I said.

The instructor agreed. 'Unfortunately true. Children need protection most of all – male and female.' That startled me and I wasn't alone. Male?

He took Spirit aside and talked to her, explaining something in a voice too low for us to hear. She grinned, enjoying it. I noticed she wasn't wearing her finger-whip, she didn't want people to know about that, any more than I wanted them to know about my laser pistol.

Then they faced the class. 'I am a pirate rapist,' the instructor said, donning the grotesque mask. 'This child is the victim. Watch what she does.'

He turned on Spirit and clapped his hands on her shoulders, hauling her off her feet in the partial gravity of the Commons. 'Ha, my pretty!' he cried. 'I, fell pirate that I am, shall rape you to pieces!' He drew her in.

Spirit's knee came up suddenly. There was a solid contact. The man grunted and collapsed into a ball.

'Hey!' I cried, horrified. 'You weren't really supposed to knee him!'

But the instructor uncurled and got up, unharmed, and Spirit was laughing joyfully. 'I only kneed the outside of his hip, on the side away from you, silly,' she explained. 'In a real situation I would have aimed better.'

The class relaxed. The point had been made. Girls had knees.

The instructor came at Spirit again, quickly drawing her in so close she could not bring her knee up effectively. His hands closed about her throat, choking her. Close as he was, this was not completely effective, but it looked bad enough.

But Spirit's own hands were free. Quickly she reached up to his face. Her fingers dug into his eye – and an eyeball popped out of its socket and flew through the air.

There was a scream from the class – followed by nervous laughter. It was not a real eyeball; it was a painted Ping-Pong ball from the mask he wore. But again the point had been made: Girls had fingers, and rapists had eyes.

A third time the instructor grabbed her. Now he pinned her arms under his own and held her close against him as they fell to the deck. No knees, no fingers were free. His leering one-eyed mask face thrust down against hers, as for a brutal kiss.

Spirit opened her mouth, jerked her head up, and bit into the huge plastic nose. The instructor roared in simulated pain, but she ripped the nose from the mask. Third point made: Girls had teeth.

The instructor let her go and got up. 'So who is going to rape this child?' he asked rhetorically. 'If not the nose, the tongue, or the ear. Chew hard, taste the blood, and rape will be forgotten. But when he lets go of you, flee for your life!' He paused, then added a sober qualification. 'But if you are one and they are many, or the rapist is very strong, you cannot prevail. Hurt one and the others will kill you. In that case, it is better to submit. There are worse things than rape.'

Which, again, was what Helse had said. The entire complement of the bubble was conscious of rape now, and trying to defuse it, to make it seem less evil. But the memory of Faith's ordeal remained fresh in my mind, and I wondered.

We practised other techniques of self-defence, but they were less dramatic. Both throws and strikes were less effective in partial gravity than they would have been in full gravity, and we were more conscious than ever of our vulnerability to the superior weapons of the pirates. We were now much better prepared for the next pirate raid, assuming one came, but not very confident about our ability to fend them off.

Meanwhile, my father's crew kept tinkering with the gravity-lens projectors, shielding us against Callisto gravity and leaving us open to the backward pull of the sun. It took constant adjustment, but we seemed to be on schedule, and that was important, because our half rations would not last longer than we had budgeted. My description of our ongoing activities may make it seem as if we were lighthearted, but this was not the case; we were distracting ourselves from the fundamental grimness of our situation.

I brought Spirit in for a quiet conference with Helse. 'You're a girl?' Spirit exclaimed, round-eyed. 'I don't believe it!'

Helse opened enough of her shirt to show her strapped breasts. This was the first time I had actually seen them, and I felt guilty, and slightly irritated for that feeling.

'Hope has asked me to teach you how to be a boy.' Helse

130

said.

'I don't want to be a boy!' Spirit protested. 'I'm just barely getting ready to start being a girl!'

'If the pirates come again, you be a boy,' I said firmly. 'After what happened to Faith, and what Helse has told me of the appetites of some men—'

Spirit nodded soberly, not continuing the argument the way I had expected. 'I'll do it. I saw those pirates too, you know. Poor Faith! Why don't you go talk to her now, Hope? She needs you.'

Surprised, I went, leaving Helse to teach Spirit whatever was needed privately. I knew Spirit would pick it up rapidly, for she had hardly begun to develop and was boyishly lanky. She also had that spirit of adventure that made her good at new things.

Faith was alone in cell 75, and cell 76 was empty for the moment, as my parents were busy elsewhere. None of our other neighbours were in their cells. We could talk in fair privacy.

Seeing her was a shock. My older sister had always been beautiful, but now she was not. The past two days had made an unkempt wretch of her. Her fair tresses were tangled, her clothing was creased and dirty, and her eyes were hollowed and staring. I had stayed away from her, knowing I had nothing to offer except guilt for my neglect, knowing that only my mother could do what little might be done.

'Faith . . .' I said tentatively, afraid she would screech at me to be gone, as perhaps I deserved. I had heard her crying, faintly, on and off, through the cell walls, and so had known she was not resting easy. That had intensified my guilt but not my courage. What could I say to her, really?

She looked up at me. She was not catatonic, as I had half feared. 'Hope!' she said, her face brightening as she reached for my hands. 'I missed you.'

'I failed you,' I said. 'I'm sorry.' That was grossly inadequate, and suddenly I was hopelessly choked, the despicable tears pushing through my eyes, and I tried to pull my hands away from her. In some times past it has been socially acceptable for a man to cry, but not in this century.

'No, no!' she protested. 'You tried, Hope, you tried! No one could help me. I brought it on myself.'

'The pirates did it!' I ground out bitterly. 'I'll kill—'

'Am I still your sister?' she asked, not loudly.

Startled, I paused for reflection. What did she mean? I am a good judge of character, but this was a matter beyond my compass.

She was looking at me, and I realized that I had to answer. She placed great importance on this matter, confusing as the implication might be. 'Of course you're my sister,' I said. 'How could it be otherwise?'

'I'm not what I was,' she said.

She thought the rape had degraded her! 'The fault is not yours!' I exclaimed. '*No* fault is yours! You were the victim of—'

Again I paused, suffering an ugly realization. 'Of a male.' I concluded. My sister had been shamefully abused – and I was a member of the species that had done it. I had a penis, the weapon of the male; I was culpable. I had experienced an infernal excitement as I watched the horror of her humiliation; I could not pretend otherwise. It had been the same when I helped Helse in the head; my member was eager to follow the course of the pirate's.

We talked more, and I think I helped her feel better. It was the least I could do. She was still my sister, but I was not sure I was still her brother. The seed of self-aversion had been planted in me, and it grew with a smoldering persistence. I hoped God would smite me if I ever had another erection, or even thought of touching a woman sexually. Male lust had destroyed my lovely sister, and I could not afford to share any part of that evil.

9

Massacre

Jupiter Orbit, 12-2-'15 – We were hungry, but we were closing on the Jupiter ring system. In three more days we should be there.

Another ship overhauled us. My father looked worried. 'Friend or enemy?' he asked.

'We can't take the chance,' Diego said. 'We must assume we have few friends in space. We'll have to set an ambush.'

'But if they're friendly – we do need food.'

'I didn't mean we'd attack them unprovoked, señor. We just need to be armed and ready – and if they manifest as pirates, we'll jump them, and this time we won't let them go. If they're not pirates, we'll never show what we're ready for.'

My father nodded. 'Sounds good to me. That means we'll have to act normal, with the women and children in evidence.'

'Yes. But at the same time we must be armed and ready. We know the penalty for failure!'

'We know,' my father agreed grimly. He hardly showed his reaction to the rape of his daughter, but I knew he had been deeply wounded. I think he maintained a firm presence because he was afraid my mother would collapse if he did not. I would have considered this mutual bracing in crisis to be a good object lesson in human nature had it not been my own family concerned. So my father carried on in a nearly normal manner, while my mother stayed mostly out of sight, and I think I understood them both and respected them for the way they handled it. Naturally I had to carry on too, so as not to weaken the family effort.

The ship closed and locked onto our main air lock. I wished there were some way to prevent this, but the designers of bubbles had not anticipated the problem of piracy in deep space. Any ship could attach to and board a bubble; all locks were interconnectable. Thus the best of intentions led to the worst of errors – as far as we were concerned.

The lock opened, being worked from the other side, and gaudily garbed, bearded men trooped in. They certainly looked like pirates!

My father went up to them. 'We're glad you have come! We're trying to get to Jupiter, but we're short of food—'

The man hardly looked at him. 'Bind the men. Line up the women – the young ones. We'll loot after we're sated—'

Diego needed no more. These pirates weren't even making any pretence at honest dealing! He drew a penknife and slashed at the nearest pirate, cutting his sword arm. The pirate screamed.

Our other men pounced, two to a pirate. In moments, almost bloodlessly, our forces had made the pirates captive. Our preparation had paid off handsomely!

Then something strange happened. There was a thin, keening sound, not exactly painful – but somehow I lost volition. I had been sitting with Spirit, who was now garbed as a boy, where we could keep an eye on both the pirates and cell 75, where Helse and Faith were. We were keeping both of them out of the action, just in case, though the rest of the bubble thought Helse was male. Now I watched the pirates turn on Diego and my father and throw them against the wall near the air lock – and somehow I didn't react.

García was near us. 'Oh, no,' he muttered. 'They've got a pacifier.'

A pacifier. I knew what that was, though I had never before experienced its effect personally. It was an electronic

135

gadget that broadcast a semi-sonic wave that interfered with the human nervous system. It did not damage people or knock them out; it merely diluted their concentration or their will to action. It was like a soporific drug. Some rich men used these devices as sleeping medication, and they were supposed to be useful in prisons and mental institutions. And yes, I had heard of them being used illicitly to make women unresistive to rape. They were far too expensive for peasants to own; the pirates must have stolen one in the course of their routine marauding and kept it in reserve for just such an occasion as this. Probably someone in their ship had orders to watch and turn it on when things went wrong for them – as had been the case here.

I cursed that instrument – but not vehemently, for vehemence was not possible while it functioned. I damned myself for my failure to overcome the ennui, but could do no more than that. I just sat there and watched my father get knocked about and bounced into the wall.

But Spirit had more resistance than I did. She had always been a spirited girl, true to her name, though she had been named long before the trait manifested. Somehow her neural chemistry differed; she was able to assert partial free will. She began to move towards the pirates.

'They will hurt you,' I warned without particular emphasis. I knew intellectually that we faced disaster, but I just couldn't get emotional about it. I was intellectually furious, but not emotionally. It was like watching a person in a drama do something stupid and identifying with that person, while being unable to influence his action.

'They won't notice me,' she replied. She didn't sound excited; the pacifier was working on her, but not quite as effectively as on me.

'Why doesn't it affect the pirates?' García asked, as though this were a matter of idle curiosity. Then he answered his own question: 'The field can be disrupted by certain countercurrents. The pirates can have little genera-

136

tors on their bodies, giving them protection.' It was strange to be discussing this so calmly, while doing nothing about it.

Then a pirate messenger came through the lock and whispered to the leader. The leader looked alarmed. Then he set himself and started giving orders.

The pirates who were rounding up our unresisting men paused, then turned them loose. The leader raised his voice and addressed us all. 'There is a Jupiter Ringuard patrol boat approaching. Now, we don't want any trouble with them. If they send an officer aboard, we want you all to convince him that we are traders, making a business deal with you. We're selling you food, and we're haggling over the price, but it's friendly.'

He paused, looking around. 'Fetch me some children.' he ordered his henchmen.

The pirates ranged out in search of children. They took Spirit and me, and we went unresisting, though I saw Spirit grimace. It was uncertainty that restrained her rather than inability to act; she wasn't sure what would happen to the rest of us if she resisted.

They took Helse out of the cell, thinking her to be a boy my age, but left Faith, who looked disreputable at this time. One tiny silver lining for her, perhaps! They rousted out several smaller children. Soon eight of us were standing together before the air lock.

The pirate leader drew a great long dagger of a knife. He caught a six-year-old girl by the hair and yanked her head back, exposing her neck. He set the blade against her throat. 'Now hear this!' he cried to us all. 'I'll slit this throat myself, the moment anyone squawks. And my men will do the same to the others.' At his gesture, the other pirates drew their blades and menaced the rest of us.

'So you'd better convince that officer, folks,' the pirate leader concluded. 'Unless you figure I'm bluffing. Then you do what you want, and we'll do what *we* want, because there's a price on all our heads if they recognize us, and we won't have anything to lose. If that officer catches on, he'll be dead too. So you can just take your choice between the robbery we have in mind – and your children.'

The worst of it was, he wasn't bluffing. It did not require my talent to fathom that. These men really were killers, worse than the first bunch; they had made no pretence of being anything other than pirates from the outset.

'Now we'll turn off the box,' the pirate leader concluded. 'You will have volition – but we have your children.'

The pirate by the air lock turned off the box. Suddenly I had strength of will again. But there was a blade at my back, and I knew it would be worse than futile to bolt. We had no way to co-ordinate, to run together, and nowhere to go if we did run We had all been disarmed – and half of us really were children. Despite all our preparations, we were helpless.

That bothered me, I think, almost as much as our predicament. The fact that we had been caught unprepared, after thinking we were ready. Now an officer of the law – Jupiter law – the very type of person we most wanted to meet – was coming, and we could do nothing.

Three pirates took the two smallest girls and a baby boy through the lock into their ship. The boy whimpered and his mother moved nervously, but he went along. These were the ultimate hostages: the most vulnerable of our number. I could have identified all their parents by their reactions, had I not already known. Until we had these children safely back, we were completely nullified.

I glanced at our martial-arts instructor and saw him standing with a grim expression. He knew better than anyone that the pirates' device of protection was too effective. All we could do was co-operate and hope for a favourable break.

The space officer arrived. He was wearing a conventional space suit emblazoned with the red ball of the Jupiter

Service. He was the representative of the foremost power in the Solar System – but in person he was a small, somewhat pudgy man, seemingly uncertain. He would have been nothing, if it weren't for the devastating guns of the Navy ship trained on both our vessels. How easy it would be to alert that ship, and maybe get us all blasted to pieces! But that would hardly be to our advantage. We had to gamble on the lesser evil of the pirates' mercy.

Lesser evil! There would be more than one woman raped this time, I was sure, and anything we had of value would be taken, and some of our men would be beaten. God, I hated this!

'What are you up to here?' the officer asked in English, the language of the dominant power on Jupiter. There are, of course, four major languages used on Jupiter, but the speakers of the other three – French, Spanish, and Portuguese – did not maintain space patrols. That made English the most truly interplanetary one in Jupiter-space. Thus did economics translate into culture.

The pirate chief smiled ingratiatingly. 'We are only traders, sir, peddling staples to these travellers.'

The officer turned to face our group. 'True?'

'We are doing business,' my father said in halting English. This hurt me too. My father was lying, at the behest of our enemies, and I hated to see him thus demeaned. I have never liked lying, and I felt unclean for him. At the same time, I knew we had no choice. Even if Spirit and Helse and I were to bolt and escape our captors, as we might reasonably do if we acted in unison, we could not save the three smaller children, and their deaths would be on our hands. It was like a finger-bending hold that a bully puts on another child, to force him to tell the teacher the two are only playing. I hate that sort of thing, but the only practical answer I ever found to it was to avoid the situation. Once your finger is caught, it's too late for sensible solutions; you have to go along. So I understood the situation exactly – but a special kind of rage seethed in me. Pirates like this should be extirpated from the face of the universe!

The officer's brow wrinkled. I realized he did not understand my father's strongly accented English. Quickly I spoke up, in better English. 'My father says we are doing business,' I explained. And realized that now I shared the lie directly. Damn! How I hated every aspect of this!

'Drug business?' the Jupe officer demanded.

'No drugs,' my father assured him, honestly enough, in Spanish, and that negation needed no translation.

'See that you don't. We'll be watching you.' The officer turned abruptly and departed. It seemed his shuttle craft had latched on to the other port of the pirate ship, so he had to pass through that ship to leave us.

In a moment we felt the tremor of the shuttle craft disengaging and jetting away, back to its mother ship. That test was over, but I did not feel much relieved.

'Now release our children,' my father said.

The pirate leader considered, and in that moment he reminded me uncomfortably of the way the Horse had pondered, after we had turned his men loose. 'Ah yes, the children.' He turned his head and yelled into the ship.

'You through with the brats?'

'Just about,' a voice called back.

Just about? I experienced a new chill. What were they doing with these children?

Then they brought the children back. The two little girls were naked and crying. A pirate carried the baby boy, who was also naked, but silent. The man stepped out and threw the boy to the floor.

A paroxysm of horror passed through our group. The boy's eyes were open and staring, and his chest was still. He was dead!

Now it was apparent that the little girls had been raped. It seemed every man in our group launched himself at the

140

pirates. But then the pacifier box came on again, and the charge became a shambles, its impetus gone. The broadcast interference was not psychological, it was physical; no amount of determination could overcome this paralysis of the voluntary functions.

The pirate leader drew his sword, smiling grimly. He seemed to be enjoying this. He had *wanted* us to see the children, and to react as we did, and to be cut down to helplessness again. 'You made trouble for us. We don't like that.'

My father was closest to him. The pirate raised his sword in a two-handed grip and swung it savagely. I saw, as if it were in slow motion, the blade cut into my father's side. It sliced through clothing and rib cage and into the lung, and the blood poured out like the living thing it was.

I knew in that moment that we should have blown the whistle on the pirates when the Jupe officer was here. We had been held passive by a threat to hostages who were even then being savaged. We had had nothing to lose, had we but known it. We had been too trusting – and now were paying the hideous price.

Would the pirate really have dared to kill the Jupe officer? Now I doubted it, for it would have meant the end of the pirate ship, possible complete destruction by a military missile.

Now it was carnage. Ruthlessly the pirates hacked apart our men, who were unable to resist. They left none alive. Such was the enervation spawned by the devil-box that all we could do was moan in soft horror. We couldn't *act!*

They hurled the bleeding bodies into a pile, then sheathed the swords and came after the women. Some, unsatisfied with what they saw, started rechecking the cells. I saw someone open the panel of number 75, where Faith still hid. I remembered that Helse had taken the opportunity provided by the presence of the Jupe officer to return to that cell; no one had been paying attention to her, among the pirates, so she had gotten away with it. But that minor escape had accomplished nothing, for there was the pirate at the cell.

The man looked down, then paused as if struck. Then he closed the panel and went on. What had happened? The pacifier box prevented any attack against any pirate.

Meanwhile, another pirate took hold of my mother, bringing my attention back to closer events. The cell, well around the curve of the Commons, was difficult to see anyway. I had positioned myself to have it in view without being close enough to attract attention to it.

The pirate literally tore the clothing from my mother, while she tried feebly to pull away, crying. I felt a truly terrible rage – but still it did not translate to my body. My nerves might as well have been cut, so that my limbs would not respond. It was hard enough just to turn my head.

There was a crash. My head jumped around. Spirit, possessing more volition than the rest of us, and perhaps more common sense, had reached the unguarded box, picked it up, and smashed it. Suddenly we all were free.

I ran to help my mother, who was on her back, the pirate tearing at the shreds of her underclothing as he came down on top of her, Neither he nor she realized that we refugees had been freed to fight. I leaped to land on his back, my hands reaching around to his head, trying to pull him back though my weight bore down on him. I was so crazy with grief and rage and horror that I remembered none of the precepts we had been drilled in; I just put his head in a bear-hug and shoved with my feet.

Angrily he shook me off, half rising and reaching for his sword. He was so powerful I couldn't possibly hold him. I realized belatedly I should have grabbed a hammer or something and smashed him on the head. Now I was in trouble.

But the pirate grunted and collapsed. My mother had remembered one of the lessons and jerked up her knee the moment she had leverage, and scored on his crotch. The fight was mostly out of him.

There followed an amazingly savage conflict, as the other women and children recovered their volition and sought revenge for the brutality of the pirates. They clawed at faces and bit at hands and kicked at anything in reach. The pirates were burly men, accustomed to violence and bloodshed, but they had not before been betrayed by their pacifier box. They weren't used to having the victims fight back.

There were a dozen pirates in the bubble; five times that many women pounced on them, like vicious harpies. I saw one woman kneel on the head of a pirate while another drove an iron knitting needle into his ear as deep as it would go. It took only a moment for the man to stop jerking and screaming. I saw another trying to castrate a pirate with a sharp letter opener, an antique that had surely been saved as an heirloom, since letters had not needed such service for centuries. An immense and truly horrifying well of violence had been tapped, and I saw that we were in our deepest essence no better than our enemies.

Injured and bleeding, the surviving pirates beat a disorganized retreat and slammed the air lock closed. In moments their ship disengaged and fled.

We were left with our victory – and our grief. We had had sixty grown men in our complement; all had been slain in the pirates' orgy of killing, while we were helpless. Three pirates also lay dead in their blood, and the baby boy. The two raped little girls stood staring, not grasping any of this.

I went to my father, hoping somehow to discover him alive, but knowing better. I looked down through burning eyes at his corpse. How terrible his fall, how ignoble the deed! Nothing in my father's life or philosophy justified this dreadful termination. And I, by getting my family into the trouble that forced our exodus, had been the cause.

In a moment I felt someone at my side. It was Spirit. I

clutched her to me, sharing my agony with her. We had never dreamed of desolation like this.

Now the women were scattered across the Commons, suffering their separate reactions. No trace of their violence of a moment ago remained. The departure of the pirates had excised the savagery in us. Some had found their husbands and were keening their grief, kneeling and bending their torsos forward and back, letting out part of their pain. Others were standing absolutely still and silent, just looking down. I realized that there is no set formula for the abatement of intolerable loss.

'We must do something,' Spirit said.

I wrenched myself away from my horror, realizing she was correct. We had suffered an appalling disaster – but disorganization would only exacerbate our situation. We had to have a new leader who would see to whatever had to be done. But who, with no men remaining among us?

'Use your talent, Hope,' Spirit told me.

She sounded so practical that I looked at her. Her eyes were staring out of her head like those of a little automaton, but she was right again. Her shock simply had not yet progressed to her vocal cords. How she would react when the full impact affected her I did not know. Some horrors, like some joys, seem to be too massive to grasp all at once.

I thought a moment, then recalled a woman of grand-motherly age, huge and ugly and competent. She was Concha Ortega, a dark-skinned widow who was travelling with her three grandchildren. Not one of those children ever misbehaved. None of them had been among those taken hostage by the pirates, which perhaps would enable her to be more objective than she might otherwise have been.

I saw my mother making her way towards us. She was an awful sight. Her hair was ragged, her clothing shredded, and there was a glazed look about her. 'Take care of Mother,' I murmured to Spirit, and departed. I knew my little sister would do what little could be done.

I made my way to Señora Ortega, who was hauling the body of a pirate towards the air lock. 'Excuse me, Doña Concha,' I said to her. 'I am Hope Hubris, Major Hubris's son. You must be our new leader.'

She viewed me contemplatively. 'By what authority, Don Hope, do you appoint me to such office?' She was extremely imposing, with half-cropped grey hair, line-encased eyes, and much mass of body, and I felt like the stripling I was as that gaze fell on me.

'It's just that I know,' I said. 'All our men are gone, and you are the best woman. You understand discipline, you know what to do. You must lead, or we shall be leaderless, and perish in space.'

She pondered briefly. 'You are right, little man,' she said. 'It must be done. I have suffered no recent losses; I can put my mind to this problem.'

'Thank you, Doña,' I said, retreating.

Señora Ortega raised her voice, addressing the entire bubble. 'We must provide proper burial for our dead,' she announced. 'We must show proper respect.'

Proper respect – she had hit a note that resonated. Grief was piercing, but respect was vital. It was the dues paid the dead.

Under Señora Ortega's direction the bodies were moved to the vicinity of the rear air lock and laid out there in such style as was possible, considering the absence of facilities and the scantness of gravity in that region. The survivors closed the eyes of the men, washed the bodies with sponges from the heads, and reclothed them for burial. The signs of devastation were removed as much as possible, so that the men appeared to be sleeping.

There was a problem with the bodies of the three pirates. No one wished to do *them* honour! We hauled them to the front air lock and dumped them unceremoniously. We closed the lock and made ready to use the override control to open the outer port without first decompressing the lock. That would hurl the bodies into space unburied, unlamented.

'No,' my mother said, looking up from my father's body.

'Speak, Charity Hubris,' Señora Ortega said. 'What would you do with this rubbish?'

'I would use it to greet the next pirates who come,' my mother said, and there was a note in her voice that sent a chill through me.

There was a murmur of surprised agreement among the women. How confidently would a pirate enter if he discovered three of his kind, mutilated and dead, in the air lock of the bubble supposedly waiting to be fleeced?

'Excellent notion, Doña Charity,' Señora Ortega agreed. I noticed how careful she was to employ the ceremonial address, providing respect to the living as well as to the dead. She was indeed the proper leader. 'We shall save those bodies for such use. We shall post the warning of the skull on the stake.' For in Earth's past, savage tribes had demarked their ranges by such means, plain warning to intruders.

Then she paused in thought. 'Should we evacuate the air from that lock?'

Even the children knew the consequence of leaving bodies in air and warmth. There would come a horrendous stench.

Grimly, the women decided to leave the air in the lock.

That ugly business done, we returned to the rites for our gallant men. Normally death is a family affair in our culture – but not all the men had adult kin here in the bubble, while some families had made this trip without men, so everything was awkward, and it seemed best to handle it as a community effort. We arranged to have all the men suitably prepared, and we tore up one black gown donated for the purpose into strips for black armbands of mourning for all. Even though we were all Hispanic, there were differences in the details of our customs, so again we compromised on the single uniform service. There were suggestions of the Roman rite and the Gothic rite, with our scant and precious incense burned and the lips of some men anointed with oil. Doña Concha led us in singing the psalm *De profundis*: 'Out to the depths have I cried to Thee, O Lord . . . I trust in the Lord, my soul waits for His word . . . ' Oh, it moved me; I had to believe that the Lord would accept my father and treat him kindly. Then a few complimentary words were spoken for each dead man, and there was general praise for the group of them. Doña Concha did a good job; she had been through it with her own husband, who had died some years before, so understood the needs of the families though she had not herself been touched this time.

I fancy myself as being not superstitious or overly emotional, but that quiet, sincere service helped me tremendously. When she praised my father, calling him Don Major and describing in a few words his integrity and bravery in leading our group towards Jupiter, tears of sheer joy mixed with those of grief in my eyes, and the terrible burden of his loss eased significantly. It is truly bad to lose one's father, but it is best that he suffer a hero's demise. I'm sure the others felt the same as she spoke of their own men.

It was of course impossible to bury them in a sanctified cemetery or to place them in crypts with flowers or to kiss the earth as it was thrown into the coffins, and we elected not to use the few simple candles we possessed, not wishing to tax the air-recycling system with so much open flame. We decided to do the best we could: to bury them temporarily outside on the bubble. A select crew donned space suits and took the bodies one by one out the rear lock. We were not relegating them to space, but securing them to the outside of the bubble in plastic wraps and whatever else could be made to serve, so that they would be preserved by the cold and vacuum until the time they could be properly interred on planetary ground. We could not keep them inside the bubble, of course, and outside was as perfect a deep-freeze as exists. They would be preserved intact for Eternity, out there.

So it was done, and we sang the canticle *Benedictus* with the antiphon *Ego sum resurrectio et vita*, I am the resurrection and the life. The earth had, figuratively, been thrown into the graves, and the necessary formalities were over. Señora Ortega explained gently that though we all should normally be permitted to retire to our justified grief, it was nonetheless necessary for us to keep the bubble functioning and on course; we would never be able to give our men proper burial if we did not survive ourselves. So she declared an end to formal grief, leaving only the armbands, as if a year had suddenly passed. She asked those of us who were able to function to join her in operating the bubble. This would not, she assured us, signify any lack of feeling or any affront to the dead, but rather our recognition of what had to be done in a most difficult situation. The way she expressed it, it was easy to agree. We had chosen well in this leader.

When a small crew of those women who had some grasp of the principles of gravity-shield navigation had been assembled, Señora Ortega dismissed the rest of us to our cells. 'The best thing you can do right now is mourn your dead in privacy,' she said. 'Send them to heaven with your prayers. I know what you are feeling; my own grief is long behind me, and it occurred in better times than these you suffer now, but I remember.' In this way she returned informally what she had denied formally: the timely expression of grief.

We went to our cells, but it was not a simple retirement. I realized abruptly that my mother should not be alone in her cell. I spoke to Faith, who had remained in her own cell throughout, thus missing much of the horror of the pirate encounter. It was not that she lacked feeling for our father, but that the full appreciation of his death added at this time to her existing state could have destroyed her. Yet I feared for the welfare of our mother too. 'Please join her,' I asked Faith. 'You can understand and comfort her better than I could, for you are a woman.'

Faith looked at me with a head-tilt of startlement, then swept back her hair and climbed to the next cell. She knew her own dismay had been preempted by a greater one.

But now Spirit ws alone. I hesitated, knowing this was not right for her either.

Helse arrived. 'Go with your sister, Hope, ' she said. 'I am not bereaved, except to the extent I knew and respected those members of other families who died. I will try to help someone who needs it.'

I felt a warm surge of gratitude towards her. 'Thanks.' I joined Spirit in her cell.

Spirit abruptly flung her arms about me, buried her face in my shoulder, and bawled. It was at that moment of let-down that the enormity of our tragedy struck me. Until then the continuing exigencies of our situation had caused me to hold much of the horror at bay, except when I thought specifically of my father.

Now it overwhelmed me too. I clung to my crying little sister and sobbed as vehemently as she

10

To Love And Be Loved

Jupiter Orbit, 14-2-'15 – but a person cannot cry forever. Spirit bounced back first, somewhat wasted, having washed much of the first rush of grief out of her system. I know she still suffered, but already she was coming to terms with it. I had to follow her in that recovery, for I was now the oldest (and only) male in our family, and that is a thing of special significance. I would not presume, of course, to order my mother around, but it would be my position to formulate family initiatives and make suggestions that I knew my mother and older sister would take seriously. So I forced my own continuing agony of soul into a compartment, like the cell I slept in, closed the panel on it as well as I could, and required myself to function. My mother and sisters could grieve; I would have to endure.

There were meals to be fetched and distributed, though our shortage was now, ironically, less acute because of our diminished number. Señora Ortega asked me to resume my prior capacity as food distributor, and to expand my activities as necessary, since I was now the oldest male in the bubble. Oh yes, that woman knew how to make a young person do her bidding! I agreed and got to work, and found that there was indeed reprieve from grief in work.

We had to reorganize the heads, for it was senseless to reserve half the bathrooms for males who no longer lived. I asked Spirit to explain to women how they might be able to use the male facilities by assisting each other as I had assisted Helse – but cautioned her that she should present this as her own idea, and to leave Helse out of it, as Helse

150

was still considered a boy. If Señora Ortega suspected that Helse was older than I, or that she was female, Señora Ortega did not say. I think she did suspect, and did us both the quiet favour of assuming that Helse was a boy a few months younger than I. Women of grandmotherly age can be discreet; they have had a great deal of time to learn that art.

There was further cleaning to be done, removing bloodstains from the floor and walls of the Commons. Helse and Spirit and I helped with it all, keeping ourselves constantly busy.

It may seem that my grief for my father was shallow, since I was soon functioning in virtually normal fashion, and am not referring to it in every paragraph of this narrative. I protest that this was not the case. My father was much in my mind, but I knew I could not bring him back, no matter how much pain I felt, and it is pointless to grow repetitive here. I worked to help alleviate the suffering of the living, including especially the members of my own family, and I hope I succeeded in this. I discovered that in this effort was the most effective reduction of my own pain. So do not slight me for my seeming neglect; I have written as much of this aspect as I care to, though it hardly does justice to the reality.

Spirit had found another girl her age who, of course, had suffered similar loss, and they spent the next night together. That freed me to return to Helse – and I needed to do that, because she maintained her masculine masquerade, and only I could help her in the head. How she managed that one night by herself I do not know; perhaps she borrowed a mop handle to push against the far wall and hold herself in place. It cannot have been comfortable.

The first night I was back with her, after the slaughter, I found it difficult to relax, let alone sleep. I tossed about in the partial gravity, but it was not my own discomfort that haunted me so much as my father's. He was outside in the cold, now; was he shivering? Did he gasp for air in the cruel vacuum? Of course not – yet as I drifted off to sleep, I phased into a dream awareness of Major Hubris, alive and well, to my gratified surprise. But I knew, even in the dream, that it was not so, and that if I embraced him I would feel the absolute chill of space in his flesh. I felt it my duty to advise him of the truth that he was evidently not yet aware of, for my father always preferred to be in touch with reality even when it was not pleasant. Whereupon, surprised, he turned slowly to a staring corpse with a great red wound in his side. He looked in that instant like Jesus Christ, and I could not scream in horror lest I defile an image I was not worthy to approach.

I shuddered awake, finding Helse holding me. Oh, death is no thing of joy! 'I would help you if I could,' Helse murmured. 'But this is not like the other, not like the case with Faith. I have had no direct experience with death.'

'Leave me alone!' I snapped. I shouldn't have done that, and don't know why I did it, and was sorry immediately, but unable to apologize. Grief is like that, too. Grief is not necessarily any prettier than death, and the grief-stricken do not wander like lambs grateful for the shepherd's guidance. They can be more like wounded wolves, snapping at those who would help them.

She did leave me alone, and I slept intermittently again. But I had not escaped my nightmare. It came at me again and again, like a ravening monster, its moist teeth seeking to rend my flesh. It was guilt, the personification of my neglect. Could I have done something to avert the tragedy? Why had I had such ennui when the pirates were slaughtering our men? Why had I stood silent when the pirates hoodwinked the officer from the Jupiter patrol? Certainly the pirates had held three children hostage – but those children had been doomed anyway, and by my neglect our entire group had become vulnerable. Why hadn't I screamed the truth to the officer? It seemed so simple in retrospect. I had known the pirates were not to be trusted. I banged my fist against the wall in frustration.

I woke again, feeling Helse's restraint on my arm. 'Hope, you'll hurt yourself!' she protested.

'I ought to kill myself!' I flared. 'I let my father die!'

'But there was the pacifier. You tried to—'

'Shut up!' I shouted, and spun through the same cycle of self-reproach and inaction as before.

She shut up, and again I tried to sleep. If I did, I got no satisfaction of it, for the horror and guilt stalked me relentlessly. Gradually I realized that the truths I cached away in emotional compartments during the day only gained strength to conquer me at night when my resistance was down. And the most fundamental truth was the one I had glimpsed before, when Faith was raped: A man was a creature of murderous lusts, and I was a man. I might as well have raped my sister and murdered my father myself. Only circumstance had put me in the camp of the victims rather than that of the perpetrators. I was a damned creature, because of my anatomy and nature.

I contemplated my erect member and cursed it. 'You are the cause of all this!' I ranted. 'You don't care who you hurt!' For I knew that a sword is but a symbol of the phallus, and when it plunges into a living body and causes blood to spurt, that is a symbolic sexual act. That is why women are not much for violence; they lack the weapon. 'I ought to rip you out by the root!'

Again I woke to find Helse's hands on me, preventing me from attempting what I had threatened in the dream. My rage was replaced by chagrin, for of course she had seen me handling my aroused private.

But she said nothing, and I remembered that the male member was no stranger to her. She knew better than anyone else the nature of the lusts of the male. I turned my back on her and struggled back to a semblance of sleep once more. This time I made it fairly well through the arbitrary night of the bubble.

The following day was gruelling. My intermittent night's sleep left me ill-prepared to fend off the emotional horrors. I went about my business in grim silence. Spirit tried to speak to me, but I repulsed her, then cursed myself for it when I saw her silent, hurt tears, but I did not try to make amends. It was as though my emotions were under the type of interdict the pacifier box had instilled, so that I could lash out verbally but not apologize.

I saw that there were others as morose as I, and some refused to come out of their cells to eat. One woman went into the head and did not emerge; when someone finally checked, they discovered her dead. She had cut open an artery in her thigh and bled to death on the bidet. Suicide.

I knew exactly how she felt.

Helse guided me to our cell early. 'Hope, you are dying on your feet,' she told me. 'I think I can help you, now.'

'Nothing can help me,' I muttered, but I was so tired and dazed that I offered no resistance.

Then, perhaps as much to hurt her as from curiosity, I asked: 'That pirate who started to go after you and Faith – why did he quit?'

'I spoke the word,' she said.

That was what I had suspected. But had the pirate left them alone because he feared QYV – or because he thought they were two teen-age boys? I resented the fact that my parents had had no such magic word to protect them. What grief we all might be spared if we could deter malice with a single spoken syllable!

When Helse had secured the cell and had me alone, she used some cloth to block the faint light spilling in around the panel, putting us in darkness. Then she dropped to the floor and moved about, away from me. Two metres cubed is not a lot of space for two people, but I was in the corner and she was in the opposite corner. I could hear her without seeing her.

In a moment she was back. 'Please remove your clothes,' she said.

'What?' I asked dully.

'I am nude. I want you to be too.'

'I don't understand.'

'I know. I can help you sleep well.' She came to me and took hold of my shirt and started to remove it for me.

I resisted. 'Helse, if anyone should look in here – '

'I told them I would talk to you and straighten you out. You have been bristling at everyone. No one will look, or listen – and anyway, I've blocked the cracks. They can't see in from the Commons.'

'They could wrench open the panel, idiot! If you don't have your clothes on – they will know – '

'Spirit already knows.'

'She's a child.'

'Yes.' Again she worked at my shirt.

This time I let her do it. I didn't know what she was up to, but it was better than the nightmares I faced when I slept.

After she got the shirt off, she worked on the trousers. Now I was afraid to stop her, for she seemed to know what she was doing, while I was a mass of confusion. She bid me stand, and I stood, and she undid my belt and took my clothing down. I simply let her continue until she had me naked.

She ran her hands lightly over my body in the darkness, not excluding the genital. I was aroused, of course; it could hardly have been otherwise. There was something about being undressed by a woman this way. She evinced no shock or surprise, and I was reminded again that she had done things with men I had never imagined. But such would not be the case with me; I was no pirate or seducer of children.

She made me lie on the floor, using some wadded

clothing for cushioning, then lay down on her side beside me. Her warm bare thigh touched mine, and her cool soft breast rested against my left arm. I hardly dared breathe.

'Hope, I want to tell you about sex,' she said. 'I've been listening to you talking in your sleep, and I think I understand your problem. You saw the pirates rape your sister, and you think it's your fault. You think all men are like that. You're afraid one day you'll rape someone.'

She was right on target. I said nothing.

'Well, you won't,' she said. ' I'm not as sharp as you are about judging people, but I do know something about this. All men are not alike, in any way. Some are terrible, like the pirates – but some are so gentle and nice they would never hurt anyone. Most are in between, like your father – and you. They all like sex. That has nothing to do with the way they are. But the bad ones use sex to hurt people, and the good ones use it to make people happy. The pirates were not getting pleasure of Faith, they were punishing the people of the bubble. That's different. Just because you have this' – at this point she put her hand firmly on my rigid genital – 'it doesn't mean you're bad. I know you, Hope; I know you as well as I possibly can, in a week. I know you are good. You get angry, you make mistakes, you suffer – but you are good. You have done nothing to hurt me – or anyone.'

Still the vision of the pirates raping my sister haunted me, and of the one trying to rape my mother. Between those two was the murder of my father, inextricably linked. I never wanted to share any part of the life or lust of those pirates! I remembered how my member had swelled when I saw Faith raped, and it damned me at this very moment similarly. It had a will of its own, and I could not trust it.

'It's the difference between a theft and a gift,' she continued. 'When you steal something, or take it by force, you hurt someone. But when you accept a gift, you hurt no one, and both the giver and the receiver profit. The gracious acceptance of a gift is a gift in itself. All you have to do is decide never to steal, never to cheat or deceive or force, and always to accept a proper gift. Then you will know you are not like those pirates, and never will be. You will know that you have tamed the fire in you, and turned it to proper advantage.'

I pondered that. It seemed to make sense, 'All right.'

She waited, but I did not move. I was holding my fire tame. 'I don't think I've convinced you yet,' she said. 'You will still have nightmares. You still think you can hurt me if you let yourself go.'

'Yes.' I was afraid that if I moved at all, I would do something terrible.

'I'm going to make you know it's not true,' she said. 'This is the one thing I can do for you, to repay you for helping me, for keeping my secret.'

I thought she was going to talk to me again, explaining how I was normal and it was all right to be normal. But she didn't speak. She shifted herself about, climbing on top of me. I refused to move a muscle, not from any antagonism to her – it was impossible to feel that now, for her sleek woman's body electrified me wherever it touched my flesh – but because any motion at all would represent a commitment, one way or the other.

She held herself above me, then lay full length on me, her breast resting on my chest, her thighs falling outside mine. She brought her head down and touched my lips with hers, and it was as though I was being propelled through space without moving at all. I had never known that mere touch could have such an effect. Still I did not move.

She shifted herself again, getting her balance, then used one hand to catch and guide my member, pointing it the way she wanted. She raised her hips, then slowly settled on me again. So gently and easily that I could hardly believe it was real, I found myself inside her.

'Now tell me this is evil,' she murmured, letting her

thighs settle all the way against me, and bringing the rest of her body down so that she lay as she had before, her breast pressing me down. Only one detail had changed, a small detail, yet with an overwhelming significance.

Still I would not move or speak. It was fear as much as stubbornness. I really did not know what to do, and was afraid that anything would be wrong, and would make her angry or hurt her.

'Tell me you are raping me,' she said, putting her hand behind my head as her whole body pressed more tightly against mine. Her weight was light, less than half-gee; it might have been uncomfortable in full Earth gravity, but even so, her body was the most wonderful thing I could possibly know.

'Tell me you love me,' she whispered, and now her tone of challenge had become one of urgent pleading. When I still was silent, she dipped her head and kissed me again, but this differed, as the other position differed from before, from the prior kiss. This time her mouth was open, and her tongue came through to touch mine.

I was at last overwhelmed. 'I love you!' I breathed around our tongues, and was transported by a paroxysm of amazing sensation.

I woke, it seemed, an eon later. Helse lay beside me, her hand holding mine. She squeezed my fingers, and I knew she was awake.

'What is it that you want, that cannot be bought?' I asked, remembering what she had said before.

'You know it now.'

I knew it now, I discovered. 'To love and be loved,' I said. 'But why me?'

'You're a decent person, and you need me,' she said simply.

'I need you,' I agreed. And slept again, my hand in hers, without ill-dream.

In the morning, bubble time, I found her still beside me,

sleeping. Still I could not see her, except as the vaguest outline, and I discovered I did not dare touch her body, for fear that everything would turn out to be illusion. I realized that she had been kind to me, and more than kind; she had shown me in an absolutely believable manner that sex itself was not evil. In the time following, that realization was to expand and deepen, becoming a fundamental aspect of my philosophy. This was Helse's invaluable gift to me: my honest acceptance of my male nature.

But right then I did not perceive that essence so clearly. I was only aware of Helse herself, and of my need for her. Had she given me her body for a night, to tide me through the storm of my guilt and grief, or was there more to it than that? I had said I loved her, and indeed I did, in that overwhelming flush of feeling that a person my age and temperament is capable of; it was sudden but profound. But she, she had not said she loved me, and she was a year older than I . . .

In my desperation to know, I reached out and found her shoulder. She woke immediately, and caught my hand in hers.

'Helse,' I said, but then could not find the phrasing for the question.

'Yes, Hope,' she murmured.

'Is – will there be another time?'

She brought my hand to her lips and kissed it, sending a sweet tingle through me. 'If you ask me.'

'Ask you?' I repeated, perplexed.

'I won't do it for you, next time, Hope,' she explained. 'You will have to ask me. Then I will do it,'

That wasn't enough of an answer. I struggled to formulate my objection, 'I don't want your acquiescence. That could be for any reason. I want your love.'

She frowned against my palm. 'I never said I loved you, Hope.'

'I know. But I love *you*!'

159

She sighed. 'You are less experienced than I am, Hope. You mistake rapture for love. Your emotion is shaken by tragedy. It is right for me to ease your confusion in my fashion, but not to ask too high a price. When you are able to put it in perspective, you will know love is not made in a single night.'

I jerked my hand away from her, hurt.

She apologized immediately. 'Hope, I did not mean to imply your emotion is not real or strong. Only that it is too soon to distinguish passion from love. I have been loved for a night by many men. By day they have other interests. Had I loved any of them, I would have been hurt, for my love is not just for a night. Give me leave to protect myself from heartbreak, as I protect my body from abuse by concealing it from strangers.'

I began to understand a little better, 'But you could love me, if you were sure of me?'

'It is my dream, to love and be loved.'

Still that gentle evasion. She was being honest with me, and I appreciated that, but still it was hard to accept. I sat up, disgruntled, wanting more than I had any right to ask.

'May I kiss you?' she asked.

'I would like that,' I said, somewhat stiffly.

She got to her knees, leaned across, found my face, and kissed me. Her lips were warm and moist, and her body where it touched mine was wonderfully soft. 'When you ask, and it is granted, it is good,' she said.

'I wish I could ask for your love.'

She smiled, a faint gleam of teeth in the dark, and separated. We dressed, then went out in the guise of two boys to visit the head. Helse had opened a door to a new dimension to me, the dimension of love, but some things had not changed.

11

Sacrifice

Jupiter Orbit, 15-2-'15 – Bubble life was routine, as far as possible. I still felt the terrible loss of my father, and knew it was worse for my mother and sisters. Helse had taken a huge segment of my aroused emotions and turned it positive, so that I had a kind of internal counterbalance. But my mother and sisters lacked that. I realized that, thanks to Helse's gift, I was now stronger than they, like a shipwrecked sailor who has found a barrel to cling to while others had nothing. I could not share my support with them, and could not even confess its nature, for they believed Helse was a boy like me.

Except Spirit. She caught me alone in the course of the day, and had to needle me. 'How was it, brother?' she asked snidely.

A host of flip answers escaped before I could formulate any of them verbally. 'I love her,' I said simply.

She glanced at me a long moment, having the grace to be embarrassed. 'I'm sorry.'

I put my arm about her shoulders, forgiving her. 'I know how it is,' I said, remembering how snappish I had been before, when my internal problem radiated sparks at other people. I had no need of that any more. 'You're still my sister. You're the only one who shares that secret.'

'Still, I'm jealous,' she admitted.

'You have no need to be. You aren't competing with her.'

'Yes, I am! If you had to throw one of us into space, which would it be?'

The way to counter a question like that is to reverse it. 'If

161

you had to throw Faith or me into space, which would it be?'

'That depends who I'm mad at at the moment.' But Spirit turned sober, considering the implication.

'When you grow up and love a man, I'll try not to be too jealous,' I said.

'Oh, go ahead and be jealous!' she muttered. But she smiled. Then, in the treacherous way she had, she returned to her opening question. 'Tell me what it's like,' she begged. 'Please, Hope – I really want to know.'

Spirit was twelve. Did I have the right to tell her about sex? I had just learned about it myself! Of course we both knew the sterile mechanics as taught in school, and the applicable terms; we also both knew that such things had almost nothing to do with real sex or love.

I remembered the way older children, both male and female, had teased me in the past years about my curiosity and ignorance. It seemed to be a conspiracy of silence, and I had never believed it was justified. I resolved not to do that to my sister. 'I was inside her,' I said carefully. 'And heaven was inside me. I wish it could have lasted forever.'

'What about all the pain and blood?' she asked, and I saw that she was really worried. She, too, had seen the rape of Faith. I should have been aware of her natural reaction before. I had to reassure her about the other side of sex, as Helse had reassured me, so she would not fear it.

'There was no pain or blood. Nothing but joy.'

'But –'

'Give me your hand.' I took her small hand in mine and squeezed it cruelly.

'Ouch!' she shrieked.

'That's rape,' I said. Then I took her hand again, smoothed it out caressingly, and kissed it. 'That's love.'

She looked at her extremity. 'But that's only my hand!'

'Just one part of you – and me,' I agreed. 'Another part was used to hurt Faith terribly – but last night I used it to love Helse. The difference is in how you use it. That's what she taught me.'

Spirit smiled quirkily. 'I thought you used it to pee.' She was being humorous, resisting the notion, as I had resisted it during the night. Too simple a telling does not necessarily get the point across, because the listener isn't ready to believe. So I took stock again, pretty much as Helse had.

'That too,' I agreed. 'But not last night. Just about every part of the body has more than one use, like the mouth that is used to eat and to talk or the nose used to breathe and smell. You just have to keep in mind which use you want.'

'Yes, it's hard to talk with your mouth full,' she agreed. She still didn't accept it.

I caught her shoulder, making her face me, suddenly finding it vitally important to spread the new message. 'When you grow older, Spirit, and you love a boy, and he loves you, don't be afraid of his body. What he has for you is not cruel and not dirty; it's a form of love. The great crime of the pirates is that they take something perfect and abuse it, making it terrible. Don't judge all men by them!'

'Oh, I don't judge our father by – '

'And how do you think you and I came to exist?'

'There is that,' she agreed, with a wan smile. But her brow furrowed again. 'Still, I don't know.'

'Ask Helse,' I said. 'She will tell you.'

'I will.' Spirit left me. I hoped I had not wished something on Helse she would have preferred to avoid.

I talked with Señora Ortega, to learn how we were doing on our voyage. She squinted at me. 'You're the lad who appointed me captain,' she said with the trace of a grim smile. 'Yesterday you looked ready to die; today you are alive.'

'You're the right person,' I agreed. 'That funeral service really made me feel better. And I had a good night. I'll be all right now. Are we on course?'

'A good night,' she repeated. 'If I didn't know better, lad,

I'd think you had discovered love.' Maybe she was teasing me; it was impossible to know how much she had guessed.

She got down to serious business quickly. 'No, we're not on course,' she said frankly. 'Our girls aren't as apt as the men were; we haven't had the training. The mechanism is simple, but the application takes practice. So we're handling the vectors clumsily. Oh, we're getting there, but it won't be on the original schedule. We'll have to stay on half rations.'

Well, it could have been worse. I moved on to talk with children. I did not consider myself a child any more, and certainly it had been a man's duty I did with Helse, but my talent related well to the young folk. I tried to cheer them, for they had the least resources to comprehend or deal with the calamity that had befallen us all. We set up games in the Commons, even organizing a soccer match, using a tightly wrapped bundle of paper refuse for the ball. It really wasn't much, in this confined and curvaceous space and with the trace gravity, but it did bring a few smiles to some faces and kept the kids occupied. I felt this was the most useful thing I could do, for now, spreading some of the balm Helse had provided me, as it were.

Helse joined me in the afternoon. She still looked just like another boy, but now I fancied I could perceive feminine contours and mannerisms in her, hidden from other eyes. I still had not seen her body clearly in its natural state, and now I wanted to, knowing the rapture it offered me. 'I have been talking with your sisters,' she said with a wry smile.

'I don't like keeping secrets from Spirit,' I said, knowing my little sister had wasted no time on her fact-finding mission.

'She said you said you love me, and had great joy last night.'

'It's true,' I admitted. 'She asked me and I told her. I wouldn't lie to my little sister. I didn't think you would mind. Spirit's curious about everything, but she never betrays a confidence.'

'Then you don't mind if I tell her – ' She shrugged. ' – Anything?'

'No, of course I don't mind! I sent her to you. I don't want her to be afraid.'

She shook her head. 'You are remarkably open.'

I frowned. 'No, I'm not open with everyone. Spirit is special. We don't deceive each other. We fight sometimes, but we always understand. If she had a similar experience, she would tell me. Now that she's seen her sister raped, she needs to understand that it doesn't have to be that way.'

'Yes, of course. I was surprised, that's all. Men usually talk about such things to other men, not to their sisters.'

'Spirit is different,' I repeated firmly.

'Not Faith?'

'Faith is more like an ordinary sister.'

'She braced me,' Helse said. 'I had to tell her my secret.'

'I don't see why,' I said, annoyed. 'I try to protect Faith, but I don't share secrets with her.'

'She really cares for you, Hope. She appreciates what you've done for her. The siblings are much closer in your family than they were in mine; I envy you that. Faith saw the change in you today, and she worried.'

'But I didn't talk with her today!'

'Still, she noticed. She's not out of it, Hope; she's recovering. Your support really helped her.'

'Oh.' I was pleased. 'She must have figured it would take more than a talking-to to put me back on track.'

'Yes. She guessed there was a liaison. And she thought I was male.'

I felt myself abruptly blushing. 'She thought—?'

'She hoped it wasn't so. But she feared for your orientation, right now, under this terrible stress. So I had to tell her.'

'I guess you did!' I agreed, still embarrassed. 'I'd better

talk to her.'

'No need. She was relieved. I think she thought she could be responsible for you turning away from the opposite sex, because of the rape.'

'She was concerned for my reaction to what happened to her?' I asked, amazed. 'Rather than for her own horror?'

'She's got that basic Hubris spirit of unity. It's a precious quality. She would do anything to spare the others in her family the humiliation she suffered.'

'I guess I didn't give her enough credit,' I said ruefully. 'She, worried about me!'

'I was concerned too, maybe in a slightly different way. That's why I acted.'

'You sure did!' I agreed. 'In one hour you changed my life forever.'

'I think Faith and I are going to be friends.'

'Yes, I think so.' I was both embarrassed and gratified: embarrassed for the way I had evidently seemed to those who were close to me, and gratified for the way they had tried to help.

After that I talked with Faith myself, explaining what Helse had done for me. 'I'm not ashamed to be a man.' I told her. 'I don't for a moment condone what happened to you, but – '

'It's all right, Hope,' she said. She looked better now; she had washed herself and brushed out her hair. She was indeed recovering, having more inner strength than I had credited. 'We have all had a terrible education in the past few days. I'm glad you found her. I should have known better than to worry.'

'How is Mother?' I asked cautiously. I was glad to see Faith regaining her equilibrium, but I wasn't certain how far it went.

'Hope, we have to take care of her! I thought I was badly off, until – it's so much worse for her!'

'What can we do for her?' I asked, surprised by my

166

sister's animation. Faith had always been relatively sedate and retiring; Spirit was the wild one in our family, and I was in between. Now Faith was turning more decisive. Could her awful experience have changed her outlook?

'Helse told me a pirate tried to rape Mother, and you fought him off.'

'More or less,' I agreed. 'Spirit smashed the pacifier box. so the rest of us could fight. I wasn't very effective. Spirit really saved us all.'

'I don't want – that – to happen to Charity Hubris,' Faith said firmly. 'She's our *mother*, Hope! So if the pirates come again, and we can't stop them – ' She broke off, evidently not finding it easy to speak her thought.

'We'll stop them somehow!' I said with a certain bravado.

'If they have that awful pacifier box, or something – ' She took a breath and swallowed. 'If it comes to that, Hope, I want you to send them my way, not Mother's way.'

I stared at her, horrified. 'Faith! You know what they do!'

She smiled wanly. 'I think I know as well as any woman can. But what have I to lose, now? Hope, we can't let our mother be defiled.'

'I hate even to think of this!' I exclaimed. 'We should kill every pirate who comes into this bubble!'

'Yes. We should. But if we can't – then we must handle them another way. Promise me you will do it, if it needs to be done.'

I resisted, but she kept at me, somewhat the way Helse had, and in the end I had to yield and give my promise. There is something about the way a woman can importune a man, even if she is his sister. But I felt unclean.

Perhaps it was prophetic, for within an hour after that the pirates did come again. Not the same ones – but already the term 'pirate' was generic.

We did not know at first that they were pirates. Their

ship was in good repair and bore the emblem of the Mars Merchant Marine. That did not signify much, because for reasons of interplanetary commerce many non-Martian vessels elected to register with Mars. Martian taxes were less than those of Jupiter, Uranus, or Earth, and fuel was cheap there, as the so-called Red Planet had much of the fuel of the Solar System. But mainly, as I understood it from my school studies, Mars had extremely lax laws governing the wages and treatment of spacemen. The large trading companies could operate more profitably by economizing on safety measures and payrolls and retirement benefits, so they enlisted with the planet that permitted this. The maritime powers of Jupiter professed to deplore such shoddy mechanisms – yet quite a number of their ships operated under the emblem of Mars. So a Martian trader ship could be anything. Except, we naïvely supposed, a pirate.

They locked onto us and opened the air lock. There was a pause before the inner door opened, and we knew they had discovered the dead and spoiling pirates. But soon the inner panel slid aside, and a man in a white uniform stood before us.

We had an innocent-seeming group of women near the lock to greet the intruders. Hidden around the curve of the Commons we had armed women, ready to fight viciously if that proved to be necessary. Normally women were not warriors, but the brutal experience of rape and murder had forged a new temperament in many. Before we allowed more of the same, we would fight and kill. We all understood that. Twice we had overcome intruders, and twice had our situation reversed – and twice suffered grievously. Experience is a cruel but effective teacher.

Spirit, garbed as a boy, was one of the display children. They were innocently playing – but she was armed with her finger-whip, and the others had small knives. If the others turned out to be pirates, she and the children were supposed to scream in simulated or genuine panic and flee, clearing the way for our fighting force. If anything resembling a pacifier box made an appearance, Spirit would go for it. But if the children were caught, they would fight. We had to give the outsiders a chance to prove they were legitimate, just in case they were, for we were in desperate need of food and help. We dared not alienate legitimate visitors.

'You folk must have had a bad time,' the Martian officer said in Spanish, looking about as his men followed him through the air lock. All were clean-cut and wore sidearms, not swords. 'We discovered quite a mess in your air lock. It's all right now; we dumped the stuff in space and fumigated the lock.'

My mother was in the 'innocent' group of women. She had roused herself from her grief to participate in this, for she knew she was only one of many who had been abruptly widowed, and that someone had to carry on. Even as we children had to protect her, she tried to protect us. That was part of what it meant to be a family; I was coming to appreciate the full significance of it in this adversity. Major Hubris had been lost, but his family carried on, as if his strength had been bequeathed to each of the survivors. 'We were raided by pirates,' she said. 'All our men were killed.'

'Well, that's over now,' the officer said. 'We shall carry you on in to Jupiter, where you will be granted refugee status. Collect your things; we're on a schedule and haven't much time. Don't bother with extra clothing; we'll issue you uniforms from our stores.'

Slowly I relaxed. This was almost too good to be true! If they towed us the rest of the way in to Jupiter, our hunger and fear was over!

I turned to meet Helse's eyes. The two of us had been relegated to the centre chamber of the bubble, the doughnut hole. We were deemed too old to be innocent children and too young to fight. But we would fight, if it came to that, to protect the precious remaining food stores. As it was, we were out of the action but could see everything plainly.

Helse did not seem to share my relief. Her eyes were squinting, her mouth grim. That renovated my alarm; did she know something I didn't?

Uncertain, the women in the Commons below looked at each other. 'Leave the bubble?' my mother asked, and I realized the officer had not actually spoken of towing, but of carrying.

'Obviously you can't remain here,' the officer said reasonably. 'Drifting in space, your supplies diminishing, vulnerable to the vagaries of fate. You are fortunate we spotted you. Fetch your valuables; you don't want to be classed as paupers when you arrive.'

The women seemed almost reluctant to believe their good fortune. Slowly they dispersed while the merchant-men smiled at the children. One man produced a box of bright candy balls and proffered it. He was promptly the centre of juvenile attention, as the youngest flocked to accept the goodies. We had not seen candy since leaving Callisto! Even Spirit, suspicious at first, in due course sidled close to the friendly man and accepted a treat.

My mouth watered. I was not yet so old that candy didn't appeal. 'Look what we're missing!' I muttered.

'Never accept candy from a stranger,' Helse said grimly. I thought at first she was joking, then was doubtful.

The smallest child abruptly sat down. She had been greedily consuming the candy. She did not seem sick, but she did not get up.

Another child joined her, then a third. Soon all of them were sprawled on the deck. Spirit was one of the last to go, and I could see she was fighting it, but her knees buckled and betrayed her.

Senõra Ortega marched up. 'What is the matter?' she demanded, alarmed.

The officer faced her. 'The candy is drugged. But don't worry; we have the antidote. The children will not die if it is administered within an hour.'

'Drugged!' Señora Ortega gazed on him with wild surmise. 'Then you are—'

'Merely men who labour hard on short wages, and who have been too long in space,' the officer said. 'You are the leader here? Have your women deposit their valuables with us.' His eyes travelled across the others, who were now frozen in horror. They had actually fetched their most precious things at the behest of this man! 'We are not bad fellows, if you treat us right. We are not interested in killing anyone, or even hurting anyone. We believe in honest quid-pro-quo. Any woman who desires a unit of antidote may purchase it from one of us.'

My mother was one of the first to understand. 'My child is among those drugged. How may I purchase her reprieve?'

'You have money?' the officer inquired. 'Gold? Gems?'

'None,' my mother replied.

'Then you must earn it.' The officer glanced meaningfully at his men.

After a pause, a burly older crewman stepped forward and gazed at her. For a moment I saw her through his eyes: a woman in her forties, no young thing but still a fairly handsome figure of her sex. The kind a middle-aged man would find comfortable. I began, inwardly, to curse the condition of masculinity, then felt Helse move slightly beside me and remembered her lesson. The evil was not the use, but the abuse!

'I'll give you my little vial of fluid, woman,' the crewman said. He held a small bottle, but his *entendre* was obvious. These were more sophisticated rapists; they compelled the women's co-operation without overt violence. But for all its non-violence, it remained rape. My muscles clenched.

'Don't do it!' Señora Ortega cried to my mother. 'They're bluffing.'

171

The officer shrugged, glancing at the collapsed children. 'We are not killers, certainly; that decision is yours. We can only remain with you for an hour – after which time it will hardly matter. Any woman who prefers to take a chance with her child is free to do so. As I said, we do not wish to coerce anyone.'

The hypocrite! I started to move, but Helse put her hand on my shoulder and though her touch was light, it held me back. Helse had known better than I about the candy; her judgment probably remained better. I sank back, my teeth clenched.

My mother looked at Spirit, who was now unconscious. She wavered, afraid to gamble with her child's life. Probably the men were bluffing and had only put knockout medicine in the candy. They seemed more like unscrupulous opportunists than hardened killers. Surely men who spent much time in space did get hungry for women, though why they didn't bring women along with them in their ship was a mystery. But they were also pirates, and we knew how careless of life pirates could be. If they were not bluffing – I felt the same stress my mother did. That was Spirit, my little sister! If I let her die when any action of mine could save her, how could I even endure myself?

I tried to use my talent to determine the intentions of the men, but I simply had not interacted with them enough to judge. I could not tell to what extent they were bluffing.

'I will buy her life,' my mother decided.

The crewman smiled. I started climbing down into the Commons, going through the hole in the netting and using one of the guy ropes that held the netting in place so that I would not sail down sideways and attract unwanted attention.

'No!' Helse hissed. 'Don't do it Hope! You can do nothing except make it worse!'

I paused, knowing she was right. Yet how could I remain idle while my mother prostituted herself to save my little sister?

While I debated this, hanging on to the guy rope, my other sister, Faith, approached me. She had put on make-up and arranged her luxuriant hair, and looked like a goddess. She wore a rather tight skirt and blouse. The half rations seemed not to have diminished her at all; probably she accepted them as just another diet. 'I can't let this happen,' she said.

A new horror gripped me. 'Faith, stay out of it!'

She met my gaze. 'You understand, Hope.'

The terrible thing was that I did understand. Faith felt she had nothing to lose; now she could redeem her lost honour in some measure by saving her mother and sister from this awful dilemma.

'You promised, Hope,' she reminded me.

I could not say her nay, though I hated every aspect of this. Slowly, unwillingly, I nodded.

Faith made a tiny quirk of a smile. I had, in my fashion, given permission, and this was a thing she required. I had implicated myself in the decision, and would have to defend it. I was sending her in to be raped – again.

Faith took a breath and walked up to the men. She was slender and full and lovely and young, standing out like a beacon amidst gloom, and in a moment all their eyes were locked on her. It was obvious that none of these men would choose any older woman if he had a chance at this young one. I could appreciate the feeling myself, shamed as I was by the thought; *I* would choose a girl like Faith instead of a woman like my mother. God! What abominations infested my thoughts!

'How many children can I buy?' Faith asked them softly.

'Faith!' my mother exclaimed, shocked.

'Better me than you, Mother,' Faith replied. 'I am already lost; you must care for the family.' And Charity Hubris could not deny her, any more than I could.

Faith turned back to the men, breathing deeply – and when she did that, she was spectacular. 'How many?'

'All of them' the officer said, impressed. 'Given time.' His gaze flicked to a lieutenant beside him. 'See to the valuables.'

'No,' Faith said. 'You shall not rob us also.'

'No?' The officer seemed amused.

'Take me – on your ship. Nothing else.'

'Faith!' my mother repeated.

The officer glanced again at the other men, whose mouths were virtually drooling. Yet again I could appreciate their thoughts, though I resented my very ability to do so. To have a creature like this with them all the time, no one-hour stand—

'You drive an interesting bargain, young woman.'

Faith half turned, and her body accented itself. Somewhere along the way she had learned a lot about sex appeal! 'What pittance does anyone here have, compared to what I offer?'

My mother put her hands to her face, but did not speak again. She knew what the rest of us knew; it did make sense.

Once more the men considered. 'It's the same deal I made as a child,' Helse murmured in my ear. I had not seen her climb down to join me, since I had been distracted by the uncomfortable drama of the Commons. 'I think these really are merchantmen, pirating on the side. It's not necessarily a bad life, if they like the girl. These aren't really violent men; they just don't think it is wrong to coerce a woman into sex.'

'But she's not doing it because she wants to!' I protested somewhat irrelevantly.

'Yes and no. Few decisions in life are completely voluntary. She's doing it for her family. She is making a sacrifice for your benefit – and for every other person in the bubble.'

I had to file this away for later digestion.

'Take this young woman aboard the ship,' the officer

said. 'Give her decent accommodation.' He reached inside his jacket and brought out a packet of vials, passing it to my mother, who stood in seeming shock.

The men left the bubble and Faith went with them. I feared I would never see her again.

The ship disengaged and jetted towards Jupiter. Faith had bought our reprieve with her body. I could only hope it was a fair deal.

My mother's eyes were glazing with the reaction, but she took a vial and opened it and tilted its liquid into Spirit's mouth, carefully, so the child would not choke. Other women did the same with their children.

I shook myself and went to the group. Several vials were left over. I opened one and put a drop on my tongue.

The fluid was completely colourless, and tasteless. It could have been pure water.

I thought about that, then left without speaking. If it was only water, it meant one of two things. Either the children would die – or the drug in the candy was not truly toxic. Either way, the merchant-pirates had deceived us. But what else had I expected?

Helse rejoined me. 'What is it, Hope?'

'Water,' I said in disgust.

'I'm not surprised.'

'You suspected? Why didn't you say something before?'

'All men are pirates at heart.' She caught herself. 'I mean figuratively. Some are violent, like the outright pirates. Some are disciplined and honourable, like your father. Most are in between, as I told you before. They take what they can get, but they prefer not to have too much of a fuss. They don't mind lying to get their way. If they can get a woman to submit without violence, without any real danger of hurting the children, such men consider this to be smart management. That's just the way they see it.'

'But then Faith sacrificed herself for nothing!'

Helse caught my hands in hers. 'No, Hope. She did it to

protect her mother and sister from risk or shame. She refused to gamble with their lives.'

I knew this, yet felt constrained to argue. 'But if—'

'If we had called that bluff, those men could have turned savage and raped the women violently. They were armed; they could have killed anyone who tried to stop them. The danger was not just in the candy; it was in the men. Honourable men would never have used coercion. Faith understood that. So she offered them something better. Because she was beautiful and willing to deal, they accepted. They weren't all-the-way bad, they just wanted sex. She made it easy for them to be generous.'

'They're still pirates!' I hissed.

'They're fallible men. There's a difference.'

'But my sister condemned to horror—'

'Your sister is so lovely, I think some ranking officer will soon claim her for his own. I have told her some of the arts of pleasing men. In time—'

I turned on her ferociously. '*You* told her!'

Helse stepped back. 'Hope, she asked me. She wanted to know. I think she suspected something like this could happen, and she felt guilty for hiding when your father was killed. She had to redeem herself. She had to make the sacrifice the others were making.'

I clenched my fists, not answering.

'In time she may command an officer's love and be well treated,' Helse continued. 'Her future may be more secure than ours is.'

'By practising the arts of prostitution!' I gritted. 'As you practised them on me!'

I was sorry the moment I said it, but Helse only smiled. She had learned to accommodate my moods. She must have done the same as a child, with Uncle. 'We do what we must to survive, Hope. Women don't have the brute power of men. Compromise is forced on us all our lives. I practised my skills on you to help you, not because you forced me. Do not be angry with me, my lover.'

I was angry, but mostly with myself. 'If you taught my sister well enough, she will have the captain of that merchant ship in thrall.'

'I hope so.' She drew on my arm, turning me to face her as we stood above our cell. 'Please understand, Hope. Faith was publicly raped. She believed she had been rendered forever unclean, worthless for marriage. This was a psychological thing, not a logical one; it was part of her self-image.'

I remembered how Faith had asked me whether she was still my sister. Yes, I understood about self-image; I had been going through a similar mill myself. Logic alone is not enough to change such deep perceptions.

'All that was left to her was to do some good thing for her family,' Helse continued. 'She really cared for the rest of you, though she thought herself unworthy. She found the thing she could do, and she did it – and that key sacrifice may ironically bring her as much good as what she did for the rest of us. She would never have married a man she considered to be good, for fear she was unworthy of him. But a bad man is all right – and if he turns out later to be a good man, she will be able to accept that too. Because she *did* make her act of expiation. It was her dishonour she was sacrificing, for the best possible cause.'

I was not sure I followed her logic or agreed with it, but I hoped she was right. How much better it would be for Faith to be happy than miserable, by whatever rationalization. But still I hated the way it had worked out. Helse was educating me in the real ways of men and women, and it was not an education I liked. Yet I knew, deep down, that I did have to come to terms with the realities of the human condition.

Worse was to come. Hardly six hours passed before we were raided again. We saw the ship bearing down on us, and it was no merchant vessel. This time we hid all the children in the cells with orders to remain there until the pirates had gone, no matter what. Helse and I were included, but we were sent back to the doughnut hole with the remaining food packs. Perhaps the women did not realize how well we could see what was going on from that vantage. Spirit, still groggy, went with us, as it didn't seem wise to confine her alone.

The pirates burst in with drawn daggers, and it was obvious from the outset that resistance would be futile. Evidently news had spread that this was a helpless bubble, and they were flocking in to take advantage of it. That, too, caused me to seethe with suppressed outrage. Why couldn't they have flocked in to *help*, or at least signalled the Jupe authorities where we were so they could fetch us? I was ashamed for my species – the male species.

The women fell back, cowed by the blades. They had no equivalent weapons, and there were too many men to overwhelm by force of numbers.

'It's submit – or die,' Helse murmured. 'And if the women die, the children are alone, and maybe dead too. They know that.'

'That's my *mother* down there! My sister just sacrificed herself to prevent—'

'Yes. It is ironic. Don't blame your mother for what she does.'

A week before, I never would have understood. Now I did. Whether I would have without Faith's recent sacrifice or Helse's present help I don't know. But now I understood that the women had to do what they had to do, to stay alive and protect their families.

I understood, but my revulsion overcame me as I saw a hairy, dirty, pirate strip the clothing from my unresisting mother. I launched myself towards them, determined to kill the foul rapist.

Helse caught me around the shoulders, her inertia shoving me into the containing net. I tried to fight her off, but she clung with a strength in that moment equal to my own, and even in my desperation I could not bring myself to apply real force on her. Still, I managed to achieve a partial disengagement, and soon would get away from her.

'Spirit!' she whispered. 'Help me hold him!'

My sister snapped out of her remaining stupor, throwing off the lingering effect of the drug. She bounced across and caught me about the legs. In this trace gravity I could move her about by flexing my body, but I could not dislodge her. 'But our mother's getting raped!' I hissed. None of us dared talk loudly, for fear we would only bring the knives of the pirates to bear against ourselves.

'I know it,' Spirit said, and did not yield.

I continued to struggle, and Helse was tiring. She was as big as I, and weighed as much, but the distribution differed. I had more muscle and better leverage, because I was male, and now my advantage was telling.

But Helse managed to get hold of my head. Her shirt had torn open, and her chestband had slid askew in the struggle. Now she hugged my head to her half-bared chest. 'If you go, I will follow!' she rasped.

There is something uniquely compelling about the breast of a woman. My will to fight was sapped. I lay with my face half against the net, half against her breast, and did not move.

But in that position I could see a woman below. Probably she was not my mother; I could not tell, for most of her naked body was obscured by that of the pirate on her. Even if her whole body had been clear except for her face, I might not have been sure, for I had never seen my mother naked. Only by the face could I recognize her, and that I could not see. Yet if she was not my mother, she was someone else's mother, and she was getting raped. It did not matter that she was not resisting, for to resist was to die.

I struggled again, determined to do something to stop it. But Spirit took a tighter hold on my legs and Helse nearly smothered my face. In retrospect, I think that might be the nicest possible way to die, smothered by a breast, but at the time I was almost tempted to free myself by biting her. Thank God I did not!

'Let it be,' Helse whispered. 'Let it be, Hope. Those women are trying to save our lives!'

'At the expense of their honour!'

'Their honour is not of the body! It is of the spirit!'

That coincidental use of the word that was also my sister's name had a strange effect on me. Suddenly I knew that if there was one person I had to protect more than my mother, it was my sister.

Helse took my silence for negation. 'Please, Hope! Give over! It must be!'

It was a woman getting raped, and here were two girls urging me to let it proceed. They should have protested more vehemently than I did – but they were more realistic than I was. A man fights, a woman compromises: It was true in this microcosm as in the macrocosm.

The pirate thrust, and the woman's body jumped. I tried again to launch myself.

Helse clung to me with her divine death-hug. 'I'll tell you I love you!' she breathed pleadingly.

She didn't love me; I knew that. She was older than I, and more mature in more than the physical sense; I was beneath her. But she cared enough to pretend she loved me, in order to protect me from myself. That small share of love seemed inordinately precious. Why should I struggle, here, as if indulging in my own rape, when I could please her by relenting?

I relaxed and turned my face in to her. Helse squirmed about, sliding her breast down, and met me with a kiss. It was savagely sweet. I wanted to believe that she loved me, at least a little, for I surely loved her.

But at the same time I knew that I was forcing Helse to do something untrue, to sell a profession of love as another woman would sell her body. That wasn't right. And this acquiescence of ours was permitting my mother to get raped. Now my other thought, comparing our situation to that of my mother, returned more strongly. In an ugly transmogrification, my love for Helse seemed to identify with my mother's horror. It was as though the flesh so tightly against me was my mother's. As though I was participating in that rape. I knew it wasn't literally so, but it was figuratively so, and the stigma was there, emotionally.

I'm sure the time was not long, but it seemed an eternity. Then the pirates were gone, and the air lock was closed, and we children were free to return to the Commons.

Helse restored herself to her boyish state, resetting the band about her chest and pinning her shirt together. 'You sure are pretty when you show,' Spirit remarked to her. I had to agree, silently; this was the first time I had actually seen Helse's breast.

'You will be too, very soon,' Helse told her, patting her strapped bosom as if it were a thing to be allocated impartially among females. 'Thanks for helping me.'

'I had to. My crazy brother would have gotten us all killed.'

I was silent. They were probably correct.

We climbed down. I expected to find the women dishevelled and sobbing and hiding their faces, and I was afraid to face my mother, but it had to be done.

I was completely surprised. All the women were in good order, clothing intact, hair brushed out, eyes clear. No one was crying or hiding. It was as though nothing had happened.

Helse caught on before I did. 'Say nothing!' she whispered in my ear. 'Nothing about – you know.'

We found my mother. 'Oh, I'm so glad you're safe,' she said, smiling at us.

'We were sleeping in the loft,' Helse said.

My mother glanced at her with the merest suggestion of

irony, knowing it was a lie and thankful for that lie. 'Of course, young man,' she agreed.

Was my mother really still ignorant of Helse's sex? Or was she competent at keeping secrets? Perhaps she had seen more of our struggle in the loft than we realized. If we honoured her privacy, she honoured ours.

Later, in our cell, Helse explained it to me in more detail. 'Degradation is mainly in the mind. She doesn't want you to share her humiliation, because that could further hurt the family. The kindest thing you can do is to forever refuse to acknowledge that any man but your father ever touched your mother. There must be no stain on the honour of Hubris.'

'Is the whole universe made of hypocrisy?' I demanded, hurting anew.

'Sometimes it seems so,' she agreed. 'But it is a good thing your family does for itself. I wish I had belonged to a family like that.'

'So soon after Faith sacrificed herself to prevent this very thing!' I exclaimed.

'What Faith sacrificed herself for has been preserved,' Helse reminded me. 'Never say otherwise.'

I was blind at that moment to the significance. 'And you – you told me you loved me, just to keep me quiet! You're a woman too!'

'I'm a woman too,' she agreed.

I was perversely furious at her, but I loved her too, and maybe for much of the same reason. 'And will you do what you did before, just to keep me quiet? Will you give me your body, and pretend to like it?'

'Yes.'

'Oh, damn!' I cried, and then it was literally crying, the tears flooding from my eyes. Helse held me and comforted me, and in time we did make love, and she had the grace not to profess love, only caring, and it was wonderful. I couldn't accept what she was doing, in one part of my conscience, but in another part I knew it had to be and that I couldn't live without her. So I accepted what had to be accepted: her sacrifice, and mine.

12

Food

Jupiter Rings, 24-2-'15 – I wish I could skip over this period, but it would not be honest to do so. It had seemed our situation could not get worse, but we had a cruel re-education coming.

Our problem was composed of two things: food and travel. We were still short of food, but might have managed if we had floated to Jupiter on time. But the women didn't know how to operate the gravity lens efficiently, so we were making little progress. That meant our food was less than adequate. We had assumed we could get by on half rations, but as the day passed and Jupiter loomed larger with appalling slowness, we knew we could not. All of us were losing mass, though we were not starving. We conserved bodily energy by sleeping much of the time, but still our food dwindled.

We cut to quarter rations, trying to stretch it out a few more days, but our progress past the rings of Jupiter seemed maddeningly slow. It was gradually apparent to even the most unwilling eye that we were not making it.

I spent a lot of time in the cell with Helse, sleeping in her arms. But hunger vitiated sex, if not love. It was enough for a time just to be with her, talking and resting and enduring – but inevitably the need for food intruded. I dreamed of discovering some hidden cache of food packs that would allow us all to glut ourselves. But it never was true.

Spirit took it worse than I did. She was a growing child, and she needed proper sustenance. She spoke of big rock-candy mountains and oceans of chocolate syrup and gingerbread houses. When she started longing for potatoes and spinach I knew it was serious. She had never liked spinach. We had to do something – but what? We could not conjure food from vacuum.

I took to staring morosely out of the portholes. The Jupiter ring system is not nearly as spectacular as Saturn's, but it is extensive enough. It reaches out almost as far as Saturn's rings do, but it is so diffuse it is hardly worth noticing. In fact, for many centuries the astronomers of Earth were not able to see the ring systems of Jupiter or Uranus or Neptune, so assumed there were none, with the typical logic of our species.

The primary ring is fifty thousand kilometres inside the orbit of Amalthea, and that's where the Jupiter border patrol operates. Amalthea is just a rocky ball, 24 kilometres across; its gravity is so slight that no one has bothered to put a residential dome on it – there's not enough gravity there to focus effectively, you see, since next to nothing concentrated tenfold is still next to nothing – but there is a space depot. Amalthea is just beyond Jupiter's political territorial limit, so we had to get inside its orbit.

The rings really weren't obvious even from up close; most of the particles were the size of large grains of dust. A ship travelling at high relative velocity through the rings might suffer abrasion, but our gravity-sailing bubble just nudged through the diffuse field harmlessly. Some particles were large enough to spot from some distance, just hanging there in their orbit blithely minding their own business, and I would trace them with my eye as long as I could.

Was this an analogy of the human condition, I wondered? Every individual travelling alone, going his own way – yet caught in the gravity well of some huge primary. Each person thought he was unique, and perhaps he was, differing as much from his neighbours as each particle differed in outline from other particles. Yet in the aggregate we were indistinguishable. Did it really matter which of us survived and which did not? No single particle made a perceptible difference to the ring.

Helse came up beside me and touched my shoulder. She never did more than that when in her boy disguise, but it was enough. It carried the implication of all she was when we were alone.

'We can't go on this way,' she said.

I looked at her, startled. 'We can't?'

She smiled. 'Not we you/me. We the-whole-bubble. The food is almost gone.'

I was foolishly relieved. I had come to depend on Helse's love, whether real or feigned. It was like a beneficial drug to which I was addicted. But of course the problem of the food was critical. We had all known a crisis was coming – but none of us had any solution except to hope that we would be spotted by some random swing of the Jove Patrol and rescued. Woe betide the pirate ship that got in our way this time! We would not again allow our rescue to be baulked that way. But we knew we weren't far enough in yet. Space is huge, and Jupiter is huge, and we were a mote among motes, lost. We still had to clear the outer ring, pass the orbit of Amalthea, and reach the primary ring, the territorial limit. At the rate we were proceeding that would be at least another week – and we had food, at quarter rations, for two more days.

Spirit arrived. 'Another head's clogged,' she announced brightly. She looked drawn, as we all did, from slow undernourishment, but her spirits remained reasonably high. She had always been that way, venting her angers and griefs rapidly and stabilizing at an optimistic level, and I had always liked her for it. She was generally good company. Most brothers and sisters fight a lot, but we fought less than most, and now not at all.

'That cuts us down to three heads,' I said. 'The tanks are full, probably. If we'd had full rations, there'd be *no* heads left working now.'

'Why not change the tanks?' she asked.

'We have no replacements. It's usually done planetside. The full tank gets traded for an empty one, and the contents go to the organic soil bank. Valuable stuff, you know; you don't find fertilizer like that floating around in space.'

She wrinkled her nose. 'I should hope not! But we ought to do something about—'

She broke off as if realizing something, then elevated a finger. 'Floating in space! Why not?'

'What are you talking about?' I demanded. Spirit's foolish notions were likely to have some sense in them.

'Why not just dump the stuff into space? Then the tanks'd be empty, and the head'd work again, and we wouldn't have to double up.'

'Sure,' I said. 'Why don't you just volunteer to suit up and do that?'

'Okay, I will!' she said defiantly, and pushed off.

'She will, too,' Helse said.

'Don't I know it!' I headed off after my impetuous sister. Sarcasm can be dangerous with Spirit.

In this manner all three of us ended up volunteering for the tank-evacuation detail. We suited up, and Helse handled the safety ropes while Spirit and I went out on to the hull. You see, the bubble was spinning, one revolution every ten seconds or so, so what was partial gravity inside was like partial repulsion outside, as the same centrifugal force tried to hurl us away at a tangent. So we had to be guyed, and that meant someone had to pay out the rope, or take in the slack when necessary, so we could operate without snagging or tangling. It was the sort of job the regular crewmen would have been good at – but of course there were no experienced people among our remaining number.

We used the front lock, since the merchant-pirates had cleared it out. I carried a bag of tools from the bubble toolshed, while Spirit clambered out with juvenile agility to catch the first rope in the question-mark-shaped eyelet provided for it. Bubbles have sets of such projections for just such emergencies; now I appreciated the foresight of the design. Even a child could figure out these things – and that was a good thing for us! We were actually better fitted to come out here than the women were, because of our size and alertness, which was part of why we were permitted to do it. My mother's natural protectiveness had to yield to expedience, as it had in other cases.

Once the line was secure, Spirit waved me on, and I handed myself along to join her. It was a bit like mountain climbing in my fancy – naturally, I have never climbed a mountain, there being none on Callisto – for the moment I left the null-gee region of the lock the outward pull began. The farther I progessed towards the bubble's equator the stronger it got, tugging me at an angle. Of course it was slight, even at its worst, but I was not at peak strength because of the reduced food, and the psychological effect was considerable. The whole universe was *down* and turning; that made my perch seeme precarious indeed.

I paused at the first eyelet, hanging on and looking out. First I saw the bright distant sun, really a super-brilliant star I could readily block out with my smallest finger at arm's length. Still, it emitted enough light to make it day in space. That light might be only one twenty-seventh as intense here as it was at Earth, but we were used to it the way we saw it, and it was quite enough for all normal purposes.

Then there was Jupiter, so vast my whole spread hand could not block it out. Yet I knew that the enormous planet was subservient to the little star. I could hardly blame my primitive ancestors, thousands of years ago on Earth, for believing otherwise. I understood that from the Earth, Earth's nameless moon looked the same size as the sun. That meant that each looked, very roughly, half again as big in diameter as Ganymede looked from Callisto. The moon I could understand, but I had no mental picture of the sun seeming that size. What a brilliantly blazing ball it must be!

Spirit nudged me out of my reverie. I get that way sometimes, thinking too much at a time, and have to be corrected. I nodded, and she scampered on around to the next eyelet, while I made sure the rope did not snag. Now the curve of the bubble concealed Spirit from Helse, though I could see both. I waved to Helse, who waved back; then I followed the rope to Spirit.

The location of the refuse tanks was clear enough, as they were intended to be serviced from the outside. There was an effective airlock-type mechanism in each that prevented any direct aperture through the hull from being opened. All I had to do was release the pressure of the tank-enclosure chamber, then unbar the tank itself and slide it out. It seemed simple enough. Yet I knew that things were seldom as simple in practice as they were represented to be in the instruction manuals.

I hooked my toes – that reminded me, for some obscure reason, of the manner I used the head inside – and got to work on the first one. It didn't matter whether it was one of the working ones or one of the clogged ones; they all would need cleaning out soon enough. I brought out the big wrench, hooked its safety line around my wrist – everything had its own safety line out here! – and adjusted it to the pressure-release valve. You see, the matter in the tanks is deposited at close to the same pressure as the interior atmosphere; the suction of the tubes is mainly forced ventilation. That pressure can't be released from inside; even if the bubble were opened to space and all its air puffed out, the toilet-locks would prevent the tanks from exploding into the interior. That's a necessary safeguard, for an obvious reason. These bubbles are pretty sophisticated devices, when you think about it, safety-rigged in so many ways that it is, literally, possible for a crew of

189

ignorant refugees to sail in space for some time with little to fear from error. Of course their ineffective piloting could lead to an extended trip and starvation, and they could be at the mercy of merciless pirates, but the bubble itself was pretty safe.

Suddenly the valve let go. These things were corrosion-proof, of course, and reliable; they worked as they were supposed to work, even on an ancient bubble like this. A jet of vapour shot out, catching me in the chest and shoving me away from the hull. Even a small shove is effective when you're not braced for it! I sailed out, turning end over end until my safety rope brought me up short.

Helse reeled me in; that was what she was there for. But though I had been in no actual danger, I was shaken. Had I not had the rope, I would have been flung into deep space and no one could have recovered me. Outside space was dangerous, in its completely passive way, and now I experienced the fear of it. This did not incapacitate me; I shoved it into that corner of my mind required for unpleasant refuse, my emotional toilet tank, and proceeded with my job. But the new, enhanced awareness of space remained with me, and now I felt vulnerable. I think, in retrospect, that this was more significant than I was aware of at the time.

Helse brought me to her, reeling me in hand over hand, put her helmet against mine, and made a kissing expression. Then she hugged me clumsily in the suits, spanked me, and sent me back to finish the job.

I got back to my location. The pressure had been depleted; now the tank was conveniently loose in its socket. I slid aside the retaining bars and drew it out. Spirit helped, for the thing was large and awkward. I held it pointed at space, while she took the wrench and loosened the emptying lid. This was a matter of turning a nut, then swinging out a bar; nothing came all the way free, because of the danger of losing it in space. The tank itself had a tether chain, long enough to give us sufficient freedom to operate. Perhaps the designers had anticipated this need to dump in space also.

When we had the lid off, we had to get the refuse out. This was a dense brown mass. There are chemicals or enzymes in the tanks that commence the processing of the matter the moment it enters, so this was already part of the way composted, but it remained faecal matter. I saw Spirit wrinkling her nose inside her helmet, though of course there was no smell here in the vacuum. Odour, like sound, requires atmosphere or some other direct conduit.

Now, how were we to get it out of the tank? We had no tool for this, and neither of us was inclined to reach in with our hands.

But the problem solved itself. As I clung to the tank by its base, the far end of it swing out centrifugally, and the matter in it was drawn by that same force into space. I almost thought I heard a sucking sound as it escaped the tank, but of course that was illusion. Such a sound could have been transmitted to me via metal and suit, but no sound existed. Vacuum does not have to move about the way air does; vacuum *is* – or perhaps it is more correct to say vacuum is not. I can picture someone reading this and protesting, 'But how did the vacuum squeeze in from space?' That person is a fool.

As soon as the mass emerged, it fragmented. Tiny bubbles of gas shoved it apart. The large chunks sundered into small ones, which in turn broke into smaller ones. In moments it became a cloud of particles, drifting slowly away from us. Even if there had not been some remaining internal pressure, it would have fragmented because of the tidal force of this orbit, causing that portion of it closer to Jupiter to move marginally faster than the portion more distant. The tide – it was the same thing we experienced within the bubble, I think, in reverse, our feet being carried around faster than our heads.

191

Spirit put her helmet against mine. 'Jupiter rings!' she exclaimed.

And of course it was so. We had initiated a new ring system – of base material. Very base. That might be a real surprise for some party scavenging for ice or minerals in space! Just let him bring it into warmth and atmosphere . .

We reloaded the empty tank and bolted it tight, then went on to the next one. The job was easier and faster, now that we were familiar with it.

The eight tanks made a double circle beside the equator, four to the north (whichever pole that was), four to the south. As we worked on the ones farthest from our air lock, we could see the bag containing the bodies of our men. Nothing showed, for the bags were tied, but even that much instilled in me a certain quality of dread. We were alone with our dead!

We kept on working, for there was nothing else to do. We dumped a second tank, and a third and a fourth. But the awareness of those bagged bodies was on me. I wondered which one was my father. Sadness welled up in me, the realization that Major Hubris was gone, that I would never see him again. He had been my bastion against the uncertainties of life, the backbone of our family; without him we were largely formless. There was now a void in my life, an emptiness in the physical and spiritual form of my father, and out here it seemed as intense as the void of space around me. Major Hubris would have known what to do about the squeeze between travel and food.

I saw Spirit clinging to the hull, and knew by the attitude of her body that she felt it too, and that she was crying. She might have bounced back readily, but the onus of loss had not forsaken her. I climbed across and put my suited arm around her suited shoulders, squeezing her comfortingly. We had lost our father and our sister, but we still had each other. And our mother.

Then we went back to work, doing tanks 5 and 6,

watching their contents merge with the ring system of Jupiter. Some of those particles we had sown might remain in orbit for a billion years! It was slightly awesome to realize that my frozen refuse might outlive me by that length of time. It reminded me of a facsimile exhibit I had seen in the Maraud Museum, of the faecal deposit of a dinosaur that had been ossified or petrified or whatever and preserved intact for eternity while the reptile that made it was gone. A faecal fossil. Maybe eventually some creature from galaxy Andromeda would come and take a soil sample from this ring, run it through his alien laboratory, and draw conclusions about my nature. Would he assume I was nothing but a big chunk of faecal matter?

My gaze came to rest again on the bagged bodies, as if drawn by some spiritual gravity. The women had strapped the bags to the hull irregularly, using the same eyelets we were using. We had to reset our ropes for each pair of tanks, and for the last set we had to route the ropes past the field of bags. I did it, leaving Spirit clinging to the equator.

As I brushed by one of the bags, my equilibrium suffered. Maybe it was the vertigo of shifting weight and torque as I rounded the hull towards the pole, the air lock where Helse waited. Most of the bags were near the rear air lock, but some were here. I paused to let the sensation pass – but it did not pass.

The feeling intensified until the whole universe seemed to spin crazily about me, and I was spinning too, opposite it and opposite myself. My head and feet were curving through each other, moving without motion. I realize that doesn't seem to make much sense, but that's the way it was. My head seemed to be orbiting one way and my feet another, and the separate portions of my body each travelled different and mutually incompatible ways. In retrospect I conjecture that my days on half and quarter rations were taking their toll, as well as the shifting forces of rotation I was being subjected to. I was nearer breakdown than I thought at the time. But maybe it was other than that.

For a moment this disorientation was pleasant, but then it frightened me, for I was afraid I would fling loose of the bubble with such force the rope would snap and I would be forever lost. I was losing what little control I had over my destiny, and that was frightening. A person can bear up under a lot more stress if he believes he has reasonable control than he can if he feels completely subject to the uncaring whim of fate. I screamed in my helmet and clung to the the nearest solid thing.

It was the body in the bag. I felt its human contour. I reacted with horror, but my clutching fingers would not let go. I felt the tears of grief and terror on my face, and was ashamed for them, but it was as if none of my body was subject to my mind any more.

Then the bag moved. I was so far done I did not even scream again. I clung to it, wrestling it, perhaps trying to put it back flat against the hull where it belonged. If there is one thing more appalling than death, it is undeath – the revival of a corpse.

But the thing pushed back against me, and got me clear and sat up – except that up was down, here, or at least sort of sideways – and shed the bag. The frozen head turned to face me – and it was my father, Major Hubris.

'Son, you are starving,' he reproved me. 'You must not go on this way.'

I had to answer him. 'We are out of food,' I explained. His remark was so reasonable, as my father's remarks had always been, in life.

He shook his head. 'No. Hope. You have food, if only you will use it. Shed the scales from your eyes and eat.'

'What food?' I asked, bewildered, much as I had been as a child when he was instructing me in some new thing. 'We have searched the whole bubble! There is nothing!'

'I will not permit your mother and sister to starve

because of your ignorance,' he said firmly. 'You are now the man of the family, and so it is your responsibility to see to their welfare. You will provide food for your mother and your sister and that lovely girl of yours – and yourself. You must all eat well, to restore your strength for the ordeal to come. The worst has not yet passed. You will do what is necessary.'

'But there is no food!' I wailed.

'Son, you know better than that,' he reproved me, becoming mildly annoyed at my obtuseness. He had always encouraged me to be intelligent, not in the sense of remembering long series of numbers, but in the sense of perceiving the obvious, 'There is plenty of food. You must make a fire, of course, to cook it. You can handle that.'

'Cook it?' I asked, bewildered. 'What food? Where?'

'Here,' he said, and extended his hand to me. But the hand was empty.

I thought about it for a long time, but could make no sense of it. Surely my father would not suggest we feed on vacuum! Then I heard a screaming in the background; it went on and on. Then slowly the whole scene faded out, and I was blank.

When I recovered awareness I was back inside the bubble. My mother was tending me. 'Thank God!' she breathed when she saw my eyelids flicker. 'He wakes!'

I dislike sounding stupid, but this seemed to be the occasion for it. 'What happened?' I asked, discovering as I spoke that my voice was hoarse.

'You were wrestling with a frozen corpse,' my mother said. 'And screaming.' I watched her face as she spoke, and saw how lean it had become; the fractional rations were costing her her health. She had been gradually becoming plump as the years passed; she was losing that mass now, and, though it lent her an ethereal beauty, I knew it was not good.

Then I picked up on the other thing. That screaming I

had heard – of course it had been mine! I had really strained my vocal chords, by the feel of my throat now. But why had I been doing it?

'I spoke again. 'How—?'

'Helse and Spirit brought you in unconscious,' she explained. 'They thought you had overextended yourself and had a breakdown. We got you out of the suit and wiped the blood from your mouth.'

No wonder she had worried! Then I remembered another thing. 'We didn't finish emptying the tanks!'

'Spirit says you did six. That's enough, for . . '

My mind was not yet clear. 'For what, Mother?'

'For the time we have,' she finished reluctantly.

Then I remembered my father's message. 'We have food,' I said. 'Only I don't know where.'

She asked me what I meant, and I recounted my experience outside. 'It was a hallucination, I know,' I concluded. 'But it certainly seemed real. He was so sure – but I couldn't understand it.'

'Not a hallucination,' she corrected me. 'A vision.'

'But what was he showing me?' I demanded. 'His hand was empty!'

'It was never your father's way to tease,' she said seriously. 'He always spoke his mind. You still do not understand?'

I shook my head. 'It makes no sense to me. If there had been something – but there wasn't.'

'Then it was a true vision. Your father did not mean you to understand directly.'

'But then why should he—'

'Major Hubris spoke through you – to me. He knew I would understand.'

'I don't see how that can conjure food where there is none!'

My mother only smiled sadly. 'Your father has spoken. I thank you, Hope, for conveying his message.' She stroked

196

my forehead. 'Now rest, my son. You have done well. There will be food.' She got up and went to consult with Señora Ortega.

I slept again, for I was weak. Exertion and hunger had debilitated me more than I had supposed.

When I woke, Helse and Spirit were with me in the cell. Helse was dressed in a dark blouse and skirt, so that now her full figure showed, and her hair hung down about her shoulders. She had always kept it pegged up somehow, before, so that it looked boyishly short. She had been losing weight like the rest of us, but her youth was better able to accommodate the loss, and she was now almost as pretty as my sister Faith had been, in a different way.

The two girls had evidently been talking, but they stopped when I started hearing. I almost wished I had feigned sleep a little longer, to listen; but I rebuked myself immediately. I had no need to spy on my friends! 'What's up?' I asked. 'You look serious.'

'We have food now,' Spirit said gravely. 'You can smell it.'

I sniffed, and caught the odour of roasting meat. 'That's great!' I said. 'Why aren't you eating it instead of sitting here with me?'

Spirit looked meaningfully at Helse. 'We're not sure we should use it.'

My mind came fully clear. 'Where is it from?'

Helse laughed somewhat abruptly. 'From your vision, Hope!'

I scowled. Hunger had not improved my sanguinity. 'You think I made that up?'

'No,' Spirit said. 'I saw our father sit up and talk to you.'

'I hauled him up,' I said. 'He couldn't have moved or talked in the freezing vacuum of space, even if he had been alive. I must have gone crazy. I can't even say for certain it was Major Hubris; it could have been any of them.'

'But I do believe you,' Spirit said. 'Father gave you a

message, and Mother understood it. We're a family; that's the way we work together.'

'He showed me an empty hand!'

'He showed you his hand,' she agreed, her eyes now fixed as if she were going into a trance herself.

I turned to Helse. 'What does she mean?'

Helse gazed at me with a kind of translucent horror. 'Your father offered himself – for food.'

Something awfully cold closed in on me then, as if I were still in space and the heating element in my suit had quit. I felt the screaming working up again, like a rising gorge. 'His – hand?'

'That was your vision.'

'To eat his – but I never – that's cannibalism!'

'Your father expressed to you his will. He told you to feed your mother and your sister and that lovely girl of yours and yourself. Are you going to go against your father's expressed will?'

Something else jarred. 'Lovely girl?' I asked. Then I realized. 'Oh, no! I told my mother the whole vision! I gave away your secret!' I hung my head in chagrin, 'I'm sorry, Helse! I never intended to – my word is sacred – I was so overwhelmed by the vision that I never thought—'

'I know,' Helse said. 'You kept my secret, Hope, and so did Spirit. It was your father who told on me. He never gave his word.'

'But he didn't know! He died before he—'

'His ghost knew,' she said. 'You can't hide truth from a ghost.'

'But—'

'Your mother asked me,' Helse said. 'So I changed my clothing. I would not try to make a liar of your father. He was a good man.'

'That's how Charity Hubris knew it was really Major Hubris speaking,' Spirit said. 'He knew something the rest of us did not.'

'*You* knew!' I said.

'But I never told. Anyway, Mother consulted with Señora Ortega, who suggested this was a test of the vision, and when they saw that Helse really was a girl, they agreed it was a true vision, and we would have to do as Father said. So now we have food, as Father intended. He probably mentioned Helse deliberately, so everyone would believe.'

I thought about the way Concha Ortega, that too-knowledgeable grandmother, had remarked on my improved attitude; surely she *had* suspected, and she was clever enough to play her hunches competently. I thought about the way my mother had submitted to rape to preserve her children from the threat of rampaging pirates, and then pretended that rape had never happened. Now she was taking my vision at face value, though it was logically suspect. We had gone along with her before, because family pride was better than the reality. Now Helse and Spirit were going along with her again – because we needed the food. It was, after all, pointless for us all to die when there was food available. So there was sense behind my vision, and sense behind their endorsement of it. Yet it seemed to me that more than sense was operating here.

'Are you ready?" Helse asked.

'You sacrificed your secret – for this,' I said to Helse.

'How could I seek to refute your vision, Hope?' she asked innocently.

'You stand by me the way my mother stands by my father."

'Women do what they must. You know that.'

'And you too,' I told Spirit, taking her hand.

'I saw him sit up, out there,' Spirit said. 'I saw him hold out his hand to you.' And perhaps she had, or believed she had. Spirit was always my staunchest supporter when it counted.

'Then I must be ready,' I said. How any of us were going

to choke down what the brave women were serving I didn't know, but it had to be done. Too many sacrifices had already been made for it to be otherwise.

13

Refugees' Welcome

Jupiter Rings, 2-3-'15 – choose not to dwell unduly on the following days. I did get sick, and so did Spirit, but we both came back and tried again, and again, until we were able to retain what we consumed. The meat was perfectly fresh, of course, and clean, for no spoilage occurs in space. The women served it well-cooked in very small portions, so that it was impossible to tell from what part of what animal it might have come. The women ate too, with the same affected unconcern they had evinced after the mass rape. I had always suspected the female sex of being weaker than the male, but I did not think so any more. Strength is so much more than muscle!

After the first few meals, it was not so bad. I even started helping with the cooking, by foraging for fuel for the fire. First they had used the precious candles saved from the funeral service, but soon these were gone and other combustibles were required. There was wood in the bubble for furnishings, and the packaging for the original food packs was flammable. It was a very small, controlled fire, for we could not afford to overload the air-recirculation system with a lot of pollutants, so we did have enough fuel.

But it was always a grown woman who donned a suit and went outside for more meat; to that extent we children were preserved in our innocence.

Señora Ortega and the other women chose to accept my vision as they had interpreted it. Not one of them broke ranks on this, though I was sure not all of them really believed in supernatural visitations or messages. They knew what had to be done, and they did it without fuss or fanfare, exactly as they had throughout their married lives. What a fundament of strength was thus subtly revealed!

So we survived and even began to regain weight, thanks to the gift of our men. We all knew, I think, that had any of those men been alive to speak their wills, they would have told us to do exactly what we were doing. The bubble had been forged by necessity into one large family, as close as any other, united by a complex of vital compromises and secrets.

We navigated and studied and slept and played games of all sorts, for morale was as important as physical condition. Slowly we drew nigh the primary ring of Jupiter. Now that we knew we would make it, our attitudes improved.

We spent more time staring at Jupiter, swelling to giant size, its cloud bands more prominent than ever, violently coursing past each other with bubble-storms at the interfaces, the details constantly changing in an overall pattern that was unchanging. As we watched, the great red spot came on the horizon, like a monster eye trying to orient on us. Ah, Jove, the ruler of gods! Our hopes expanded in direct proportion to this image in our sky. All would be well once we achieved Jupiter, the kindly colossus of space! Jupiter, within whose bands of clouds floated so many enormous bubbles, each one a great city spinning like our little bubble from internal gravity, since they could not stay afloat if they used normal gravity. The city-bubbles did not have to worry about vacuum outside, instead they faced the phenomenal pressures of Jupiter's atmosphere. Yet they were the most highly civilized cities in the Solar System, and the lifestyle of ordinary people within them was reputed to be fantastic. We dreamed, a little afraid, and longed for what we hoped would be.

This is not to suggest that everything was smooth now. Conditions of enduring stress and confinement tend to accentuate and at times exacerbate interpersonal relations.

and we of the bubble were not exceptional in this respect. All of us shared an unspoken guilt that tended to sublimate itself in those ways that were permitted expression. I have heard sublimation spoken of as a useful alternative to unsocial behaviour, but I don't believe that. When an emotion is suppressed, it tends to manifest in something very similar to the forbidden thing, and perhaps sometimes it would be best simply to accept the forbidden instead. Thus we had the smaller children saving their faeces and sometimes eating them, mocking the food that could not be identified. That sort of thing I need not explicate further.

I spent time with Helse openly now, for my father had seemingly blessed our association. No one objected overtly to our sharing a cell, though perhaps there were private qualms. But she and I did fight on occasion, if only because I wanted her to love me, and she would not let herself go that far. To her, the body was a thing to be used as expedient, but the heart was special – which was one reason I wanted her heart. I suppose I was greedy, but that is the way of love.

Spirit, especially, got difficult. She had always been close to me, and remained so, but now she came to resent the time I spent with Helse. It seemed that when Helse had masqueraded as a boy and Spirit had shared the secret, that was all right. She was part of it. But now that Helse was openly female and there was no secret, Spirit felt excluded. I should have been alert to the symptoms, but, as is so often the case, I wasn't paying attention until too late. I was caught up in my own concerns, which were more immediate but less important than the psychological welfare of my sister, until too late. I hope not to make that error again.

Spirit burst in upon us once, when Helse and I were sleeping in our cell in deshabille, though not actually making love. I had discovered that the adolescent fantasy of continuous sexual activity was exactly that: fantasy. Helse would make love any time I asked her to, and, knowing that, I found that usually it was enough just to be near her. Sex is less than love, but more than the act; often mere closeness suffices.

'There you go again!' Spirit cried as we sat up groggily. 'Father's gone, Faith's gone, Mother's alone – and you're busy fooling with her!' There was a vicious freighting on the word 'fooling'; it was intended as an obscenity, and in that context it became so.

There wasn't much I could say. Of course I was guilty, at other times if not this particular time, and as I just explained, the technical act was only a fraction of it and not worth arguing. I did not want to get angry, because that would proclaim my guilt, but I didn't know how else to react.

Helse handled it with better grace. Her age and experience enabled her to navigate certain difficult passages more readily than I could. 'I do not take your brother from you, Spirit,' she said. 'I can never do that. You are of his blood and I am not. I do not love him as you do.'

Spirit faced her defiantly. 'That's space-crock! You love him more than I do!'

I started to chuckle at her miscue; obviously Spirit had not meant to say that. Prompted by Helse's statement, Spirit had reversed the emphasis, inadvertently arguing against her own interest, as can happen when a person's emotion overrides her tongue.

But Helse reacted as if she had been stabbed. 'Oh!' she cried, and scrambled to her feet and up out of the cell, not even pausing for her clothing.

I stared after her. So did Spirit, her anger forgotten. 'I vanquished her!' she exclaimed, amazed.

'But you misspoke yourself!' I protested.

Now it was Spirit who reacted oddly. 'Oh, I shouldn't have said that! I blabbed her secret!'

'What secret? She doesn't love—'

I stopped, looking at her with a dawning surmise.

204

Spirit, flustered, reached for the exit panel. 'I'd better go try to apologize. I lost my stupid head.'

I caught her, preventing her from going. 'You mean she *does* love me? She always told me she didn't, and my talent enables me to know—'

'Oh, you don't know half what you think you do!' Spirit snapped. 'When your emotion is tied in, your talent cuts out!'

She had stabbed me as deeply as she had Helse. I knew immediately that she was correct. I had no basis to judge Helse's state of emotion, because my own was suspect. It was as if I was trying to move a heavy suitcase in free fall: my effort moved me back as much as it moved it forward. I had to be firmly anchored before I could be sure of the effect of my effort. I think the laws of the mind are similar in this respect to the laws of matter.

'She's older than I am,' I said falteringly. 'It makes sense that I am less to her than she is to me. If she felt otherwise, why should she deny it?'

'She *had* to deny it, dummy!' Spirit said. 'She thinks men don't love women who love them back. She's always been used by men who only wanted her body, no matter what they said at the time, and when her body changed they didn't want her any more. So she knew if she really liked someone, she shouldn't ever, ever let on, because—' She wrenched, trying to break free of my hold on her. 'Let me go, Hope! I could kill myself! Helse's an awfully nice girl, and I've got to tell her – I don't know what, but I've got to!'

I let her go. I sat against the wall, meditating on what my sister had said. It explained a lot. I should have caught on to it myself, with my vaunted talent for understanding people. But, ironically, this failure was a valuable lesson for me, for it revealed the glaring weakness in my talent. *I had to be objective.* I resolved never again to make that error.

But I realized that I couldn't patch it up with Helse by trying to reassure her of my undying love; she was constitutionally incapable of believing me. Her past experience could not be left behind. The same thing that made her so well able to please a man made her unable to trust him. Oh, I knew the power of an emotional fixation! I had been ready to swear off sex forever after the rape of Faith, and only Helse's timely and forceful action had turned me about. But I could not reassure her about her own fixation; all I had were words, and she would not believe them. The men who had used her body during her childhood had not harmed her body; they had poisoned her mind. I was way too late to re-educate her subjectivity. What, then, could I do?

I mulled it over, and finally worked it out. My mother, actually, had shown me the way. The reality of our inner belief does not have to match that of our external professions.

In due course Helse returned. She remained unclothed; probably no one in the bubble had noticed or cared, since I was the oldest male in this limited community. If anyone realized that we were having a difference, that person knew enough not to interfere. She looked resigned.

Evidently Spirit had caught up with her – it could hardly be otherwise, in such limited space – and apologized for blabbing. Spirit could be exceedingly winsome when she was contrite, and surely her apology had been accepted. But Helse believed the damage could not really be undone. She had returned bravely to confirm the disaster.

I gave her no chance. 'I must apologize for what my sister did,' I said before Helse could speak. 'She said she loved me more than you do, and of course that's true, but it was extremely unkind.'

Helse paused, taken aback. 'That isn't what she—'

'Oh, maybe she garbled it,' I said blithely. 'But I know you don't love me, and I'm learning to live with that. I'm sorry Spirit misinterpreted – well, she *is* my sister, and she has a hot little temper, and—'

'But I'm trying to tell you—'

'Please, Helse,' I said, holding out my arms to her. 'I need you so much – don't tease me any more! Let me hope that one day you'll feel about me the way I feel about you. Don't deprive me of that one illusion.'

'Illusion!' she exclaimed. 'Hope, I—'

I continued to extend my arms to her. She hesitated, then came to me. I kissed her passionately, and after a moment she responded in kind. We proceeded naturally to the act of love.

Yet there was a certain difference, perhaps I should say diffidence about it, on her part and on mine, because we each knew we were deceiving the other. It may even be that that reservation made the experience sweeter. Certainly, for me, the term 'love' was no euphemism for any other thing; love was exactly what it was.

When the desperation of our merging eased, she drew apart a little, her face showing concern. 'Hope, this isn't honest. I—'

'Don't say it!' I cut in again. 'Leave me with at least the dream that some day you'll change your mind!' I was perhaps overplaying it, and she knew it, but this was a unique situation for me. The message I had for her was other than the one I professed, and she knew it.

She smiled, defeated. 'That one illusion,' she agreed, and kissed me softly, and in that single gesture there was more joy than in all our prior congress. We chose to share the illusion of illusion.

Jupiter was now so big that it was no longer an object in space; it was becoming our primary, in perception as well as physics. So close, so close – our ordeal was almost over!

And yet – and yet! If we reached Jupiter and were saved, and found places in that great society – what then of the relation I had with Helse? She would have to report to Kife, or QYV, and who could say what would become of her thereafter? Or the new situation might simply change her attitude. She was a pretty girl and I a mere stripling; she could do better than me, in that society. The illusion of her non-love for me might turn out to be no illusion there. So I viewed our potential rescue with a certain undercurrent of apprehension, for the love of Helse had become more important to me than life itself. Right now, while we sailed the waves of gravity in space, she was mine.

A day later the Jupiter Patrol found us. At first we feared it was another pirate ship or an opportunist merchanter, but soon we saw the big round Jove circle with the red spot in it, and recognized the lines of a ship of the Space Navy, and knew this was authentic. Contact at last!

They locked on and boarded us. The officer who spoke to us was a sleek, neat, brisk, correct woman. There would be no sexual solicitation here! 'Please identify your origin,' she said in English.

Naturally the representative of the mighty Colossus did not bother to learn the language of mere refugees! But we were in no position to complain. I spoke up, since my English was as facile as any. 'We are refugees from Callisto fleeing the oppression of our government. We seek sanctuary at Jupiter.'

The woman frowned. 'Perhaps you people are not aware that there has been an election on Jupiter, and extra-planetary policy has shifted. Political and/or economic refugees are no longer being accepted. You will have to go elsewhere.'

I was stunned. 'But there is nowhere else! We used our last reserves to get here! We are out of food, our batteries for running the life-support systems are low. Our men were killed by pirates, our women raped—' I broke off, realizing that I shouldn't say that. Maybe I could qualify it. '*Some* of—'

'Yes, we are familiar with the standard refugee story,' she snapped. 'You people expect us to believe that all of space is infested with ancient buccaneers in pirate hats and pantaloons, holding you up at sword-point for gold. This is the twenty-seventh century, and we are not so credulous. We will give you supplies to take you to Europa or Ganymede, and we shall tow you out beyond our territorial limit. That is all. It is high time you moon folk started taking care of your own problems, instead of foisting them off on us.'

Appalled, I translated her words for the others. I could hardly believe it myself. Here we had finally arrived at the political sanctuary of mighty Jupiter, the planet of all our dreams – and were not welcome. What had happened to the great melting pot of the Solar System!

It is terrible to have one's hopes so brutally dashed. I think we were all in something like a group trance. We stood there unprotesting as the Jupiter work crew swarmed over the bubble, emptying our refuse (muttering in English they thought we could not understand that now they knew we were liars, because we could not have come all the way from Callisto, because the refuse wasn't enough for such a trip), restocking our supply of food packs, replacing our oxygenation units and the batteries for our general environment-maintenance equipment, tuning the gravity-lens generator, and replacing the water-recycling filters. They were so competent it was small wonder that they did not believe we could have made the trip we claimed; we were, after all, only incompetent refugees. They evidently assumed that some ship had towed us here and rehearsed us in the story to tell, in an attempt to play upon sympathy. They were also so efficient they hardly checked the bags tied to the outside of the bubble, assuming them to be junk storage: another evidence of our sloppiness.

Yet we needed all of their help, for only luck had prevented something crucial from failing. But we needed help less than we needed the enormous gift of sanctuary on Jupiter. They were generously giving us trifles instead of the essence. Now they could write up a report about all the good they had done for thankless refugees.

Oh, yes, they were as good as the female officer's word. (I refrain from applying the vernacular description for a female of questionable ethics, tempting as it is.) They towed us out beyond the orbit of Amalthea, to the outer ring, and turned us loose with the admonition not to return to Jupiter territorial space, on pain of being blasted out of it. Poverty-stricken foreign freeloaders, they let us know politely, were not wanted in the decent God-fearing territory of mighty Jupiter. After all, we didn't even speak the language.

Maybe they were bluffing about the blasting-out-of-space. We were unlikely to risk it. Certainly they had the physical capacity to do such a thing. The Jupiter States possessed the mightiest military force in the Solar System, excepting possibly that of the Saturnine Republic.

My mother shook her head as she absorbed my translation, looking abruptly haggard. She had been prepared for anything except this! 'And we thought we had known rape!' she said.

I pondered that, and concluded she was right. I may have overstated the phrasing of the Jupiter rejection, for the female officer's speech was always politely delivered, but the essence is accurate. They definitely did not want us. So what could have been more cruel than the abrupt destruction of our aspirations? Physical rape came and went; it was possible to cover it up, to pretend it never happened; but this rejection could never be undone. Now we had, almost literally, nowhere to go. We knew that none of the major moons of Jupiter would give us safe haven. They were all overpopulated, poverty-ridden and oppressed by the autocratic governments that seem to sprout like weeds in the wilderness of the so-called Third System.

Jupiter, in fact if not in theory, hoped we would simply disappear in space and never appear again. We were not Jupiter's problem, and we could be ignored.

For this my father had died and my mother had submitted to degradation. For nothing!

I found Helse looking out a port, watching magnificent Jupiter whirl by, shrinking visibly as we were towed from it, like the shrinking of our dream. 'Give me your tired, your poor, your huddled masses yearning to breathe free,' she murmured, quoting from memory the historical sonnet, 'The New Colossus', whose tradition the United States of Jupiter supposedly carried on. 'The wretched refuse of your teeming shore . . ' She was crying, of course, and so was I

14

Hell Planet

Space, 5-3-'15 – We held a group meeting in due course to discuss our situation. We were the wretched refugee refuse, yearning to breathe free, who had learned the hard way not to believe all that was quoted in the geography texts, but we still had to decide on some course. Where were we to go?

Well, we would not go hungry. We had a full supply of food packs now, courtesy of the surplus stores of rich Jove, and the bodies of our men remained anchored to our hull. I wondered whether the Jupiter Patrol workmen might actually have spotted the nature of those bags and played stupid so as to avoid the awkwardness of having to dispose of them, perhaps even giving them decent burial. It might be politically inexpedient to accept bodies while rejecting living people. Had they inspected those bodies, they would have discovered how they had died, and it would have been more difficult for the Jupiter Patrol to maintain its official ignorance of the pirate problem. Jupiter, like our women, preferred to ignore certain unpleasant realities. Probably they had the physical capacity to deal with the pirates, but lacked the political motivation. It was all understandable – in its sickening fashion.

We knew we could not return to Callisto. Starvation in space would probably be preferable to what the authorities there would do to us to cover their own embarrassment at our very existence. We were, after all, tangible evidence of the failure of their system. They might not care to correct that failure, but they would certainly labour diligently to cover it up. Everywhere, concealment seemed preferable to correction!

Ganymede and Europa were little better. Io was largely uninhabitable, and its few residential domes were reputed to be horribly overcrowded. No salvation there!

That left the outer moonlets – who would hardly be likely to welcome our motley assemblage of women and children. Yet we did have to go *somewhere*, for we could not live indefinitely in space.

'Hidalgo!' Spirit exclaimed.

Señora Ortega's head turned towards her, and we all paused for consideration. Out of the mouths of babes . .

We discussed it. Hidalgo is a planetoid no bigger than Amalthea, in a stretched-out orbit between Mars and Saturn. But it was no ordinary fragment, for a couple of centuries ago Jupiter assumed sovereignty over it, and more recently Hidalgo had become an actual state of the United States of North Jupiter, the only non-planetary body to be granted that status. It was now a major tourist region. Huge pleasure domes were set on it, spinning on their bases to provide the kind of gravity the tiny planetoid could not. The population there was not Hispanic, but was polyglot and multiracial. Our kind could surely merge with their kind. There was always work for domestics, and that was one thing our women could handle. Our children could get superior schooling there and grow up as free citizens. Hidalgo, we reasoned, was so far out from Jupiter proper that the ban against refugees might not apply. Spirit, in her intuitive fashion had come up with a truly intriguing prospect.

But there were formidable problems. Hidalgo did swing out past Jupiter's orbit, which was the basis for Jupiter's claim in it, but that did not mean it was close to Jupiter physically. It was a tiny, tiny mote in space, virtually impossible to discover by random search with a clumsy bubble. We would need an ephemeris, a detailed listing of the locations of bodies in space and time. These locations were given as triple co-ordinate sets, computer-calculated, so that it was possible to pick a precise date and time and get the exact spacial co-ordinates of the desired object, relative to the sun and its position in the galaxy. Without the ephemeris, we could look until we died of old age for that grain of sand in the immensity of solar space.

We also did not have a drive system capable of getting us there. The jet we had was barely enough to move us around the Jupiter ecliptic – that is, the plane of the equator and inner moons – and Hidalgo is far outside that. The efficient Jupe workers had recharged our jet, for it, like everything else associated with this bubble, was near exhaustion, but no matter how fresh the jet was, it was grossly insufficient. We needed a powerful ion drive that would accelerate us at a significant fraction of gee, to aid our gravity lenses. To put it in simplest terms: we needed to add a more powerful motor to our sailboat. We could not simply centre on a distant speck like Hidalgo and fall in to it; there was not enough gravity there to bring us in within a century or so.

And we needed more supplies: food, oxygen, electricity, all for a much longer journey. Lots of things like that, if we wanted to get there alive.

That was why we decided to raid an outpost on Io. That planet might not be worthwhile to settle on, but it would do just fine for a supply raid. The badlands section had all sorts of technical facilities for monitoring the volcanoes and radiation intensity and such, and there were many study foundations there performing obscure research. They were well funded and surely had plenty of supplies to spare. Io is the most active planetary body in the Solar System, bar none, and that sort of thing is a magnet for scientists. We knew they had huge supplies of food and medicine, and surplus equipment for every type of bubble and ship. Most important, they had complete libraries of ephemeridae.

I think it did not occur to any of us consciously at that time that what we contemplated was, in fact, piracy. All we knew was that we would die in high space if we did not float to a haven somewhere, and that the Jupe authorities had rejected us. It becomes much easier to justify strong measures, even illegal ones, when your life depends on them.

We also could not afford to doubt that everything we required for our extended journey through space would be available on Io. For if we made our play and did not achieve our needs, we were doomed. We were, in fact, making a gamble whose boldness would have appalled us a month before. Experience had altered our horizons drastically.

The period of revolution for Io is one and three-quarter days. You might think that would make it easy to intercept; just park for a day and wait for it to swing around. But it doesn't work that way. We were in orbit ourselves, and as we knew, orbits are not lightly shifted. So we had to use our precious jet to jockey around, letting Io catch up to us, using its gravity to wrestle us back in line. An expert navigator could have done it in a few hours; it took us two days, but we did get there.

Io was formidable as it loomed close. One volcano was bright shades of yellow, orange, brown, and red. The whole planet looked as if it had been recently scrambled – and, geologically speaking, it had.

You see, Io is not like other worlds. That may be the understatement of this narrative. It resembles them as a maddened sabre-tooth tiger on ancient Earth resembles a sleeping denatured pussycat. Other worlds, such as our own Callisto, may seem almost dead; Io is screamingly alive. The closer we got the more I remembered about it, and the less I liked what we planned. It wasn't the human opposition I feared; it was Io herself.

There's really too much to tell here; I'll try to touch on the essence only. Io, just over four hundred thousand kilometres from Jupiter, should have one face locked on

Jupiter, the same way it is with Callisto and the others. But Europa, the next moon out, interferes, forcing Io into an eccentric orbit. That means her circuit isn't round and her velocity isn't constant. She moves at different speeds, and turns her face back and forth as though bothered by someone hovering just behind her shoulder. This has to do with the fundamental physics of the situation. Tidal forces develop, and these are not mere little tugs; it is more like a giant hand squishing an overripe orange, making the juices squirt and the peel buckle. That tidal action generates heat, keeping much of the interior of the planet molten. This in turn means constant change. New volcanoes keep popping up and spewing out their stuff and dying down, and the ground shifts restlessly. So maps are soon outdated, and no one can really say ahead of time what the details of the landscape will be – especially on the active face facing Jupiter. That's the bad face, the Gorgon-face, the uninhabitable one that spits sulphur in your eye and pollutes the whole region of space with radioactive debris. The one we were headed for.

But what choice did we have?

We glided in. It was night locally, with the inside face away from the sun, but glowing with its own savage vents. Truly, this was Hell we were comning to! Io is one terrible lady.

We floated along at a reasonably safe elevation, looking for our target. We had to select it by night, then hide the bubble and make a foray afoot, so there would be no hint of our intent. We agreed there should be no violence. We were raiding for what we had to have, but we were not criminals. We would pretend to be a scientific party that had got isolated by a vagary of volcanic activity – a completely credible story on wild Io! – and once inside the dome, we would hijack the crew, using a mock bomb, and make them provide the supplies we needed. Peaceful hijacking had for centuries been a staple tool for the impoverished desperate.

It was indeed a desperate strategy. But if we won, it would give us our fair chance for refuge. If we lost, at least it would be quick. We had to do it.

We spotted a dome, but it was too small; it wouldn't have enough supplies. We moved on, and spotted another – too large. We didn't want to tackle any more than we had to; even our minimum requirement might prove to be more than we could handle. Finally, near a massive rocky escarpment, we discovered a medium-sized observation dome with several transport bubbles docked beside it. This was our target.

We floated down behind the escarpment, which resembled a wrinkle in that orange I mentioned before and seemed to be an ideal place to hide our bubble. But as we closed on it, we discovered that perspective and darkness had deceived us; this was a far more massive outcropping than thought. It was a mountain range, with the highest peak some eight or nine kilometres tall. Back on Callisto we had seen no hills beyond a few hundred metres high, so this was awesome. None of us had had any experience with this exaggerated type of terrain. This is probably why we erred so disastrously.

We landed in a comfortably small niche in the mountain, tucked down well out of sight of the dome we stalked. Even an observation dome with the most powerful telescopes could not see through a mountain of sulphur. We weren't sure we could complete our mission before dawn, so we wanted the bubble to be properly concealed.

Helse and I were in the raiding party, because we spoke English, the common tongue of scientists in this region of space. My mother and Spirit stayed behind with thirty-four women, while twenty-five women formed the raiding party, in addition to the two of us. Señora Ortega led us. I think we all felt the excitement of adventure – but also knew it was grim business. I had heard it said that a person is most truly alive when death is near, and I think there is some truth in it.

Our first problem was getting down to the dome. We had parked near the base of the mountain – but that little ledge of a kilometre or so became abruptly gargantuan when we approached it afoot. Again, we had perceived it as it would have been on Callisto, a very gradual decline, much broader than it was tall. It was not so. It was the other way around.

The cliff was of sulphur dioxide ice, yellow underfoot. Maybe there was other rock beneath, but that was the surface. It wasn't slippery, fortunately, but it was unfamiliar, and we didn't trust it. There were small cracks and pocks and crevices in its layout, visible in the generous light of Jupiter, but we feared these could mask more dangerous nether flaws in the structure. But we traversed the more or less level portion without untoward event, headed towards the drop-off.

The descent was horrendous. We took one look over that awesome cliff and hastily roped ourselves together like ancient mountain climbers. I think we all suffered from agrophobia in that moment. But we had to get down to the base, where we could proceed on the level to the target dome. We let ourselves down the cliff on the rope, paying it out one person at a time, watching the party leaders step-slide down the steepening slope.

Helse and I were in the middle of the party. Even so, it was one frightening descent. The projecting edges of the mountain were like the blade of a pitted cleaver. We had to chip away the sharp corner and form a niche for the rope, so that it would neither slide nor fray. We wanted it to feed through exactly where and when we wanted it to.

Gravity here seemed to be more than on Callisto, though it is possible our time in low-gee had distorted our perception. Though Io is a smaller moon, it is far more dense. One might suppose that surface gravity would be the same for two worlds of equal mass even if their diameters differed, but that is not so; the smaller one has greater surface gravity, because that surface is closer to the centre. So, though Io actually is slightly less massive than Callisto, it is almost twice as dense, and that makes the difference. Io is sized like Earth's lonely moon, but is a little more so in diameter, density, and mass, and a lot more so in activity.

Apart from this, the suits made us clumsy. A suit in vacuum, in a familiar region, is manageable; but in atmosphere and on an awkward surface it becomes more clumsy. There is environmental resistance. There was very little planetary atmosphere here, but we felt it nonetheless.

But mainly, our problem was the sheer height of our start. I hesitate to repeat myself, but it is difficult even to rationalize the impact this elevation had on us. From space a niche in the foothill of a mountain may seem minor, especially when it is down near the larger plain. But one kilometre is, after all, a thousand metres, and that is awesome up close. It seemed that if we fell, we would fall forever – and somehow, perversely, my apprehension made me almost *want* to fall, to get it over with. A fall at quarter-gee would not be nearly as ferocious as one at full-gee, but my nervous system had evolved on Earth, and it reacted as it would have on Earth. I was almost paralyzed with the fear of that height.

'Close your eyes,' Helse told me, helmet to helmet. 'Pretend it's only a few yards. Metres.'

Coward that I was, I did, and it helped. But soon I was looking again, reminding myself that I hadn't been agrophobic while in the bubble. *On* the bubble had been another matter – but I believe that was understandable. Out here it was the feel of weight and the uncertainty of the rope that jittered me, rather than the actual elevation. Had I, for example, been using a reliable flying suit, this same elevation and slope would hardly have bothered me. At least, this is what I now prefer to believe.

So I scrambled over the dread ridge in my turn, just as if I felt no fear, and Helse followed me, and with the conquest of my hesitancy, my apprehension abated without actually disappearing. Commitment does seem to help. The women before and after us seemed to have no problems, though I was sure each experienced similar qualms.

The vista below was dramatic. The surface of Io was a tapestry of orange even in the reflected light from Jupiter. Dark runnels showed where some recent flow of sulphur had passed, and bright flame – or whatever it should be called, since no fire as we know it can burn in near-vacuum – showed at a roughly circular vent to the right. The observation dome was near this vent, partly sheltered by a lesser escarpment. It looked precarious to me, but I suppose there's no way to gather significant data on a sulphur volcano except by sitting beside it for a while and making on-the-spot notes. I wondered what the life expectancy of such researchers was. Probably that was a super-strong, super-insulated dome, able to withstand what it had to. But probably, too, the researchers possessed a certain quality of courage. A person did not have to be a muscular warrior to be brave, as the women of our bubble were showing.

We were step-sliding down the steep slope at about five kilometres per hour, so we had a half-hour descent to do. That was all right. But what, I wondered, about the return trip? And how much rope did we have? Not any kilometre length, for certain!

Sure enough, the rest of us had to set ourselves against the slope, clinging to sulphur-ice, while our end-person separated herself and us from the anchor at the top. She left a trailing length, so that we could use it to haul ourselves up the vertical portion of the slope and over the lip, but that was all. On our return trip we would have to climb unaided to that point. I didn't like it.

Now that we were no longer anchored, we proceeded

more swiftly. Too swiftly – I tried to brake, for safety, but the onrush of sliding women hauled me along. In moments we were out of control. Inexperience was telling.

I think someone screamed. As I mentioned, it is not a complete vacuum on Io; the sulphur dioxide gas is around, especially near the hot vents where it can't freeze out, so sound is theoretically possible. Maybe it was conducted along the ground, or the rope. Anyway, there was reason to scream. We were sliding towards a sharper drop-off – and, judging from our present angle, this one had to be virtually vertical.

I dug in with my feet with renewed desperation, chewing up a mass of chips and dust. So did Helse and the women. But the drag of those in front, who were completely out of control, was too great. We were all being hauled to that dread brink.

Then a women towards the front drew a knife. She sawed at the rope, and in a moment it parted. Then she dug in her heels, and the rest of us did likewise, and this concerted effort was effective at last, and slowly we slowed.

But as we crunched to a nervous halt, we watched the first five women tumble over the brink, led by Señora Ortega.

Maybe it was just an irregularity, leading to a gentler slope below. In that case they would be all right, just bruised and perhaps angry at the rest of us for cutting them loose. It was an anger we could accept.

We worked our way sideways, finding a better slope, avoiding the ledge. We each jammed our heels in at each step, making sure we would not get out of control again, though this slowed us enormously. Then we moved down. When we got below the level of the ledge we looked across anxiously, to see what had become of our leading segment.

There was nothing. The ledge overhung a developing crevice that widened into a channel for an avalanche, almost vertical. Those women might as well have fallen straight down.

What could we do but go on? We could not even see the lost women, let alone reach them, let alone help them, in the highly unlikely chance they survived. Even the time it took to make the effort would prejudice the success of our mission.

All of us had known this trek would be dangerous; now we had the proof. A similar fate would befall the rest of us if we didn't complete our mission.

So we paused, helmets bowed in silent mourning for Doña Concha and the others. That was the best we could do.

Io had taken her first victims. I was very much afraid they would not be her last ones.

We continued down. There were other ledges and other crevices, none of them having been evident during our approach in the bubble. We proceeded slowly and avoided them. Once bitten, thrice shy! This mountain had a great deal more character than we had anticipated, and now every trace irregularity loomed monstrously. Had we had any inkling of the enormity of the challenge the descent would represent, we would have landed elsewhere and avoided such a hazard. But that was most of our problem: ignorance and inexperience. Both were being rapidly abated, and we did at last make it to the base. But it took us almost an hour, twice as long as budgeted.

We untied ourselves and marched across the orange surface. The woman who had cut the rope was now our leader. I didn't know who she was, and suspect most of the others shared my ignorance, but it didn't matter. She had tried to decline the title, but the rest of us insisted, by gestures. She had saved herself and the rest of us by her quick action. Her snap judgments promised to be most reliable. There is indeed a place for hasty decision, and that place is the surface of Io, for there simply is not time to consider all aspects of many alternatives at comfortable leisure.

Our new leader sought the ridges, not trusting the snow-filled recesses. But these ridges, though only a few metres high, were irrregular and fragmented, so our firm footing exacted a price of devious routing. We had to jump over crevices, and some of them were pretty wide and deep. Even with low gravity, this was nervous business.

Sure enough, one of our women slipped as she jumped over an especially bad one and fell down into it. The crack was about thirty metres deep, closing into a dark crease. She was wedged down there unmoving.

We started to lower a rope to her, to pull her out. Then we saw her suit: It was deflating. The fall had punctured it; perhaps it had snagged on a sharp projection. Her air was gone. Further effort on our part was pointless. We could not reach her in time to do any good.

As it happened, I recognized the suit of this woman. She was the mother of one of the smaller children. Her loss became more poignant in that moment, as I thought of what we would have to tell that child.

Señora Ortega's grandchildren, too, would have to be told. There was a grim business coming after we returned to the bubble, even if we completed our mission without further casualties. These were real people, not strangers, who were dying.

After that we avoided the worst cracks, though this meant risking the yellow snow. From some of the low areas fumes sprayed up, making little domes of frozen gas and particles like decorative waterfalls. These were really miniature volcanoes, I realized, harmless as long as we didn't step in them. This was the land of volcanoes.

We tramped on for hours, sacrificing time in favour of safety. Dawn came, as the moon's rapid orbit brought it a quarter circle around Jupiter in ten hours – which hours we had used up in our pre-landing survey and then in our suiting-up and organization and slow descent and march.

We had grossly underestimated the time such routine required.

On Callisto, dawn outside the dome is pretty but unremarkable since we have our own day-night schedule inside the domes. Here dawn was immediate and forceful – in fact, more savage than we had imagined.

Sulphur dioxide sublimates to gas in the ambience of day on Io. It is frozen only during the night. With the first touch of sunlight, the snow around us began to heat and convert. As that light slowly intensified, this conversion became explosive. The gas expanded upward and outward, filling the vacuum, swirling past the irregular features of the landscape. We were soon amidst an upward-flinging storm.

In addition, the ground quaked. Io was now in the close, swift phase of its orbit about Jupiter, and the tidal force was manifesting. The entire body of this world was being squished – and her molten interior was squirting out of every available pore. This was not a volcano, it was an entire planetary face of eruptions. We were caught in an awakening hell.

And this surely was the physical location of Hell, I realized. Hell did have to be somewhere, if it had any reality at all, and this was conveniently located. Satan could ship the newly damned souls out here at light-speed by the busload, less than an hour's trip from Earth, and dump them out amidst the burning sulphur and leave them to their own miserable devices. Where could they go? And we, like the unlikely fools we were, had come here voluntarily. Our souls would not have far to travel when they departed our bodies.

We had to rope ourselves together again, lest the rising winds of the filling vacuum blow us away. New crevices were yawning, and the constant shaking of the ground was as deeply unsettling to our attitude as to our bodies. We were accustomed to a stable planet. Where could we hide – from this?

We ploughed on towards the target dome, huddling against the titanic forces of nature being unleashed about us. When a person fell, two more picked her up. When a segment of our line of people was blown towards a crevice, the rest of the line dug in instantly and pulled them back. We were learning to react correctly.

But vicious Io would not permit us to continue so readily. She opened a battery of jets almost beneath us. The ground cracked open, and a line of ejecta spewed out immediately behind Helse. The sulphur sand and gas rose like the cutting edge of a knife – and what it cut was our rope. Suddenly the last eight women in our line were separated from us; we perceived their suited outlines dimly through the haze.

We tried to rejoin them – but now the vent widened, as if seizing on its advantage, and the wash of gas and sand expanded. The ground beneath the eight of them broke up; fragments of it were blasted out, raining down in a larger pattern. A central plume of eruption formed, surrounded by an envelope of swirling gas. We could no longer see our friends – and I suspected that was just as well. They could not have survived that blast.

It may seem that I lacked emotion as I watched my companions perish. I think this was not the case; my emotion was stifled, suppressed, voided, because I knew there was nothing to be gained by it, for me or the others. I had concerns of survival too pressing to be dissipated by the energy of emotion. So I watched with a kind of numbness, unable to comprehend the larger significance of what I saw, and plodded on.

The woman before me doubled over. I saw her suit deflating; a particle from the eruption had holed it. I tried to clap my hands over the puncture, but it was useless; her remaining pressure leaked out around my clumsy gloves and she was dead before I knew it. I saw her face inside the helmet, bloating out, the eyes – oh, God, depressurization is a terrible thing!

My numbess suffered another jolt. I realized that there was absolutely no merit in my survival. That particle could have holed my suit as readily as this woman's; only pure chance had dictated that she had occupied that spot in its trajectory instead of I. Had we been moving ahead a trifle faster, I would have been there; slower, and the woman ahead of her would have been there. Similarly, it had been luck that cut off the eight women behind us; it could as readily have been nine.That would have taken out Helse. At that point my speculation baulked.

There was nothing to do but salvage the dead woman's oxygen tank. Fumblingly I moved it to my suit as a potential spare for whoever might need it. My suit had had about twenty-four hours of service remaining at the start of the Io adventure, but some of the other suits might have less. I disconnected her body from the chain and we went on. Already I wished ardently that we had never landed on terrible Io; but it was far, far too late for any change of mind.

The angry planet was not through with us. She would not be satisfied, I realized, until every one of us was dead. A new gas vent opened, this one at a slant, and its blast shoved the twelve of us who remained rapidly forward towards the dome we were headed for. This might have seemed fortuitous – but we already knew the danger of too-swift progress and didn't like this. We tried to slow down, to control our route and our destiny – but the vent only increased its exhalation, while the ground shook violently, impeding our footing, and we had to move at Io's will, not our own.

The consequence of this loss of control was not long in coming. We found ourselves charging a vent overflowing with sulphur lava, the viscous bright-yellow material flowing slowly across our path. It would have been easy enough to avoid – if the wind behind us had not been shoving us directly into it.

We saw it coming and tried to veer left to get around it.
But the lead women were already too close; they were
carried right into the glowing mass. Their suits inflated like
bubbles and burst with the sudden heat overload.

One women, just at the edge of the flow, managed to
brace her feet and turn and point left. Helse and I and the
woman now in front of us scrambled desperately left – and
the braced woman pulled on the rope, helping us crack the
whip, so that we could gain impetus to avoid the lava.

It worked, and we scrambled to relative safety – but the
woman who helped us could not maintain her footing and
was carried on into the lava. She fell headlong; her suit
immersed for a moment before the rapid heat expansion
lifted it to the surface and popped it. She died helping us to
live – and so did several of the women closest to her. The
rope burned through, setting our end free.

More sacrifice for us – and we didn't even know their
names. They had surely known ours, though, for the
sacrifice had been too deliberate; they were preserving us so
we could speak English to the scientists of the dome and
complete our mission.

I don't care if Io is literal Hell. I am sure those gallant
women went to Heaven.

Helse and I and three women cleared the lava. We
survived – we five, of the twenty-seven who had started this
trek. And we still weren't at the dome.

The lava flow was following a great U-shaped channel.
We were now in that channel, ahead of the flow, and knew
we had to get out of it quickly. The lava was moving slowly,
but that could change quickly – or a reverse gust of a gale
could drive us back into it. All low ground was treacherous
while lava was spewing!

We spotted the edge of the escarpment that sheltered the
observation dome. This rose into a mountain not more
than two kilometres high, but it was as jagged as the other.

There should be shelter from wind and lava in its lee, as this was not a volcanic structure. It seemed that solid rock floated on the half-molten crust of the planet, much as continents were supposed to do on planets like Earth. We were very glad to have this solidity amidst this horribly living surface. Security was hard to come by, here in Hell!

It was effective. The wind cut off as we passed into the mountain shelter, and the ground was more stable here. We stayed at the base, close in, knowing better than to try to climb the impossibly steep slope looming beside us. Therein was the final error in our judgment of Io.

The foot of the mountain was not a straight line; it wound in and out in a series of sculptured bays. It was really quite pretty in its fashion, with the sulphur changing shades of orange depending on the angle of the sunlight and shadow and the direction from which we viewed it. Massive and sombre, an island of stability in this ocean of violence, it seemed almost to lean over us protectively. The sun rose slowly higher as we walked, further warming the region. The yellowish atmosphere was thickening.

Then the avalanche started. I think a volcanic tremor set it off, but it was the softening sulphur snow that made it ready to happen. Too late, we realized what we had been flirting with when we cozied up to this mountain.

The entire face of it seemed to slide. Snow flew up in a yellow cloud, obscuring the more solid motion, but we could tell by the rumble that shook our bodies through ground and vapour that there were massive boulders within it. This probably happened every morning as the mountain warmed, while at night the sulphur dioxide solidified and coated it again. The mountain was more or less eternal, as this region went; not so its clothing of snow.

I knew that avalanches tended to flow in channels, as the material took the easiest route down. Thus it would concentrate mostly in one bay or another, by the time it struck the bottom. But which bay? Our survival depended on our choice of locale.

By common consensus we drew into one bay. We would ride it out together. But Helse, at the end, suddenly unlinked herself and bolted, terrified. She had panicked and done the worst possible thing.

I set out after her – and was brought short by the rope that linked me to the three women. With anger and desperation I untied myself, while the rumble swelled around us. Then I launched after Helse. I didn't know whether I could catch her and fetch her back in time, but I had to try. I suppose that was brave of me; I really didn't think about that at the time. I just knew I had to save Helse.

I sprinted after her, making better time than she in the clumsy suits because I had more power. But by the time I caught her, it was too late. The avalanche was upon us.

I wrapped my arms about her and threw her down, seeking to protect her with my body, though knowing it was useless. The mass of the falling material would crush us both to death in an instant. My last thought was that this was as good a way to die as any: embracing the woman I loved.

But – it didn't happen. A few chunks of discoloured snow fell beside us; that was all. The noise was all about us, however, swelling to a crescendo – which then stifled out. The horrendous fall of sulphur had come – and we were alive.

We climbed back to our feet, somewhat dazed. I wondered how I had been able to hear so much, and realized that the atmosphere had filled out considerably as the snow sublimated; sound was indeed possible in the normal fashion, now.

The avalanche had settled in the other bay, where the three women waited. Now that bay was filled with the rubble of the mountain.

We examined the monstrous orange pile, cogitated a moment, and went on. As usual, Io had given us no other course.

We trudged on, burdened more by the horror of twenty-five women dead than by the fatigue of the trek. But now we walked some distance out from the base of the mountain, though that put us at the fringe of the wind and belching ground. We knew how far out we had to be to avoid the main mass of an avalanche, because we had just seen an avalanche. We could walk within that range, but had to be ready to bolt out of it at the first sound of a slide.

Sure enough, before long we felt the rumble of another avalanche, and saw the clouds of yellow snow. We were clear of it, but I was developing a profound dislike for that colour. I think for the rest of my life I will associate yellow with Hell.

We were beyond the threat of the snowslide, but sympathetic vibrations in the ground opened new crevices at our feet, and we hastened right back towards the mountain snow. Scylla and Charybdis, the perils of the left and right – we had to be alert and quick to avoid them both!

Then we rounded an outcropping and spied the station dome. Never had a structure looked more beautiful to me! We bounded up to it, to the tiny-seeming lock at its base – and were met by a suited man.

He didn't even try to question us. He conducted us right inside, and soon we were in a blessedly warm chamber, breathing fresh air, feeling full Earth gravity. The gravity around the dome must have been reduced, as it was wherever a gravity lens focused the waves, but we hadn't noticed. That shows how far gone we were.

Best of all was the feeling of security. There were no storms in here, no jetting vents, no lava flows, and no avalanches. We could relax without risking prompt extinction. It was like a crushing burden evaporating from our bodies.

The head scientist showed up immediately to question us.

He was an older man, obviously from Jupiter. He had short grey hair, large spectacles that would have been fashionable half a millenium ago, and of course he spoke nothing but English.

Our original plan was no good, despite our ability to speak the language. The fake bomb had been lost with our companions and we had no way to hijack this station, even if we had wanted to carry through. Too much had happened; we did not care to honour the memory of the women who had sacrificed themselves by the commission of a crime. Perhaps this was illogical, but it was the way I felt, and I believe Helse agreed. So we simply told the scientist the truth.

The man shook his head in polite amazement. 'They actually towed you back out to space?' he asked, referring to an earlier part of our story. 'I find that awkward to believe!' That was the word he used: awkward. He was trying to avoid implying that we were not telling the truth.

'Believe it, Mason,' an associate told him. 'The new administration has instituted a get-tough policy on immigration. No more Hispanics.'

'But the governments of the moons are notoriously repressive!' the scientist said. 'What other recourse do these people have?'

'Evidently to die in space,' the other returned wryly. It was obvious that the scientists were humanitarians, unacquainted with the specifics of political policy.

The scientist, Mason – I was not certain whether that was his given or his surname – returned his attention to us. 'So you plotted to hijack this station to obtain supplies – to go where?'

'Hidalgo,' I repeated.

'But that's impossible! Hidalgo is on the far side of the Solar System at the moment!'

'We had planned to get an ephemeris to locate it exactly,' I said. Such details hardly mattered, now that we had failed.

231

Mason went to a computer terminal. 'Here is our ephemeris,' he said, punching buttons. The screen illuminated, showing three-dimensional co-ordinates. 'See – Hidalgo is just about as far away now as it is possible to be. You could travel more readily to Mars or Earth at the moment.'

My weight seemed to increase. 'We didn't know. We thought it could be close to Jupiter.'

'It *is* close – in season. You happen to seek it at an inopportune time.'

'Then we have nowhere to go,' I said, thinking again of the twenty-five women who had given their lives for this hopeless mission. We had never had a chance, from the outset. Perhaps some other year I would be better able to appreciate the irony.

Mason pondered. 'Politics is not my speciality. But I think you would be well advised to seek asylum on Leda. There is a Jupiter military station there whose commandant is of Hispanic descent. I suspect he would interpret the law more liberally than did those you encountered before.'

'You're not arresting us?' Helse put in.

The scientist refocused on her. 'Arrest you? For what you have told me? That would be self-incrimination! As I explained, I am not a political man, and if I were, I suspect I would not endorse this particular brand of politics.' He shook his head, smiling. 'Besides, you remind me too much of my niece.'

Helse's face froze. I realized she was thinking of the supposed uncle-niece relationship she had had as a child prostitute. For all the apologies she had made for that system, it was evident that she wanted no more of it.

'Leda,' I said quickly. 'The next moon out from Callisto, but too small to house a population . . .'

'Indeed,' Mason agreed, returning his attention to me. Helse relaxed, realizing that the scientist's remark had been innocent. 'Its diameter is hardly ten kilometres. That would be about six miles in your measurement.'

'No, kilometres is fine,' I said. He really didn't know our culture. I realized that scientists, while certainly intelligent people, were not educated in things beyond their fields. Miles was *his* culture's unit of measurement, outside the scientific and technical arena, not mine.

He smiled. 'Leda would fit within the shadow of one of our sulphur mountains here! But if you can reach it, I think it would be worth your while.'

'We can reach it,' I said, optimism returning. 'If we can get the supplies we need, and an exact course. It's pretty far out.'

'Eleven million kilometres from Jupiter,' he agreed, checking his figures on the terminal, though he surely knew them in his head. 'About twenty-five times as far out from Jupiter as is Io. But I think we can let you have a good drive jet and sufficient supplies.'

Helse came alive again. 'You can?'

The scientist smiled. 'We suffer frequent losses here, owing to the violence of the geography we study. This is one loss I shall be glad to sustain.'

'But we were going to hijack you!' she cried, chagrined.

He looked at her pretty face. 'You did, my dear, you did.' Then, perceiving her reaction, he asked: 'Did I say something wrong?'

I realized we would have to tackle this head-on. 'Do you have a picture of your niece?' I asked.

Perplexed, Mason gestured to a desk. There was a picture of a family of three. 'My brother and his charming wife, and their daughter Megan, a charming girl.'

I stared at the picture. There was an uncanny resemblance between Helse and the pictured Megan. The scientist had not been joking about being reminded of his niece.

'How old is she?' I asked.

Mason considered. 'I do lose track of time, in a place like this. I can tell you quickly about the past five eruptions of Vent 37C here, but mundane details like the party of my brother's politics or the age of his child – let me see.'

'You have it on file,' his associate reminded him.

'Oh, yes. Thank you.' Mason punched more buttons, and got the information. 'She was born in '95; that would make her twenty now, if I have not lost track of the date this year. I fear my picture is becoming dated, too.'

So the resemblance was illusory, or at least misplaced; Megan was four years older than Helse, instead of the same age as the picture showed. Still, they might resemble each other in the manner of sisters. But I saw that Megan was full Caucasian, not mixed Latin as Helse was.

Nevertheless, this was enough to reassure Helse. Mason really did have a niece, and obviously adored her, but she had never lived with him, and if she had, he would not have abused her. He reacted to Helse the way he would to a true niece; there was no untoward aspect. My talent told me this now. Sometimes experience makes us overly suspicious.

Helse was blushing now, evidently pursuing a similar series of thoughts. The scientist set about providing us with what we needed, drawing on the expertise of his staff to do a far better job of it than we could have done. Our mission, it seemed, had, after all, been successful.

15

When Will It End?

We had to wait till evening for the atmosphere to freeze out so that a bubble could safely float across the dangerous landscape of Io. By day, a chance volcano could sweep it right out of space.

Helse and I ate and slept comfortably, revelling in the civilized facilities of the dome and the kindness of the scientists, who seemed rather pleased to be entertaining young folk like us. I think, in retrospect, that this was the happiest period of our odyssey, despite the recent deaths of the women, for now we had genuine hope. Not all men were pirates or callous officials. I think if I ever have occasion to do any scientist, anywhere, a favour, I will do it unstintingly.

At last, refreshed, we set off. A technician transported us along with the supplies in a small bubble. In minutes we traversed the distance it had taken us dreadful hours to cover afoot. We came in sight of the nestled home bubble.

Helse touched my arm. We were not in our space suits now; they were unnecessary. 'Hope – how are we going to tell them?'

Somehow that aspect had been suspended from my awareness for several hours. Twenty-five women were dead, the mothers and only surviving parents of so many of the children. What could anyone say to soften that tragedy.

'I'll have to explain,' I said. The idyll of the day ended like the illusion it had been, and cruel reality returned.

We watched our small bubble close on the larger one. 'When I spooked and ran, there at the avalanche,' Helse murmured, 'why did you come after me, Hope?'

Preoccupied by the grimness I was about to have to convey, I answered her absently. 'I had to try to save you, idiot. Without you, I might as well be dead.'

'You thought we were both dead when the slide struck.'

'Yes. Shows how much I know about avalances. You turned out to be right.'

'Blind luck,' she said. 'I panicked. You were ready to die for me.'

'And instead, the sensible women died,' I agreed. 'Pure chance. Neither of us knew what we were doing.' That bothered me even in my distraction – the reminder that no merit of mine accounted for my survival. It had bothered me briefly when the woman in front of me had her suit holed; now it hit me harder, because I had no immediate distraction of survival. I was no better than any of those women who had died; only a freak of fate had preserved me. It was as though a man's boot landed on the ground where live ants walked, and three were squashed and two were spared, without the men even noticing. At times like this I wondered whether I believed in God. Surely God was not like the booted man, heedless of human welfare or merit. But if He were not, then what was He like? If He had decreed, after due consideration, that sixty men and twenty-five women should die while trying to do the right thing, while brute pirates prospered, what kind of a Deity was He?

'I think I love you,' Helse said.

The bubble nudged into contact with the other, and the air locks kissed and held. We had arrived.

Something penetrated my distraction. 'What?'

Helse smiled. 'Never mind.'

'Did you say—?'

She shrugged, and now the air locks opened, and my onerous duty was upon me. I could not question Helse further. But perhaps I did not need to.

We were met at the lock by a small group of women. 'Oh,

236

they found you, Hope Hubris!' one said. I had to concentrate to remember that her name was Señora Martínez. 'We were so worried, when neither party returned—'

Neither party? 'I – we have bad news and good news,' I said.

Señora Martínez peered past me. 'Where are the others?'

'That's the bad news,' I said. 'Only Helse and I made it. All the others—'

'Your mother did not find you?' Señora Martínez asked, her face drawn.

The cold of the outside closed in on me. 'My mother – went out?'

'She led another party of twenty-five. She had a premonition you were in trouble. That there would be deaths in your party if someone didn't come to help.'

Helse turned a staring face to me. 'Oh, no, Hope . . .'

'There were deaths,' I said dully. 'My mother and her party – did not return?'

Señora Martínez shook her head. 'We thought – she would be with you.'

'When did she leave?'

'At dawn.'

That meant the second party had been out on the surface of Io all day, following our route. All day in Hell.

'We could look for them in the bubble,' Helse suggested.

The station technician who had piloted us here spoke up. 'Anyone travelling afoot on the surface leaves a trail. The eruptions and evaporation of the day obliterate it, but if they are still alive and moving, that new trail will show up now.'

I knew with a sick certainty that nothing would be found. The odds were against any human party surviving a full day on Io's inner face. How well we knew that! Yet we had to look.

Quickly we transferred the supplies and installed the new drive-jet. This one was much larger and heavier than the old one, and was fashioned in a circle. It would blast a ring of fire, or more properly a tube of fire, surrounding the rear air lock. It was securely fastened in place; we would not be able to move it to the bubble equator to institute spin in space. But for that we still had the old, little, single-jet drive, which we could store near the lock inside when not in use. 'Be careful not to short the lead wires when it's inside!' the technician warned us. 'It will jet in air as readily as in space, and you wouldn't want that to happen.' Yes, we were sure we wouldn't!

The technician finished and bade us farewell. The locks sealed and the two bubbles separated. Then both took off and floated low across the hellish surface of the planet, looking for a trail.

There was nothing. Our own trail of the morning had been obliterated, of course, and no other evidence of life showed. Sulphur was condensing on the mountain slopes and settling like snow on the plains below, leaving clear spaces around the active volcanoes. New tracks should have been evident in that fresh snow. The second party of women was gone with no more trace than the first. Killer Io had had another feast.

'We did not know how bad it was!' Señora Martínez said tearfully.

None of us had known.

At length the second bubble parted company with us, having done what it could.

My memory of this period becomes hazy. Spirit and I sat in the cell our mother had used, trying vainly to comfort each other, to ease our common loss. Helse brought us food from time to time, but left us mostly alone. It had been terrible when our father died, and numbing when Faith sacrificed herself, but this was the worst – because our mother, Charity Hubris, was all that we had left of our family, except each other. There was an amorphous, intangible ambience of emotion that had to coalesce

238

somewhere, like sulphur dioxide precipitating at night, and now, for each of us, it had no object except the other. That settling out had to be accomplished, but it took time.

When we came out of it a few days later, like two survivors of holocaust, we went about the bubble and took stock. It was a disaster area. We had hardly been alone in our mourning; the children of those other forty-nine women had been coming to similar terms.

Some of them hadn't made it. I had never thought of children as suicidal types, but I could not condemn them for it. Spirit and I had had each other; some of the others had had no siblings. To be entirely alone – I had come near enough to that abyss to comprehend its nature, and I understood. The bodies of those children joined their fathers in cold storage on the hull of the bubble.

So we were spiralling out towards Leda, our only remaining hope, using our strong new jet to accelerate our orbital velocity, which in the normal paradox of such travel caused us to proceed outward at reduced velocity. We knew where we were going, thanks to the spot ephemeris the kindly scientist Mason had printed out for us, and had only to follow instructions to take advantage of the gravity wells of Europea, Ganymede, and Callisto to boost us to much better outward progress. So, even though Leda was a tiny mote, far out from Jupiter, we expected to reach it in a month of floating. This would have been impossible for us before, for Leda's sidereal period is twenty-four days, and we could have taken that long just to catch it once we reached its orbit. But a good drive unit makes a tremendous difference. When one adds a powerful outboard motor to a sailboat, one ceases to worry as much about the wind. We had really become a crude spaceship. In fact, the trip might have been impossible, regardless of schedule, without that new drive. This was because the gravity lenses kept us within the Jupiter ecliptic, the disk of space extending outward from its equator, where the rings lie. But Leda, like all the outer moons, has an inclined orbit, twenty-seven degrees tilted instead of falling within one degree of that plane like the inner moons. So we had to go that far out of the ecliptic or we would never have a chance to align. The scientists had plotted it out for us; otherwise we should have been lost.

Our bubble complement was now ten grown women and seventy-two children, counting Helse and me as children. The women had done an excellent job, but they had been under strain, piloting the bubble and caring for the majority of us who had sunk into the depression of new orphanism. I would have grieved longer, but I saw how selfish that would be. It was time for me to pull my weight.

Helse had been helping all along. Now Spirit and I moved in, taking instruction from Helse, and helping her teach the other children. We learned to take sightings on Jupiter and Ganymede and Callisto, three-dimensionally triangulating our relative position by using the little hand computer the scientists had provided for this purpose, then modifying the gravity lenses to correct our erring course. For our course was never precisely on target by itself; it always had to be adjusted. Naturally we could not simply orient on Leda and jet towards her; Leda not only was not visible from here, she wasn't *there*. She would be there only at the precise date and moment the ephemeris indicated. So we had to take triple sightings on familiar objects in space, get our angles precisely, check the time to the second, use the ephemeris to pinpoint exactly where those three objects were, so we could calculate exactly where *we* were, then calculate how far that deviated from where we should be. Fortunately the scientists had also provided idiot sheets that spelled out the steps in very simple bite-sized statements, complete with blanks for the new figures. We learned to set the degree of thrust of the drive unit, again according to computations. It was a challenge, and in its fashion it was fun; we felt like little spacemen, and we were. Soon the grown women were able to retreat into purely nominal supervision and get some needed rest.

But now we were passing through the mid-reaches, and pirates still clogged the ecliptic. We spied a ship overhauling us and knew it was trouble. We held a quick council of war, and decided to offer no resistance. Normally sex was all the pirates really wanted, and it no longer seemed like a prohibitive price to pay. We would have been glad to have any of the lost women back from Io, if sex was the price of her rescue. What is one act, compared to life?

But Helse took the precaution of changing to her boy costume, and she set up half a dozen of our oldest girl-children, including Spirit, similarly. Then most of us retreated to our cells and left the ten women to do what they had to do. With luck, no one would be hurt, and each woman would not have to service more than two or three or four men.

It came to me then how far our attitudes had progressed, or regressed, in the course of our savage experience. We no longer even expected anything other than piracy and forced sex from strangers, and hardly considered any course of action other than that which would get us through with the smallest loss. The children of the surviving mothers took it for granted that prostitution was the proper course, just as they accepted the cannibalistic consumption of their fathers to abate their hunger. We had suffered more than physical degradation! Yet at the time it seemed right – and in retrospect it still seems right. We did what we had to do. How can that be wrong?

'I should be out there,' Helse muttered as we heard the lock open. 'I'm old enough and God knows I've had experience.'

I reacted with horror. 'Never you!' I breathed. 'I love you!'

'And did you love your mother?' she asked.

I swung my arm up, hitting her. The action was

unpremeditated and the position awkward, so my arm only grazed her head in passing, but I was immediately chagrined. Of course I knew what she meant, as my second thought caught up with my first. I had loved my mother, and let her prostitute herself; why should it be otherwise with Helse? There was an inconsistency in my philosophy.

'I'm sorry,' I whispered.

She smiled wanly and put her arm around me. 'I understand, Hope, I understand. But you must accept that it is not only your family that can make sacrifices for you. That woman at the lava flow threw away her life for us. Those women meeting the pirates now are not our relatives, but they are doing it for us. You must permit me to do for you what I can, and for the others of this bubble.'

She was right, but I could not say it. The thought of some foul pirate embracing her, treating her as the Horse had treated my sister Faith, filled me with a blinding horror. 'I love you!' I repeated, as if that had any logic.

'I know you do, Hope. And I love you. There need be no pretence between us any more. I know you are the one man who would never hurt me.'

Her words filled me with a blaze of emotion that I felt physically in my chest, radiating through my body. I know the biologists say the heart is not the true font of love, that it is all in the mind; I sometimes think biologists doubt that love exists at all. But what I felt was in my breast *and* brain. I leaned over and kissed her, and fire seemed to play about our touching lips.

Then we had to break, for we heard the tramp of pirate feet along the Commons, and if anyone saw us kissing, Helse's masculine ruse would quickly enough be discovered. 'I will never hurt you,' I agreed passionately. And I believed it.

What terrible ironies fate inflicts on us!

They were pirates, all right. We heard their guttural exclamations as they examined our women, who had gone

242

so far as to make themselves as reasonably attractive as possible, donning dresses and loosening their hair. I hated all of this, but knew it was necessary. It was better than the violence and bloodshed that otherwise would come.

These were real brutes. It seemed they weren't interested in acquiescence. They wanted violence. I heard them hitting the women; I heard the screams. I started to get up, to go out there in a fury – but Helse held me back. She was correct, of course, as she had been before, when my mother had been out there. My headstrong reaction was sheer mischief. I settled back, shivering with rage. And I realized that Helse *was* doing service with the older women: it was her chore to keep me out of the action. To save my life, if nothing else, from the consequence of my adolescent folly.

One woman was thrown on the deck immediately above our cell. We heard the thump of her body and that of the pirate who bestrode her, and saw their fuzzy outlines through our ceiling panel. I wished I could slide open the panel and stab a blade upward into the pirate's body.

Then the woman screamed, and it was an ugly sound. She had been terribly hurt! Still Helse held me back, and of course I could not even get out of the cell while the bodies lay astride it. Once more I waited in silent shivering fury, while Helse clung to me and stroked my hair as she might the fur of an aggressive but imperfectly disciplined guard dog.

The pirate finally got up and moved away. We heard screams elsewhere; it sounded as if cells were being opened, children hauled out. Our programme of accommodation, of pacifism, was not working!

Helse issued a stifled scream. I looked at her, startled. There was blood on her shirt.

As I watched in the dim light, I froze for the moment, and watched it dripping down from our access panel. Helse happened to be under it, so had caught the first drops. How bright red that blood was!

We exchanged a horrified glance. The blood had to be coming from the woman who still lay above us, and it could not be the result of any minor scratch. The pirate had stabbed her!

A new scream rent the air, close and loud. 'Spirit!' I cried with instant recognition. The pirates were hauling her out!

This time my rage could not be constrained. I jumped for the panel, shoving it violently aside. Blood dripped down on my head as part of the woman's body sagged into our cell. I had to push her out of the way. I saw her staring eyes and the terrible wound in her side; she had been cut so deeply she had already bled to death, or perhaps her heart had been pierced.

I hauled myself up, my vision tunnelling to only one thing: the pirate. His bloodstained blade was jammed in his waistband, and he was half-lying on the deck, reaching down into Spirit's cell.

He cursed, suddenly slapping his face, and I knew Spirit had used her finger-whip on him. That reminded me of my laser pistol, which I had not thought to have about me, idiot that I was. Now I needed it! Then the pirate scrambled forward, dropping into the cell as I cleared mine.

I dived after him. I caught him about the head, trying to draw it back, trying to choke him, but my strength and weight were too slight. He roared and brought a hairy hand back, catching me by the hair, yanking me forward.

'Spirit!' I gasped.

She reacted as if she were a part of my own body. She pounced on the knife at his sash and snatched it out while he was preoccupied with me. This was like our fight with the scion, so long ago – one month ago, an eternity! – but this was more serious. This man would kill us!

I brought up my knees as the pirate pulled me over his head. I clamped my legs against his ears, resisting him. Upside down, I saw Spirit take the knife and survey her prospects. I felt a kind of chill, right through the heat of the

244

combat, at the calculating way she considered. I have said before that I would not care to oppose my little sister when she was really angry; it remains true.

Then she gripped the knife in both hands and stabbed the pirate in the belly.

He grunted and let go of me. He grabbed at Spirit, but she drew back as far as she could in the cell, jerking out the knife so as to let him bleed. The pirate roared, stalking her, evidently not seriously damaged, or at least not sufficiently aware of it. What brutes these men were!

I knew the noise could summon his companions. They would ignore the screams of women and children, knowing they were merely victims, but the pirates might come to the aid of one of their own in trouble. We had to shut this one up until we got him safely dead!

I tried to circle his bull neck again, but he threw me against the wall. That distraction, however, laid him open to attack again. Spirit launched herself, her feet pushing off violently from the walls of the corner, her two-handed knife spearing towards the pirate's face. He saw it coming and reared back, trying to protect his eyes – but there really is little room to manoeuvre in a cubed cell, and he banged into the wall, and though the knife missed, I grabbed him once more by the head.

Spirit thrust again – this time for the throat. She scored, for there was nothing weak or halting about her fighting nature, once aroused. The blade slashed into the exposed neck, cutting it open from front to side, digging deeply.

Blood spurted out in a horrendous red jet. She had severed not only the jugular vein, but one of the deeply buried carotid arteries.

The pirate collapsed. There was not much else he could do, in the circumstance. I extricated myself from his body and took the knife from Spirit's lax hand and shoved her up and out of the panel exit. There was blood on her, of course – but there was blood everywhere.

It was chaos on the Commons; no one noticed us. I got us both out and slid the panel closed. Then I hauled the woman's body over, laying it across the panel, sealing off that cell. Then I shoved Spirit down with Helse and jumped in myself, and slid the panel closed. 'If anyone looks, play dead!' I snapped.

We played dead anyway, the three of us. It wasn't hard to do, for we were smeared with the gore of the woman and the pirate. Spirit was sobbing, for she was not yet so hardened to the new reality that she could slaughter a man without reaction, but she was fairly quiet about it and I knew she could stifle it the rest of the way if the panel opened. She could do what she had to do; she had always been the best at that, in our family. I held one of her hands and Helse held the other, lending her what little emotional support we could. We all knew the pirate had deserved it; that he was a murderer who had raped and killed, virtually simultaneously, one of our women who had offered him no resistance; that he had then tried to get at Spirit for similar atrocity; and that she had slain him in self-defence. Still, she had killed him, and she was only a twelve-year-old female child. Justification did not make it easy for her.

Time passed and and the bedlam above diminished. No one looked in, though we cringed in fear as footsteps passed close. Eventually the pirates departed and disconnected their ship. It was over.

Apparently that cut-throat crew was so disorganized that the pirates didn't even make a count of their departing number. Or maybe they were used to taking losses and simply didn't care.

I climbed out. It was even worse than I had feared. All ten women were dead. The pirates had callously raped and murdered them, apparently as a matter of course, leaving no adult witnesses. Non-resistance had been disaster this time; we might as well have fought them from the outset, at least taking more of them with us. As it was, they had made a literal wreckage of our bubble, and of our hopes for sanctuary. Panels were broken, walls were dented, and food packs were ripped open and strewn about the Commons, the crumbs soaking up some of the blood that puddled around the equatorial region.

Helse joined me. Spirit, overcome by the horror of the killing she had done, remained in the cell. I would return to her as soon as I could; right now I had to determine the extent of our losses. I didn't know whether anyone survived, besides the three of us, or whether we had any supplies remaining, or whether our equipment still functioned. In short, whether we had any reasonable prospect for continued survival.

More of us had survived than I had thought at first. Other children had been overlooked in their cells, and others had thought to play dead. Even so, twenty-seven children had died. Our total number was down to forty-five, all children, some of them in the almost-suicidal reaction to being newly orphaned. Only one pirate was dead, the one Spirit and I had killed.

I knew Spirit would be missing or dead now, if we had not dealt with that brute; I was shaken but had no honest regret for what we had done. As it was, we had been lucky. Lucky we had managed to kill him, and lucky we had been able to conceal his body and ourselves. It had been a narrow and ugly thing, amidst the battlefield carnage that was our bubble.

We held an impromptu, crude service of mourning, then 'buried' the bodies on the hull, bagged with the men. Helse and I did most of it; we were now the two oldest survivors. In addition, we were relatively unscathed by this latest slaughter, odd as it may seem to say it. My parents and older sister had been lost before, so I had a head start on adjusting, while Helse had always been alone in the bubble. The children who had just lost their last parent had a more immediate shock to bear. How well I understood!

There is no need to dwell on what followed. When the necessary cleaning up was done and our supplies were surveyed, I assumed the leadership of the bubble. It wasn't that I was any natural leader; it was that there was no one else. Helse was the oldest, but she was no leader, and the children somehow expected the commands to issue from a man or a grandmother. They would follow me.

I assigned the most competent surviving children to navigation duty; they did know how to do it, once their shock of emotion backed off. I assigned others to mess duty, handing out the food packs. There were enough of these; though a number had been destroyed in wanton vandalism by the pirates, our diminished number more than made up the difference. But this was no casual assignment, because I knew and they knew that if the rations ran short again, these would be the ones to select and haul and thaw and carve and cook the meat. They had to be tough, realistic kids, and they needed time to prepare themselves.

The most important thing I was doing was unspoken. I was trying to establish a viable social order. These orphans had to have something tangible and social to relate to, to replace their lost families. Now we had a group family, much tighter than before, because the need was greater than before, with discipline and caring and stability, and that helped them to survive emotionally as well as physically. It was my talent, coming into its own at last, exerted as a life-promoting force. I tried to come to understand the specific needs of each member of our family, and to accommodate that need as well as was possible. When a child cried, someone was always there to hold his hand or hug him or talk to him; when a child stumbled, someone always came to help him up. When he laughed, someone laughed with him; when he mourned, someone mourned with him. When he went to the head, someone accompanied him, for the accommodations were sized for adults, so a child alone could have trouble. Helse and I took turns telling stories, inventing whatever fantasies seemed most to appeal, for there is immense comfort in group story-telling, as our prehistoric ancestors knew. Many of us took to sleeping on the Commons floor, for it got lonely at night in the individual cells. Sometimes we formed big circles, and slept holding hands in a sort of daisy chain. Even for me, that helped; my dreams were less nightmarish when I felt the touch of other hands in mine.

It worked amazingly well. In hours, it seemed, we had become fused into a desperately close community. We knew this was all that lay between us and the physical and social void beyond.

We survived. But what would we do when the next pirates came? When would it end?

16

Violation Of Trust

Jupiter Ecliptic 17-3-'15 – We planned cynically for the next pirates. We knew, now, that pirates were as random and savage and uncaring as sulphur volcanoes and should be treated with similar dispassionate respect. If we wanted to live and to reach sanctuary at Leda, we would have to accommodate that reality. We had a gauntlet to run, and we could not avoid it, so we had to prepare for it.

We were children – but we had lost our parents and siblings to pirates. The realities of space had forced themselves upon us in most brutal fashion. We were children who had been bloodied. I repeat this point, perhaps, in a kind of explanation or apology for the cynicism of the things we contemplated, which may disturb people who have not experienced what we had. We had, I believe it is fair to say, as fair a notion of necessity as any space crew of any age could.

We concocted plans, discussed them, and acted them out in little playlets, searching for flaws, for we knew any error or oversight could be fatal. This became, really, part of our therapy; instead of telling stories, now we were developing scenarios. The important thing is that we did this together, giving respect to all views, making even the smallest child feel important – for, indeed, the smallest *was* important.

We considered attacking pirates with knives, but realized that only a few men would get cut before the others destroyed us. We were, after all, children, and could not fight adults on any even basis, and any delusion that we could would be fatal. We thought of poisoning their food and/or water – but had no poison, and anyway, pirates didn't come to eat and drink, they came to rape and kill.

In retrospect, I marvel at the psychology of the pirates. Apparently, civilized restraints break down the moment civilized enforcement ends, at least for certain types of men. They raid and destroy simply because they enjoy pillaging and hurting, and in space the refugees are easy targets. I find it very difficult to sympathize with such an attitude, but at least I think I understand it now. The pirates are that dreg of society that is least civilized, and that mankind as a whole would be best off without. Mighty Jupiter preferred to treat the refugees as if *they* were such dregs, but that was because the refugees *were* easy targets – helpless – while the pirates would have been more difficult to deal with.

I was to spend long hours considering mechanisms to rid our species of the pirate trash, and if ever I have the means to implement any such notions, I shall do so, to whatever extent I am able. This is my promise to myself.

We went over every kind of defence, both likely and unlikely. We finally settled on a three-stage programme.

Stage one: We would present ourselves as sweet, innocent orphan children and beg the pirates not to hurt us. If they were nice, or at least not homicidal, all would be well. After all, the scientists on Io had been nice; we could not assume with absolute conviction that every man in space was evil. Many of the children did not really believe that, but they grudgingly accepted the hypothesis because Helse argued the case so feelingly, and Helse in her female dress was very pretty. I had thought appreciation of prettiness was an adult trait, but revised my thinking when I saw how she swayed even the smallest children. In fantasy tales the pretty girl is always good, and children do seem to take that on faith though it is of course suspect.

Stage two: If they were not nice (as seemed the overwhelming likelihood) and sought to kidnap, rape, or

251

kill any of us, or got angry when we rejected their candy (we had learned that lesson well!), Spirit would give a signal. She would blow a whistle provided her, at which point every child would instantly draw a knife or nail or other sharp instrument and plunge it at the eyes or nearest other vulnerable region of the nearest pirate. If that succeeded, every pirate would be blind or castrated and presumably helpless; then we could consider what to do next. Maybe we would have to kill them, but we didn't have to make that decision right now. We drilled on this, stabbing at pirate-shaped-and-sized dummies; even our smallest children could run a mean spike into a crotch. This was not the same as fighting pirates, which we knew to be hopeless; this was to be a surprise manoeuvre, occurring explosively. Two seconds after that whistle blew, a dozen or more pirates would be hurting and normally no more than that came aboard at one time.

Stage three: If for some reason we failed to incapacitate the pirates – and, realistically, we deemed our chances to be no better than fifty per cent – and the situation was critical, we would back off and Helse would say to me 'Do it!' and I would go out the second air lock, with Spirit, or whoever else was handy, standing by to cut off the drive for the few seconds I'd need to get past the ring of fire. I would make my way around the outside hull to a particular refuse-tank release bolt that had been weakened, and knock it off. That would not only release the refuse, it would empty the bubble of air – because we would have jammed the automatic safety valve open.

That would finish the pirates. It would also finish any of us who weren't in suits. So at Helse's signal, all others would have to go to their cells and get suited in a hurry. Since the pirates wouldn't have their suits in the bubble (we laughed uproariously at the joke we adapted about the pirate trying to rape a girl while in a space suit; what kind of attachment would that suit have to have? – juvenile humour gets quite fundamental), even if they caught on, they wouldn't have time to stop it. Their only recourse would be to flee immediately back to their ship and slam the air lock closed. We would try to block the lock open – just a few seconds delay in closure would be all we would need – but if we failed in that, we still would have saved ourselves from a larger disaster.

We liked this plan so well we almost hoped for an early chance to test it. We spent hours perfecting the details. Spirit had to be suited from the outset, because, though she could cut off the drive from the inside – there was a simple make/break switch – to let me out, she would not be able to do it again to let me in unless she herself survived the vacuum inside. I had to use the rear lock, because the front one might be encumbered by the pirate ship. I really didn't want anyone else performing this particular office, because if there were any error of timing and the drive came on again while I was crossing its deadly ring, I would be cleanly sliced into pieces. I trusted Spirit to make no error; I wasn't quite sure of anyone else. Spirit had always been my most reliable support, even before we started this terrible voyage.

We rehearsed all three stages until we had them down pat. We timed the last stage, so we knew exactly how long people would have to get into their suits once I used the air lock. We all got very quick about suiting up. Those suits now hung on hooks in each cell, perpetually available, and nobody touched another person's suit. We had to play it close enough to take out the pirates, and that was close indeed. A thirty-second delay in suiting could prove fatal.

There were fairly sophisticated wrinkles that we worked out. Chief among these was my physical position. I had to have my suit on a stand by the lock, so that Helse could give me the signal from the Commons. To conceal my presence, we made a baffle before the rear lock and decorated it with coloured tassles lovingly fashioned of waste paper, so it looked as if we were playing a childish game. My suit, too, was decorated so that it looked fake. Some of the littlest kids showed surprising ingenuity in the details.

So we were ready – while those of us with most sense ardently hoped that we would never come to stages two or three. If the pirates missed us, and we made it unscathed to Leda – but few of us really believed that would happen.

For a time, however, it seemed we would indeed be lucky. We floated on for several days, passing the orbit of Callisto, and no pirates came. Our rehearsals became precise, then perfunctory. We were now departing the Jupiter ecliptic, following the schedule set up by the Io scientists. Almost, I resented the time we had spent, planning and rehearsing, instead of finishing our mourning. But it would certainly be best if we never saw another pirate.

We relaxed by gradual stages. Helse, as the oldest surviving female, became a den mother, seeing to the needs of the smaller children within the framework of the community family and counselling some of the larger ones. And I, as the oldest male, found myself becoming a father figure. I resisted this aspect at first, until Helse explained to me the need of these children for someone to play this role. We could not have a group family without a father; the thing did not set right. 'Do it,' she told me. 'It must be done, and you are the one. You set up the community family, you laboured to make it work; you are indeed the father of it.'

'How can I be a father, when I'm not even married?' I temporized, half in humour. But as I said it, I felt a catch in my being. Marriage . . .

Things were going smoothly – almost too smoothly, since the distractions of our serious preparations tended to abate our horror of recent losses – and there was no present need for us to be on duty. The crew of kids was performing well enough, and it was important that they be permitted to exercise this responsibility. None of us could know who might be eliminated in the next pirate raid, so the skills had to be distributed throughout our group.

We were not needed, at the moment, on duty. Helse guided me to our cell. 'You could be,' she said when we were private.

'Could be what?' I knew she had something in mind, but I wanted her to express it.

'A father.'

I smiled. 'A father? I'm only fifteen!'

'You have proved you are old enough. I could be pregnant.'

'Pregnant!' That particular aspect had never occurred to me. I shared the ordinary adolescent's self-imposed unawareness of the natural consequence of sex. Nature does not require awarenesss, merely performance.

She laughed. 'I didn't say I was, Hope. Just that I could be. That it is possible. You could be a father.'

She was right. 'I'm not ready,' I said. 'But for you – oh, Helse, I want you forever!'

'And I want you,' she said. 'Hope, I've never dared to love before, but now I do. Now I do! I don't care that you're younger than I am, or that we were thrown together randomly. We've been through more together than any regular couple, and when you risked your life for me on Io I knew, really knew, that I could trust you, and – '

I realized that she was leading up to something, and I had a notion what, and I wanted very much to have it, but still I wanted her to say it. 'What do you mean?'

'Hope, I want to get married.'

That was what I had waited for but still I reacted carefully. 'You mean an *ad hoc* marriage, like the ones in the military sevice?'

'If you want.'

That was her way of suggesting I try another tack. 'This

isn't the military service.'

'True.'

'I'd prefer a civilian marriage.'

'Yes.' That was her way of agreeing.

'We could arrange a suitable term – '

'If you wish.'

I cut it short, unable to hold back any longer. 'What do *you* want, Helse? I want anything you want.'

'Till death do us part.'

When Helse loved, I realized, she loved completely. Now she was testing my love. I hardly felt worthy, but I was willing. I knew I loved her absolutely, and would never love another like this. 'Till death do us part,' I agreed, and suffered a momentary spell of dizziness, awed by the profundity of the commitment. There were all kinds and lengths of marriages, and this was the most binding.

'Oh, let's do it now!' she exclaimed.

'Well, it wouldn't be official without a priest,' I said.

She kissed me, and my head spun again. 'We'll do it by common law,' she said. 'We can have a wedding. It will be like a party for the children. They can rehearse it and take parts – and it will entertain the group while we travel, and –' Here she stopped and kissed me again, passionately. I had never before seen her so turned on, and I liked it. Her love had been well worth waiting for. 'Maybe I had to love a younger man,' she said. 'I've always been used by older men, so I can't relate to them the same way. But you – you're a virgin boy, and you're all mine.'

'I'm yours,' I agreed, overflowing with love for her. I suppose her description of me as a virgin boy might have been taken as uncomplimentary, yet I knew she didn't mean it to be so, and it was true. She had introduced me to love, in all its forms outside the family love I had grown up with. I don't know whether the harshness of our situation in the bubble had the effect of intensifying my emotion or whether I would have loved her as ardently anyway, but certainly this was the most positive emotion of which my being was capable. Helse was older and far more experienced – but I was the first man she had loved this way, and that was enough.

'And I'm yours,' she said. 'I will be Helse Hubris.' The cumbersome double surnaming of our culture had gradually faded out in favour of the Jupiter custom of using the masculine surname only.

'Helse Hubris,' I agreed, liking the alliteration, liking the meaning, liking every apect of it.

You might think we would have made love then, but we did not. It could only have distracted us from the greater excitement of our engagement. Sex had always had a different meaning for us; this was more vital.

We fetched Spirit and put her in charge of operations. She was delighted to participate. She had, it seemed, got over her earlier jealousy of Helse, realizing that Helse was no threat to our brother-sister relationship. Indeed Helse was not; she had stabilized me during each crisis, so that I was better able to help others, including Spirit. Yet I suspect I misjudged the nuances of Spirit's acceptance, though I doubt I will ever be certain in what way. The same emotional involvement that prevented me from using my talent to judge Helse properly also interfered with my judgments of Spirit. Of course I *knew* Spirit; she was my sister and closest companion, and would never betray me in any way; that was never in question. Still, there may have been something.

The kids set it up with gusto. They assembled stray bits of cloth into a wedding gown for Helse, and they made plans for a big cake. These seemingly simple things were not simple in the bubble! A choir formed and practised singing the wedding march. The problem of the lack of a priest was solved by working out a ceremony in which the two of us would exchange vows ourselves, in the manner of the old Quaker religion, each speaking his or her piece, and sealing the vow with a kiss. That public kiss was very important; the children planned to applaud it. I found myself getting genuinely nervous; they were making it too real!

Too real? That isn't what I meant to convey. This was ultimately real. This was the most solemn commitment of our lives. Maybe what I meant was that I did not want it to become too much of a show, as if it were *not* genuine. But weddings, as I learned, are not just for the nuptial couple; the crowd must have its satisfaction too.

It took several days to put it all together, and several major rehearsals. Spirit insisted that every single detail be *right*. We worked up to full dress rehearsals, orchestrating it right through to the kiss. That kiss had to be right, too; the imps made us do it over and over, just so, not too long or too brief, too intimate or too distant. They even practised their applause. Kids, I learned the hard way (though I really didn't mind this particular exercise, despite Helse's tendency to break up with mirth in the middle of it), are the worst sticklers in the universe for specific detail.

I wondered just what the difference was between a full dress rehearsal, with all the participants, and the official ceremony, but knew better than to raise that question. I suppose it was merely a matter of designation: This one is a rehearsal, that one is the production. Besides, this was an excellent distraction from the tedium and grief we all would otherwise have had time to dwell on. This was more than a wedding or a rehearsal for same; it was group therapy. So we didn't push the date; we let the kids extend the rehearsals as long as they had a mind to.

Helse looked wonderful in her home-fashioned patch-work wedding dress. She would have looked good to me in rags, though. I was in my space suit. You see, no one knew how to make a man's formal wedding outfit, so Spirit, in her authoritative office of manager, decreed that one suit was as good as another and insisted that I be garbed as a space captain on duty. I would tilt it back for the nuptial osculation. I felt like an ancient knight in armour, especially since the suit was decorated for camouflage. Embracing her was awkward, not nearly as pleasant as it had been in non-dress rehearsal, where her body was all soft and feminine against mine. And the inordinate laughter, when one brat advised me to remove the suit on the wedding night because it didn't have the necessary attachment – that actually made me blush, which set the little fiends off anew. But anything to make the kids happy! And though I protested the unnecessary elaboration, it was therapy for me too. It made me really believe that Helse would be mine forever.

We were amidst the umpteenth such rehearsal, and I had just noticed that some mischief-maker had pinned a label saying HELSE HUBRIS to the gown so she would be able to remember her new name when the time came, when our lookout sounded the alarm. 'Ship ahoy!'

I felt dread. 'Suit up!' I told Spirit, and she scurried off to do it. I was already suited, coincidentally; that was the lone silver lining in this cloud. The other kids milled about, uncertain what frame of mind to be in: festive or frightened. But soon they decided on both: Each fetched his or her weapon, concealed it in the costume, then returned to the wedding rehearsal. This was *stage one*, innocent children playing.

Fine for them, but I wasn't satisfied. 'Get suited!' I called to Helse.

But someone needed to keep the children organized while Spirit and I were busy with the air lock, so Helse elected to remain in her wedding dress. If a pirate attacked her, Spirit would blow the whistle. I didn't like this, as Helse in that gown was entirely too attractive, but understood the need. Even so, I would have argued, but there simply wasn't time. I was the nominal leader of the bubble, but already I had learned that leadership exists largely with the consent of the followers, and that compromise is essential, and that the true will of the majority must always be taken seriously. So I sealed up my suit, and made sure Spirit was ready to seal hers after blowing her whistle, if it came to that. We were ready for whatever might come.

The ship closed on us, matched velocities, and connected to our front portal. As I watched, it occurred to me that the mechanism of a ship and a bubble was very like that of a man and a woman. The ship was long and slender, resembling a phallus, while the bubble was round in the manner of aspects of a woman. And all too often the roles became ferociously literal.

The ship took hold and made an entry, I thought as I heard the clang of merging locks. The bubble had to receive. Sometimes this connection was pleasant for both parties, but sometimes disaster for the bubble. Perhaps there is a fundamental parallelism in all things, if we could but perceive it.

The air lock opened and the men came in – and they did look like pirates. I stood behind the baffle, watching, my hands sweating inside the gauntlets of the suit. Spirit had her hand on the whistle. How well we knew how serious this could be!

'What have we here?' the lead intruder demanded. He could have passed for Redbeard.

'We are children, seeking sanctuary,' Helse informed him prettily. 'Our parents were killed by horrible pirates. We are orphans in the void.' I hoped she wasn't overdoing it, though her words were literally true for everyone except herself. I had my helmet on, but in the ambience of air could hear reasonably well. I could also see them, by peering through the partially filled netting of the doughnut hole that was between us.

The man eyed her appraisingly. This was the first time Helse had stood before a stranger to the bubble in her female guise. Oh, I worried! 'No women except you?'

'None,' she assured him innocently.

The man consulted the one beside him, who could have passed for Bluebeard. 'Slim pickings here. What's the current market for children?'

'There's connections for small ones,' Bluebeard said. 'And girls of any age are in demand. I'd say, take all the girls and dump the boys.'

'Good enough.' Redbeard strode towards Helse. 'But this one we'll use ourselves, here and now.'

They were pirates, all right. I had a momentary vision of my sister Faith, spread out by the Horse. Spirit blew the whistle; she had probably seen the same vision. We would not let Helse suffer that fate!

Pandemonium erupted. The children drew their weapons and swarmed over the pirates. Their reactions were amazingly swift and sure. Maybe the smaller bodies of children permit faster interplay of the nervous systems. Never, in all the entertainment projections I have viewed in Maraud, including historical recreations of ancient wars, have I seen such a savage turn of events. Those children were absolutely vicious. It was as if all the pain and horror of the past month was being released in fifteen seconds.

They scored. Oh, they scored! In a moment the men were screaming, and blood was flowing. Blinded, some men staggered around, hands at their faces, the blood leaking through their fingers. Others dropped to the deck, clasping their crotches. Redbeard reeled back, blood cascading from the side of his head where his ear had been; he had suffered a near miss. Three children stalked him like rabid puppies, their knives raised, their teeth gleaming. It was nightmare, but it seemed that we had won. I had underestimated the effectiveness of our ploy.

But we had reckoned without the resources of the pirate ship. A new man appeared in the lock, carrying a solid, squat device. 'Take him out!' Spirit screamed. 'Now!'

Half a dozen children turned, well understanding the

threat of an unknown weapon. We needed no pacifier here! They charged the new pirate like little kamikazes.

But he was ready. He pulled the trigger, and the thing burped.

Something splatted against the body of the nearest charging child. It looked like brown taffy, but it spread out tentacles as it struck, wrapping around the body, pinning the limbs. The child fell, bound by strong elastic bands.

Three other children were close. The taffy gun burped again, catching each, and the elastic enfolded each. One child tried to cut the strands that enclosed him, but there were too many; though he severed two, his arm remained bound by those he couldn't reach. In time he might have worked his way loose, but everything was happening in seconds. This was a personnel control device, incapacitating without hurting, and it was effective.

The pirate swung the taffy gun around, and the children everywhere paused, realizing that they were overmatched.

More men appeared from the pirate ship. 'Take your pick,' the one with the gun said to them. 'No sense wasting taffy on brats we're going to kill anyway.'

The other men drew knives and advanced on the children. None of them seemed to care about the wounded pirates of the first wave, who were moaning and, in some cases, dying. Helse turned to face me. 'Do it, Hope!' she cried, and bolted for our cell, where her suit was.

The pirate at the air lock aimed his gun and fired. Helse fell, wrapped in taffy. Naturally they intended to salvage her!

I started back from the rear lock, appalled. But Helse screamed from the floor: 'Do it! Don't wait for me! Do it, or we'll all die!'

I knew she was right. The other children were scurrying for their suits, and the new pirates were starting after them, wary about ambush-traps. I had to do my part, and do it immediately, or everything would be lost. I could not fight off the pirates here, or even rescue Helse. I didn't even have my laser pistol, with which I might have taken out the pirate with the taffy gun; then we could have turned it against the other pirates and – but this was foolish dreaming. Already the brutes were methodically stabbing the children they had caught. We were at war.

I entered the lock, glancing at Spirit. Grimly she nodded, standing beside the old drive unit, her hand near the switch for the new one. She was ready.

Practice had made perfect. Quickly I worked the lock and moved out onto the hull, anchored by my safety line. I was afraid of the void, but I had rehearsed this and knew exactly what I was doing. I braced myself and the drive cut off on schedule, and I dived across and anchored my rope on the nearest eyelet. The drive came on again, a wall of flame as seen from this vantage; Spirit's timing was perfect. Now no one could follow me or stop me. The tricky part was past.

I clambered around the hull, carrying my massive wrench. Then I was at the key tank, exactly as rehearsed. I lifted the wrench, ready to bash off the one not holding it.

I froze. The realization hit me now with full force: *Helse was not in her suit.* Caught by the taffy, she could not get to it. If I let the air out of the bubble, she would die.

But if I didn't do this, we would be subject to the will of the pirates. Last time they had raped *and* killed.

I visualized a pirate raping Helse, as the Horse had raped my sister Faith. Then my mind's eye saw Bluebeard slitting Helse's throat. I knew this was not only possible, but likely.

'Helse, forgive me!' I cried in my helmet. Then I swung with all my clumsy force, half hoping it wouldn't work.

The wrench caught the nut squarely and bashed it off. The tank, released without first having its pressure abated, crashed out of its slot like a missile being fired. I was thrown back and flew out into space myself. This I hadn't rehearsed, of course; I had always stopped short of the final bash.

17

Female Mystique

Space 22-3-'15 – Spirit was tending me when I woke. I clutched at her arm. 'Was it all a dream?' I demanded desperately.

'I wish I could lie to you, to give you ease, my brother,' Spirit said. I saw the marks of tears on her face, and on her soul. 'It was no dream.'

'Helse – '

'Dead.'

The confirmation was no longer a shock; I had known my love was dead. I had killed her.

'Hope, you must seal it off, the way you did for the others. We need you to pull us through. Otherwise Helse's sacrifice is for nothing. Remember, she told you to do it. She knew.'

There was only one thing worse than losing Helse, and that was losing what she had fought for. She had died as bravely as any of the other women had. She had indeed known, and had not faltered.

I cast about for something to lean on that would support my failing equilibrium, and found it in an oath:

'I shall extirpate piracy from humanity,' I swore.

I had not honoured my oath never to hurt Helse, but if I lived, I would somehow honour this one. I had no notion how or when, but I would do it.

From that point I strengthened. Helse had been my support before; now it was Spirit. Spirit was stronger than I. I do not pretend this was steady or sensible; I gyrated wildly. But when I screamed with grief, Spirit understood, and when I was lucid she talked with me, and when I could function, she encouraged me. My oath and Spirit; these were the pillars of stability during my nightmare sequence. The wildest tempests of my confusion and grief beat about these pillars and did not topple them, and in time I was able to function again.

I may be presenting this as more coherent than it was. I am human; I seek to flatter myself and tend to avoid what damages my self-image, however much I try to be objective. So if this narrative is a construct of favourable distortions, it is as it must be in order to exist at all. This narrative is itself therapy, clarifying the elements of my existence and thereby enabling me to accept them with less abrasion than otherwise. My talent is judgment of others; to this degree I try to judge myself, however suspect my result may be. So I may record a somewhat enhanced version of my nadir, and wish it had been so. Without a certain amount of beneficial illusion, very few people would survive.

I put away my grief for necessary periods and did what had to be done, and gradually these portions of equilibrium lengthened. I helped the survivors bury the dead on the hull, all except Helse; others did that, for I could not look upon her ravaged face. They buried her in her wedding gown, saving only the little cloth tag with the name HELSE HUBRIS; that they gave to me as the final physical memento. Helse had loved me at the last; this tag was the evidence of that, and its value magnified accordingly. O my Love, my Love! It was not to save yourself you died, it was to save me, for you were not afraid of rape but of my wild reaction to it. And so I killed you, indirectly as well as directly, because you knew me too well, too well. I thought I loved you with the ultimate devotion possible, but your capacity was greater than mine, and your love was better than mine.

We cleaned up the blood and excrements of explosive decompression. Very little of it had escaped the bubble, for the aperture of loss had been narrow, not permitting the egress of substantial solid bodies. Little items like pencils and combs were lost; bodies and food packs remained. This was messy but just as well, for we needed our supplies.

Spirit, of course, had unjammed the valve in the head, and allowed the air tanks to represssure the bubble before she went out to haul me in on my line from where I dangled in space. She had cut the drive for that duration, so that she could work alone. I marvel still at her courage and competence in that adversity; I owe my life as well as my equilibrium to her. She was, in this instance, a twelve-year-old adult.

Only eight of us survived: Spirit and me and those six children who had reached their suits in time. I remember their names but prefer to leave them anonymous; I do not care to put a name to each individual aspect of my pain.

Our rehearsed plan had gone astray because of the interference of the pirates; I don't know how we could have prevented that, since we had no knowledge of the taffy gun. Perhaps I should have anticipated the unexpected and kept my laser pistol ready. But it had very little charge left, and the crisis occurred so suddenly, interrupting our wedding rehearsal – I don't even know whether such excuses are valid. Certainly I could have done more, had I thought it through better. Still, our final stage had been effective.

That was another part of the guilt I bore: I had killed more children than the pirates had. As nearly as we could figure it, they had slaughtered fifteen; the vacuum had strangled twenty-two.

But we had taken the pirate ship with us. Their air lock had been locked to ours, fixed open; our vacuum had become theirs. All forty-five pirates were dead. Their losses were greater than ours. Oh, yes, we had struck back – but it had been a Pyrrhic victory. We could not afford another such battle.

After we cleaned out our dead and said what perfunctory

services for them we could, we did the same for the pirate dead – with less honour. We dumped them in a chamber of their ship. Then we searched that ship throughout.

Much of it was ordinary stuff, clothing, food, knick-knacks. But some of it was booty from other vessels: gold, precious stones, spices, fine watches, and small sealed containers marked with letters of the alphabet: C, H, L, A.

I considered the last, trying to figure out what the letters might stand for. But Spirit solved it. 'Drugs' she exclaimed. 'Of course pirates are into the illegal drug trade! These letters stand for English abbreviations: Cocaine, Heroin, LSD, Angel Dust.'

Now I saw it. 'Their real business would be shipping this stuff. They only raid bubbles like ours for entertainment.'

She was uncertain. 'Why mess with poor refugees, when they can buy anything they want? They obviously are rich.'

Excellent question! It put me in mind of Helse's QYV mystery.

O, Helse! I reeled.

Spirit steadied me, and I fought back to sanity. Helse had been used to convey a message of some kind, perhaps to a pirate – and here were pirates shipping drugs and seeking children. Was there a connection?

'We can go back to the bubble.' Spirit suggested, mindful of my fadeout.

'No, we'd better finish this job,' I said. Only two of the other children were with us here; the remaining four were sleep-suffering in their cells. All of us understood that need! They had lost siblings and close friends and most of their peer group, and the pseudo-family structure we had so carefully nurtured had been shattered. Helse had become like a mother to them – Helse, Helse! – and so they had been orphaned again, when already vulnerable. Oh yes I knew that feeling! But I had to function, and I had in Spirit a support of amazing strength, a child/woman who perhaps at this stage was more truly our leader than was I.

'We need to take what supplies we need and cast loose; we don't know how to operate this ship.'

'Supplies? We don't need mind-zonking drugs!'

'Weapons,' I said. 'We are so few, now, we must have good weapons. And replacement oxygen tanks, for ours have been depleted by the decompression.'

'Oh, yes,' she agreed, seeing it.

We located weapons, including another taffy gun – the other had been swept into the head by the decompression and broken – and brought back to the bubble several good laser pistols and a whole pile of good fighting knives. We found oxygen and nitrogen tanks, and plenty of fresh water. Then we spied food supplies, better and more varied than ours. This derelict ship was a real mine of useful things!

We were now well set – except that at this point we were just a few children, ranged against what seemed like a universe of pirates. The great majority of our refugee companions who had set out for a better world had found death instead. Even if we arrived at Leda and gained sanctuary without further difficulty, it would hardly be worth it for the survivors, let alone the non-survivors. True success was now beyond our reach – thanks to the pirates.

I remembered my oath: to extirpate all pirates. They surely deserved obliteration.

We also discovered a holo projector and a small library of cartridges. This was an excellent find; we could have entertainment to distract us from the horrors of our memories. We trundled the projector into the bubble.

Finally we found a lifeboat, fully stocked. We could certainly use this! We lacked the expertise to operate it, but we would have time to study and experiment. We couldn't move it by hand, so we used rope to tie it to the bubble, hoping to haul it clear of the pirate ship when we separated. We had to string our lines so that they did not intercept the blast of the drive unit; we used three, hooked all around our equator, each trailing back a hundred metres to intersect at the lifeboat. If that didn't work, then it didn't work.

At last we cut loose. The pirate ship was now adrift, its life-support facilities repressuring it automatically and warming it when the air lock sealed, but with no living men aboard. There would be a stink in there soon enough! Maybe it would drift forever in space – or maybe some other ship would discover it. Then they might ponder the mystery of an operative ship that had lost its entire crew to suffocation. We knew that such mystery ships had been found before, for we had seen stories about them; now we had an answer. In this one case, the rabbit had killed the wolf.

We moved on through space alone, trailing the lifecraft on its triple tether. I had to do more of the work of maintenance and navigation, for we had lost key personnel. I had a lot of learning to do, but that was good, for it kept me almost too busy to think.

The kids eagerly set up the holo projector and tried a cartridge marked *Animal Fun*. We thought it might be a juvenile fantasy about animals, or a documentary on the ways of wildlife as it once had been on unspoiled Earth. Either way, excellent distraction for children.

The scene formed, a three-dimensional image in air that could be viewed from any side. It was a comely young woman and a donkey. Good enough; the riding of animals was a popular subject with children; the few equine animals on Callisto were always in great demand for two-minute rides.

But in a moment the kids' delight turned to dismay. I left my position by the lens control to see what was the matter.

The woman in the image had stripped naked, and – well, no need to detail it further. It was a porn show. I should have realized that pirates would stock that sort. If our bubble had been filled with animals instead of people, the brutes would have been raping and killing the animals,

270

hardly noticing the difference. 'Turn it off,' I said, disgusted. 'Check all through the cartridges. Maybe there are some regular family shows in the pile.'

But now that the children realized that this was susposed to be forbidden adult material, they got interested. They wanted to know exactly how a woman could do it with a donkey, and why she would bother. I gave up and returned to my station, not caring to admit that I was curious too.

Actually, I needed no hard-core holos for my forbidden entertainment. It came to me unbidden when I slept. Some dreams were inchoate, almost formless fragments of horror that seeped out of the locked chamber of my mind like oozing blood and invaded that lonely illuminated spot of consciousness where I huddled. It had been bad when my father died, and when my mother died, but Helse had braced my equilibrium. Now Helse herself was dead, and all the shock of loss she had shielded me against, by interposing her marvellous love, now swept down on me in an avalanche of sulphur.

I tossed about and scrambled and woke – and found the waking nightmare was as bad as the sleeping one. I had come to depend almost completely on Helse, on the love we shared, and she was there no more. I retreated from that reality into sleep – where the oozing blood and sulphur lava were assuming shapes more awful than the shapelessness had been. I screamed again.

I don't know how many times I cycled through it before Helse came. I must have been in an in-between state of consciousness, for I knew she was dead. But she was welcome any way she chose to appear. 'What brings you back?' I inquired almost socially.

'Hope, I finally realized,' she said.

'Realized what?' I asked, knowing this was crazy, that it was no more than a vision like the one involving my father, but so eager for her presence that I clung to whatever shred of interaction it offered.

'About the tattoo. Why it protected me. It identified me as a courier.'

'A courier?' I didn't follow her line of thought.

'I was conveying something to Kife. Something very valuable and secret. So I had his name and the mark, so no one would interfere with me, It is death to mess with a courier, and every criminal knows it. Kife must be very high in the hierarchy of thieves. So I was safer than I thought; I probably didn't need to masquerade as a boy.'

'I'm glad you did,' I said. 'That way, I got to room with you, and to love you.'

'You are the first I loved,' she said. 'But about the tattoo – you can protect yourself too, Hope. Draw the letters on your thigh, and when a pirate attacks you – '

'But I'm no courier!' I protested.

'They won't know that. They won't dare take the chance. I think Kife would destroy anyone who bothered even a fake courier, just to make his point. Of course, then the fake would have to settle with Kife. That might not be fun.'

'What were you carrying?' I asked. 'The man gave you no message – '

'Now I remember something I heard once,' she said, becoming more real and lovely moment by moment. She wore her patchwork wedding dress, and oh, I loved her with an agony of intensity. 'They do not tell the couriers what they carry, so the couriers can't give away the secret. It is carried in little bags that they swallow, which adhere to the lining of the intestine and can only be detached by a certain formula in solution. So when the courier arrives, he or she is given a drink, and the bag is freed and passes on out harmlessly. The bags can hold anything – diamonds, secret code messages, concentrated drugs – but whatever it is, Kife wants it, and only he has the formula to collect it without hurting the courier.'

Now my own memory confirmed what she was saying. I had heard about this long ago and forgotten it. 'So you were engaged in criminal activity,' I cried, appalled. 'Perhaps drug-running!'

'Hope, I didn't know!' she protested.

'Of course you didn't,' I agreed immediately, hating to hurt her even in death. 'Kife used you, exactly as the pirates used the others.'

'They must have fed me the bag while I was unconscious,' she said. 'And when I got to Jupiter, Kife would have collected—' She cut that off. 'I'm glad he won't collect. Don't let him get my body, Hope.'

'I won't let him get your body.' I promised.

'Thank you.' She began to fade.

'Wait!' I cried. 'I must apologize! I promised never to hurt you – but I killed you!'

'I forgive you,' she said, smiling. 'I know you didn't want to kill me.' She faded further.

'Don't go!' I cried, leaping to catch her. 'Stay with me, Helse, to love and be loved!'

That got to her, of course. In life or in death, in reality or in vision, she lived to share love. She reversed her fade and intensified, and became preternaturally natural, and suffered herself to be drawn in to me. I kissed her, and she hesitated, as she often had, being afraid to confess love. But I kissed her more passionately, and then she melted, as was also her way, knowing she could trust me not to betray her.

Not to betray her? *I had killed her!*

But she caught my mood, and took me in her arms as I started to draw away, and comforted me. 'I told you to do it, Hope, to let the air out,' she said. 'We had rehearsed it. It had to be done. I love you, Hope.'

'And I love you,' I said. We proceeded to the natural act of love, and she was a little unresponsive, as though it was harder to do this in death, but I took it slowly and it finished well enough. Her body did not even feel cold; it was warm and soft, and in the end she was moving with me, hugging me as if there had never been any gulf between us.

Then I slept, and the turmoil of my dreams eased, as it always did when Helse comforted me.

I woke alone, of course. But I knew I had not been alone. My vision-dream had become too real, the culmination too complete. One of the distinctions between illusion and reality is the element of surprise, of things happening not precisely as expected, and I had had that experience. Helse had been with me.

I lay there and thought about it. Helse had been with me in spirit, of course, but not in body. Her body was frozen in a bag on the hull. Yet there had been a body; I was sure of that. A man may dream of love, and of sex, and his body may respond to the point of nocturnal emission – but the experience Helse had given me while she lived enabled me to .know the distinction between fantasy love and reality. For one thing, there was no stain of emission in my clothing, as there should be in fantasy sex. There had been a physical girl with me. I thought.

Helse was dead, and surely I had not visited her on the hull. So if not Helse, who? Who had shared that physical expression of the longing of the spirit?

Spirit? That was my sister's name!

I recoiled, from the thought, disgusted. But it seeped back at me, refusing to be banished merely because it was detestable. *Had* Helse been with me – in Spirit?

My nightmares of darkness paled as the nightmare of day came forward more strongly. In my agony of loss I had suffered a vision, as it seems I was wont to do. I could have acted out that vision physically. I should have known there was something wrong about it while it was happening, but reason is not my strong point when I'm hallucinating. I had not understood the message from my father at the time, and I had not understood the significance of Helse's warmth and solidity and seeming unfamiliarity with the act. I could not entirely condemn myself for my ignorance of the moment.

Spirit, however – how well did I understand her motives? If she had been present, as she could have been, she would have been awake. She loved me as a sister, but she had been jealous of Helse. She had inquired about the nature of what Helse and I did together. I had explained to her the distinction between voluntary and involuntary sex – but did she appreciate the distinction between woman and girl, or between romantic love and family love? If she saw me hallucinating and heard me crying out for Helse, and she thought she saw a way to come to my rescue, as she had when I fought a man – what would she do?

I fought against it, but could not completely deny the conclusion that Spirit could have done it. I was not sure that she *had* done it, just that she *could* have, emotionally and physically. That perhaps she *would* have. I really could not judge her reaction in this respect; she was inscrutable, opaque to my talent. The only way to know was to ask her.

I sat up – and Spirit heard me and came to the cell. I opened my mouth to ask her – and could not speak. I was abruptly aware how preposterous my question was.

'Are you all right, Hope?' she asked solicitously. She was neatly dressed in blouse and pants, her fine dark hair brushed out, and she seemed well rested. I realized that she had not suffered the loss I had, once she had come to terms with the fact of our orphaning. My support had been Helse, who was now gone; Spirit's support was me.

Had she or hadn't she? I had to know, yet could not ask.

She landed lithely on the floor of the cell. Low gravity made such acrobatics easy, yet she seemed healthy enough. And she was maturing; her blouse did not conceal her nascent breasts, and her pants fit her tightly enough to reveal a developing posterior. She had a distance to go, yet she was definitely on the way. She would be a handsome girl in due course, perhaps not beautiful the way Faith had been, but cetainly enough to please any man.

Had she already pleased a man? Damn it, I had to know!

'Spirit,' I said. 'Were you with me when I slept?'

'Hope, I will always be with you,' she replied. 'We are family.'

'No, I mean—'

She looked at me with disconcerting directness. Was it a stare of challenge. 'You mean what?'

'I mean *with* me. When—'

'When you screamed for Helse?'

Why did the way grow more difficult, the closer I got? 'Yes.'

'Hope, I tried to hold you down, so you wouldn't hurt yourself. I knew you were having a bad dream. You were banging on the wall, the way you did after Father died. Finally I got you quiet, and then I left you. I had to check the lenses.'

How had she quieted me? I knew how Helse had done it. 'Did I – hurt you?'

'You can't hurt me, Hope.'

That was no comfort; it was what Helse had said, the first time we made love. 'I mean—'

She took my hand, squeezing it gently, as I had squeezed her when I explained the different types of sex. 'Hope, I am your sister. I will do anything I have to, to keep you safe. I would die for you, as Helse did. Does anything else matter?'

She was not giving me any direct answer. She would die for me; I believed it. She would more readily do lesser things, by her definitions. Other things *did* matter – but did they matter to her the same way they did to me? 'There are things you must not do for me, Spirit.'

Her gaze was innocent. 'Like what?'

'Like—' But I choked again.

'Like lying to you?' she asked. 'Ask me anything Hope; I won't lie.'

Wouldn't she? I wasn't sure. To her, a lie was a lesser thing than death. If she believed a lie would safeguard my mental health, she would probably use it. Again I realized

276

that Spirit was made of tougher fibre than I was. I found I could not pursue this matter further – for fear she would lie to me . . . or that she would not.

'You are my sister,' I said, squeezing her hand.

'Always.' She kissed my cheek.

Then she was off again, running the bubble. I knew I would never know the answer to my question. Perhaps I did not want to know.

Did it matter, really? Spirit was one terrific sister, who it seemed, understood how to do what was necessary and how to conceal what was necessary. She had learned such arts from her mother. She had just faced me and backed me down, and I could not fault her for it.

Could I afford to let my courage be less than hers? I climbed out of the cell and went to help her run the bubble.

18

Pirate Treasure

Space, 27-3-'15–We travelled another period, settling into routine. It wasn't that we mourned our lost ones less, but that there was nothing to do but go on and to keep ourselves busy, so as to keep the nightmares away. Even if we hadn't been out in blank space, away from the Jupiter ecliptic, in peril for our lives if we miscalculated the vectors of the enormous reaches of space, we would have to keep ourselves active until the spectres faded. There were few pirates out here, for this was off the travel lane; we almost missed them! But we had set up another refuse tank for quick-vacuum, just in case.

However, we were not left long to our own devices. Yet another ship overhauled us. Our luck had changed, and we wished it hadn't; this almost certainly meant more trouble.

We set up as before, except that we cut our crew of 'innocents' to two, so the other six could have a better chance to survive the decompression. We didn't like taking losses, but had to play out our play, if only to lull the pirates so our trap could spring. We knew we had a defence that worked, and we didn't want to compromise it.

The ship docked, the lock opened, and the first pirate entered. I could not see around the curve of the Commons, since I was stationed right at the rear lock and our doughnut-hole chamber was well restocked with supplies, obscuring my line of sight, but I heard them. Spirit was halfway around, able to see both locks.

Spirit blew the whistle.

The two children attacked; I heard the scuffle.

278

'Hey, what—?' I demanded, amazed. There had not been time to ascertain the intentions of the intruders.

'It's the Horse!' Spirit hissed. '*Move*, Hope!'

The Horse! I stood frozen, remembering the rape of my sister Faith. I had sworn to kill that man!

The men caught the children before suffering more than scratches, and disarmed them. Two children could not attack five or six men with the same effect possible for thirty children attacking the same number. We should have realized that. The sounds penetrated my consciousness as if from a distance. The Horse, come to our bubble again!

'Do it!' Spirit snapped, and closed her helmet.

That finally jogged me out of my stasis. I closed my own helmet and jumped into the air lock. Already the pirates were coming around the Commons, and Spirit was backing towards the drive-control panel, almost tripping over the old, small drive unit parked beside it.

I closed the lock, decompressed it, opened the outer panel, and swung out, ready to cross when the drive cut off. We would lose two, this time; the innocents, who would not be able to get to their suits. They had known the risk, and it had to be done. I waited – but the drive did not cut off.

At last I realized that the pirates had caught Spirit before she could use the panel. I had no way to cross the ring of fire that was the drive. With the old, small columnar drive there would have been no problem. Or we could simply have cut off the new one when the pirates docked. So many little things we could have done – but it was now too late. We could not spring our trap.

Then I remembered something else, and that made me feel worse yet. We had weapons now – lasers and the taffy gun. Why hadn't we thought to use them? One kid behind that gun, shooting taffy at the pirates – we had never needed to go the vacuum route at all! What had possessed us to overlook that?

Grief and shock, that was what. We had had the sense to

279

fetch the weapons, but then had lapsed into our suffering, and had never done the hard intellectual work of devising a new strategy of defence. What a colossal error! Even Spirit had missed it.

There was nothing to do but go back inside. Bad luck and poor planning had foiled our grand play. Maybe I could get to the taffy gun yet, however.

It galled me that it should be the Horse who had us at his mercy a second time. The one who had initiated our descent into horror. Objectively I knew he was not the worst of pirates; he was a rapist and robber and opportunist, but not a wanton killer. But he was a symbol in my mind, and he had to be destroyed. For the sake of my sister Faith.

Now, I realized, I might see him rape my sister Spirit. Unless I found a way to get at one of our power weapons so as to take him out.

I re-entered the main bubble. The Horse was there, his laser pistol pointed at my midriff. He was garbed exactly as I remembered him: black shirt, yellow pantaloons, bright-red sash, and broad buccaneer hat – all of it worn and dirty. he stank the same too; no wonder they called him the Horse!

We were all captive, exactly as before. All our savage experience seemed to have changed nothing. They bound us and set us in a line against the wall of the Commons, near one of the operative heads. The two innocents were some-what battered, but the others weren't hurt. Spirit and I had been removed from our space suits; no hope of escaping to the hull now! But maybe some chance would come to get a weapon.

I shifted my wrists. Two pirates had bound us with lengths of rope about the crossed wrists and crossed ankles. They had a light touch, and had made the knots only tight enough to hold us effectively, not enough to interfere with the circulation in our extremities. They obviously knew what they were doing. I didn't recognize either of them –

but of course we had seen so many pirates since our first encounter, that they tended to fuzz in my memory. But for what it was worth, I didn't think these particular two had raped Faith, while I thought the two standing with the Horse had done so. That provided me with a set of priorities; whom to attack first, when I had the opportunity.

The interrogation began: Where were all our other people? How did we get the pirate weapons and supplies? Where were we going, since we were now spiralling away from Jupiter and out of the ecliptic? The Horse knew there was something strange about us, and he sought to turn it to his advantage. I realized that he was basically a scavenger, seeking whatever other pirates had missed.

We did not answer him. We all remembered his prior visit. We owed him nothing.

'Then we shall do it the harder way,' the Horse said. 'I'm not much for torture and killing, but I do like to turn a profit and I don't like being baulked.' He looked us over. 'You,' he said, pointing to me. 'You're the oldest, and as I recall, you had a fine piece of a sister you've managed to hide somewhere. You will answer my questions.'

I remained silent. It was the only way I could get back at him, at the moment.

He pointed at Spirit. 'Strip her,' he said.

The two pirates beside him went over and hauled my little sister out, untied her, and ripped off her clothing, though she struggled and tried to bite and scratch. Then they held her upright and naked before us.

The Horse studied her. 'Not quite old enough,' he said with evident regret. 'Another year and she'll be fine, but I don't get my kicks from children. Anyway, that won't make this kid talk; it didn't before. We'll have to go the other way.' He drew his knife.

I broke out in clammy sweat. I had somehow been braced for rape, much as I detested the notion, but this was

281

worse. He was going to torture Spirit!

The Horse faced me 'This is your sister, by the look of her. Put her in your clothes and she could be your little brother. I don't want to have to hurt her, but I will if you don't talk. I ask you once: Will you tell me everything I want to know?'

'He won't!' Spirit exclaimed.

Guided by her, I remained silent. Maybe the pirate was bluffing, trying to scare me into talking.

The Horse sighed. 'Okay, we'll start with a finger.' He grabbed Spirit's left hand and wrestled with it until he had hold of her smallest finger, while the two other pirates held her legs and other arm, preventing her from struggling effectively. It struck me how similar this process was to rape.

Then, without ceremony, he brought the knife up and sliced into the base of her finger, near the knuckle.

Spirit screamed with ear-deadening intensity, and wrenched with all her strength, but the pirate hung on and kept carving. Blood spattered out. I rolled over, trying to break my bonds, and the children on either side of me started crying. They had been toughened to the wounds of combat, but this was different. I could not get free; I landed on my side, my head on the deck.

Something landed before my nose. I stared crosseyed at it. It was about five centimetres long and tattered at one end.

It was Spirit's little finger.

I looked up, my eyes hazed by tears of shock and fury. I saw and heard Spirit sobbing, her hand covered with her own blood.

'I ask you again,' the Horse said, grinning. 'Are you ready to talk?'

Now I knew he wasn't bluffing. He would keep cutting off parts of Spirit until she died. Then he would start on another child.

What did it matter, what he knew of the adventures of our bubble? We had no secrets worth dying for.

But I tried one more thing. 'Kife,' I said.

Suddenly I had the complete attention of all the pirates. 'So you're into that, are you?' the Horse asked, licking his lips. 'All right, show me the mark and I'll turn you loose.'

'I have no mark,' I said. I hadn't thought to mark myself, and probably that wouldn't have been convincing since it wouldn't have been a tattoo. A lie would get me nowhere, and I really didn't have much taste for lies anyway. Lies were for pirates and scions.

The Horse squinted at me cannily. 'Not everyone knows this, but I do: There's always a mark. That's to stop imposters from making claims. If you can't show me the mark, you've got no claim. And even with the mark, you can't protect anyone else. You're the only one exempt. So show me it, and I'll put you in that lifeboat you're towing and send you off, and I'll interrogate someone else here.'

The trouble with the Horse was that he was canny. My bluff had failed. I couldn't save Spirit anyway. 'Let my sister go, and I'll tell you everything,' I said, capitulating.

'I won't let her go, but I'll let her be,' the Horse said. He gestured to the pirates holding Spirit, and they let go her arms and stooped to bind her ankles. Crying brokenly, preoccupied with her mutilated hand, she did not try to escape, and of course it wouldn't have done any good if she had. She tried to put her fist in her mouth, but the blood was still flowing, and she only smeared it on her cheek.

Oh, Spirit! Better had they raped you.

One of the pirates who had tied us went over and gave her a bandanna, and she wadded it against the stump. All the fight had gone from her. They put a blanket over her and let her sit down, and she huddled in it. The pain was evidently diminishing – but never again would she have that finger.

I swore again, to myself, to kill the Horse, who had

savaged both my sisters – but until I had the chance to do that, I would have to co-operate. I could not watch Spirit be tortured any more.

I talked. I told the pirates everything, summarizing our entire misadventure in the bubble. The Horse was especially interested in the QYV aspect. 'And the body of the courier is frozen on the hull?' he asked.

'Yes,' I agreed shortly.

'So you were the one who killed her, not a pirate.'

'Yes.'

'Which means you will have to settle with Kife.'

I hadn't thought of that. 'I suppose so.' I said, resenting the very fact of agreement with him. If I ever encountered Kife, however, I knew it would not be amicable.

The Horse smiled. 'I will make sure you go free, then, I wouldn't care to be the one to deprive Kife of his vengeance. He's an ugly one.' He pondered. 'Still, I understand those couriers carry some really good stuff. We'd better take a look it it.'

'No!' one of the other pirates exclaimed. 'It's death to mess with—'

'With a dead courier?' the Horse asked. 'Whose body will be lost in space, tied to a drifting bubble? I think even Kife knows where to cut his losses. He'll deal with her killer and let it go at that.'

'I don't know,' the other pirate said.

'That's why I'm the leader here,' the Horse said. 'I'll take the responsibility. I'll never have another chance to see exactly what a courier carries.'

It occurred to me that if the Horse let me go and Kife caught up with me, Kife would learn from me of the Horse's part in this. Then the Horse would be marked for vengeance too. I had killed Helse to save the bubble; the Horse would be interfering with the privileged material itself. Surely the Horse realized this. Therefore he probably intended to kill me and the other children, once he had all

284

the information we could provide, so we couldn't implicate him. If Kife tracked the bubble, without any living witnesses, he would discover that the great majority of the refugees, including Helse, had died in prior encounters with pirates; there would be no evidence that the Horse had ever intercepted the bubble a second time. He could probably get away with it.

It all depended on our being dead. I *had* to kill him – to save us all. But still I had no way.

Under the Horse's direction, two pirates suited up and scrounged on the hull for Helse's body. It took them some time, for there were many bodies there and they had to inspect each one naked for the mark. I had told them Helse was female, but evidently they weren't sure of me, so checked males too, just in case. Actually, it was probably hard to tell until the corpses were pretty well stripped, anyway.

They found her and brought her inside the bubble. I had never looked at Helse after her death; now I had to. This, I think, is the most visceral grievance I have against the Horse: I had known Helse was dead, intellectually, but some part of my romantic mind had remained hopeful that she might live. Now no part of my mind could doubt any longer. My last faintly fond illusion had been banished. The utter bleakness of reality took its chill hold on my soul.

I looked, terribly compelled. It was appalling. They had cut away her wedding dress and brought her in naked. She was not pretty at all in this state; she was frozen like a statue, her eyeballs and tongue protruding grotesquely, her body bloated by the decompression that had occurred before it froze. I would not have recognized her at all, if I had not known it was her. But it was; the aspects of familiarity loomed larger as I slowly perceived them. Her brown hair, her breasts, the QYV mark at her thigh – oh, Helse, the woman I had loved!

They tried to cut her open, but she was like rock. They

had to thaw her – and that was the worst thing of all. We had thawed the bodies of our men for food – but the adult women had handled that, concealing it from the children as much as possible, and I had not cared to watch. But I understood that they had selectively heated only those portions they intended to carve, leaving the main part of each body intact. A leg, for example, could be heated and even cooked to a certain extent while on the bone, and when it was soft enough to carve, the edible flesh was stripped and the still-frozen remainder of the body was taken back out to the hull. Helse, in contrast, was being thawed entire. This was a much slower and uglier process, for they did not use fire for fear of destroying what it was they sought: the container anchored to her intestine.

In fact, it took several days, as I reckon it, for the body to thaw to their satisfaction, for the ice in the central body cavity melted very slowly. For all that time we had to wait and watch, tied and guarded by the pirates. They released us periodically to eat and drink, one at a time, and to use the head, but watched us so closely that we never had a chance to escpae.

Even poor Spirit, a shadow of her former vitality, was permitted to rummage for bandaging material and replacement clothing only under the eye of a pirate. She searched inefficiently, unlike her normal manner, and found nothing suitable, and finally had to settle for soft underclothing from her own belongings. She fastened these garments clumsily against the stump of her finger and anchored them to her hand with elastic so that it looked as if her whole hand had been amputated. She refused to take any pirate pain-killer, for that was marked H. My heart went out to her in her misery and agony, but I was helpless. She was so pale I knew the loss of blood had hurt her. I couldn't even talk to her, couldn't comfort her. My little sister was dying, in her sad way, before my eyes. The strength I had perceived in her was gone; defeat and pain had robbed her of it. Even the two halfway decent pirates seemed sorry for her.

We slept at irregular intervals while the ice melted, though we felt the chill of it as the air in the vicinity lost its heat in the contact with the deep, deep freeze of space. There was nothing else for us to do. My mind ran over every possible plan to escape, but all foundered in the face of the reality of being both bound and watched. I wondered why they were taking the trouble to keep us alive for this period, and could only conclude it was for further questioning in case some new mystery arose in connection with the courier's body. The Horse was a thinker, in his fashion; he did not discard things before he was quite finished with them, including lives. That made him more dangerous than the more directly brutal pirates. Once the capsule was recovered and opened, our lives would be surplus. So the thawing of Helse was in fact a countdown on our own lives, and when the chill of her body had dissipated, the chill of our bodies would commence.

When I slept, I dreamed, and it was not fun. I seemed to march through an inchoate crowd of faceless people, all walking towards the brink of a yellow sulphur cliff, all stepping over it and falling to their doom. Only I could perceive the oncoming disaster, and I tried to talk to them, to urge them to stop and turn about, but they did not seem to hear me. I discovered that they were roped together and I was roped with them, my hands bound together; I was being carried over the cliff too.

I woke sweating in the cold. I was indeed roped, along with the others, and we faced the slowly warming body, and smelled its faint but growing aroma. We were approaching that cliff of doom, and the dream was no fantasy, but a rendering of reality. My dreams or visions had a disturbing propensity that way. I looked covertly at the pirate guarding us, but he was alert; no chance there.

I slept again, huddling into myself, and thought I woke

to find the guard sleeping, and nudged myself over to him and managed to get my fingers on his knife. He woke then, and opened his mouth to scream, but I had the knife, and my bonds unravelled before its blade, and I brought it up and stabbed him in the face and saw the blood geysering out of his nose, splashing across my hands, which looked oddly like Spirit's hands, and I woke, and it was only sweat on my hands, and the guard remained alert.

Next time I dreamed I slipped my bonds and made a noose of the rope, flung it about the head and neck of the guard, and garrotted him mercilessly, watching his eyes and tongue bulge out of his head, and it felt good, it gave me a feeling of power to do that to him – but I woke, and it was the head of my beloved Helse my gaze was fixed on, not the garrotted pirate. Still she thawed . . .

I dwelt on that for a while, compulsively. Helse was dead and my heart with her, and now her body was becoming more of a horror to me than her death itself had been. She had at least died quickly, and probably not suffered much; decompression in space, horrible as it may look, is about as clean a demise as a person could seek. I understand consciousness is lost in the first second, so the rest is never felt. Now she was being restored in a fashion, and her restoration would destroy us all. I felt anger, frustration, guilt and grief for her death, but had to some extent confined these emotions before they ravaged me beyond recovery. I knew that any breakdown on my part could lead to death for all of us, so had not had the luxury of prolonged grieving. But as I watched her body slowly soften, it all came back with appalling and gruesome force.

All that we had suffered in the bubble – was it worth it? Could it ever be worth it? Or would it have been better if we all had died? In that case, the Horse would be doing us a favour when he killed us, ironically.

I drifted to sleep again and dreamed of my family alive, as they were at the beginning of this travail, and I was explaining to my father how I wanted to marry Helse, but he was perplexed because he thought she was a boy. 'No, she is a girl,' I said, not even wondering how it was he did not know, when he had known before and had told my mother, and I drew off her clothing so he could see. But what was revealed was not the sweet soft shapely flesh of the living woman, but the cold hard horror of the corpse, and I stared in shock – and was awake again, my eyes fixed on the reality. Waking was no escape from nightmare!

Where had it all gone wrong? How could I have avoided the unmitigated horror of this outcome? I knew the answer: I should have avoided contact with the scion in Maraud. That had been the start of the whole terrible chain of events. Had I only drawn my sister Faith aside, hidden her from view – yet this scion had come looking for us, having seen Faith before. How could I have prevented that? I simply was not competent to deal with the problem I had faced.

Incompetence. There was the root of it. Had I had competence, I would have found a way to alleviate the situation. Had I had more experience, or had a more knowledgeable person been there to guide me—

But now I realized that if I had somehow dissuaded the scion without offending him, so that the crisis had never occurred, it would have solved only part of the problem. We, the Hubris family, would have survived, never having to take the bubble off-planet – but all the other refugees would have proceeded as before. Helse would have been aboard, and had to seek another roommate, and perhaps had trouble from the outset, and the pirates still would have raided and raped and murdered, and the Jupiter Patrol still would have rejected the refugees. The end would have been the same: death for all on the bubble, including Helse, one way or another. And I would never have met her and loved her, and she never would have loved me. A fantasy that saved my family without saving Helse was no good. It was not the scion I had to settle with, it was the pirates.

I slept again, and dreamed of the end of this dread sequence; the thawing was complete, and the fell pirate Horse reached his gross dirty hairy hand up between Helse's spread thighs into her soft body, raping her with his hand, for raping was his business, and rammed his gross fist around and around inside there while she struggled against the pirates holding her arms and legs, and at last with a gloating gasp of satisfaction pulled out what was inside her. It was large and green and shaped like a baby, the baby I had planted in her, but no, it was not mine, it was Kife's, he had raped her first, putting in her the seed of her destruction, putting his brand on her tender body. I had a vengeance to make against QYV, could I but survive to pursue it. This whole pirate trade, using and abusing innocent people—

Now the capsule, as the Horse held it up to the light in lustful victory, was small, its proper size; in my dream I was not concerned about such superficial changes of reality. The pirate's small eyes gleamed as he viewed the prize, the ultimate pirate treasure, the burden of the courier. What did that container contain? And I was curious too, and guilty for that curiosity, for by experiencing it I seemed to be supporting the death of my beloved, even as my bodily reaction at the time of the rape of Faith had seemed to support that act. Even in my private mind, where I could conjecture freely, I could not find an answer to my guilt. How much better to have Helse alive and leave the mystery intact! I had no right to want to see the content of that capsule! Yet I did.

The Horse broke it open and an object fell out, a blob of something, soft like mud, green mud. It fell on the body and spread out across the flesh like taffy. The Horse, fearing to lose it, tried to pick it up, but it broke apart and part of it adhered to his fingers.

He stared at his hand, watching his fingers dissolve, and I

realized that the green blob was a living thing, some kind of alien being that fed on human flesh and now was consuming both the corpse and the pirate. It had been quiescent until freed from the confining capsule; now there would be no stopping it. It would gorge until they were both gone, the dead woman and the living man, and then it would start on the rest of us. Already a pseudopod of it was extending across the deck towards me.

I woke in a new sweat, and nothing had changed. The body still thawed, the odour of it slowly intensifying, the dread cold still reaching out to touch me, and the pirate guard still watched. The Horse and one of the other pirates had returned to their ship, no doubt preferring to rest well away from the grim scene there. Spirit slept fitfully to one side, sometimes moaning faintly, the bloodstained under-garment enclosing her hand. She looked so wasted and frail! Would this slow horror never end?

The sequence was interminable, but in two, perhaps three days, perhaps more – I really don't know how long it took that body to thaw completely, everything is conjecture – it ended. As we watched dully, knowing the end was coming in more than one sense, that the reprieve Helse had provided us by taking as much time as she could to thaw was over, the Horse returned from the spaceship. He inspected the now limp and discolouring corpse, nodded approvingly, and took out his knife. He cut carefully into Helse's abdomen, as if performing surgery. The cutting was largely bloodless, and I could not see all of it – indeed, I did not want to see *any* of it, but couldn't control my eyes – but I saw enough. They had set her on a table, raised a metre or so, so the Horse wouldn't have to squat down awkwardly. The curve of the floor of the Commons lifted me somewhat, but still I had no clear line of sight to the incision.

He laid her open like the carcass of an animal, severing skin and muscle and linings to get at the intestines. This was just as bad as my dream! Then he drew out the guts of her in dark lengths, intact, squeezing and peering until he found the position of the capsule. He made an incision in the intestine at that point and cut free the prize. It was not as messy an operation as my horrified imagination had hinted, but was more horrible in other respects. Maybe this was because my dream had portrayed it as a kind of rape, while this was surgical. My abhorrence of rape had been muted somewhat by the education Helse herself had provided me, but my reaction against the onslaught of the knife remained unabated, for I had seen my father killed by the sword and the finger of my sister cut off. But mainly it was the actual *cutting* of the flesh of my beloved. Had she been alive it might have been an operation. We tolerate much more profound violations of our bodies in the name of medicine than we do in the name of pleasure.

The pirates crowded close, intent on the capsule as the Horse proudly held it up. It was about two centimetres long and half a centimetre in diameter. Not impressive, physically – but its content could be invaluable.

The child next to me nudged me. Slowly I turned my head, interrupting my own morbid fascination with the proceedings. Spirit was looking at me, seeming much more alert and alive than before, and when my gaze met hers, her eyes flicked down to her bandaged hand. I looked there – and saw she had a tiny blade, hardly more than a sliver from some razor blade the women used to remove hair from their legs when they were allergic to depilatories.

When she saw that I had seen, she hid the knifelet. I realized that she had cut her bonds during the recent distraction of the pirates. She must have picked up the blade while foraging for bandaging material and hidden it in the gore from her finger. No wonder she had had so much trouble finding what she needed in the way of bandaging – it had been this she was really looking for. The pirates, thinking her completely broken, had not considered her any real threat, so had not watched her as closely as they had the rest of us. Even in her shock and pain right after the loss of her finger, my cunning little sister had been alert for some way to free herself and us. No wonder she had fooled the pirates; she had even fooled me! Now Spirit was ready for action, and she knew it had to be soon.

The children between us fidgeted as if uncomfortable. Then the one beside me presented the tiny blade, shoving it towards me with his bound hands. The children between Spirit and me had not taken time to free themselves; they knew I needed to be freed first. They had the discipline of desperation. We would have only one chance, and we had to make it good.

I moved slowly, using the blade to saw through the rope about my feet. Then I realized this was foolish; the hands had to be first. I nudged my companion, and he moved his bounds hands to mine, and I sawed at his rope. The blade was sharp, for these items are fashioned in the factory bubbles of Jupiter to last almost forever, and my leverage was good. The strands parted, and in a moment his hands were free. Then he took the blade and severed my rope. My hands, too, were free. While I had dreamed vainly of such an escape, Spirit had taken practical action to make it possible. But I could not move my hands freely, lest the pirates see. I arranged the rope so it looked tied, and moved as slowly as before.

Meanwhile the pirate awe of the QYV treasure abated enough to get practical. 'We have it, but we have a problem,' the Horse said. 'We don't know what's in it. Could be a diamond – or could be an ampoule of Quintessent H, worth two million – or could be a deadly virus Kife means to use to wipe out a major bubble. Do we gamble, or don't we?'

'Where'd she come from?' a pirate asked, glancing at Helse's body. 'Do they have virus labs there?'

'Callisto, the boy says,' the Horse replied. 'No advanced

293

technology there. No precious minerals either.'

'But she could have been a second-stage courier. It could have started anywhere. Maraud is a centre for bootleg re-transfer. The Jupiter Patrol is watching for drugs on the regular ships from the inner worlds, but pays no attention to refugees. So it figures Kife would use one of them for something really important.'

'But Jupe's bouncing refugees now,' the Horse pointed out. 'Why use a courier who can't get through?'

The other pirate shrugged. 'I don't know. He must've figured she *would* get through, for some reasaon, and it fouled up. She would have been pretty enough, alive.'

Pretty enough, Yes, that figured. Faith might have got through, and Helse too, if some male Jupe officer spotted them. Regulations could be bent or ignored for that sort of thing. Yet I wasn't sure. I had seen no evidence of corruption in the Jupiter Patrol, and it had been a woman who turned us away. So the mystery of Kife's strategy remained.

I freed the hands of the girl on my other side and passed the blade on. Covertly, we all worked on our foot-ropes, though the pirates were now so engrossed in their debates over the capsule that they were paying no attention at all to us.

But I knew it would take more than our bare hands and one tiny blade to overcome these rough pirates. We had no real weapons, and the men were so much larger and stronger than we were they could have overcome us bare-handed. There were weapons farther around the Commons, but we would be caught long before we could reach them, assuming the pirates had left them in place. What could we do to save ourselves?

I worked it out as my feet came free: Someone would have to distract the pirates while someone else reached the weapons. We had no chance to plan this out before we would have to act, so I had to hope our minds ran in similar channels. I could make the best use of the weaspons, but I was farthest from them; Spirit was closest.

I looked again at Spirit, making a little signal with a finger. She should go for the weapons. She nodded.

'To hell with that,' the Horse exclaimed, settling the pirates' dispute. 'We could debate it for years and never decide. I'm going to open it.' And, while the other pirates shrank back apprehensively, he twisted the two halves of the capsule.

It burst apart and an object fell out, giving me a shock of *déjà vu* relating to my recent dream. The pirates shied away as if afraid the thing would explode, but it bounced harmlessly on the deck. The Horse stooped to pick it up.

When should we make our move? Now, while the pirates were distracted? Or should we wait till we had no choice. I decided that sooner was best. But we did have to give the remaining children time to get free. The more of us who burst loose at once, the better.

'A key!' the Horse said, disappointed. 'A stupid little plastic key!'

'A key to what?' one of the others asked, edging back towards it.

'How should I know? Maybe to a safe that got shipped by some other route and has a booby trap to blow it up if any key but this is used on it. Probably a magnetic pattern imprinted in it, no way to fake it. But we don't have that safe!'

'Then what good is this to us?'

'No good at all!' The Horse threw down the key in a fury. 'We sure ain't going to Kife with it! Three damn days gone – for this! For nothing!'

Spirit got up and started walking towards the weapons.

For a moment the pirates did not even notice. Spirit walked exactly as if she were going to the head. She had marvellous composure. All the time I had thought she was broken, she had been planning this!

Then the Horse spied her and caught on. 'She's loose!' He started for her. 'Who forgot to tie—'

I launched myself towards him.

We didn't have a chance, of course. There were eight of us and five pirates in the bubble at the moment – but each of them was a match for two of us unarmed, and there were more in the pirate ship that would come at the sound of the commotion. But we were desperate; we had nothing left to lose.

I ploughed into the Horse, who wasn't looking at me. My impact spun him around. In a moment he recovered, grabbed me, and threw me aside. Scowling, he drew his laser pistol.

Why hadn't I grabbed for that pistol first? I might have got it, if I had concentrated on that alone! I had bungled my only chance! Now, as if it were in slow motion, I saw the ongoing panorama of the action. The Horse, drawing his weapon. The other pirates, turning to face the rushing children. One of the bad ones reaching for Spirit at the fringe of the group. But no, he wasn't catching her, he was clapping his hands to his face! She had flicked him in the eye with her finger-whip!

Then the Horse realized what was happening and brought his pistol around to bear on Spirit instead of me. I tried to roll into his feet, to jar his aim, but was too slow. But Spirit fooled him by leaping up into the storage compartment, neatly curving through the hole in the net and disappearing among the packages of food up there. His shot burned a package but missed her. It was that curvature of the jump that had thrown him off; we were used to it, but he wasn't.

Unfortunately, we had no weapons stored up there. Spirit was safe for the moment, but we had lost the war because the Horse was striding towards the cache of weapons.

I scrambled to my feet. Maybe I could still get to a

weapon first, if I dived for it. But I knew this was unlikely.

I was passing Helse's body on the table. I reacted almost without thinking. I picked up the corpse, entrails and all, lifting it readily in the partial gravity, and heaved it at the Horse. It was strange, touching Helse's dead flesh, which was not soft but rather stiff, but I knew she would approve of being allowed to participate in the fight this way.

The body struck the Horse. He spun around, firing his laser into it, not at first realizing what it was. Then he realized, and his face snarled with disgust. A length of intestine had strewn itself across his arm, and he brushed it away and backed off.

Meanwhile I was making progress towards the weapons thanks to Helse's intercession. My dead love had given me a better chance.

'Down!' Spirit cried from the far side of the Commons. She had sailed right through the centre compartment and out the other side! 'Flat!'

I didn't know what she had in mind, since there were no weapons over there, but knew better than to ignore the warning. I spread myself flat against the deck, hoping this was not all a bluff.

'Someone shoot that brat,' the Horse cried. Then he turned and aimed his laser at me. I could hardly move to avoid it, since I was lying down.

There was a horrendous roar, an ear-hurting sound, and a blast of hot air. Fire exploded in the baggage-storage section and the netting disintegrated. Burning packages rained down, curving in their fashion as they fell. The pirates, amazed, tried to dodge them.

Had Spirit detonated a bomb among the packages? But there was no bomb!

A pirate near the air lock screamed. I looked – and saw him bathed in fire. His hair and clothing were puffing into bright ash, and his body was blackening. He spun to the side, his skin flayed from his body.

A jet of flame shot through the centre of the bubble and down through the air lock, directly into the pirate space ship. There were screams as it fried unseen pirates there.

A laser? That would have to be a laser cannon, the kind mounted on a Jupiter Navy battleship. We had nothing like that on board!

Then it cut off, after only a few seconds, leaving us bathed in heat and gasping for air. The metal of the air lock glowed red where the jet had touched it, and the odour of burnt flesh was strong. The pirates were standing motionless, staring, and I think some were temporarily blind. Those of us on the deck were better off, being farther from the flame.

Now I realized what it was. Spirit had ignited the small rocket drive! She must have braced it against the rear lock and aimed it down towards the front lock, searing through everything between. It was a little, weak jet when used to move the mass of the full bubble, externally – but here inside it seemed devastatingly powerful. She probably had it set on the lowest level of thrust; otherwise she would not have been able to hold it at all. But even that level, which from outside might seem to be a pallid jet of half a dozen metres, was enough to incinerate what remained in the storage compartment and to char what did not. The ferocity of its passage heated the air explosively, and the jet showed in air to extend the full sixteen-metre breadth of the bubble and beyond. It had been perhaps a five-second burst – and the bubble was in a shambles.

'Get their weapons!' Spirit called.

I scrambled up – but the Horse reacted as quickly, swinging his pistol about again. 'Spirit!' I cried, throwing myself flat again and trusting the other children to follow my lead.

The jet of fire came again. It wobbled, and part of it struck the side of the air lock near the pirate. Fire refracted, forming a curving sheet of flame and sparks that caught the standing pirates glancingly.

It cut off a second time. 'I'll burn you all, if you don't get those pirates!' Spirit called.

But this time the pirates had been harder hit. The Horse was staggering, having been brushed in the face by the flame, and I got his pistol without resistance. It took a third blast from the rocket before we had complete control, but we did have it.

When I reached Spirit, I discovered the price she had paid for her valiant move. She had been very close to the rocket, and the thing was no toy. She had held it in place by hand, her extremities shielded by bandage-clothing, but her hands were burned and her hair singed. She had closed her eyes tightly, protecting them, but her cheeks were blistered. When she saw me coming and knew we had won, she fainted.

Poor, heroic little girl! I scavenged for balm for her skin and tried to get her comfortable, then tended to the other pressing business.

We didn't push our luck. We sent the two least obnoxious pirates – the ones who had tied our bonds loose rather than cut off the circulation of our hands and feet, and who had let us use the head with reasonable frequency – out the cooling lock with instructions to close it behind them and separate the pirate ship from the bubble. Then we dealt with the Horse and the two remaining pirates.

I had sworn to kill the Horse, and now was my chance, but I found I was unable to do it directly. I was not, when it came to the test, a calculating murderer; I killed only in the throes of desperation. Yet when I looked at Spirit's stump of a finger and at Helse's mutilated body, and remembered Faith, I suffered a helpless secondary rage. We could not simply let these criminals go!

Spirit had recovered consciousness by this time. She was in pain from her new injuries and unsteady on her feet, but her eyes bore on the Horse with singular malignancy. Faith was her sister too, and Spirit had suffered even more directly and recently from the villainy of the Horse. Spirit was no forgiving cherub. Wordlessly she held out one burned hand for the laser pistol.

I gave it to her, not knowing what she would do, but aware that she had more guts to do it than I did. I saw that it hurt her just to hold the weapon, but she gritted her teeth and took it in her left hand, the one with the lost finger, though she was right-handed, and she aimed it and steadied it and fired – into the crotch of the Horse.

He screamed and jumped, but the damage was done. Spirit had castrated him with the laser.

Then we forced the three into the trailing lifeboat, after hauling it up to mate with the freed front lock. We had not killed the Horse – but blind and burned, he might not live long anyway, jammed into the lifeboat with his two cut-throat companions and set adrift in space. Certainly he would suffer to a certain extent the way we had. Certainly he would never rape another refugee girl. Maybe his pirate ship would search out the boat and pick him up; maybe it wouldn't bother. His fate was now in the hands of his associates, as perhaps it deserved to be. His blood was not, technically, on my hands. That perhaps is my ultimate confession of weakness.

We had not actually lost any children this time, but half our supplies had been destroyed and we all had emotional and physical scars. Several children had bad burns from the rocket, and I feared Spirit's face would never be pretty, for there would be blister scars on it when it healed. But we survived, and we had a little portion of our vengeance!

We bagged Helse's remains and returned her to the hull. I saved the mysterious plastic key, hiding it on my person, my last memento of Helse. That and the HELSE HUBRIS tag.

We cleaned up the rest in the usual manner; it did give us something to do. We settled down to travelling our route and tending our injuries. Spirit, tough little creature that she was, started recovering right away, but I refused to let her do any real work until her skin scabbed over and started healing. She was, I still believe, the toughest one among us, and she had earned her rest.

19

The Final Raid

Spirit eyed me speculatively one day. 'Hope, you're getting too old.'

'Old?' What was she up to now?

'You're thinking about starting a beard.'

Oh. 'Men do, you know.' I ran my finger along my chin, but there really wasn't anything there.

'What if the pirates come again, to slay the men?'

She had a point. If women were subject to rape, men were subject to murder. It was best to remain young. I fetched some depilatory from the diverse supplies that remained and went over my face, rendering it fully boyish again.

'That's not enough,' she said. 'All they want is girls.'

'To rape!' I exclaimed.

'You should be safe from that,' she pointed out.

Startled, and not entirely pleased for a reason I could not define, I had to agree. It might indeed be smart for me to learn to masquerade as a girl, just as it had been useful for Helse to masquerade as a boy. If pirates came and blazed away at males and spared the girls, this could give me my only chance to survive long enough to blaze back at them. We would all have lasers ready next time, of course; still, we had so often been betrayed by circumstance that we had to consider any possible advantage that might be available.

Spirit got to work happily. She had a marvellous ability to invest her whole attention in immediacies, bypassing the horrors that tormented my more reflective mind. She found a dress my size and made me change into it, while the other children offered enthusiastic suggestions. I even had to put on pantyhose to cover my hairy legs, and girlish slippers. Naturally the brats fitted me with a padded brassiere to make my front look right, giggling fiendishly.

I had become the entertainment of the hour. They brushed out my hair, which had grown longer in the past month, and they tied a pretty ribbon in it, and instructed me in girlish nuances of expression and stance. I was surprised by the amount the little girls knew about this sort of thing; evidently they took their sex roles seriously from an early age. I was not really enjoying any of this, but they found it hilarious. Still, it would be pointless for me ever to attempt such a masquerade before pirates unless I had it down pat, so I did work at it, trying to satisfy the piercing cynosure of the children. When they began to nod approval, I knew I was getting better.

Spirit insisted on making it more of an ordeal. She donned male clothing and postured before me in a gross parody of masculinity. Her ravaged face did help, here. 'I am your brother!' she declaimed. 'I am here to stop you from getting raped, unless you really want to be. Say 'sir' to me, sister!' The other kids laughed as if that were the humour of the century. Was this really the way the typical male came across to the opposite sex?

'Ship ahoy!' the lookout cried.

That *would* have to happen at the time I was ludicrously garbed! Just when we thought we were free of pirates, well off the ecliptic, another came!

I rushed for my space suit, not sparing time to change; every moment might count. Spirit did likewise – but of course she didn't mind her garb the way I did mine. It was awful for me, cramming the damned dress into the legs of the suit. Spirit had it easy; male clothes are designed for space suits, or vice versa. In this respect it really is a male universe.

The other kids hesitated, then decided to go for their

suits too. They were alive now only because they had been lucky enough to avoid the pirates and get their suits on in time; they didn't want to gamble that way again. But that left us without any innocents to test the intruders. We all had laser pistols now, so the innocents could attack with much better effect, but still we all lacked confidence in that. So it was to be suits for all. A few children in a bubble – the suits would not be too surprising. Bubbles didn't leak, but some people worried that they did. Then the innocents could simply slam their helmets on, if we had to go the vacuum route.

I stationed myself near the rear air lock, and Spirit joined me, while the others scrambled. We two were the fastest, because we had drilled specifically for this, many times; our suits were hung right by the air lock, supported so that we could almost literally dive into them feet first. We had everything tight except our helmets. My slippered feet tended to slip around in the big suit-feet, though, and I hated the way my skirt wadded up around my middle.

'You sure look cute, sister, in your suit and ribbon,' Spirit teased me.

I put my hand to my head to remove the damned thing, but my suit gauntlets were clumsy.

There was a crash. The entire bubble shook, almost knocking us off our feet. 'They crashed into us!' I exclaimed, shaken in two senses.

There was another crash, worse than the first. 'No – they're shooting at us!' Spirit screamed. Then she jammed her helmet over her head.

I followed her example. The automatic seal operated and the suit's air puffed on.

The third shot punctured the hull on the side of the bubble opposite us. The air sucked out with gale force. I couldn't see the puncture, but knew its nature from the direction of the rush of air.

Spirit and I were drawn along with it – but we were

farthest from the leak and were affected least. I grabbed the netting above the Commons as I flew by, and Spirit did the same. She had had prior experience with explosive decompression; I had not, since I had been out on the hull before.

The opening was small, for bubble-hulls are tough, designed to withstand pebble-meteorites and to self-seal to some extent. But of course space artillery is designed to penetrate exactly such hulls. The shell had formed a tube that let the air out; it took about thirty seconds, with diminishing intensity as the pressure dropped.

Spirit and I survived it – but I realized that the other children probably had not. They had required more time to suit up, and their reactions were less certain. They might have paused in surprise, listening to the collisions of the shells against our hull – and that would have been fatal. Once again we had been betrayed by the unexpected.

I looked at Spirit through our helmets. Why had the pirates done it? To hole a bubble – that was the deliberate murder of all within. No rape of women or kidnapping of children was possible.

Now the pirate ship docked against our air lock and the men used it, keeping their ship sealed. Suited men appeared and began checking around inside our wasted hulk. It seemed that all they wanted was salvage.

What should we do now? If the pirates saw us, they would surely kill us. But we couldn't remain in the holed bubble long; it was now useless. We had no way to repair such a leak, assuming the pirates left us any food or life support equipment when they finished. We seemed to have a choice between a fast death and a slow one.

Spirit had the answer. She handed herself to a rent in the net and took hold of an armful of food containers. She meant to pretend to be a looter!

Would it work? It might. Our suits were standard, similar to those of the pirates; in the confusion of looting, we might manage to get aboard the ship. After all – well, first things first.

I took an armful of food packs, enough to cover my face panel somewhat, and followed Spirit down to the air lock. I really didn't know whether this would work, but didn't see any alternative.

We came to the lock, and the pirate there waved us on in. He closed the lock behind us, and we stepped into the pirate ship.

It took me a moment to realize what was strange. This was very like the bubble, here: just a chamber for access. We had explored a ship before, when we cleaned out the pirates with our vacuum, so this was reasonably familiar, but this present one was a larger and probably better ship. We floated through the chamber and down a short hall, toting our burdens. Then we came to something different.

The vacuumed ship had docked nose-on, so that its spin matched the bubble's spin and the whole thing had been like one extended passage from our lock. Indeed, in the case of the Horse's ship, our drive jet had fired right down its throat, the length of the ship. But this present ship had docked at the centre, so its nose and tail sections were projecting to either side, and it was spinning around endways to match the bubble's rotation. It was always easier for a ship to match rotations, since it would have taken energy to stop the bubble's spin, not worth it for a temporary connection. Here, it is best to make a set of diagrams:

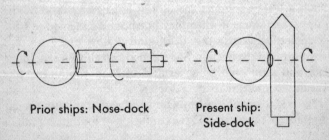

Prior ships: Nose-dock   Present ship:
                                  Side-dock

I have drawn a centre line to show the axis of rotation in each case. As should be clear, the two modes of docking lead to quite different dynamics within the ship. Actually, the rate of rotations does not have to match, as the air locks have a built-in slip mechanism that allows opposite rotations to bubble and ship. But what would be the point? Certainly it was impossible for the ship to maintain a long-axis spin while connected to the bubble, so it had either to go to no spin, meaning null-gee, or to rotate end over end, as it was doing.

This seemed unnecessarily clumsy. My mind cast about for the rationale. Could it be that these particular pirates were accustomed to difficult manoeuvres in space, and performed them routinely? That would imply a really professional crew, more like a military unit than a motley collection of malcontents. Their completely callous holing of our bubble implied the same. We were up against no-nonsense raiders this time – probably a ship that deserted from a planetary navy.

And there was the explanation for the manoeuvre: This ship had not docked at the nose because it couldn't! It had a projectile cannon mounted in the nose instead of an air lock. No other pirate ship had fired at us, because such military hardware could not be mounted on ordinary space vessels; they had to be designed for it. A projectile cannon attached to the side of the hull of a spinning ship would be virtually useless, and would severely shake the ship when it fired; it had to be on the axis line, so it could be fired without affecting either the spin or the balance of the ship. Since boarding became so awkward, no chances were taken; the victim was rendered completely helpless before the approach was made. This was like a pirate with one arm, afraid the girl might resist and hurt him, so he shoots her just before he rapes her.

Why was it that each pirate vessel we encountered seemed worse than the last? Even the Horse had been worse the second time!

Now we were at an intersection. On either side a long passage extended down. That's right; we were floating at the null-gee axis, and the opposite directions were both down, because of that endways rotation. We had to pick one or the other without delay, for a pirate was coming through the lock behind us. I saw an arrow pointing, decided that would be towards the residential section (for no good reason; male intuition is suspect), and jumped. Spirit followed.

Of course, we did not sail blithely down the centre of the passage. That is not the nature of free fall, as our experience in the bubble had amply shown. We slid down one wall, and as the pressure of that wall increased our angular momentum – that is, the speed of our revolution around the axis – our centrifugal force increased, and we slid faster. The process fed on itself. So it was a bit like being on a giant slide, whose slant increased as it progressed, so that not only one's velocity but one's rate of increase of velocity quickened. Soon we were bumping along at an uncomfortable rate, and had to catch the inset rungs to break our falls. The packages sprang from our arms and went tumbling on down ahead.

A pirate emerged from a side hall – just in time to be pelted by the onrushing packages. He did not take it well. A laser pistol appeared in his hand, pointing with excellent accuracy at me as I clung to the descent ladder.

So we were caught. But that had been inevitable. So far, we survived.

I lifted back my helmet, surrendering for the moment. There was no point in getting shot, or in getting Spirit shot. Perhaps we could talk our way into something less unpromising.

'A woman!' he exclaimed in English.

I still had the red ribbon in my hair! I started to protest, but Spirit nudged me. 'So what'd you expect my sister to be – a frog?' she demanded.

The pirate's lips quirked. It seemed he had some minor sense of humour. 'You escaped from the derelict bubble?'

'Derelict?' Spirit demanded. 'It wasn't a derelict! Not until you blasted a hole in it!'

'So it would seem.' The pistol still covered us. 'Come in here and get out of those suits.'

We entered his chamber and climbed out of our suits. I had a problem with modesty, as my dress tended to snag above my waist; how did girls stand it? Of course my bloomer-panties protected the essentials. I lost a slipper in the suit and had to fish for it. I realized now why girls often seemed so inefficient; their costumes did it to them. But at length I stood, somewhat bedraggled, before the pirate. Spirit, in masculine attire, was better off. I knew that only the seriousness of our situation prevented her from teasing me about my feminine ineptitude.

'How old are you?' the pirate asked. He was evidently an officer, as he wore some sort of insignia and seemed better spoken than the usual brutes. Probably he originated from Uranus, whose moon Titania was the home of the English-speaking people, and which moon had a long-standing Navy tradition. Mainly, he was calmly self-assured.

'Fifteen,' I said. No point in concealing that fact.

'Twelve,' Spirit said.

He gazed at me appreciatively and appraisingly, and I became aware of one reason women can cringe under the cynosure of men. I wished I could be anywhere but here.

'You are young,' the pirate officer said. 'But that perhaps makes you cleaner. You will serve one man per night, commencing this night. You will co-operate gladly—'

'No!' I cried, horrified with better reason than he could know.

'Otherwise your little brother will be flogged – by the man you do not please – and you will go without food or water till the next. I believe in time you will co-operate willingly enough.'

I was silent. These pirates certainly knew how to make a girl perform! All we could do now was stall for time.

The officer raised his voice to address the other pirates that were arriving now. 'Take these two to the guest room. You will draw straws for order of satisfaction.'

Stunned, we went to the indicated chamber. It was near to the end of the ship, where gravity approached one gee. It occurred to me that this end-over-end rotation could be the normal mode for this ship, as a slower turning rate led to greater effective gravity at the extremes, compared to the other mode. We had enough trouble establishing half or quarter gee in the bubble; the ship's smaller diameter would force a very high rate of spin to get similar effect, and the difference in effect as a person moved inward from the hull would be formidable. Just standing could be uncomfortable. But the present way, there was relatively little differentiation; it was almost like standing on a planet. When not accelerating or shooting at a helpless bubble, this ship needed no specific orientation in space. And when it was accelerating, that would provide temporary gee. So this odd mode wasn't nearly as odd as it looked. I had never seen it in holo shows depicting navy vessels, but probably those were censored to avoid the undramatic aspects.

The guest room was set up in the fashion of an antique boudoir of the salacious version, with mirrors on walls and ceiling and virtually the entire floor covered by the mattress. Evidently these pirates had entertained women before. This was intended for only one type of guest. I realized that this was the type of situation my sister Faith had walked into.

For a moment we were alone, while the pirates drew their straws. I looked at Spirit. 'We're in trouble,' I said, in a gross understatement.

'*You're* in trouble, paleface!' she quipped. But she turned serious immediately. 'I can take your place. We can change clothes—'

I tried to conceal the extent of my horror at the notion. 'No good,' I said. 'They won't fit.'

'We could make it dark—'

'I won't stand by and watch you be raped!' I said.

She sighed like an adult. 'That too, of course.'

'Maybe we can overpower the first pirate—'

'I could ram a knitting needle in his ear,' she said. 'That works pretty well. If I had a needle.'

'Still no good. They'd be on us when he didn't come out.' We no longer had our laser pistols; the officer had competently deprived us of them at the outset.

'We need to get to the captain and hold him up and hijack the ship,' she said.

'If we could get to the captain, and if we could make him do our will,' I said. 'Spirit, these are pirates! They'd as soon kill us as rape us! We just don't have the—'

The panel opened. A gross, burly, bearded pirate came in. 'Girl, get on the bed and spread 'em!' he said to me. 'Boy, get to the side and watch. When you get old enough, you'll get to do it too; meanwhile you can learn.' He started to strip.

Spirit's gaze darted about the room, seeking some possible weapon, but I knew there was none. Her finger-whip had also been taken from her; pirates knew about such things. Her finger-stump had been sprayed with plastic bandage; they knew about that sort of thing too. These were English-speaking pirates, but they differed from the Spanish-speaking ones we had encountered only in their language and efficiency. Maybe we had floated from the Hispanic territory to the British; elsewhere in Jupiter-space there might be French-speaking pirates too. Certainly there had been in the past, in Callisto's history.

I hesitated. I really wasn't taking time to think all these things out as lucidly as I present them here; our fleeting thoughts may be more suggestive than complete. I could use the anti-rape measures against this man, poking his eyes out – but that would surely mean a most unpleasant death for Spirit and me. There had to be a better way.

'Move, girl!' the pirate cried, grabbing my arm and yanking me onto the bed. I fell, and he jumped on top of me, his clothing only partly undone. His liquor-sodden breath seared my face as his foul hand grasped at my padded front. Yet again I appreciated the position young women may be placed in; no person in her right mind would enjoy this approach! Helse had been very smart to conceal her gender.

'Kife,' I said. I hadn't known I was going to do it, but the chain of thought leading to Helse had led naturally to her identity as courier, so brutally fresh in my mind. This did seem worth a try.

The man froze in mid grasp. 'Oh, no!' he muttered.

'You think a girl survives in space because of her muscle?' I asked, following up my advantage. I could tell the man was really shaken. Evidently QYV's notoriety extended throughout piratedom.

He backed off. 'Why didn't you say something before?'

'Kife wants it private,' I explained. 'I'll probably get in trouble just for giving away my status.' And, really, I had become Kife's courier, for I retained the key in the capsule. 'Take me to your captain.'

'Damn!' he swore. 'I'm tempted to—'

'Yes, I heard about someone who did that once,' I said blithely. 'Thought he was real smart, thought Kife wouldn't know. But Kife always knows. You know how long it took that man to die, once Kife caught him?'

The pirate was uncertain again. 'Look, girl, I just drew straws! I didn't know—'

I saw Spirit smirking. 'At the end, he couldn't even scream,' I said. 'Though he sure was trying to! Because of the blood, you know, in his throat. They ran a hose into him, up his nose and down his windpipe, so he wouldn't choke to death on the gore before they were ready. Kife doesn't like it when someone dies before he's ready. They hadn't done the eyes yet, or the liver—'

The pirate retreated farther. 'What do you want, girl?' He had evidently forgotten my demand to see the captain, or hadn't taken it seriously. I decided to play with this some more. I was hurt and angry about the holing of our bubble and the callous murder of the other six children. This might be a small vengeance, but it helped.

'I just thought you'd like to know what you're missing. They gave me one of his gonads for a souvenir, pickled in brine. 'Course it was sort of ragged, because he kicked some while they were pulling it off—'

I don't think I ever saw so rugged a man look so sick so suddenly. 'I never touched you, girl! I didn't know—'

'Take me to your captain,' I repeated, tiring of this sport. But mixed with my fiendish glee at the nature of this reprieve was my sense of irony. Had Helse employed her weapon of the name more freely, she need never have died. She hadn't really known what she had.

Thus we found ourselves in the presence of the captain, called Brinker. He was not one of the bushy-bearded types; he was clean-shaven and his jacket fitted well. He was small, but looked very much like a Nordic officer, with pale blond hair and sharp, almost chiselled facial features. I became more certain than ever that he had deserted from the Titanian navy, taking his ship and crew with him. I understood such things happened. Space around Uranus wouldn't have been safe for him, so he had crossed to Jupiter and taken up the trade of piracy. He seemed completely self-assured and carried a needle-laser sidearm in a holster visible in his left armpit, its butt forward. I wondered how this physically unprepossessing person maintained discipline over rough pirates, now that he was not supported by the weight of military law and custom. This was obviously a fairly taut ship.

'Say the word,' Captain Brinker said to me.

'Not in public,' I said, aware that I was being tested.

I did not see Brinker's hand move, but abruptly the pistol was in it and there was the tingle of heated air beside my left ear. Suddenly I saw how Brinker kept discipline. He must be the fastest gun in space! He could have burned me instead of firing past my head, and I would not have had time to blink. The pistol was already back in the holster.

But I sensed that it would be wrong to back down in the face of such a threat. Captain Brinker did not respect those he could readily cow. That much my talent of human understanding indicated, though we had not interacted long enough for me to gain a clearer comprehension of the captain's nature. So though I was frightened, I bluffed. 'Shoot me. You know whom you will answer to.'

The pistol appeared in his hand again, its lens-muzzle bearing on my right eye. But I had never been daunted by such threats. Afterwards, when I had time to consider, I might shudder with reaction, but at the time of crisis I always stiffened my opposition when threatened. This wasn't courage, just the way I am. Some circuit in my brain cuts out under pressure. So I stared into that lens and waited, unspeaking.

Again the weapon snapped back to its holster. 'Very well,' Brinker said. 'You shall have your private interview.'

The pirate guards left, the panel sealing behind them. My sense was continuing to operate; there was something amiss about the captain. I had felt a similar unease when first meeting Helse in her guise as a boy.

That was the key. 'Spirit,' I said in a normal voice. 'Do you remember Helse's secret?'

She looked puzzled. 'I remember.'

'Another shares it.'

Her brow furrowed, then straightened. She was catching on. 'Are you sure?'

'Almost. In a moment I'll tell.'

314

Captain Brinker frowned. 'What are you talking about?'

'You asked me to say the word,' I said while Spirit unobtrusively moved away from me. 'I can do better than that. I can write it out for you.' I glanced about the chamber, the captain's small office. 'Do you have something to write with?'

'Just spell it,' Brinker snapped.

That, of course, was the test. If I spelled Kife the way it sounded, I would show up as an imposter. But I had another ploy now. I saw that Spirit had gotten herself close to an anchored metal cabinet, so might have a baffle. I took the plunge. 'F-E-M-A-L-E,' I spelled aloud.

The pistol was back in the captain's hand, aiming at my eye. 'Explain yourself, girl.'

'I suggest you not fire until you consider the consequence,' I said evenly, though the cold clutch of fear almost brought me down. I dread the thought of blindness! 'If you are not concerned with the vengeance of Kife, you should think of the more immediate result of action against us.' I had slipped in the other key word deliberately, so that it would seem like no bluff, with the spelling held in reserve. 'The secret you value most will be exposed if you kill us. This chamber is not completely sound-proofed; one of us will scream the word while you kill the other.' I glanced towards Spirit, who now stood behind the cabinet, out of the line of fire. 'Your men will hear, and wonder – and when they discover the nature of our bodies, they will understand the potential.'

'You are speaking gibberish,' the captain said.

'No,' I said. 'Here is the secret: None of the three of us here are the sex we seem.'

The captain did not seem to react. 'Be more specific.'

'I am male,' I said. 'Spirit is my sister. And you—'

'Show me,' the captain snapped, the laser still zeroed on my eye.

I lifted my skirt and dropped my bloomers, displaying

my masculine parts. This was hardly the occasion for modesty! I signalled to Spirit, who stepped out and started to drop her trousers.

'Enough,' the captain said. 'You have made your point. How did you know?'

I covered my private region, straightening out my dress. 'I have had experience with transvestism, as you can see. I have learned to recognize it. In my profession, such abilities are often necessary. My employer does not like to have his name bandied about, so I avoid the use of it when possible by using other means to conceal my nature.' Again I was implying that my position as courier was to be taken for granted.

'In a dozen years, no one has realized I am a woman,' Captain Brinker said, putting away the pistol. 'I killed any who suspected. If my crew knew, I would lose my command – and more.'

'Much more,' I agreed. 'It is not to the advantage of any of us to have our natures revealed. Shall we deal on that basis, and leave Q-Y-V out of it?' Now at last I spelled it, to remove the last trace of doubt about my connection.

'What do you want?'

'I want my freedom,' I said. 'To pursue my mission. If I fail my mission, I will have to seek a very fast, very sure extinction. I also want the freedom of my sister.'

'She is a courier too?'

I was aware that she was testing me again, so I steered clear of unnecessary elaboration. 'No. Couriers don't travel in pairs. She is only my sister – but I will not make any agreement unless she is free.'

'If I set you free, I have no guarantee of your silence,' Brinker pointed out. 'Rather than risk that, I will destroy the whole ship.'

But first she would try to eliminate us cleanly, hoping somehow to conceal our natures and hers from her crew. I saw that she could not be moved on this aspect. 'That would certainly protect you from my employer's vengeance,' I agreed. 'I trust you have no blood relatives he can trace. Yet I would rather live, and you would too. Is there no compromise?'

'Yes. I will give you the lifeboat. Your sister remains with me.'

As hostage! It did make sense, as I would never betray the captain's secret while my sister was subject to her will, and the captain would not kill Spirit as long as Spirit's life guaranteed my discretion. Yet I could not do it. Spirit was all I had left, the only remaining barrier between me and total desolation. 'Make another offer,' I said curtly.

'No other offer,' the captain said, now assured that Spirit was important to me. 'I may neither kill you nor let you go entirely free without imperilling myself. It must be all or nothing – or this. Take the compromise – or the consequence.'

'Hope, she means it,' Spirit said. 'Do it. She will not harm me, for I have the same secret. I can be the cabin boy, and I will not be molested. You must go free – to complete your mission.'

My non-existent courier mission! 'My father, my mother, my fiancée – all sacrificed themselves for me!' I exclaimed in anguish. 'You are all I have left, Spirit! I cannot let you go!'

'Hope, I said I would die for you,' Spirit replied. 'This is not nearly as bad. We may someday meet again.' And I saw the tears on her face, and knew she was determined to make this final sacrifice for me. I had to do it.

'Agreed,' I said to the captain, almost choking over the word. Spirit – I did not know whether I could survive without her, or whether I wanted to. Yet it seemed it had to be done. 'We are children and you are pirates – but we have seen as much of death as you have. Do not test us unduly. I refuse to use my courier status to win free; find another pretext to put me on the lifeboat.' I was serious; I was on the verge of throwing it all in, screaming out the captain's secret, and letting things follow as they would.

'We understand each other,' the captain said. 'I will send you back to the bed. You will hijack the ship instead, using our detonation-control panel. Your sister will have to do it.' She glanced at Spirit. 'You have the nerve, girl?'

'I have the nerve – girl,' Spirit replied.

'No more of this!' I said immediately, knowing that mayhem was in the near offing. Either of those two would destroy the ship if pressed, herself with it. 'You are both male, henceforth. And I will exit as I am.'

'Then listen, lad,' Captain Brinker said to Spirit, and my sense informed me that she was not entirely displeased about this development. I realized that it must be a lonely thing, being the only woman in a crew of cut-throat men, anonymously, unable ever to let down her guard lest she be relegated to perpetual slave duty in the guest room. She surely had to sleep in a locked chamber. She might wish for the company of her own kind, while preserving her secret – and we had handed that opportunity to her.

Brinker was letting it be understood that she was compromising in the face of necessity – but in reality she was arranging exactly what she wanted: to be rid of me and to keep my sister. This insight did not dismay me; it reassured me. The captain had no reason to betray us.

The captain tersely explained how to arm the detonator panel, so that the pirate ship would be blown up if anything happened to the one in control. Then we were ready; I would not need my space suit in the lifeboat, and I already had a fair notion how to pilot it, and where I was going. Except—

'The ephemeris!' I exclaimed. 'I must have that!'

'You know how to get it,' the captain said.

I nodded. I looked at Spirit.

'One thing,' Spirit said to the captain. 'If my brother doesn't make it safely away—'

318

'You will do what I would do in the circumstance,' Brinker finished.

'Yes.'

'Spirit isn't bluffing,' I said.

The captain smiled grimly. 'I think we shall get along.'

I thought they would, too. There was an underlying similarity between them.

I embraced Spirit. 'Beloved brother – farewell,' I said, not caring that a feminine tear showed on my face.

She looked so small, trying to be brave, her face scarred, one finger missing. But I knew she would blow up the ship if she had to.

'Beloved sister,' she responded. 'I love you.' She kissed me with a passion that disconcerted me.

I turned to the captain. 'You will see that my brother is well treated,' I said, and was surprised at the coldness in my voice. I had the fake weapon of QYV and the real one of the captain's secret, but in fact I believed I would find a way to come for Brinker and kill her in the most humiliating and painful way if she harmed Spirit, and this was manifest in my tone. I would somehow in due course destroy all pirates; this I had already vowed. But Spirit was special.

'You can be sure of it.' Captain Brinker was no gentle creature, but she understood. There was no bluffing in any of this; we were all killers.

The captain activated her buzzer, summoning the guard pirates. 'Take the girl back to the guest room; her protection is fake, and she will have to co-operate. Leave the boy with her for now; we'll lock them up together until we tire of her.'

The arriving pirates smiled broadly. 'Yes, sir!' one said, crunching my elbow with his huge hand. I must have made a very fetching image of a girl! The other grabbed for Spirit, who looked so cowed it was obviously not necessary to hold her securely.

I had seen that cowed look before. That was when Spirit

was most deadly dangerous.

We accompanied the men docilely enough. I noted how other pirates nodded; their captain had come through again, penetrating the difficult matter of the Kife ploy. It was not just Brinker's ready laser that compelled respect; it was her ability to solve the tricky problems, protecting the ship when some other person might have blundered. Brinker was a good captain, setting aside the issue of legality. Even the way the bubble had been holed – that had defused our trap before we had a chance. Brinker took no unnecessary chances.

We entered the longitudinal hall – and Spirit exploded. She kicked her guard pirate in the leg, punched him in the gut, and used him as a brace to shove off violently. In a moment she was plunging down the passage towards the control room at the end.

'Hey!' the man cried stupidly, going after her. My own guard kept his hand on me, and I, being supposedly female and helpless, made no move.

He hauled me towards the control room. We passed through the door and stood on the floor, which could serve as a wall when the ship was accelerating. Our heads were pointed towards the centre of the ship, far up the centre passage.

Spirit had made it to the Destruct Control panel and stood with her small hands locked on a lever. 'Let my sister go!' she cried, spying us.

The pirate on duty gaped. 'That's the detonator!' he said. 'One tug on that lever and all our ammo blows!'

Spirit smiled and tugged the lever down. Every pirate in sight blanched. 'Tried to fool me, huh?' she demanded. 'I've seen these things before. Now I've armed it; if I let go, it'll snap back, and that'd blow a hole in your ship, wouldn't it! See how you bastards like breathing vacuum, same's you did for our people. Turn my sister loose!'

Hastily, my guard did so. I rubbed my elbow. 'Brother,' I

asked, 'do you know what you're doing? We'll die, if—'

'But we'll take all these apes with us,' she said zestfully.
'That's the way I like to go!'

I spoke to the pirates. 'I know my brother. He's a power-crazy brat. He thinks killing people is a game. He used to smash all his toys for the fun of it. He's not afraid of death.
If you don't do what he says—'

Captain Brinker appeared. 'What?'

'We're hijacking your ship, sir,' Spirit called. 'You pilot it where we say, or I'll blow it right out of Jupiter orbit!'

'You ungrateful brat!' Brinker exclaimed. The laser pistol appeared in her hand. 'I spare your life, and you pull this. Get away from that panel!'

'Go ahead, kill me!' Spirit gibed. 'When I let go of this handle, we'll *all* go! Boom!'

'Sir!' a sweating pirate cried. 'It's true! We can't take the chance!'

The captain's weapon swung to cover him. 'Don't tell me what to do!' Brinker snapped. 'Who let that brat go?'

The pirate closest to Spirit turned, his face turning waxy.
'It was so quick—'

The beam of the laser speared him through the right eye.
Steam and fluid puffed out as the eyeball was burned and punctured. The man staggered back, clapping one hand to his face.

'When I give an order, I expect it to be carried out competently,' the captain said. 'I had this matter settled, and you have bungled us into a problem. She turned back to Spirit. 'What do you want, boy?'

'Pilot this ship to Leda,' Spirit said.

'The Jupe military base? They'd blow us out of space! You might as well turn that handle loose now and get it done with.'

Spirit looked at the handle. 'Oh. Well—' She made as if to let it go, and again the pirates blanched.

I stepped in. 'The captain's not bluffing, kid. We can't

321

hijack this ship there.'

Spirit scowled. 'I know. But I sort of like explosions anyway.' She let go the handle – and caught it halfway back.

A pirate grunted in horror, but the captain didn't flinch. It was evident whose nerves were steadiest. 'We'll give you safe-conduct to our lifeboat,' Brinker said. 'It's fuelled and stocked; it can easily reach Leda.'

'No good,' I said. 'We can't even find Leda without our ephemeris, and we don't know how to pilot a spacecraft.'

The captain spoke to a pirate. 'Suit up, go to the bubble and fetch its ephemeris.' Then, to me: 'There are instructions on the boat. It is designed to be operated by any fool who may survive disaster in space, even a teenage girl. You can operate it, if you can read English.'

'I can read English,' I said. 'Spirit, maybe we should—'

'Okay, take my sister there,' Spirit said. Then she did a dismayed double-take, fine little actress that she was. 'Oops – how can *I* go? I have to keep my hand on this handle!'

'I will hold the lever for you,' the captain said.

Spirit laughed so hard she seemed almost to lose control of the handle. Even I, who knew her propensity for such seeming mischief, was alarmed. 'Oh, no, you don't, sir! The moment I quit this handle, you'll shoot me and plant my sister in that bed!'

Captain Brinker smiled, and the pirates smiled with her. This was rough humour they understood. The captain, too, was playing to an audience. Obviously I ran the danger of the bed. 'Then it seems you must remain here, guarding your handle, while your sister departs. Is that good enough?'

'But I can't stay here forever,' Spirit said, playing it out with uncomfortably accurate intuition. 'Once my sister's gone, the moment I quit, my life'll be out the air lock!' She shook her head. 'I guess I just better blow it up now, and be done with it.'

Again the pirates froze nervously. No one liked being subject to the whim of this vacillating child. Again the captain interceded with a skilful compromise. 'I could use a nervy lad like you for my cabin boy. Spare the ship, and I'll see that you're protected.'

Spirit considered with childlike solemnity. 'Will you make a Pirate's Oath on that?'

'Pirate's Oath,' the captain agreed. 'Now just let me have that lever—'

'Oh, no, you don't, sir!' Spirit repeated, grasping the lever more tightly and lifting it part of the way back. 'Not till my sister's safe! You're probably lying, but at least I can save her!'

'Accuse me of lying again and I will burn you where you stand,' the captain said evenly.

'The captain's right, kid,' a pirate called. 'He never breaks a real promise.'

So now the pirate crew knew that the captain had to keep her word, or stand diminished. Cleverly played, indeed! There would be no backtalk or grumbling when Spirit was spared. And of course it was true: Spirit *was* a nervy kid, and would make a good cabin boy.

The pirate returned with the ephemeris. I took it. 'Thanks, brother,' I said to Spirit. 'Don't blow up the ship until I get clear.' I revelled in the expression of the nearest pirate. We had them scared, all right.

I took one last look at Spirit. She met my gaze squarely, and somehow it reminded me of the time I had tried to question her about the events of the night. It wrenched my heart to part from her.

Then I turned and moved towards the passage to the lifeboat.

20

Salvation

After that it was routine. I found myself in the lifeboat, and the instructions were there, and the controls were simple. Those instructions made all the difference; had we had them for the last lifeboat, we could have mastered it as readily. The captain had kept her word.

I activated the drive and jetted off. 'Farewell, Spirit!' I cried as I saw the pirate ship and attached bubble receding behind me. I did not yet know how to work the radio, so could not broadcast any message, but it wasn't necessary. Anyway, such a broadcast might have alerted other pirates to my presence, and I didn't want that.

I watched the pirate ship for some time, making sure it didn't explode, as if my concentration could affect it. As time passed, I was reassured that the rest of the bargain had been honoured. Spirit was now becoming the captain's cabin boy.

Now I let the tears flow. It hardly mattered; I was dressed for it. It was all right for a girl to cry.

I have no heart to detail my journey to Leda alone. The mechanics of it were absolutely boring, and the mental and emotional aspect was horrendous. Now I had time to realize that I had in fact sold my little sister into more than a masquerade. Captain Brinker evidently had no use for men in the emotional sense – which meant she might have use for women. Cabin boys, historically, had been notoriously employed as homosexual objects. Now the captain had a cabin girl. Why hadn't I thought of that before?

Because I could not afford to jeopardize my escape? Had I forced my sister into that bed after all, to benefit myself? I could not be sure, but there was no joy in the contemplation.

I was the sole survivor of the original bubble-trek to the better life. All the others had sacrificed themselves, many of them directly for me. At this stage I hardly seemed worth it. Over and over I rehearsed this in my mind, trying to come to terms with my fundamental unworthiness. On Io I had known that no merit of mine justified my survival; now, as I neared Leda, I had no better assurance.

Slowly I concluded that though I was unworthy, I might be able to redeem myself in part. I resolved to dedicate my life to the justification of the sacrifices that had been made for me. I did not know exactly how I would do it, but somehow I would. I would make the universe know that the lives of all the gallant refugees had not been in vain.

With the powerful jet of the lifeboat, I made it much faster than would have been possible in the bubble. I radioed ahead, having mastered the radio by this time, and they gave me landing instructions and took me into custody when I turned off the jet and emerged. They took me in at the station, listened to part of my statement, and told me there was no proof for it, because I was a minor and there were no corroborative witnesses. What irony! There were no witnesses because they all had been captured or killed! No wonder the pirates had free rein in space!

They shipped me to a refugee-detention-camp bubble orbiting Jupiter not far above the roiling atmosphere, and dumped me in with a thousand other refugees gleaned from all around the Jupiter system. I had had no idea there were so many! We had never seen another bubble during our odyssey, but they must have been there. If each of these people represented the lone survivor of an expedition like mine, bounced back from Jupiter on the pretext of a changed policy when in fact they had merely come to the wrong station for admission – it was appalling. What monsters ran the government of mighty Jupiter?

We were strangers to each other, yet not strangers in experience. The others had indeed suffered grievously, and learned in the harshest possible way the realities of space. They were not necessarily nice people, these survivors. Like me, they had learned to steal and lie and kill, just to get by. They had eaten human flesh. They understood full well the horror of our situation. I did not like being among them; I would have felt more comfortable in the company of the nicer people who had made the sacrifices, such as my own parents and sisters and fiancée. Part of the horror of my situation was the knowledge that if I had been a better person, I would long since have died.

The commandant of the detention centre summoned us all to an assembly to announce that current United States of Jupiter policy, which was relevant for us, would admit only those refugees who possessed viable commercial or artistic skills, and therefore would not be a burden on society. The rest would be returned to their planets of origin.

Returned to Callisto! Or for the others, to Ganymede or Europa or some lesser moon. Horror overwhelmed us, and the assembly became a riot. They had to flood the bubble with sleep gas to break it up. We well knew the fate most of us would face on our home moons. Few of us would be kindly treated – and those who were would still be locked into the very situation they had risked everything to escape. I, personally, would face a charge of attempted murder, because of the scion. The verdict was sure.

Callisto meant death for me. I was not concerned so much for myself, as death had brushed past me too many times to be any spectre of the unknown. I was concerned for my mission: to vindicate the effort of the refugees who had already died. I was the only one of our original party who remained to make that attempt.

Yet I seemed to possess no skills or arts the authorities considered worthwhile. They weren't interested in information about Halfcal history or culture. They had passed out assorted tests in Spanish, and many forms, and I had duly filled them all out – but they were coded by numbers, not names, and the authorities weren't paying much attention. I wasn't sure they were even reading the completed forms, or whether the number designated for me actually matched the one on the forms I had been given. Probably my answers had been credited to somebody else and vice versa. This sort of thing happens when men are treated like cattle.

My name was duly posted on the list of scheduled returnees. I would have perhaps a month longer here, while the remaining refugees were processed and the bureaucracy ground its inefficient wheels to produce the necessary transportation. Then a Jupiter ship, in the name of the Home of the Brave and the World of the Free, would deliver me to my doom.

So I am whiling away my time by writing this private history, as it may become the only record of the travails of my family. I have all day, every day, to rehearse my memories and piece it out to the best of my ability. Probably these poor sheets, written in English to prevent comprehension by other refugees – somehow I value this immediate aspect of my privacy, for all that I do want my story to be known after I am gone – will be destroyed with the other refuse of our camp, once we are excised from the detention globe. That will be a secret tragedy. But even so, this writing is a necessary therapy, a coming to terms with my situation. I am about to be eliminated, and my dreams and vows with me. I must tell *someone* of my pain, even if only a sheaf of papers. At least, for a little while, this enables my family and friends to live again, if only in my appreciation.

Perhaps I can arrange to mail this manuscript anonymously to the scientist of Io who helped us, Mason.

Editorial Epilogue

Here the manuscript ends. The final page is discoloured, surely by tears, and a full paragraph of text has been obliterated. It is a point of curiosity what the washed-out text contained, but the words are largely beyond restoration. Only a few are decipherable; among them, twice, 'Spirit.' The HELSE HUBRIS name tag is absent, long since lost.

Hope Hubris, at the age of fifteen, had seen all his family lost or dead, and he believed he was also slated for death. It is not surprising that he was depressed, and that the poignancy of his accumulated memories overcame him.

The official records for this period in the life of the Tyrant are scant, as the affairs of refugees were not at that time deemed important. There is no listing of his presence in the detention bubble. Yet other details of his narrative have been corroborated, such as the appearance of two Hispanic refugees at a scientific observatory on the hellface of Io and the four-year residence of a pretty child in the mansion of a prominent politician of Callisto, so there seems to be little reason to question the general authenticity of the document.

We take editorial licence to recreate the following sequence, as the narrative seems incomplete without it.

An official discovered Hope Hubris at his cramped table formed from a surplus crate, his head on the last sheet of his holographic manuscript. (Clarification: Holographic is used in its sense of 'wholly hand written' rather than in the more common contemporary sense of three-dimensional projection of images, though perhaps that also in a sense applies.) 'Hey, kid, are you sick?' he asked in clumsy Spanish.

Hope raised his dark head to stare dully at the man. 'No, sir.'

'You can go to the dispensary for a pill.'

'No, thank you, sir. I am merely tired.'

'What's that you have there?'

'Nothing, sir. Just some papers.' Hope tried to put them away.

'Say, that's English! Where did you get that?'

'Sir, it's unimportant. I was just writing – a letter.'

'In *English?*'

'Yes, sir. I studied your language in school.'

'Let me have that.' The official moved to pick up the papers, thinking they were stolen.

'Sir, please – it is mine!'

The official paused, then tested the bedraggled young refugee. 'You are fluent in English?' he asked in that language.

'Yes, sir,' Hope answered in kind.

'Let me see you write something in English.'

Hope took a separate sheet, and wrote: *This is my statement that I am literate in the language of the Colossus Jupiter, from whose fair and promising clouds I am barred.*

'I'll be damned!' the official exclaimed. 'Don't you know that English-language literacy is grounds for status as an alien resident in Jupiter?'

The eyes in the dusky face widened. 'No one informed me of that, sir.'

The official shook his head. 'Maybe that form got lost in the shuffle. Happens all the time. Anyway, it's true. Come with me; you are about to have your status changed.'

And so this manuscript, *Refugee*, written in the depth of despair, saved the young life of Hope Hubris, and thereby altered most significantly the history of mankind. It is not possible to say whether it happened precisely this way, but certainly it was the chance discovery of his literacy in

English that qualified him for alien residency; a subsequent reference by the Tyrant himself confirmed this aspect. The existence of this particular manuscript was not then known, and it is very tempting now to suppose that this was indeed the document that did it. There would be poetic irony in having the narrative of his failure convert that failure to success.

This aspect, of course, also resolves the mystery of Helse's use as a courier: She too was literate in English, having had an excellent private education, so she also would have been granted sanctuary if she had survived. Her employer surely knew that.

We trust this clarifies the early nature of the later Tyrant of Jupiter. He was not at all the monster his political and cultural enemies have claimed. He was very much a victim of violent circumstance. The marvel is not that he emerged emotionally scarred, but that he retained his sanity and power of character.

Conjecture is precarious, but some further speculation on the concluding, unreadable paragraph of his manuscript may be in order, as this relates to a further mystery of his character. Obviously this paragraph concerned Hope's little sister Spirit, and great emotion attaches thereto. One must wonder why, when one short paragraph is devoted to the memory of parents, older sister, and fiancée, all dead or degraded, there should be a much longer passage devoted to the younger sister, who perhaps survived best. Objectively it would seem that Spirit was the least important figure of this number, and suffered least (though still considerably); why then should she apparently be mourned more than all the rest? It does not seem to make perfect sense.

The motives of the Tyrant, however, have always made sense, when properly understood. He was a most intelligent, forthright, and practical person, not given to emotional foolishness. He was never known for extreme subtlety or deviousness. He related with rare precision to the needs and feelings of the average man; that is one secret of his inordinate success. What he felt, *everyone* felt. Few, for example, failed to applaud his savage campaign against the space pirates – and this manuscript makes clear his underlying motivation there. He was fulfilling his vow. One must therefore conclude that if he wrote most feelingly about his little sister, the state of his awareness warranted it.

It would be easy to take this as proof of the incest with which he has been charged – but again, this may be unwarranted. Direct evidence for such incest has never been presented – and there have been those who certainly would have presented it had they been able. Every investigation has foundered on uncertainty. Yet it does seem likely that Hope's greatest emotional concern was with his sister.

Probably the truth is this: Though Hope Hubris loved his parents and older sister in a family way, and loved his fiancée Helse romantically, his closest actual companion was Spirit. She understood him, she fought for him (sometimes with devastating effectiveness: he literally owed his life to her), she may have slept with him one time to ease his agony of bereavement, and she deliberately sacrificed herself to free him from the last pirate. She was the embodiment of blood relative, friend, and perhaps lover. She was his strength – and when he lost her, his competence as an individual suffered severely. One can be sure he would not passively have awaited shipment back to Callisto, had Spirit been with him at the end! The two of them would have found a way to compel sanctuary. Note how rapidly the manuscript concludes once Spirit departs from it; it was as though Hope's normally acute interest in detail and personality left him at that point. Helse could have been his support – but he knew her only a month or so, while he had known Spirit all her life. This Spirit was in fact the most

332

significant figure in Hope's life, and it was her loss that affected him most profoundly.

This insight may be critical to proper comprehension of the subsequent career of the Tyrant, though no other biography has remarked upon it. Others treat her presence as incidental to his career; this was, as the following manuscripts will demonstrate, grossly in error. Hope Hubris loved, honoured, and needed his sister Spirit – all of his life.

This document is presented with compassion and pride by Hopie Megan Hubris, daughter of the Tyrant, 6 June, 2670.

The world's greatest science fiction authors now available in Panther Books

Piers Anthony
'Cluster' series

Vicinity Cluster	£1.95	☐
Chaining the Lady	£1.95	☐
Kirlian Quest	£1.95	☐
Viscous Circle	£1.95	☐
Thousandstar	£1.95	☐

'Tarot' series

God of Tarot	£1.50	☐
Vision of Tarot	£1.50	☐
Faith of Tarot	£1.50	☐

'Split Infinity' series

Split Infinity	£2.50	☐
Blue Adept	£1.95	☐
Juxtaposition	£2.50	☐

'Bio of a Space Tyrant' series

Refugee	£1.95	☐

'Incarnations of Immortality' series

On a Pale Horse	£2.50	☐

Other Titles

Phthor	85p	☐
Chthon	£1.50	☐

Fritz Leiber
'Swords' series

The Swords of Lankhmar	85p	☐

Other Titles

A Spectre is Haunting Texas	£1.25	☐
Ship of Shadows	£1.50	☐

To order direct from the publisher just tick the titles you want and fill in the order form.

All these books are available at your local bookshop or newsagent, or can be ordered direct from the publisher.,

---

To order direct from the publisher just tick the titles you want and fill in the form below.

Name _____

Address _____

_____

Send to:
Panther Cash Sales
PO Box 11, Falmouth, Cornwall TR10 9EN.

Please enclose remittance to the value of the cover price plus:

UK 45p for the first book, 20p for the second book plus 14p per copy for each additional book ordered to a maximum charge of £1.63.

BFPO and Eire 45p for the first book, 20p for the second book plus 14p per copy for the next 7 books, thereafter 8p per book.

Overseas 75p for the first book and 21p for each additional book.

Panther Books reserve the right to show new retail prices on covers, which may differ from those previously advertised in the text or elsewhere.